TOO MANY MEN, NO, TOO MANY BOYS
HAD IGNORED HER KIND OF
BEAUTY FOR TOO LONG

Well, he'd just see about showing her.

Slowly, he closed the distance between them. "Can you see what I see? Or do you only see what the boys here in town see? Your beautiful sister who will eventually transfer to a four-year school, leaving you here with Bobby. Because that's what I bet you see."

His arms went around her, drawing her close. Those shoulders were as broad and as solid as they had looked under his jacket earlier in the day. For one moment, Angie thought about closing her eyes and giving in. He saw her indecision and lowered his mouth to hers.

BOOK YOUR PLACE ON OUR WEBSITE AND MAKE THE READING CONNECTION!

We've created a customized website just for our very special readers, where you can get the inside scoop on everything that's going on with Zebra, Pinnacle and Kensington books.

When you come online, you'll have the exciting opportunity to:

- View covers of upcoming books
- Read sample chapters
- Learn about our future publishing schedule (listed by publication month *and author*)
- Find out when your favorite authors will be visiting a city near you
- Search for and order backlist books from our online catalog
- Check out author bios and background information
- Send e-mail to your favorite authors
- Meet the Kensington staff online
- Join us in weekly chats with authors, readers and other guests
- Get writing guidelines
- AND MUCH MORE!

**Visit our website at
http://www.kensingtonbooks.com**

FALLING IN LOVE

PAULINE TRENT

ZEBRA BOOKS
Kensington Publishing Corp.
http://www.kensingtonbooks.com

ZEBRA BOOKS are published by

Kensington Publishing Corp.
850 Third Avenue
New York, NY 10022

All Kensington titles, imprints, and distributed lines are available at special quantity discounts for bulk purchases for sales promotion, premiums, fund-raising, educational, or institutional use.

Special book excerpts or customized printings can also be created to fit specific needs. For details, write or phone the office of the Kensington Special Sales Manager: Attn. Special Sales Department. Kensington Publishing Corp., 850 Third Avenue, New York, NY 10022. Phone: 1-800-221-2647.

Zebra and the Z logo Reg. U.S. Pat. & TM Off.

ISBN-13: 978-0-8217-8141-8
ISBN-10: 0-8217-8141-3

First Printing: February 2009

10 9 8 7 6 5 4 3 2 1

Printed in the United States of America

To Rachel Grace,
Kaitlyn Nichelle, and
Trinity Lynn—
the next generation of women.

May you find love and yourselves
without having to compromise either.

Acknowledgments

Acknowledgments are fun but tough, especially, I suspect, for first time authors. I know I want to gush and thank everyone I ever met and to whom I ever mentioned wanting to be a writer. Instead, I will narrow it down. Just know, even if you're not listed here, I probably thank you.

First and foremost, to Shanna and Andrew Goldberg. None of this would ever have happened if it hadn't been for them and their patience, love, friendship and support. To my New Jersey family: Miss Phyl, Judy, Bunny & Richard, Natalie & Che, and Nina & Chris, for being so supportive from the very beginning. To Mitchell—whose contribution to my work and my life cannot be overstated, Christine—whom I cannot imagine life without, Ed and Scott, all four of whom prove over and over that family doesn't have to be about biology and that home is wherever your fuzzy pink slippers are. To Michelle, for being indispensable and so much more than that. And finally, to my dear David, for making it so easy.

Prologue

The boys were forgetting they were in danger. That's what two weeks without action could do to even the best-trained men. And his guys *were* the best-trained men. You didn't get to wear the Green Beret because you were lazy or slow. Still, for two weeks they'd only had routine patrols. Village life was becoming a routine of ball games with the kids, harmless flirting with the women, and civic improvements—building walls, digging wells, anything to keep them busy—with the men. It was enough to dull anyone's senses, even Green Berets'.

God forgive him, but when the intelligence came down about insurgents in the area, he had been grateful. Not to counter the boredom—no true soldier ever hoped for action just because he was bored—but to counter his boys' complacency. They needed to remember why they were here and what was really at stake.

According to the intel he and Champ had received just the day before, unfriendlies were moving into the area and, while they probably knew there were US military personnel encamped in the village, there was no indication they knew *who* those military personnel were. He smiled, tight-lipped, not even showing teeth through his camouflage paint. Well, they would find out soon enough.

It would be quick. It would be quiet. Easy in and, if things went according to plan, easy out. And things *would* go according to plan. His boys were that good, and the unfriendlies had no idea what was coming up their ass. Even the moonless night was with them.

Looking right, he could barely make out the figure of Edwards, his senior weapons man. Looking left, he caught Champ's eye. The captain nodded. It was time. He turned to motion to Edwards . . . and his gut exploded.

He hit the ground, soundlessly, clutching his stomach. Around him, muzzle fire lit up the night. The figure that had been his friend, Edwards, was writhing on the ground, not even five feet away. Screams filled the air—but whose? He didn't know.

A thud and there were knees on the ground next to him, straddling his head, and muzzle flashes providing cover, protection, until one of those legs was hit. The blood splattered his face. It was warm, soothing even. And his gut didn't hurt so bad anymore. Then there were hands on him, pulling on him, lifting him, and the pain exploded. It ripped a scream from his throat and brought on blackness.

He floated for a while. Hours? Days? He didn't know. Once, he'd seen his grandfather, Pops. The old man was young, though. Smiling but sad. Before Pops could speak, another voice started yelling, "You stay with me! Goddammit, First Sergeant, you stay with me and that's a fucking order!" Pops disappeared in a flash of pain, and he floated again.

The same voice, not yelling now, not angry. Just insistent. Too damn insistent to be ignored. "First Sergeant! Open your eyes. Come on."

He squinted. The light was too bright. The pain too much. He wanted to float.

"Montgomery!" Getting angry. "Open your eyes, you son of a whore!"

"Guh . . . guh . . . good . . . woman," he croaked.

"Well, it took you long enough," the voice replied.

He opened his eyes, blinking at the light. Champ sat next to him. "You with me, First Sergeant?"

He nodded, tried to swallow, and choked instead.

"Yeah, sorry 'bout that, but Doc says nothing but IV yet."

"What . . . ?" His voice wouldn't work.

Champ squared his shoulders. "Ambush. Bastards knew we were there, knew we were coming. Bad intel."

"Who?" he croaked, knowing his captain would understand.

"You got gut shot, as you've probably figured out. McCoy and Reynolds were touch and go but made it. We lost Edwards." The captain's voice was low but matter-of-fact.

He closed his eyes, remembering in spite of himself. Jim Edwards . . . writhing only five feet away but too far. . . . And then . . . knees at his head. Opening his eyes, he looked at Champ. *You*, he thought but couldn't get the words out. He pointed instead.

"I took one in the leg. Nothing serious. A couple shots of tequila and I was fine."

He nodded—but knew better. Knees at his head . . . Cover fire before the blood . . . Hands pulling at him, refusing to leave him behind . . . His eyes started to close.

Champ reached out and touched his arm. "Rest now."

He did.

Chapter 1

There was a fire in Lambert Falls. The smell in the air was unmistakable. Angie Kane paused in front of the diner door, keys in her hand. Someone definitely had a fire going. Normally, this would not be noteworthy. It was, after all, late January and, contrary to popular belief, it got chilly in winter even in North Carolina. Two things made Angie stop. First was the fact that it was 4:30 A.M. and usually there were no signs of life when she arrived to work. Second was the fact that, in looking around, she saw the smoke from the fire was rising from the chimney of the old Montgomery place.

You couldn't actually see the old plantation. It was high enough on the hill and hidden by century-old trees. But above those trees rose three of many of the house's chimneys. And smoke was rising from one of them. Angie had lived in Lambert Falls her entire life, all twenty-five years of it, and it had stood empty almost as long.

She was intrigued. *No*, she chastised herself. She wasn't intrigued. That was too strong. Perhaps curious was better. Even mildly interested. But not intrigued. She would leave that emotion to the ladies of the town. Besides, she couldn't help but smile to herself, she would get all the speculation and gossip from those same ladies as they came into the diner over the course of the next few days. So, without another glance up the hill, Angie opened the diner door and went to work.

The thirty minutes between the time she arrived at the diner and the time it opened were busy, if comfortably monotonous. She had been opening up Tuesday through Saturday for three years now and could do it in her sleep. Some mornings, she thought she might have done just that. The industrial dishwasher that Joey had started last night as he left needed unloading. The coffee, both regular and decaf for when the Jones sisters came in, was started. At 4:45 A.M., Alvin, the morning cook, arrived with his iPod headphones still in his ears over his skull cap in the winter. In the summer, the headphones would go over his Atlanta Braves baseball cap. Whatever the season, he would exchange his seasonal headgear and iPod for his white cap and cook's apron and head back to the kitchen to set up the grill. He and Angie would chat amicably about nothing in particular over the first cup of coffee of the day until it was time for her to turn on the overhead fluorescent lights and flip the CLOSED sign on the door to OPEN. At 5:10 A.M., Bobby Granger, the sheriff, would come in to get his coffee (black with sugar) and two slices of wheat toast with butter and strawberry preserves.

Bobby's wife had passed away several years ago, and breakfast at the diner was his way of getting company outside of the station and his deputies—and every single woman over the age of forty in town. When Bobby came in at 5:10 every morning, Angie's day officially started.

Bobby was finishing up his last piece of toast when the Jones sisters came in. They made a point of studying the menu. Then Mary ordered her one soft-boiled egg with dry toast and Margaret her two fried eggs with biscuits.

"Angie, dear," Mary spoke, "did you see the smoke coming from the Montgomery place?"

"We noticed it as soon as we stepped out of the house," Margaret continued.

Angie figured people had probably once gotten the two women confused for each other. And strangers in town might still, but the locals knew them apart. "Was there a fire on the hill?" Angie asked innocently as she poured their decaf coffee.

"No, dear," Mary explained, "a *house* fire. . . ."

"In the *fireplace*," Margaret continued for her.

"Someone *living there*," Mary said.

"After all these years," Margaret finished with a shake of her head.

The two women looked at Bobby simultaneously, and each lifted an eyebrow. Bobby swallowed the last of his coffee. "Can't say I noticed either, Angie," he said. Angie knew he was lying and knew he was on to her, too. People tended to sell Bobby short because he was a small-town, Southern sheriff. He played the good ol' boy role when he needed to, but he was sharp and wouldn't have missed anything so obvious. Just as he knew Angie wouldn't have either.

He picked up his hat and dropped a tip on the counter. "I'm sure there's no great mystery. Angie, thanks for the coffee. Ladies . . ." He tipped his hat as he put it on. Three construction workers held the door for him as he left and Angie started pouring coffee.

Bobby headed to the station without another look at the old Montgomery place. He'd seen the smoke, of course, but would deal with that in a bit. For now, Jimmy had worked a double and probably needed sleep.

The deputy was behind the desk, on the phone, when Bobby walked in. Bobby nodded to him and crossed to the coffee maker. As he turned back, two steaming mugs in his hand, Jimmy hung up and stood.

"Hey Boss." Jimmy took the coffee Bobby offered him. "We're getting calls about smoke on the hill."

Bobby nodded and sat down in the chair Jimmy had just vacated. "Figured we would be." He sipped at his coffee, thumbing through the pink slips of paper Jimmy always used for phone messages. There were indeed more than usual. "What else has been going on?"

"But Boss . . ." Jimmy started.

Bobby interrupted him. "The chimney smoke's taken care of Jimmy. Nothing you need to worry about. The sooner you fill me in on the rest, the sooner you can go home and get some sleep."

Jimmy shrugged. He *was* tired but more importantly, he trusted the sheriff. If the boss said it was nothing, it was nothing.

The exchange didn't take long; Jimmy was good at his job and didn't leave many loose ends for Bobby to handle. And the night had been a quiet one—at least until the early birds had woken up to a good reason to gossip. Bobby considered asking the other man to stay given the number of calls they were getting but couldn't bring himself to do it. Hand to God, the kid looked dead on his feet. The answering service could manage the concerned citizens of Lambert Falls when the time came. Until then, he would.

He spent the time finishing up some paperwork and, as expected, fielding calls about the old Montgomery place. After a couple hours, he was actually grateful to be able to forward the phones for a little bit.

Clipping his radio to his belt, he stepped out into the weak morning sunlight and looked up the hill at the cause of concern. Normally, he would've told Jimmy what was going on but Jimmy would've wanted to stick around and Bobby needed him to get some sleep. Plus, there was the other man to consider. If he knew it or not, he was the cause of enough speculation already. Both of the town's officers of the law showing up on his doorstep . . . well, the man didn't need that, too.

The man the whole town was interested in was old Doc Montgomery's grandson, Chris Montgomery. Chris had called Bobby a few days ago and asked Bobby to do a quick drive-by of the old house before he came to town. Bobby had done so and had found the outside of the house, at least, in remarkably good condition. Sure there had been a couple broken windows and the whole place was in desperate need of paint, but there were no holes or visible leaks. Considering how long the place had stood empty, it was amazing.

When Bobby had called the young Montgomery to give him the information, Chris had invited him up for a visit. According to Bobby's watch, it was time to meet Christopher Montgomery in person. Bobby approached the plantation in his car. Normally, he would have made the visit on foot, make it look and feel less formal, but that driveway was a half mile long if it was a foot, and he wasn't about to hike it without reason. The lawns were no longer manicured and well kept after so many years of the house being empty, but even that had a raw beauty to it. Short of torching the place, Bobby wasn't sure this property could be anything but beautiful.

He rang the bell and waited. Looking at his watch again, he knew he was on time. He was just about to reach for the bell a second time when footsteps sounded behind the massive oak doors. Christopher Montgomery opened the door.

Bobby's professional eye took over and he made a quick assessment of the man. He was medium height and lean. Green-brown eyes, slightly guarded, that would miss nothing. Brownish red hair still worn short from habit, Bobby assumed. White T-shirt that was comfortably worn, soft faded blue jeans, bare feet. This was a man who was comfortable with himself and his environment but always just a little wary, just a little "on." That was to be expected though, Bobby thought, given the nature of his past.

"Sheriff Granger?" Chris asked, extending his hand. "Chris Montgomery."

Bobby shook his hand. "Pleased to meet you in person, Chris. And it's Bobby."

Bobby's handshake was strong but not challenging. Chris appreciated that. So many men felt they had to try to prove something or play stupid games with him. He had been a little concerned about a small-town sheriff. And Bobby looked him in the eye. Again, not a challenge, just being comfortable and friendly. And smart. Smarter, Chris realized meeting the man in person, than Bobby had let on during their few phone conversations. Chris couldn't help but laugh inwardly at himself. Here he had been concerned about the stereotyping that was going to follow him around and he had been guilty of it himself.

"Thanks, Bobby. Come on in." Chris stepped back from the door, allowing Bobby access to the large foyer. Bobby couldn't help but look around. He hadn't been in the house since he was a child. The wallpaper was faded and peeling in some places, but it looked very much like he remembered. Just a little dustier, a little older. But then, he was a little dustier and a little older himself.

"Excuse the place. I've got my work cut out for me, I think," Chris said as he led them deeper into the house toward the kitchen. "I've got coffee on if you'd like."

"Thank you," Bobby agreed. He sat on a bar stool at a large butcher-block island in the center of the room. "Sugar if you've got it." Chris poured the coffee and placed a box of sugar and a plastic spoon in front of Bobby.

"I haven't had a chance to get unpacked and settled yet, but

I managed to get the necessities at a 7-Eleven last night on the way in to town." Bobby watched as Chris poured an inordinate amount of sugar and creamer into his cup before stirring it vigorously with another spoon. He took a sip and added another teaspoon of sugar. Looking up, Chris saw Bobby watching him and laughed. "I could never stand coffee, but so often it was all we had that I had to make do. Now I'm addicted. Go figure."

"Chris, let me tell you how sorry the whole town was to hear about your granddad. Doc was a great guy," Bobby said, getting it out of the way.

Chris nodded. "Thanks. He was the best. I was a lucky kid."

"I remember when we were kids," Bobby spoke slowly. "Doc and Miz Montgomery would always scare the living hell out of us at Halloween on the driveway up to the house. Lights made to look like things watching us, scary noises, the works. We'd come into the foyer certain the devil himself was on our tails. The whole place would be bright with candles and creepy music and Doc telling us ghost stories. But Miz Montgomery would always hush him up and feed us candied apples and popcorn balls."

"My grandparents always loved the holidays," Chris said. "From Halloween through Easter was big shit."

Bobby nodded. "Well, know that everyone here loved both of them and you'll be welcome here. I will warn you though," Bobby added with a chuckle, "you may be Doc Montgomery's people, but you're also new in town, so there'll be lots of curiosity and no little amount of talk."

Chris laughed with him. "Thanks for the warning. Anything else I need to know?"

Bobby thought about it for a second or two. "The best cup of coffee in town is at the diner at the bottom of the hill, and don't let Maddie over at the dry cleaners starch your pants or you can't sit for a month. I'm sure there're other things you need to know, but I'm not a great welcome wagon. Come to dinner tonight and my girls can help you out better."

Chris raised an eyebrow.

"My wife passed a while back and now I live with my nieces. They're good girls and can help you with town better than I can. Plus, Carter Anne can cook you up something a damn sight better than what you can get at the 7-Eleven. Say about five-thirty?"

"Sounds good. Thanks, Bobby."

Bobby drained his cup and stood up. They headed through the house. "We're the yellow house at the corner of Main and Peachtree. You can't miss us. Just park in the driveway if you drive it."

"I'll probably just walk," Chris said. Bobby nodded and Chris couldn't help but feel as if he had just passed a test of some sort.

At the door, Bobby noticed a small pile of belongings. There were two duffel bags, a footlocker, and a framed picture leaning up against the wall. "You travel light," Bobby mentioned.

"Habit," Chris replied.

Bobby looked closer at the photograph. Two men, one in a light gray suit and fedora, the other in military fatigues tucked into jump boots and wearing a green beret, arm in arm at an airfield. The older man had tears in his eyes.

"Hey," Bobby said. "There's the Doc."

Chris bent, picked up the picture, and handed it to Bobby. "We had just gotten back from Somalia."

"Didn't realize you fellas were in Somalia. Thought it was just the Rangers."

"Good. That's what you were supposed to think." Chris's voice was quiet.

Bobby glanced from the photo to Chris. His eyes were looking at the picture but his mind was somewhere else.

Bobby wondered if the man was even aware of how closed down he had just become. It was a look Bobby was used to seeing in criminals—and victims.

"Well," Bobby said with slightly strained cheerfulness, "it's good to see the Doc again, even in a picture." He placed it on the floor gently. "We'll see you tonight?"

Chris nodded. Bobby noticed his eyes were clear again, like he had thrown a switch somewhere inside of himself. "Five-thirty."

Chris stepped out of the house and breathed deeply. Winter air was so clean. He could easily spend all day working on the grounds then enjoying another warm fire inside. As much as he would have liked to burrow into the house and stay there until spring, he knew small towns well enough to know that the longer he stayed out of sight, the longer the locals would have to speculate. The longer they had to speculate, the greater the mystery would become, and then he'd have no chance of ever fitting in, of ever simply being at home among them.

He zipped his jacket and pulled on his gloves. If Bobby was right and the best cup of coffee in town was the diner at the bottom of the hill, then that seemed like a good place to start. As he made his way into town, he realized he was looking forward to meeting the people and seeing the places he had heard so much about from his grandfather. The Jones sisters. Apparently, Margaret had given his grandmother a run for her money years ago. Town center and the statue of Thomas Jefferson Lambert, where his grandfather had first kissed his grandmother and poor Margaret lost out, even if she hadn't known it at the time. Even Bobby had been a treat. Pops had underestimated the nice young man who might make sheriff one day, though. He had made sheriff and was obviously more than just a nice man.

Chris's thoughts took him down the hill and to the main street. He looked around and, sure enough, directly across the street from him was the diner. It was just a few blocks up from the 7-Eleven where he had stopped the night before. He must have driven by it in the dark and not even noticed. The large clock on the building across the street read 11:30. It was early for lunch but dinner would be early, too, so he figured he was fine. He needed to get on a normal schedule anyway, if he could remember what that was.

He opened the door and a bell jingled over his head. The diner wasn't very crowded, but every eye turned toward him and time seemed to stop. *Ah*, he thought with an inward smile. *The stranger makes his first appearance.* It didn't matter where in the world you went, small towns were the same. The first appearance always silenced the room. Out of habit, he assessed the situation quickly. Two older women at the first table. A mother with her baby to his right. Three young guys in worn ball caps at the counter. The old guy contingent sitting at the other end of the counter. A young woman serving coffee. The happy-looking man in the kitchen, busy at his grill. And of course, the door behind Chris, another one under an exit sign by the restrooms, and a third just visible through the window separating the kitchen from the seating area, behind the cook.

Chris sighed to himself. Hopefully one day he would stop doing a recon of every new place he entered. For now, he supposed he should forgive himself the old habit.

The young woman made her way over to him. Chris took her in quickly. She was far prettier than she had appeared from a distance. Brown hair that wasn't at all mousy as he had originally thought but that shone with highlights, shades of gold and red, making you wonder what exact color her hair was. Green cat eyes that slanted just slightly and twinkled brightly. A perky nose that turned up and reminded him of a laughing storyteller statue he had seen while in Asia once. And she had curves everywhere a woman should have curves. After years of seeing women and children hungry, starving, and often dying, the anorexic look that was popular among women in the US was simply unattractive to him. Ruben had been right, in his opinion, to immortalize round, soft bodies in his art. He liked women he could get a grip on, who he wouldn't break. Who would be soft. This young woman would definitely be soft. He shook himself slightly. He had to get a grip, for Pete's sake.

Angie heard the room go silent and looked up to find the cause of it. It was obvious immediately. In the door stood the stranger from the Montgomery place. It had to be. He was also one of the best-looking men she'd ever seen in her life. Although he wasn't very tall, just a little taller than she was, he stood as if he towered over the world. His hair was light brown, almost reddish, and tousled from the winter wind blowing outside. His jaw was firm and there was a small scar on his chin, right at his jaw. Angie found herself staring at it, wondering what had caused it. The jeans he wore hugged his hips and legs, and not even his bulky winter jacket could hide the V shape between his shoulders and his waist. His brown eyes were blank, though, taking in everything and giving out nothing. She swallowed hard, smiled, and walked over to him.

"You can sit anywhere you'd like," the young woman spoke. Her voice was warm honey. She picked up a menu and motioned for him to choose a table. He walked through, ignoring the eyes that followed him. As he slid into a booth, the old man contingent started talking among themselves again. The woman with the baby went back to feeding the child, and the two older women whispered over their mugs to one another. Noise filled the diner again.

"Sorry," she said as she put the menu in front of him. "We don't get many new faces in these parts." She rolled her eyes good-naturedly. "I'm Angie. Can I get you some coffee? Or iced tea?"

"Thanks, Angie. I hear you've got the best coffee in town. I'll take that." Chris smiled up at her. The smile didn't quite reach his eyes, though.

Angie walked back to the coffeepots and filled a mug. She brought it back to him and took out her pad. "Ready to order?"

Chris closed his menu. "Can I get a burger with cheese and ketchup only? And an order of fries, please."

Angie nodded, smiled at him, and walked away. She had made sure her smile didn't reach her eyes either. Lambert Falls could be a friendly place—but honestly, you had to help a little bit. Some people were just . . . Well, she couldn't be bothered right now. The lunch crowd would be coming in soon. She had no sooner had the thought than the bell over the door jingled and the first of the bunch came through.

Chris watched, amazed, as the diner filled. It seemed he had gotten there just in time. A steady flow of people kept the bell jingling until every seat in the place, including the one separating the old guys from the young ones at the counter, was taken. By the time Angie got back with his burger, there was a line outside, shivering in the cold.

Angie put his food in front of him and refilled his coffee mug. She put his bill facedown on the table as well. "There's no rush on this." Chris looked doubtfully at the lunch crowd waiting. "Seriously. Take your time," she responded with a smile. "Can I get you anything else?"

"You can answer a question for me, Angie," Chris said. "Is this the only restaurant in town?" He motioned to the crowd and the line outside the door.

Angie laughed in spite of herself. "No, there's the Chinese place and there's an Italian place, but they're only open for lunch on Sundays. The Waffle House is over on Madison, and of course there's the Shoney's. But, as you said, we're the best coffee in town, so . . ." Angie let the sentence dangle before continuing. "I imagine we're kinda small compared to wherever you're from." As soon as the sentence was out of her mouth, she wanted to kick herself for it. Was she really becoming one of those women who pried others for personal information? Oh dear Lord. . . .

Chris took a bite of his burger, but not fast enough to hide the smile that hovered at the corners of his mouth. "But sometimes," he answered, swallowing, "small is a good thing." He wiped his hands and mouth on the paper napkin pulled from the dispenser on the table and extended his hand. "I'm Chris, by the way."

Angie put the coffeepot down on the table and took his hand. Her hand was strong but smooth. He *knew* she'd be soft. "Angie Kane. Pleased to meet you. Wave at me if you need anything else."

"Thanks, Angie, I'll do that. It's nice to have a friend in a new place." This time, when he smiled, it reached his eyes and lit up his face. Angie felt her knees weaken. She turned away quickly before he could notice.

Chris watched her go back to work. The view from this angle was as pleasant as the one from the front, he noted. She seemed to know everyone, have a kind word for each person. Watching her, he realized she was deceptive. She looked like she was moving slowly, taking her time. In reality, she was moving remarkably quickly, getting a lot done in an incredibly efficient manner. And always with that smile on her face. Chris suddenly had to admit that moving to Lambert Falls and renovating the old place took on even more appeal. He made a note to himself to ask Bobby about Angie Kane, do a little intelligence gathering, and then make sure he met her again.

Angie walked in the door of the house and kicked off her shoes. Her fuzzy slippers were waiting for her by the hat rack and she slipped them on. Once her feet weren't so uncomfortable, she took off her coat and hung it up. She slipped her gloves and hat into the pockets and shuffled into the kitchen for a soda. Grabbing a Diet Pepsi, she wandered into the living room where her uncle sat, watching television and cleaning his gun.

"Hi, honey," he said as she came in. He lifted his cheek for a kiss and she brushed her lips against it before throwing herself onto the couch. "Hard day?"

"Nothing more than usual, I guess," she answered. "I'm just tired. Busy lunch and lots of kids in after school let out. Too cold to be outside, so they all came in for sodas. How about you?"

He started to answer when Angie was speaking again. "All anybody was talking about today was the guy living in the Montgomery place, like it was unheard of to have someone move to town. I mean, it was like the president was in town or something. He didn't seem like all that much to me."

"Really? You met him?"

Angie nodded. "He came in for lunch. Said he had been told we were the best coffee in town and wanted to try it out. Nice enough fellow but not all that . . ."

"So you liked him?"

"Sure. I guess. As I said, he was only in for lunch." She took a sip of her drink and closed her eyes. "It hardly matters if I like him or not."

"Well, I'm glad that you *do* like him, though, because he's coming over for dinner," Bobby said, watching her closely.

Angie's eyes sprang open. "He's what?"

Bobby smiled at her. He had thought she had been talking strangely about Chris Montgomery and he had been right. Truth be told, this *might* have been why he had invited Chris over in the first place, but no one needed to know that. If things had already started, all the better.

She sat up straight. "Bobby, you're a scamp. Does Carter Anne know? Because there is no food in the house, the place is a mess, and I have to get changed. What time is he coming?"

Bobby took another sip of his drink, deliberately slowly. "You keep this house spotless, Angie. I picked up steaks on the way home from work, and Carter Anne told me there was a crisp put up, so that's thawing. She's bringing ice cream with her on the way home from work, and he's not due until five-thirty, so you've got plenty of time to change."

Angie looked at her watch. It was already 4:30. Well, it didn't matter. There were things to be done around the house, and if she still looked like this when Chris arrived, so be it. She crossed to the dining room and started pulling china out of the hutch. "The silver needs polishing, I'm afraid."

Bobby followed her in. "Angie, sweetheart, the silver is fine. And I can set a table." He took the plates from her and put them on the table. Turning her to look at him, he said, "Go upstairs, get changed, take a deep breath. Relax. As you said yourself, he's not all that. Just a new neighbor, not the prince of Wales."

Angie sighed. "I said that before I knew he was coming to dinner at my house with no warning from my uncle! I won't have him thinking that we're backwater hicks who can't make a person feel welcome."

Bobby bit the inside of his cheek to keep a straight face. "You seem to care an awful lot."

Angie squared her shoulders. "Now you're just bein' mean."

"Honey, have you ever noticed that your accent gets thicker when you get frustrated with me?" Bobby asked, eyes twinkling.

The two of them locked eyes, his sparkling with amusement, hers flashing with frustration. Finally, Angie humphed and turned on her heel. Bobby waited until he heard the water running for her shower before he started to laugh.

Angie had the bathroom steamed up before she ever set foot in the shower. A good hot shower would help her mood, she was convinced. She peeled out of her jeans and turtleneck and brushed her hair out of its ponytail. When she stepped under the water, she felt her shoulders begin to relax immediately. Bobby was wonderful and she adored him, but he could get on her last nerve, hand to God. Inviting someone over for dinner without any warning whatsoever. And not just anybody. This wasn't one of his poker buddies or Jimmy, his deputy. This was Chris Montgomery.

She shampooed her hair and breathed deeply the scent of the conditioner. Coconut. She loved the smell of coconut. It made her think of warm, exotic beaches. She soaped up her washcloth and began to wash away the day. That was one thing; she didn't want to smell like the diner when he got here. That wouldn't do at all. The soap was slippery and the water hot, and she was thinking about Chris Montgomery and the way his jeans fit as he had walked out of the diner. The way his jacket stretched across his shoulders when he had first walked in. How that last smile he had given her had lit up his face and made her feel so warm down to her toes. What would it feel like to have those arms around you, those lips kissing you . . . She gave in to the fantasy a moment more before pulling herself back to reality. And reality was that he was showing up on her doorstep in less than an hour, and if she wanted to be able to look him in the eye, she needed to stop thinking about him like this. Sighing, she rinsed off, turned off the water, and stepped out of the shower. Wrapping a thick, fuzzy towel around her hair and another one around her body, she left the warmth of the bathroom.

The old house didn't hold heat well, but she had, thankfully, remembered to turn on her heater before getting into the shower. Pulling out a jumper and another turtleneck, she tossed her clothes over it to warm them quickly. She dried off and pulled on her underwear. It wasn't often that she envied Carter Anne any longer. Sibling rivalry had, for the most part, gone the way of training wheels and braces. After all, God gave everyone different gifts. And Angie knew she was pretty. Everyone was always telling her what a pretty face she had. But, as Angie pulled up her functional cotton panties and fastened her sturdy bra behind her, she found herself envying Carter Anne. She could have shopped out of the catalogs or even gone into Danville to shop at the mall like Carter Anne and her friends, but where Carter Anne looked sexy and modern in her lacy things, Angie just would have looked foolish—if she could have found anything to fit her in the first place. She caught a glimpse of herself in the mirror. Good heavens, what was she thinking anyway? Why did it matter what her underwear looked like when there wasn't anyone around right now to see it? Shaking her head, she grabbed up her jumper and turtleneck before they caught fire and pulled them on. To complete the outfit, she added thick brown tights and her brown Doc Martens. So she wasn't the sexiest girl in town. She had comfortable down to an art.

She sat down at her vanity and brushed her hair out. It was still wet and she didn't have time to style it. Angie sighed again at her reflection. If only her hair was a normal color, instead of this mixed bag. Carter Anne's hair was a rich, chocolaty color . . . There she went again, comparing herself to Carter Anne. What had gotten into her tonight? She knew the answer.

The answer was Chris Montgomery and the fact that as soon as he laid eyes on Carter Anne, Angie would disappear. *Don't be silly*, she scolded herself. *It's not about him at all.* She was just tired and cranky. Probably due for her period. She always got emotional around then. Chris Montgomery was not worth thinking about. Instead, she stubbornly pulled her hair into a French braid and decided to forget about it. She made a token effort at makeup and then took herself downstairs.

Bobby was out back grilling the steaks when she came down. She could see him through the kitchen window, huddled against the cold in his work coat. There were mushrooms and onions sauteeing on the stove. Carter Anne was checking on the potatoes baking in the oven. "Hey," she said as Angie appeared in the kitchen.

"Hey," Angie replied. One look at her sister and she felt silly for having thought about Chris Montgomery at all. Carter Anne was in a blue cashmere sweater, short black skirt, silky black hose, and clunky black high-heeled boots. She could have stepped out of a fashion magazine rather than just spent a day as the elementary school's receptionist.

"Can I help?" Angie asked as she popped a cherry tomato into her mouth.

"Would you do the salad?" Carter Anne waved the spatula in the direction of a pile of vegetables on the counter before returning to the saute pan. "Can you believe he did this? Just invited this guy over without telling us first?"

"I know," Angie commiserated with her sister. She picked up a knife and started slicing. "I've already scolded him."

Carter Anne laughed. "Then that makes two of us. He didn't call me until four when I was walking out the door at work. I could have shot him if I'd had a gun, hand to God. Who is this guy anyway? All the girls at work were talking about him."

"Chris Montgomery. Seems nice enough."

Carter Anne turned from the stove and stared at her sister. "You've met him?"

Angie nodded and kept slicing. "He came in for lunch today. Like I said, seems nice enough."

"What's he look like? Some people are saying he's gorgeous, but Susan thinks he's probably a freak of some kind, sneaking in like he did last night."

Angie felt herself blush. "He's *not* a freak."

Carter Anne saw the color come to Angie's cheeks. "Oooooh!" She giggled. "Tell me, tell me quick, before Bobby comes back in."

Before Angie could speak, the doorbell rang. The two women looked at each other in a frozen moment before Angie found her voice. "Answer the door and you'll find out."

"No," Carter Anne went back to the potatoes. "He already knows you. You answer it. Anyway, I'm not leaving you to finish dinner!"

Angie laughed and headed to the door. She got three steps away from it when she realized he didn't know she was Bobby's niece. Or at least, he hadn't let on at lunch. Well, surprise kept life interesting.

Chris stood at the door, flowers in one hand and a six-pack in the other. Unless he'd *totally* missed his guess, Bobby wasn't a white wine kind of guy. The flowers for his nieces had been a little harder to find, but he refused to show up empty-handed. Gran would have come back from the grave to yell at him if he'd even thought about it. Finally, the man at the hardware store had told him about the small florist tucked away in the corner of the main strip. Chris had gotten there just at closing, but the young woman behind the counter had acted as if she had all the time in the world. He had no doubt his visit would make good gossip the next day. Ah . . . Southern hospitality.

As the door opened, Chris put on his friendliest smile . . . and froze.

"Angie?" he asked. It wasn't often that he was surprised anymore. He liked the feeling. In one quick glance, he took her in. The fading sunlight made her hair shine, each hue fighting for dominance. Her green jumper enhanced the green of her eyes and managed to conceal her curves while hinting, teasingly, that they were there.

"Chris Montgomery." Angie smiled back at him. "Come on in." She stepped back to let Chris in.

"These are for you and your sister." He handed Angie the flowers. They were modest, just carnations and daisies, but Angie smiled as if she had never been given flowers before. She buried her nose in them, breathing in their scent. Chris watched her smile go from polite to honest. Such a little thing and it brought her such happiness.

Angie looked up from the flowers, still smiling. Their eyes locked. His look was so . . . intense. Angie's smile faded, and her hand went to her throat as Chris's eyes dropped to her lips.

Bobby stood a moment and took in the scene. Wasn't this an interesting development? He cleared his throat. To the man's credit, Chris didn't even flinch, just turned his smile on Bobby. Angie, on the other hand, nearly jumped out of her skin.

"Bobby! Dammit!" she squealed. "You could scare a body half to death sneaking around like that."

Bobby controlled his laughter. "Sorry, Angie. Didn't realize walking into my own hallway was sneaking." He dropped Chris a conspiratorial wink. Angie looked back and forth between the two men, Chris masking his amusement only slightly better than Bobby.

"These need water," she said flatly and marched back into the kitchen muttering.

Bobby turned to Chris, extending his hand. "Come on in. Sorry about that."

Chris released his smile. "Warmest welcome I've had in months." The two men shook hands before Chris handed over Bobby's beer.

They walked through the old house. "Hope you like steak," Bobby spoke easily.

The two women were in the kitchen. Angie was arranging the flowers in a large vase. Lead crystal and very old if Chris had to guess. She didn't turn at the sound of Bobby's voice, but the other woman did.

"And this is my other niece," Bobby continued. "Carter Anne, Chris Montgomery."

Carter Anne extended her hand daintily. "Nice to meet you, Chris." She smiled.

"You as well. Thank you for having me on such short notice."

"Oh, it was no problem. Really." She motioned to a chair at the kitchen table, ignoring Bobby's snort. Chris sat and studied her quickly as she spooned the vegetables into a serving bowl. She was an attractive woman, he'd give her that. Her rich brown hair was styled just so, and her outfit, which clung in all the right places indeed, spoke of studied casualness. She was, well, Chris thought, a little too perfect. And too thin. He wondered if she would eat any of the dinner she was preparing.

Bobby put the six-pack in the fridge, pulling one for himself and another for Chris.

"I wouldn't say no to one of those, Bobby," Carter Anne said. Bobby handed her his.

"Angie?" he asked before he closed the door.

"No, thanks." She had turned around and was leaning up against the counter. She lifted her diet soda, showing it to Bobby. "I'm set."

Carter Anne sat down next to Chris. "And thank you for the flowers. They're lovely."

Chris started to shrug as he looked over at the vase next to Angie. But they *were* lovely. Whatever Angie had done in arranging them had caused an ordinary bouquet of midwinter flowers to be a stunning riot of color against the green of the fern and the white baby's breath. He looked from the flowers to Angie. She was watching him. The blush that came to her cheeks at being caught gave her face a warm glow. Chris smiled at her. As she ducked her head, he turned back to Carter Anne. "My pleasure. Although I didn't realize they were quite that lovely when I got them." He motioned toward the vase.

"Oh yes," Carter Anne agreed. "Angie is so talented with things like that. I keep telling her she should go into design of some sort but . . ." Carter Anne shrugged. Chris turned to look at Angie.

She swallowed the sip she was taking and spoke. "I don't want something I do for the love of it to become work."

"I can see the wisdom of that." Chris nodded. "Still, seems to me, a gift like that"—he nodded at the flowers again—"that's something that could be both. And I've always found it easier to work when you love what you're doing."

Carter Anne smiled and patted his hand. "You tell her, Chris! She certainly doesn't listen to me and Bobby."

"For now, though," Bobby himself spoke up. "The steaks should be ready. I'll be right back." He strolled outside, not bothering with his coat.

"Y'all go in and sit. I'll pull the potatoes," Angie spoke, handing the mushrooms and onions to Carter Anne. She had to have a minute. Just a minute to compose herself.

Carter Anne stood and Chris offered her his arm. "Miz Carter Anne?" She giggled, linked her arm with his, and led him into the dining room.

Angie took a deep breath. Of all the crazy things. Hand to God, she had to get a grip or she wouldn't make it through dinner. Nothing would come of this anyway. It never did. She busied herself, pulling the baked potatoes from the oven, pouring the beer and her soda into glasses. By the time she was done, she felt calmer.

Bobby came in with the steaks in one hand and she handed him the platter of potatoes for the other. Picking up the tray of drinks, Angie followed him into the dining room.

She studied the table with a practiced eye. Bobby had done well. Not only was the table set but the water glasses were full, the salad was on the table already, and the butter and sour cream were ready for the potatoes.

Carter Anne stood and took the potatoes from Bobby so he could put the steaks down. Once they were seated again, Carter Anne looked at Chris.

"So, how do you like Lambert Falls so far, Chris?" She began serving up the food, hardly looking away from him.

Chris took his plate from her. The steak smelled delicious and the potato was steaming. Yeah, he'd been living a soldier's life too long. "Seems nice enough so far. In some ways, it's like walking into a storybook. Pops talked so much about the town that I feel like I've been here before."

"Well," Carter Anne said with a smile, nibbling her plain potato, "I hope we don't let you down then."

Angie saw the smile he gave Carter Anne. It was bright and friendly . . . and it didn't reach his eyes. She didn't want to grin as she added sour cream and butter to her potato, but she couldn't quite help herself.

Carter Anne leaned into Chris. "Though the Falls must seem pretty ordinary to you considering the places you've been. You have probably seen some amazing things." She waited expectantly.

Bobby saw the shift in the young man but doubted if his girls had noticed. *He's flipped that switch again. Closed himself off.* Bobby watched and waited.

"I have been some interesting places," Chris said, slicing his steak. "I really loved the Panamanian jungle. It's warm and humid. The canopy is thick enough that it gives the light a mysterious quality. Like a cross between Sherwood Forest and Middle Earth."

It seemed to Angie that Chris hadn't missed a beat. And yet . . . had something shifted in him when Carter Anne had asked the question? His voice was calm enough and still friendly but . . . Maybe she was imagining it. And what he was talking about was so fascinating. The jungles of Panama. Made her trips to Virginia and the Outer Banks positively mundane.

"Right, Angie?" Carter Anne's voice broke into her thoughts. She sounded a little exasperated.

"What? Oh. I'm sorry. I was thinking." She looked at her sister. Bobby was watching her, and Chris, well, Chris Montgomery had the strangest expression on his face. She couldn't read it at all. She sighed to herself.

"Earth to Angie." Carter Anne laughed. "I said you and I like the beach."

"Oh, definitely," Angie agreed. "We go to the Outer Banks every summer for a week."

Carter Anne turned back to Chris with a smile. "See. We don't mind sand. Still, it's probably a little different from Afghanistan."

Angie tried to hide her shock. Had Chris mentioned the deserts of the Middle East and Carter Anne had talked about *Nags Head*? No wonder he looked like he had closed down.

"Well." Chris nodded his head toward Angie. "I don't want to bore your sister into daydreaming again."

"No! Oh, no . . ." Angie started. "That's not . . . I mean . . ."

Bobby recognized now was the time to step in. "Angie, Carter Anne, Chris was asking me about life here in the Falls. Told him you could give him a better introduction to town than I could. What should a man know 'bout living here?"

Chris busied himself with his dinner, grateful to Bobby for stepping in. The man might be a small-town sheriff, but he could read people.

Carter Anne turned her smile back on Chris. "What would you like to know?"

Chris swallowed before speaking. "I already know not to let Maddie starch my pants and"—he forced Angie to meet his eyes and gave her a wink—"where to get the best cup of coffee and good conversation." Angie smiled sheepishly at him before taking a bite of her steak. It wasn't the smile he'd gotten earlier, but at least she was looking at him again. He'd settle for that for now. "Let's start with a grocery store, movie theatre, and a place to buy a couple shirts."

"That's easy." Carter Anne started answering questions. Chris listened as she told him about the malls in Greensboro and across the state line in Danville, the first run movie theatre, the dollar theatre, and the Sears. But he was waiting for Angie to speak. Waiting for the sound of that warm honey.

"And the Food Lion is the easiest place to get groceries. It's smaller than the Kroger over in Greensboro, but it's right here," Carter Anne continued.

"That'll beat the 7-Eleven," Bobby added.

"But." There was his reward. Angie was speaking to him again. Chris turned his attention to her. "Come spring, you'll just want to shop at the farmers' market here in town on Saturdays."

"Local farmers?" Chris asked, hoping to keep her talking, to help relieve her embarrassment from earlier.

"The best," she continued. "Fruits and veggies so colorful

and ripe you'll think they come from the Garden of Eden. And fresh breads, too. There's nothing like a thick slice of bread smothered in Carter Anne's pear honey for breakfast."

"Pops used to say that the corn here in North Carolina was the sweetest anywhere."

"He was right, then," Angie agreed. She smiled. She wouldn't let herself go, though. She *wouldn't*. Nothing could come from her developing a crush on a man like Chris Montgomery. Well, nothing but her own heartache.

Chris returned her smile and she felt that quiver in her stomach again. But she *wouldn't*. "Then I'm glad I'm planning on sticking around."

"Been meaning to ask you about that," Bobby said, pushing his empty plate away and leaning back in his chair.

"Well, ask about it over coffee and dessert," Carter Anne piped up. "You boys go into the den. Angie and I will be right in."

Chris looked at Carter Anne's plate. Sure enough, all the salad was gone but half the plain potato and more of her steak remained. Angie's plate, however, was as empty as his and Bobby's.

"Let me help clear, at least," he said. Carter Anne started to refuse him, but he lifted a hand. "Please. I insist. After a meal like this it's the least I can do."

Much to his private embarrassment, Chris kept making reasons to squeeze by Angie, brushing her hip or her hand. Good God! When was the last time he'd reacted to a woman this way? Had he ever?

Finally, though, the table was cleared and there was nothing more he could do without being obvious. Even if he had been able to come up with an excuse, Carter Anne spoke up.

"Now you two"—she pointed at Chris and Bobby then to the door—"scoot. Out of my kitchen."

Bobby glanced at Chris. "When she uses that tone of voice, you want to listen. Trust me."

Chris laughed. "Yeah. I had a sergeant when I first came out of boot that used that same tone."

Carter Anne laughed as she watched the two men retreat into the den. Still smiling, she turned to Angie. She was at the counter, scooping warm peach crisp into bowls. The coffee was already brewing.

"Well?" Carter Anne asked as she pulled the ice cream from the freezer.

"Well, what?" Angie responded.

"Oh don't give me that!" She crossed over to the counter and started scooping ice cream on top of the crisps. "He couldn't keep his eyes off you." Carter Anne's voice was a whisper.

"Well, he can look all he wants to." The image of him she'd had earlier in the shower tried to interfere with her common sense, but she pushed it aside. "I'm not interested."

"Not interested?" Carter Anne's voice rose. With a quick look at the door separating them from the man in question, she lowered it again. "Did you *see* him?"

Angie laughed. "Carter Anne, I just had dinner with the man. *Of course* I *saw* him." She was preparing the coffee tray and setting the dessert bowls on another with quiet efficiency.

Carter Anne looked hard at her sister. "You're *not* interested, are you? Truly and really."

Angie took the ice-cream container and put it back in the freezer, then handed the dessert tray to Carter Anne. She felt a momentary pang of guilt. *Truly and really* was the phrase they had used between them since childhood. It signified that, no matter what else was going on, no matter what had been said or what the rest of the world thought, *this* was the truth. How many hurt feelings had been mended by the question *Do you feel that way truly and really?* Still, a momentary infatuation wasn't worth telling anyone—not even Carter Anne.

"I'm not interested, Carter Anne. Truly and really." Angie picked up the coffee tray. "Why don't you go for it if you're so taken with him?"

Carter Anne studied her sister. Satisfied with what she saw, she smiled her most flirtatious smile. "Maybe I will. I can always console him when he realizes you're not interested." She turned, flipping her hair, smile in place.

Angie gave herself a moment to sigh once Carter Anne's back was turned. It was better this way. Truly and really. Putting on her own smile, she followed her sister into the other room to join the men.

"So, there's my sister, tied to the tree." Chris was speaking as the women entered the room. Bobby was laughing so hard he had tears in his eyes. "And me, covered in my mother's makeup for war paint and my father's axe in my hand, both of us frozen in terror at the appearance of Pops and my dad."

"Oh!" Bobby laughed, wiping his eyes. "I bet Doc tanned your hide good for that."

Chris looked up as Angie set the coffee on the table. "I swear, sometimes I *still* wince when I sit down."

Bobby was still chuckling. "Yeah, I was a few years behind your dad in school, but I remember him. How's he doing?" Even focused on the conversation, Bobby realized Carter Anne had taken the seat next to Chris on the couch while Angie was in the other chair. Well damn.

"He's doing great. Expects to retire in a year or two with a star. Then Mom insists he's going to spend the next year buying and remodeling a place of their own. She's tired of military housing."

Bobby nodded but Carter Anne spoke before he could say anything.

"What about the old place here?"

Chris smiled behind a sip of coffee. It had been well done—that subtle way women had of asking the question behind the question. "Pops left the house to me," Chris answered. "Guess he figured I was the one who would want it."

"And did he figure right?" Angie asked, taking a bite of her dessert.

Chris watched her lift the fork to her lips, then met her eyes straight on. "Yeah. Yeah, he did. I think I plan on sticking around awhile."

Angie threw her other shoe into the closet. It struck the wall with a satisfying thunk before dropping next to its twin. Men! They were idiots, every single one of them, hand to God. And the evening had been going so well.

After dessert, she'd been shocked when Chris had asked her to take a walk with him. Seeing Carter Anne's smug told-you-so smile had made Angie want to say no. Until she saw the look of pleasure in Bobby's eyes. Damn the man. She'd said yes.

Angie's hand hesitated at the drawer where she kept her pajamas. Okay. Fine. Maybe there had been a quiver in her stomach that she hadn't been able to suppress. She was woman enough to admit it, she decided, pulling her favorite oversize pajamas out and slipping into them. But she'd only said yes because of that look in her uncle's eyes. She'd known at the time what would happen. And she'd been right.

"It must be nice for you, living here in the middle of town," Chris commented as they walked down the street, the lights of town center shining around them.

"It's certainly convenient," Angie agreed. "Bobby and I can walk to work practically year-'round. 'Course he takes the squad car a lot. Makes it more official."

"Of course."

They walked a few steps in an awkward silence. Chris struggled to find something to say. Anything to talk about. "But not Carter Anne? She doesn't walk to work?" He rolled his eyes, grateful for the dark night.

"No. The school's too far for her to walk dressed for the office."

"As she was dressed tonight? Yeah, she wouldn't want to walk far dressed like that. Way too nice for a walk."

Angie looked down at her oversize coat and sturdy, comfortable shoes. Why in the world was she the one out here if all he was going to do was ask about Carter Anne?

"You work at the diner. Bobby's the sheriff. What does Carter Anne do?"

They had reached the far side of town square, closer to the old Montgomery place than to her home. Angie stopped and looked at him. "She is the receptionist at the elementary school and takes classes at the community college two nights a week. Although she doesn't know exactly what she wants to do, she does know it isn't stay here and be a receptionist for the rest of her life. She's twenty-one years old and currently single. Although we live with Bobby, he respects the fact that we are both adults, so she doesn't have a curfew. You'll have to get her cell number from her directly. We do, however, only have one house phone, and when it rings after midnight, Bobby tends to think it's an emergency call, so please be respectful. Is there anything else I can tell you about my sister?"

Chris stood, mouth hanging open. It might have been a while since he had felt surprised by anything, but this woman had done it to him twice in a matter of hours. He smiled. He could learn to like this a lot.

"No." He shook his head. "I think that just about covers it.

I'm surprised to hear she doesn't have men asking her out all the time."

Angie pulled her coat around her tighter, crossing her arms in front of her chest. "I didn't say she didn't have suitors. I said she was currently single. Date too many men in a small town and you will get a reputation. She's careful about that."

"And what about you?" Chris asked. He reached out and uncrossed her arms.

"What about me?" Angie asked. She didn't think the shivers running down her arms had anything to do with the temperature. What had she missed? Hadn't he just been asking her about Carter Anne?

"Do you have . . . *suitors*?" Chris laughed at the old-fashioned word.

"Is it so funny to think that I might?" Angie spat.

"No." Chris shook his head. This wasn't going the way he'd planned. "I just . . . too much competition, is all."

"Ah." Angie nodded, stepping away from him. "I think I see now."

But Chris could tell by the look in her eyes that she didn't see. She didn't see at all. Too many men, no, too many boys had ignored her kind of beauty for too long, only seeing the beauty of the thin, perfect sister. Well, he'd just see about showing her.

Slowly, he closed the distance between them. "Do you?" he asked, his voice low. "Do you really? Can you see what I see? Or do you only see what the boys here in town see? Your beautiful sister who will eventually transfer to a four-year school, leaving you here with Bobby. Because that's what I bet you see."

His arms went around her, drawing her close. Those shoulders were as broad and as solid as they had looked under his jacket earlier in the day. For one moment, Angie thought about closing her eyes and giving in. He saw her indecision and lowered his mouth to hers. She pulled away just in time, his words *too much competition* ringing in her ears.

So, he thought she would be easier than Carter Anne because she wasn't as popular. *Didn't*, as a matter of fact, have suitors. Well, she wasn't so desperate that she'd fall into a man's arms just because he looked good, either, thank you very much. Angie drew herself up and looked up into his eyes, hard.

"You, Chris Montgomery, need to understand a few things. I *like* livin' in Lambert Falls. I *like* takin' care of Bobby. I'm *happy* where I am and with who I am." She realized her voice was rising and she made a deliberate effort to lower it before continuing. And she continued quickly before he could say whatever it was that he was obviously trying to say. "Which means, you can save your charm and your pity and your white knight act for someone who needs it. I'll tell Bobby and Carter Anne we got close enough to yours that you went on home, with your thanks for a lovely evening."

"Angie." Chris started to reach for her again then realized it would be a mistake. "Angie, you don't understand . . ."

"Good night." Angie had interrupted him with a nod, turned on her heel, and walked away.

When she'd gotten home, Bobby was on the phone, so she walked past his office with a wave. Carter Anne was cleaning up, but Angie just ignored her as she headed up the stairs into her room and changed into her most comfortable pajamas.

She lay on her bed in the dark, staring up at the ceiling. Idiots. All of them. Finally, rolling over, with an ache in her stomach, she closed her eyes and tried to sleep.

Chapter 2

". . . so call me." Carter Anne's message finished and Chris hit the button to delete it from his voice mail without a second thought. He was torn. It was the third message she had left him in the time since the dinner over at their place. Part of him knew it was rude to continue to just ignore her. Rude and hurtful. But another part of him still remembered the closed-off look in Angie's eyes when she thought all he wanted was information on her sister. Worse, he remembered the way her eyes had changed from closed off to hurt when she thought he just wanted a quick roll with her. How the hell was he supposed to be nice to one sister without alienating the other? And how had he managed to get himself into this kind of a mess in just over a week and after only one dinner? Combat was easier than dealing with women.

It *had* been a little over a week, though. He had made a strategic retreat and given Angie some room. Now, Chris thought, maybe it was time for some good coffee instead of the liquid mud that seemed to always come from his own coffeepot. He glanced at the clock. Almost two-thirty. Angie got off at four. That gave him enough time to get back into her good graces— or at least back on speaking terms—without looking like he was stalking her. And surely the diner wouldn't be too crowded at this time of day on a Saturday afternoon. Grabbing his jacket, he headed out.

His keys were in his hand instinctively. But hadn't Mrs. Hughes at the Food Lion told him almost no one locked their doors in Lambert Falls? Part of learning to be a civilian again was going to be learning to trust a little bit, learning not to keep looking over his shoulder all the time. Chris hesitated. Finally, determinedly, he shoved his keys back in his coat pocket and walked away. He chuckled to himself. He felt as if he had landed in Bedford Falls instead of Lambert Falls, where everything was good and everything was nice—so long as George Bailey had been born. Well, Chris didn't know if it was George or not, but something kept Lambert Falls good and nice. Nicer than he was used to, anyway.

The walk down the hill was easy. The wind that had brought a dusting of snow with it had died down and the winter sun shone pale in the sky. It was still cold, but without the wind, not bitterly so. And the inch or so of snow that covered everything gave the town a Currier & Ives look. He could have been in a quaint New England township or a small Colorado mountain town as easily as Lambert Falls, North Carolina. Hell, if it hadn't been for the electricity lighting the shops as he entered town square, it could have been a Nepalese village. Chris smiled. Names and faces were different, sometimes the customs varied a little bit, but small towns were small towns, wherever you went. It was one of the things he liked, why he found them so comforting.

In spite of the wind dying down, the warm air of the diner felt good on his cheeks as Chris walked in. He had guessed incorrectly about the number of people who would be here, though. Looking around, he figured the place was at least three-quarters full. Angie was working the counter and a young woman he didn't know seemed to be handling the tables. Scanning the row quickly, Chris saw three empty stools right in the middle of the long stretch of counter. He moved to the middle one and sat down.

Angie turned around, orders in each hand, and stopped cold. The turn had brought her face-to-face with Chris Montgomery. Damn! Damn and damn. It was a small town, so she had known she would run into him eventually, but leave it to him to waltz in here and catch her unawares. She nodded quickly and moved along to the other end of the counter, delivering two men their "specials all the way." Smiling, she checked in with the men to make sure they didn't need anything else before taking her time getting back to the middle of the counter. If she was going to be honest with herself, she wasn't really upset with him. She was upset with herself. She had made a fool of herself last time they'd been face-to-face and wasn't looking forward to having to look the man in the eye again let alone have conversation with him. When she couldn't waste any more time chatting with other customers without obviously avoiding him, she forced a smile on her face and stood in front of him.

"Well, hi there." She hoped her smile hid her embarrassment. "What can I bring you?" She pulled her order pad out of her apron automatically.

Well, Chris thought, she was a little too friendly to be natural, but that beat giving him the cold shoulder in front of the whole diner. He figured it was a step. "Definitely coffee. Mine's mud and I'm getting desperate."

Angie giggled. It sounded genuine. Definitely a good first step. "And what pies do you have today?"

Angie slipped her order pad back into her apron, turned, and grabbed the coffeepot before answering him. As she poured, she spoke, "A desperate man shouldn't have to wait for his coffee while he decides on his pie." Chris reached for the sugar, but Angie was already handing it to him, along with a large handful of creamers.

"A woman after my own heart." Chris put a hand on his chest and smiled at her. "Not only does she understand the need for coffee, but she remembers the crazy way I take it." He started dumping sugar by the spoonful into his mug.

"Now," Angie said, raising an eyebrow as she watched him add more sugar and at least half a dozen creams to his coffee, "if your system really can handle more sugar on top of that," she nodded at his mug, "we've got banana cream, chocolate cream, and I *think* there's one more piece of pecan back there. But I'd order that fast if you want it."

"The pecan's that good?" Chris asked, sipping his coffee. The small whimper of pleasure that came from his closed lips was involuntary and completely real. It really was good coffee.

Angie couldn't help herself. She smiled at him. A real smile that warmed Chris more than the diner and the coffee combined. "It's that good. I can vouch for it myself." She leaned down and whispered, "I had a piece at lunch."

Chris nodded and Angie started to move away, but he called her back. "Angie?" She turned, indicating she was listening. "You got ice cream back there?"

"Only a dollar more. And I can vouch for that, too."

Chris smiled. "Bring it on, then." He watched her walk away then went back to his coffee. Okay, so he'd gone too fast the other night. He could accept that. He was beginning to figure out Miss Angie Kane, and a slower approach was going to be necessary. He could do that. When necessary, he could be a very patient man.

The bell over the door jingled. Out of habit, Chris cut his eyes without turning his head in order to see who was coming in. He closed them just as quickly and took a deep drink of coffee. When he opened them again, Carter Anne was sitting on the stool next to him.

"Well hi, stranger!" She leaned on the counter, facing him. "You're a hard man to get ahold of, did you know that?"

Chris turned and smiled back. "Don't mean to be. Sorry I haven't returned your calls. I've been busy around the house and getting settled."

"Then I'm glad I ran into you and I'll ask you quick before you disappear again."

Chris took another swallow of coffee. This was not going well. He became aware of the fact that the people sitting around them were listening. Oh, everyone was being subtle about it—and they were listening nonetheless. He kept an eye on the kitchen door, not sure if he wanted Angie to come out of it or stay on the other side of it.

"Every Sunday night, Sartini's, the Italian place, has live music. I think it's his brother and nephew, honestly, but they're pretty good if you like the cheesier Dean Martin and Frank Sinatra stuff. And they're excellent when you consider the other options in the Falls."

Chris nodded, trying to appear politely interested but not too interested. Carter Anne sighed in quiet exasperation. "So . . . how would you like to take me there tomorrow night?"

Again, Chris was aware of his audience. Some of them, like the two older women in the booth directly behind them, weren't even trying to be subtle any longer and were staring at him openly, waiting for his answer. Had he just been thinking how much he liked small towns?

"I think that would be fine, Carter Anne," he answered with a smile. He wasn't sure he had any other recourse. He wouldn't turn her down in public like this. If he had only returned her phone calls, it could have been private. Then he could have turned her down without the whole town knowing about it. "What time should I pick you up?"

"How about six? Music starts at six-thirty."

Carter Anne touched his arm lightly. It was a movement that could have been simple friendship or could have been more, leaving it entirely up to the person on the receiving end to interpret it. Chris decided not to interpret it at all. And with an inward groan, he saw Angie choose that moment to come out of the kitchen carrying his pie.

Angie's heart was suddenly in her throat. Why did she keep doing this to herself when it came to this man? What was it about him that turned her into a crazy woman? They had done nothing but pass time while he ordered his pie. And for the past week—nine days actually, but who was counting—she had done nothing but tell herself she hoped to never see the man again. So why did the sight of Carter Anne's hand on his arm in such an intimate way make her want to cry?

Squaring her shoulders, Angie walked over to the two of them. "Hey, Carter Anne." She put the pie down in front of Chris a little harder than necessary but certainly not hard enough to make a mess or spill the last piece of pie so he couldn't eat it—more's the pity.

"Hey, Ang. Guess what?" Carter Anne wiggled her eyebrows at her sister. "Chris is taking me to Sartini's for dinner tomorrow night."

Angie looked from her sister to Chris and back again. "Hey, that's great." Forcing herself to look at Chris, she continued. "The food is really good. You'll like it."

Carter Anne studied her sister a moment. Something wasn't right here. She couldn't quite put a finger on it, but something was definitely not right. Still, now was not the time or the place to question Angie, so she decided to bookmark it and come back to it later. "I'll be sure to tell Bobby the two of you are on your own for dinner. Now, however, I need to go." She turned to Chris. "See you tomorrow at six," and turned back to Angie. "See you tonight, honey." Chris nodded while Angie waved her off.

Clearing her throat, Angie straightened her apron. "Well, enjoy the pie." She topped off his coffee and walked away.

"Angie . . ." Chris called to her, but this time she didn't turn.

The Jones sisters sitting directly behind him were very aware that he hadn't watched Carter Anne walk away with nearly the same intensity that he watched Angie, but no one else seemed to notice.

Bobby was sitting in front of the television, but it wasn't on. Instead, he was reading a book. Carter Anne took a moment to smile at his bowed head. It was probably some tome about some ancient empire or medieval lord. Bobby was always reading about something no one else could understand. Or be interested in, if truth were told. But, hand to God, she loved the man. He had always given her good advice, and she knew he would again this time. Had he been out of uniform or drinking a beer, she might have let it sit. Let him relax for the night. Since he was indeed still in uniform and had a soda—propped precariously on the arm of his chair, she noticed—he was still on call. No matter how absorbed he might have looked, she knew part of him was still aware, still alert, just in case his radio went off.

As if to prove her point, he spoke without ever looking up from his page. "Carter Anne, if you've got something on your mind, come on in and sit. Otherwise, you're just boring holes in the back of my head for no reason." She crossed to him and kissed the top of his head before taking a seat in the chair next to him.

He looked up as she did and smiled at her. She was dressed for her date in gray woolen slacks, a pale pink sweater, and dark boots that managed to be both fashionable and functional with the snow. Her mother's pearls lay beautifully in the V of the sweater and dangled from her ears. Bobby shook his head at himself. This is what happened to a man when he lived with young women. He started to understand fashion. "You look real nice, honey."

"Thanks, Bobby," Carter Anne replied.

Bobby looked at her harder. There was no light shining in her eyes the way there should have been before going out on a date, though. "But you've got something on your mind. What is it?"

Carter Anne sighed. "Bobby, I don't think I should be going out with Chris tonight."

Bobby closed his book and put it aside. Honestly, he was inclined to agree with her, but he wasn't sure how to say that. He bought himself more time by taking a sip of his Dr. Pepper. "What makes you say so?" He figured that was safe. She could lead the discussion wherever it was going.

"I think," Carter Anne started. She readjusted herself in the chair as if she couldn't get comfortable in it or with herself. "I think maybe Angie likes him."

"Well . . ." Bobby hated moments like this. They needed a woman's touch, not his. Still, he was all his girls had and vice versa, so he'd do his best. They had always done their best by him, the least he could do was give it back. "Why'd you ask him out, then?" Please God, his voice had sounded neutral and not judgmental.

"Because she told me she *didn't* like him. Didn't like him truly and really. And she told me I *should* try for him."

Now Bobby was just confused. Ten years he'd been married and eighteen years he'd raised these girls alone and he still didn't understand women. Not really. "Then why is there a problem?"

Carter Anne sighed with barely hidden exasperation. "Because of the way she looked yesterday when she found out we were going out tonight. And the way she hasn't talked to me about it at all today. Not at all. Every time I've tried to check with her about it, she's changed the subject."

At least his youngest niece was more observant than she often let on. Bobby could be grateful for that. Sometimes it seemed that she wandered around in her own little world, but never when it had to do with Angie. "Sounds to me like maybe you're right. Maybe you shouldn't be going out with him tonight."

"But it's almost six now!" Carter Anne's exasperation broke through. "And if she won't tell me she likes him . . ." She looked at her uncle pleadingly.

He balanced his soda again and leaned back. "Do you like him? Is that what you're telling me?" Bobby held his breath. This could get complicated. He hoped he knew how Chris was feeling. He suspected how Angie was feeling. If Carter Anne had gotten mixed up in all this, someone was going to get hurt.

"I don't know, Bobby. That's the problem. I think I could like him. I think I could like him very much. But I also think Angie already *does*."

"Carter Anne"—Bobby rubbed his eyes before looking back at her—"you're a good girl. And you're a smart girl. It *is* too late to cancel tonight. But keep your eyes and ears open. Be aware. And don't fall just because he's handsome and new."

"But Bobby." Now Carter Anne's eyes were twinkling, but with humor rather than her normal pre-date glow. "I like handsome and new."

Bobby laughed. She stood up and moved so she was standing over him. Reaching down, she took his hand in hers. "Thank you, Bobby."

Bobby squeezed her hand. Another crisis averted—or at

least postponed. The doorbell rang. "You be good tonight, Carter Anne."

She leaned down, gave him another kiss on the head, and was gone.

Chris looked across the table at Carter Anne. It had been a nice evening. Any night he spent in the company of an attractive woman, having a good meal and listening to live music, was a nice evening in his opinion. The fact that he had discovered he honestly liked Carter Anne and enjoyed her company made it even better. Although he couldn't pinpoint the exact moment she had stopped flirting with him, he knew she had. And that was fine by him. *This* woman, Chris realized, was one he could be friends with.

She fiddled with the rim of her decaffeinated cappuccino, speaking without lifting her eyes. "I feel I should apologize for the way I've behaved the last few days. You don't have to believe me, but I really don't usually throw myself at men like that."

"Carter Anne," Chris spoke gently. "Carter Anne." He repeated himself and waited until she finally looked up at him. "I know you don't. After a while, in my line of work"—Chris's voice was low and reassuring—"you learn to read people pretty quickly. You have nothing to apologize for."

Carter Anne smiled and felt herself relax again. "Thank you. I've been feeling a little foolish."

Chris smiled back. "Would it sound patronizing if I said I've been flattered?"

Now Carter Anne laughed warmly. "I'd be insulted if you hadn't been."

Chris joined in the laughter, grateful he'd handled that the right way, grateful the awkward moment between them had passed. She picked up her coffee and sat back in her chair, studying the man across from her. There was one more thing she had to know.

"You're really smitten with her, aren't you?"

Chris's hand stopped, his own regular coffee halfway to his mouth. "What do you mean?" he asked, forcing himself to sound nonchalant and take a sip.

Carter Anne looked at him. Yep. It was all there. The slight change in body language, the guarded look in the eyes. Maybe she wasn't military, but she'd been reading men since she was twelve. Well, good. She was coming to like him. It would have been a shame if she'd had to squish him like a bug.

"Angie," she said, not completely able to hide her smile. "You're smitten."

Chris laughed again. "I haven't heard that word in years. Didn't know anyone still used it."

She smiled openly this time. "You're very good at not answering questions."

"And you are very good at asking them." Chris sighed and made up his mind. "But yeah. Yeah, I'm smitten"—he tipped his coffee at her—"as you put it." Carter Anne's grin was smug. Yes, he could definitely be friends with her. He leaned in. "Got any suggestions?"

Carter Anne thought for a moment. "Go slow. And don't do anything stupid like try to make her jealous or ignore her or any of the ridiculous things men do. She won't trust it if it's too fast, but she'll never trust *you* if you play games."

Chris nodded. He realized, without *much* embarrassment, that he was hanging on Carter Anne's every word.

"Get to know her," Carter Anne continued. "As a person, not as a girl. Then she'll believe it. And"—she put her empty cup into the saucer and her eyes twinkled merrily—"stop taking her sister out on dates."

Chris threw back his head and laughed. "Oh, Carter Anne,"

he said a moment later, reaching for their check. "I can handle all that."

He paid for their dinner and the two of them stepped out into the cold. Carter Anne pulled the collar of her coat up and shivered. The wind had picked back up and the temperature was dropping. The parking lot was only at the end of the block, but it felt farther than that. She slipped her arm in his and snuggled closer, both of them comfortable with the movement, knowing where they stood.

Not many stores were still open on Sunday night, but the few that were—the drugstore, the ice-cream parlor, and the video store—gave off a welcoming glow. As they reached the door of the ice-cream parlor, it opened and Angie backed out, a large lidded sundae in each mittened hand. Automatically, Chris held the door with his free hand. When she turned around, she bumped into his chest.

"Whoops! Sorry!" she said, stepping back. Then she registered who it was. Carter Anne slipped her arm out of Chris's, but not, she realized, in time to keep Angie from noticing. If she had thought Angie would be out tonight, she would never have taken his arm in the first place, dammit.

"Hey, honey." Carter Anne found her voice first. "We were just heading home."

Angie nodded and lifted the sundaes. "Bobby thought ice cream would help drive away the chill." She laughed but still couldn't meet Chris's eyes.

"Sounds good to me," he said. "Want some?" he asked Carter Anne.

"Oh no, I try not to eat ice cream," she replied instinctively. Oh damn. She'd done it again. This was not her night. She saw the hurt come into Angie's eyes and could've kicked herself. "But maybe some cocoa." She tried to redeem herself.

Chris jumped at the opening. "Want to join us?" he asked Angie quickly.

"No, thanks." Suddenly Angie just wanted to get home. She lifted up one of the sundaes again. "Bobby's'll melt. See you at the house, Carter Anne." She nodded to them and walked off to the parking lot and her own car.

"Well, that went well," Chris muttered.

"Come on." Carter Anne held the door open to the ice-cream parlor with a sigh. "We can't go straight home now. You might as well buy me that cocoa."

Chris watched a car pull out of the lot and head toward town square. She didn't even seem to hesitate. With a sigh of his own and a wry smile for Carter Anne, he walked into the parlor.

Angie was sitting on the edge of her bed, head in her hands, when the soft knock came on her door. It had to be Bobby. A little thing like a closed door never stopped Carter Anne. If she simply ignored it, Bobby would think she was asleep and leave her be. It was tempting, but she knew her uncle would just come at her later. The next knock, a little louder this time, made up her mind for her.

"You can come in, Bobby." She looked up as the door opened and was surprised to see Carter Anne walk in.

"How 'bout me?" Carter Anne asked as she crossed to the bed and sat down next to her sister. She put her arm around Angie's shoulders. "Honey . . ." she started, but Angie interrupted her.

"Carter Anne, please don't say anything. It's my own stupid fault for getting all worked up."

"Especially," Carter Anne broke in, "since you're getting all worked up about nothing."

Angie looked at Carter Anne out of the corner of her eye.

"Seriously, Angie. Chris is a nice guy. A really nice guy, but there's just nothing *there*."

Angie turned to face her sister. "But the way you two were snuggled up . . ."

"Angie." Carter Anne's voice was amused exasperation. "Did you feel how cold it is out there? I'd've snuggled up next to . . . next to Eddie Tomlinson, if he'd been walkin' next to me."

Angie laughed weakly. Eddie Tomlinson weighed about ninety pounds soaking wet, only had three teeth God gave him, and usually smelled of the garage he owned on the outskirts of town.

"Chris only has eyes for you, Angie," Carter Anne continued.

"Is that why he asked *you* out? Or why he let you snuggle up next to him?" Angie asked, hating the bitterness in her tone but unable to prevent it.

"Angie, honey." Carter Anne shook her head. "Chris didn't ask me out." Angie looked at her sister, but Carter Anne continued before her sister could voice her skepticism. "When you told me you weren't interested, *I* asked *him* out. He was just being polite."

"Really?" Angie asked.

"Really. That's part of what I've been trying to talk to you about this whole time you've been changing the subject on me."

Angie looked down, embarrassed.

"And even if he was interested in me"—Carter Anne lovingly brushed a stray lock of Angie's hair behind her ear—"knowing what I know now, all he'd do is pine until he lost interest and moved on."

Angie rested her head on Carter Anne's shoulder. Carter Anne stroked her hair.

"So why don't you make his week and let him know you're interested?"

"You said it yourself, Carter Anne," Angie replied quietly.

"What'd I say?"

"He'll lose interest and move on."

"What do you mean?" Carter Anne asked, trying to keep the amusement in her exasperation.

"I'm not like you, Carter Anne." And she turned and looked at her. "I don't want to leave the Falls. I like it here. But him? How long do you really think he'll stay? *Really*? How long before he gets tired of having to drive thirty minutes just to get to a grocery store that wasn't built in the '80s? Or a Starbucks?"

Carter Anne watched her sister struggle to stay calm as she continued.

"This is a man who has lived everywhere and seen so much. Do you really think he wants to drive an hour to get to a *mall*?

"And how long do you think it will take him to get tired of *me*? The farthest north I've ever been is DC. My major vacation every year is Nags Head or Virginia Beach. I like it that way, but Carter Anne," Angie was beginning to lose steam. How could she make her sister understand that life wasn't always the fairy tale Carter Anne wanted it to be? "No matter how happy *I* am with the Falls, with me, how long do you think a man like Chris Montgomery will be?"

"So you won't even give him a chance?" Carter Anne couldn't believe what she was hearing.

"Why?" Angie asked. "Why, when I know I'll be the one who gets hurt?"

Carter Anne stood up. "Angie, I love you, but hand to God, that's the biggest crock of shit I've ever heard you utter."

Angie started to speak, but Carter Anne held up her hand. "No. I'm too angry. Just know I don't think you are giving Chris near enough credit, but you're too scared and too stubborn to admit it."

She turned on her heel and marched to the door. Once it was open, she looked back. "And you don't give *yourself* enough credit, either."

Carter Anne slammed out, leaving Angie staring, open-mouthed, at her closed bedroom door.

Chapter 3

Chris was waiting for her when she stepped out of the diner. His collar was turned up against the cold, but otherwise he seemed oblivious to the temperature that had dropped steadily over the course of the day. Angie, on the other hand, was trying to pull on her mittens and simultaneously wrap her scarf tighter around her neck. Seeing him, she simply stopped. Not now. Not today. She was tired, she was cold, she was grumpy, and she just wanted to go home. Her very orderly life had gotten so . . . confused . . . since he had arrived in the Falls.

"Angie." Chris stepped toward her. He saw the wary look in her eyes and changed tack immediately. *Go slow*. Carter Anne's voice spoke in his head. His tone changed from slightly flirtatious to gentle. "Hard day?"

She closed her eyes. God he was handsome. "Chris," she started before she realized she had no idea what she wanted to say to him. Definitely complicated. Still, she may be tired, but she could be polite. "Does it show?"

Chris smiled. "Maybe a little."

Angie couldn't help but smile back. "The diner is particularly crazy this time of year, I guess. Too cold for the kids to do anything but come in to try to stay warm. But it keeps us busy."

She finished wrapping the scarf around her neck and tried to burrow into it up to her chin. Why wasn't his coat even done up? Didn't he know it was *cold*?

"Well." Chris saw his opening. "Could I walk with you? I've got something I'd like to talk to you about."

Angie sighed. What was she supposed to say to a request like that? The truth had always worked in the past. . . . Squaring her shoulders, she looked up at him. "Can I be totally honest with you?" There was that smile of his again.

"I hope so."

"I'm tired. My feet hurt. But mostly I'm embarrassed about the last couple times we've met, and I would really just like to forget all about them."

Chris thought for a moment. What the hell was he supposed to do now? This was *not* what he had expected. Then it hit him and he stuck out his hand. "Hi. I'm Chris Montgomery. Aren't you Angie Kane? I know your uncle."

Angie looked from him to his hand and back up into his eyes. They twinkled, but underneath the twinkle . . . was that nervousness? Was she, Angie Kane, making a man like Chris Montgomery nervous that she might not accept what was so obviously a peace offering? He tilted his head and lifted his shoulder slightly, hand still hanging between them.

"Chris." She shook her head, chuckling. He lowered his hand, still looking at her with that questioning expression on his face. Angie sighed. "Okay. Thanks." She nodded at him, and they fell in step together, heading toward the house on Main Street. "What did you want to talk to me about?"

"Actually, I have a business proposition for you."

"Really?" Angie cut her eyes over at him.

"Really," Chris continued. "And I'm serious about this, too."

"All right. What's this proposition, then?"

"I need some help around the house." Chris spoke quickly,

counting on her sense of propriety to not let her interrupt him. "A woman's touch, I guess you would say. There's a lot of Pops's stuff left that I need to go though, a lot of clearing out to do, and the place needs to be scrubbed top to bottom. It's simply too big a job for one person. If I want to get it done in the next ten years, anyway."

Angie wanted to be able to see him, look him in the eye, but it was too cold to stop and face him. "I can see that but why not just hire someone to come in . . . ?"

"That's what I'm talking about. Hiring someone to come in." His voice held a hint of amusement.

She rolled her eyes. "Why me, then?"

"First"—Chris cleared his throat, hoping she would take it the right way—"I don't want to pay someone *that* much." Angie laughed out loud. Good, she hadn't been insulted. He continued more confidently. "Second, I want someone I can trust not to talk all over town. I'm not expecting to find anything outrageous, but Pops was a private man and I'd like to keep it that way."

Angie nodded. This was going well. "Third, and finally I guess, I'm expecting to spend a lot of time with this person, so I'd like it to be someone I already know and like. When I thought about all three of those things, you seemed like the best choice." They were approaching the house. *Please, let her see the logic in saying yes*, he thought.

She stopped them at the foot of the walk. "That last one might be a problem. I can't quit the diner, especially if you're not paying *that* much."

Chris couldn't believe his ears. She was joking with him. Angie Kane had made a joke with him. He was grateful he had already thought about the diner. "What about a couple evenings a week, after you get off work?" He was close. He could feel it. She wanted to say yes.

"How about this?" Chris kept his voice calm, nonchalant. "Think about it. Talk to your uncle. Give me a call sometime this week."

Angie nodded. "I will." Then she smiled at him. "Carter Anne has your number."

Chris waited until she had gotten into the house and thrown him a wave. Yes, he could be very patient when he needed to be.

Carter Anne was at the kitchen table, flipping through a magazine when Angie walked in.

"Looks like they're getting divorced in spite of . . ." Carter Anne stopped midsentence as she looked at her sister. Angie's brow was furrowed in concentration. "What's up, Ang?" Carter Anne asked.

"Chris Montgomery just offered me a job." Angie realized she couldn't quite meet her sister's eyes, so she crossed to the refrigerator and pulled out a Diet Pepsi.

"Doing what?"

Angie took her time getting ice and pouring her drink into a glass before finally sitting down next to the other woman. "He wants help getting the old place in shape. 'A woman's touch' as he calls it."

Carter Anne looked down at her magazine to hide her smile. Oh, Chris. This is good. She knew she had to play it carefully or she would blow it for him. Composed, she looked back up. "What does that mean, exactly?"

"I'm not completely sure." Angie sipped her drink. "Going through stuff. Keeping the Doc's private life private. Maybe some decorating eventually. He didn't really get into details."

She was intrigued. Carter Anne could tell. Oh, Chris *was* good. "What about the diner?" she asked innocently.

"I'd only help him part-time. I couldn't quit for something so temporary."

"But he *is* offering to pay you, right?" Carter Anne was all in favor of romance, but business was business.

Angie laughed. Leave it to Carter Anne to cut to the heart of a matter. "Yes. He made it clear he was offering me a job, not asking me a favor."

"Well then." Carter Anne went back to her magazine as if the matter was settled. "I think you should do it."

This was the hard part, Angie realized. "Carter Anne, what about . . . well . . . You know how I feel." She let the rest of the sentence dangle as she fiddled with her glass.

Carter Anne realized that she had to tread very, very carefully. "Honey, you said it yourself: it's an infatuation. What better way to get over it than to get to know him, warts and all. Make him less of a mystery and more of a person." She flipped a page in her magazine as if it didn't matter. "You might discover he's just an ordinary guy."

Angie reached out for her sister's hand. "When did you get so wise?"

Carter Anne lifted her magazine. "Everything you ever want to know about relationships . . ."

"I'm gonna sleep on it, but you may be right." Angie stood up.

"Dinner'll be ready at six." Carter Anne went back to reading. Angie simply nodded as she sipped her drink and headed upstairs. Carter Anne watched her out of the corner of one eye and smiled. No, Angie wouldn't find Chris ordinary. Not ordinary at all.

"Twelve dollars an hour?!" Angie gasped at Chris. She had managed to maintain her composure throughout the whole meeting, even though she'd been nervous since deciding to accept his offer. When she'd called him to discuss terms, Chris hadn't wanted to talk about it over the phone. Instead, he had suggested she come to the house and look around. Damn the man, he'd even already known Sundays were her day off, so she hadn't been able to weasel out that way.

Still, she knew she had to get used to being around him, had to get comfortable with him. Had to find a way to keep her blood from racing every time she heard his voice if this was going to work. So she had agreed to come to the house.

Now, sitting on the edge of her chair in the kitchen, Angie found herself losing any sense of calm she had found in the last twenty minutes. Twelve dollars an hour. The man was insane, hand to God.

Chris tipped his chair, balancing precariously on the back two legs, and took a sip of his coffee in order to buy some time. The morning had been going well. He had been pleased when Angie had called to discuss details. More so when she'd agreed to come over. He had expected her to take the weekend, and instead, she was here now. And he'd gotten cocky, it had gone so well.

He'd done his homework. Firms would come in to do what he wanted, but it would be expensive. The money wasn't the issue. It was the principle. He'd spent too long living simply to be comfortable dropping money frivolously, even though he could afford to do so. So he'd lowballed her, expecting negotiations. What he hadn't expected was her outburst.

"I won't take twelve dollars an hour for this, and if you think I will, then that's crazy talk," Angie continued. She was getting heated and she knew it but . . . well, twelve dollars was insulting. Like she was a charity case or something.

Chris watched her over the rim of his mug—and the light went on. She thought it was *too much*. My God. He took another sip and changed tactics. "There's enough to be done that you'll earn it. Plus"—he had a brilliant idea— "I thought you might make dinners as well. It's been a while since I had my own kitchen."

Angie sat back. There was a lot of work. And if she'd be shopping and cooking, too. . . . It was a crazy amount of money, though.

He almost had her. Chris could tell. But he couldn't do it. Not if he wanted any kind of trust between them. Lowering his chair, he confessed. "Angie, firms that do this charge twenty-five, thirty dollars an hour." He ignored her jaw dropping. "But I would be working with strangers who just saw it as another job. You know I don't want that.

"I was planning on letting you haggle your way to eighteen or twenty. Twelve dollars is nothing. So much so that I don't even feel right letting you take it."

"Are you serious?" Angie was shocked. Twenty-five dollars an hour to set up house. They were crazier than he was. Bet they dragged their feet and charged mileage, too. Still, if that was the going rate . . . She smiled at Chris. "Okay, then. I'll take fifteen. Eighteen would be taking advantage."

Stunned, Chris gaped at her then threw his head back and laughed. "You've got a deal."

Angie smiled with him. "You might want to rethink the cooking thing, though. Carter Anne cooks at home."

"Nonsense," he replied. "For fifteen dollars an hour, I want dinner, too."

"Seriously . . ." Angie started, but Chris interrupted her.

"I've been eating army chow for over ten years. It'll be okay. I promise."

Angie shrugged, trying to hide her panic. Cooking . . . Well, it was his decision. He was the boss.

Standing up, Chris took her hand and lifted her up from her chair. He didn't like the wary look that sprang up in her eyes.

Who hurt you, he wondered but kept the thought to himself. Instead, he let her hand go. Patience.

"Come on." Chris nodded toward the hallway. "I'll give you the grand tour."

Angie took a deep breath and steadied herself. What had she been thinking? That he was going to pull her into his arms? He was her employer now. Things were different and different was good. Obviously, he realized it as clearly as she did.

"Angie?" He had made it to the door of the kitchen and was waiting for her. Forcing a smile, Angie followed him.

"Have you ever been in the house, before?" Chris asked, all business.

"Not to remember. Your grandfather left when we were still little."

Chris nodded. "He packed up and moved in with us when Gran died."

"Oh." Angie didn't know what to say.

"It's okay," Chris assured her. "It was a long time ago. Anyway."

They moved from the kitchen into the formal dining room. Dust covered the sheets over all the furniture, and cobwebs hung in the corners.

"As you can tell"—Chris waved his hand at the dark room— "we've got our work cut out for us. I've made a few rooms livable since getting here, but mostly, the whole place looks like this."

Angie gasped and immediately regretted it as she got a throat full of dust. Patting her on the back, Chris winced. "I know. Pretty bad, huh?"

"No." Angie croaked, cleared her throat, and tried again. "No. It's beautiful." She walked into the room, spellbound. It was dark, dirty, and smelled of stale air, but underneath that— the ceiling soared. The windows would let light in once the heavy drapes were pulled back. And she would swear the molding was original. She itched to roll up her sleeves and go to work right now.

Chris looked at the room while watching her see it for the first time. Angie's eyes were dancing with possibility. He hadn't seen past the dust and the mouse droppings, he admitted. Not until now. But the room *was* beautiful when seen through the right eyes.

Suddenly, he remembered the room the way it *had* been. The glow of the chandelier, the warmth of the fire at dinner, the laughter of his family around the table. And he wanted it back. Not just because he owed it to Pops, but for himself.

Angie did a slow turn in the middle of the room before stopping in front of him. Her smile was wide and infectious. "The whole place really looks like this?"

He smiled back at her. He couldn't help it. "You're gonna love it."

She did. Underneath nearly two decades of dust and neglect was a beautiful home. The first floor was the living area of the house. Moving from room to room, Angie could almost hear the echoes of the families that had lived here before. Grand parties and intimate gatherings. Children running up and down the magnificent staircase or being scolded for sneaking cookies in the kitchen. The masters and mistresses of the old plantation sweeping through in silks and laces.

The second floor held the bedrooms. Designed during a time when "visiting" meant guests would commonly come and stay for days, there were four bedrooms besides the master suite. This was the heart of the house, up here. Here had been where children and adults had lived the joys and sorrows of their private worlds. Dreaming dreams, running fevers, making love, giving birth, facing death, all within these walls. Angie was overwhelmed by the power of the house and its history. She couldn't wait to bring it all back to life.

Chris kept watching her as they moved from room to room. At first, she'd asked questions. Ordinary questions about boxes and storage. As they'd made their way through, though, Angie's questions had stopped. She had started simply stepping into the room, touching the walls or clearing a small spot on a window to look out, even occasionally muttering something under her breath. It was as if she was listening. Listening to the house itself.

Finally, she stopped in the hallway. Cobwebs stuck to her hair, and Chris was sure he was as dusty as her clothes were. Although she was standing amid peeling wallpaper and tattered rugs, he knew she was seeing something very different.

"Chris . . ." Angie looked at him. "It's beautiful."

"I've saved something for last. Now, I'm glad I did." Smiling at her, he reached down and took her hand. Neither one of them noticed when she didn't pull away but just let him lead her down the stairs.

Chris crossed them through the kitchen and dining room to large pocket doors Angie hadn't noticed earlier.

"I've seen down here." Angie's voice was puzzled.

"You haven't seen *this*." Chris pushed on the doors. They squealed in protest but moved.

Angie stared, amazed, as the entire wall seemed to open in front of her. Beyond the doors was the largest room she had ever seen. It ran the length of the house and the ceiling was as high as the second floor. A carved balustrade ran around the top of the room, protecting a walkway where guests could look down on the events. Ornate spiral staircases stood in the far corners, tempting hands to brush over their tarnished iron. Marble fireplaces stood, sooty and empty, at either end of the room. The far wall was all windows, and the weak winter sun fought to shine through years of dirt. Tattered lace curtains hung limply off two sets of French doors that would lead out to a weedy, overgrown garden. It was magnificent.

"Is this . . . a ballroom?" Angie whispered. Chris thought she stepped into the room the way some people would step into a cathedral, quietly and with reverence.

"It was." He had to fight not to lower his voice to match hers. "I'm not sure what I'll do with it now. Not many people attend balls anymore. Maybe I'll use it for storage."

"You can't!" Angie spun on him. "It's too beautiful!" Her protests died in her throat when she saw the twinkle in his eye. "Bein' mean." She grinned back at him.

"Come on." Chris motioned back toward the rest of the house. "Let's talk details."

Angie took one last look at the room and sighed.

"You get to come back, you know," Chris teased gently, reading her mood.

Laughing at herself, she followed him back into the kitchen. Automatically, she reached to refill the coffee mugs sitting on the table just as Chris did as well.

"For fifteen dollars an hour . . ." Angie started.

Chris took her gently by the shoulders and sat her down. "I expect help with the house and dinner. Not a full-time maid. You serve me coffee at the diner. I can serve you coffee in my kitchen."

Angie started to protest then shut her mouth. Might as well enjoy it. When Chris returned to the table, he put her mug in front of her and took a sip of his own. Grimacing, he sat down. "Of course, if you want to *make* it . . ."

Angie laughed and took a sip of the mud Chris called coffee. "So, what exactly do you want me to do?"

"Well . . ." Chris thought a moment. "Obviously, the place needs to be cleaned within an inch of its life. Pops left a lot of stuff behind, too. We'll need to go through all of that and make decisions on it. The personal stuff will have to be my call, but the stuff that goes with the house—I'd really love your opinion on that.

"As for dinners, you can just leave me a grocery list and I'll pick things up as we need them."

"No." Angie interrupted him with a bit more force than she had intended, but she had to talk to Carter Anne about dinners before she could even think about making a grocery list. How was she supposed to know what went into a recipe? "I'll pick things up on my way over from the diner," she explained quickly. "That way I don't have to plan too far in advance and can get what's fresh or what we have a taste for."

Chris smiled. "See, I told you the cooking thing wasn't going to be a problem. You're already thinking faster than I am.

"I figure we'll start down here." Chris waved his mug in the general direction of downstairs. "That way, when we get to the things stored on the third floor, we'll know what we can use and what we can get rid of."

"There's a third floor?"

"Of course." Chris nodded. "Originally, it was for the house slaves. Then it was servants' quarters. Then Gran just turned it into storage.

"It has, of course"—Chris smiled to himself—"done duty as a pirate ship, a cowboy fort, and the site of several cutthroat games of hide and seek."

Angie smiled back. "It sounds wonderful."

"It was. Other kids used to dread visiting their grandparents during the summers, but I loved it." Chris sipped his coffee thoughtfully. "I haven't thought about visits here in years. Now it seems I can't stop."

"It makes sense, though," Angie reassured him. "How could you be back here and *not* relive those memories?"

Before the silence could become awkward, Angie spoke again. "Should I see the third floor now?"

"It's really not necessary," Chris replied, leaving behind a game of cops and robbers from when he was six. "Seriously. Consider it an attic. We can deal with it last."

"Okay," Angie agreed. "We'll start down here and work up to it. How's Tuesday?"

"How's Tuesday for what?" Chris asked.

Angie rolled her eyes. "How's Tuesday to start work?"

Chris's eyes widened. "You want to start that soon?"

"Sooner begun, sooner done." Angie quoted her own grandparents. "I can pick up the supplies when I buy the groceries and come straight here from the diner."

Shrugging, Chris agreed. "But I buy the supplies."

"I don't mind. I'm going to the store anyway. And you're paying me—"

"Fifteen dollars an hour." Chris interrupted her. "I know. And you'll earn it, Angie. I promise. You don't have to buy the supplies out of it."

"Alrigh', alrigh'. I'll stop now." She stood up and bundled into her coat. "And I'll see you Tuesday."

"Yes, you will," Chris agreed, walking her to the door.

She took a step outside and turned back with a grin. "Be ready to work."

Chris smiled back and watched her walk down the driveway toward home.

"Carter Anne!" Angie's voice carried throughout the house. She threw her coat on the hook. "Carter Anne!" It was Sunday. She had to be home.

Her sister appeared at the top of the stairs. "Did you take

the job?" Carter Anne asked excitedly as she scurried down the steps.

"Yes, I did. But come here." Angie took the other woman by the arm and led her to the kitchen. Carter Anne sat down but Angie began to pace.

"So? What does the house look like on the inside? What's he paying you? What will you be doing?"

"Carter Anne . . ." Angie stopped and looked at her sister. "He wants me to cook dinners."

Carter Anne fell silent for a moment, staring back at Angie, before bursting out laughing. "Oh no, he doesn't."

"Don't laugh, Carter Anne. What am I going to do?" Angie sank into the chair next to her. Carter Anne reached out and laid a hand on Angie's arm.

"Well, I'll just have to finally teach you."

"Oh Lord." Angie put her face in her hands.

"Tell me about the rest of it," Carter Anne encouraged. "Let the cooking part go for now."

Sighing, Angie decided her sister was right. The house was beautiful. And there was so much she and Chris could do with it. Especially once they got it back into shape. Smiling, she started speaking. "It's like something out of a book or a movie, Carter Anne. Like Tara or something. Servants' quarters and old, hidden staircases. And the ballroom . . . Oh my God, the ballroom!"

"It's got a *ballroom*?" Carter Anne asked, caught up in Angie's excitement.

"You can practically hear the music from when it was used. And get this." She stood to get a drink from the refrigerator and automatically pulled one for Carter Anne as well. Putting the cans on the table, she sat back down and grinned. "He's paying me fifteen dollars an hour!"

"What?" Carter Anne's hand stopped, her drink halfway to her lips. "To set up house?"

"That's what I thought, too!" Angie grinned wider. "But he says the professional firms charge even more than that, so he's actually getting a deal."

Carter Anne shook her head and took her sip. "I'm in the wrong business."

"Yeah, but"—Angie's face fell again—"he's got me cooking, too."

"Look," Carter Anne spoke reasonably. "We can start with very basic meals. Things that don't take much skill. You can practice on me and Bobby until you get the hang of it."

Angie laughed. "You might want to run that by Bobby first."

"Run what by Bobby first?" The man himself spoke from the doorway. "Those words never mean much good is about to happen." He walked into the kitchen, giving both girls a kiss on the head before pouring himself coffee and joining them at the table.

"Angie's going to be doing some of the cooking for a little while is all." Carter Anne flashed her brightest smile at her uncle.

Bobby's face never changed. "Well, if that's what she wants to do." He took a deep sip of his coffee. Hand to God . . . He loved the child, but cooking? Maybe Jimmy could start bringing him dinner by the station at night. And maybe even the occasional lunch. He'd have to ask. "Why the sudden interest in cooking, Angie?" He looked at her; she was biting her lower lip. Didn't seem this was something she was too excited about.

"I took that job for Chris Montgomery I told you about."

"Did you now?" Bobby nodded. "Good for you."

"And he's paying me fifteen dollars an hour."

Bobby sipped his coffee again. "Seems a bit steep, but it's the man's money."

"Well"—Angie swallowed—"for fifteen dollars an hour, he wants me to cook dinners, too."

If Bobby had ever been more grateful for his poker-playing days, he couldn't remember it. "Seems reasonable to me. Guess you *are* gonna be doing some cooking around here for a bit." He stood up, coffee in one hand, the other tucked into his back pocket. "Well, might as well start tonight." He looked from Angie to Carter Anne. "Might want to start with spaghetti. Sticks to a man's ribs. I need to go give Jimmy a call. Check in about some things."

Angie waited until he left the room. "He seemed to take that well."

Carter Anne nodded.

"But you know," Angie continued, "he's going to call Jimmy to see if he'll start bringing food by the station."

Laughing, Carter Anne stood up and crossed to the cabinets. She pulled out a large pot. Turning to Angie, she held it up. "Okay, lesson one. This is a pot. It can be used to boil water."

Angie laughed and stuck out her tongue. Then she stood up and joined her sister at the stove. It was time to learn to cook.

Chapter 4

Holding the bag of groceries in her hands, Angie approached the door to the old Montgomery place. How long would people refer to it that way, she wondered? Around these parts, probably a long time. Technically, it still deserved the name since Chris was a Montgomery, but somehow she felt it would be called that even when he sold it and moved on. Once at the door, she stopped, wondering what to do now.

Before heading over, she had gone home and quickly changed out of her work clothes and into some grubby jeans and an old sweatshirt. She had even tied a bandanna around her head to keep her hair out of her face. So what if the real reason she had stopped was to make one last panicked call to the school to talk to Carter Anne? Her sister had been understanding, if a little exasperated.

"Angie, just add the seasonings we talked about and brown the beef. You'll be fine."

"Bobby drank nearly a gallon of water with dinner the other night, though, Carter Anne."

"Well . . ." Carter Anne had paused. "Go a little easier on the salt."

And with those last words of encouragement, Carter Anne

had hung up. But they hadn't talked about what Angie was supposed to do now. Should she ring the bell? Go on in? *For God's sake*, Angie thought to herself. *You're a grown woman who has functioned perfectly well for twenty-five years. Stop acting like a silly teenager with a crush.* Giving herself one last mental shake, she opened the door.

"Chris?" she called, moving into the kitchen to unload the groceries. A radio played country music at earsplitting volumes. Legs stuck out from under the sink, and the voice that echoed from inside the cabinet warbled along with Tim McGraw, only slightly off-key. "Chris?" Angie spoke a little louder. Nothing. Putting the groceries on the counter, she leaned down and touched his leg. "Chris!"

Chris moved faster than Angie would have thought possible. And, she realized, had it not been for the counter he had so obviously forgotten, it would have been an impressive and graceful move. As it was . . .

"Who . . . Shit!"

Angie backed up, trying to control the laughter bubbling up inside her. "Chris, it's just me."

He appeared from under the sink, scowling, one hand on his forehead. "There's nothing *just* about you, Angie," Chris growled. He closed his eyes and breathed deeply. When he opened them, the room grayed ominously. "Okay, new rule," he spoke, trying to regain a sense of balance and clear his head. "No sneaking up on me."

Angie knelt in front of him. "Chris Montgomery, I have been calling your name since I walked in here. Just because I wasn't louder than Tim here doesn't make it sneaking." She was managing to control the laughter but, oh, it was hard. Especially with him looking so pitiful sitting there.

"Please, Angie." He looked up at her. "Leave me some pride."

"Okay." She laughed then, unable to control it any longer. "No sneaking."

Her laughter died as blood began to seep through his fingers. Reaching for him, she moved his hand away from his head and blood poured out of him.

"Let me see that."

"It's nothing, really." Chris tried to cover the cut again but winced. "Head wounds bleed badly, that's all."

Angie moved his hand away. "Chris, you're *bleeding*. Let me look. Hold on." She stood and with easy efficiency, found the paper towels, wet one, and was kneeling in front of him again before Chris could even think about standing up. Her hands were as cold as the water as she wiped away the blood.

She smelled clean, like coconut. Wisps of hair had slipped loose from the faded blue bandanna she had tied around it to keep it out of her eyes. They framed her face, brushing against her skin. Chris breathed her in. Man, he'd hit his head harder than he'd realized. That was the only explanation for his lightheadedness. It had to be. And surely that was why he wanted to brush those wisps of hair away from her eyes, just to see if it was as soft as it looked. And place small kisses on the corners of her mouth where it was currently pursed in concentration. It was the knock on the head. It had to be. Damned if it was.

Angie rocked back on her heels, still studying the cut. "Well, you don't need stitches. But we should clean it." Her eyes met his, dark and cloudy. "And you'll, you'll . . ." When had the heat come on? Surely it hadn't been this warm in here when she walked in.

"I'll what, Angie?" His voice was as clouded as his eyes. Slowly, carefully, Chris reached for a tendril of hair, his fingertips barely grazing her skin as he brushed it aside.

Angie stood abruptly, the shock of his touch bringing her to her feet. What was she thinking? This was Chris Montgomery. Worse, this was Chris Montgomery with a blow to the head. He couldn't think straight, so she'd have to.

"Where . . ." Angie cleared her throat and tried again. "Where do you keep rubbing alcohol?"

Chris took a deep breath to steady himself and the room grayed again. Yeah, he'd gotten himself good, all right. He motioned carefully to the corner. "That shelf."

Angie turned and opened the cabinet he'd indicated. Her medicine cabinet at home had Tylenol, alcohol, Band-Aids and Pepto. Here, she was faced with bandages, sterile gauze, medical tape, epinephrine, pure aloe, and, unless she missed her guess, a suture kit.

"Wow," she managed. "Do you just have Tylenol or something in here?"

"There should be some ibuprofen in a baggie somewhere." Chris's voice was directly behind her. Angie spun around.

"Chris Montgomery! You shouldn't be up!"

"Angie." Chris sighed. "It's a bump on the head. Trust me, I've had worse."

"Well, it's a bump on the head that's bleeding like a stuck pig. And I wasn't around for the worse, but I am around for this." She put her hands on his chest and pushed gently. "So go sit down."

Laughing gingerly, Chris backed up. "Yes ma'am." His head was spinning, but damned if he'd let her know that.

Rummaging, Angie found a baggie containing pills large enough to choke a horse, labeled "800 mg." She shrugged. They didn't mess around. Taking that, the alcohol, some gauze and tape, she moved back to Chris. His head was bleeding again through the paper towel.

"Really, Angie," he protested. "You don't have to make a big deal over this."

"I caused it by sneaking up on you." She stressed the words with a playful grin. "The least I can do is fix it. And I'm not whipping out the suture kit and performing surgery."

"I suppose I should be grateful for tha-AAAT! Dammit woman, that hurts!" Chris exclaimed as Angie touched the alcohol to his forehead.

"What happened to 'I've had worse'?" Angie tried not laugh.

"I was unconscious during the alcohol-into-the-open-wound part of it." Chris groaned.

Angie pulled back and stared at him. "You were what?"

Chris sighed. This wasn't how he wanted to be known here. "I was unconscious."

"That's what I thought you said. You're serious, aren't you?"

Chris tried to nod but it hurt too much. "Yeah. I am."

Angie stepped forward again and continued to gently clean the cut.

Chris waited as long as he could. "What?" He finally spoke. "No questions?"

Angie chuckled as she taped gauze over his forehead. It really wasn't too bad once she'd stopped the bleeding and gotten it clean. "Not all women from small towns are hungry for gossip." She smiled. "Besides"—she filled a glass with water and brought it to him with one of the horse pills—"if you want me to know, you'll tell me."

Chris swallowed the pill, watching her as she sat in the chair across from him. She continued to surprise him. Delight and surprise him, if truth be told.

"Now," Angie continued, matter-of-factly, holding up three fingers. "How many fingers am I holding up?"

"Three," Chris said definitively. "And before you ask, my name is Christopher James Montgomery. It's February seventeenth and you are Angela Kane, the most un-nosy small-town girl I've ever met. While I can't tell you your middle name, it's okay because I didn't know it before you snuck up on me."

Angie giggled and held up her hands. "Fair enough, Christopher James Montgomery. No concussion. You're good as new. And it's Lambert."

"What's Lambert?" Chris asked.

"Maybe not good as new," Angie teased, lifting an eyebrow. "You're usually quicker than that."

Chris winked at her. "Nice you think so, Angela Lambert Kane." He felt the bandage carefully. "Pretty good. How'd you learn to do that?"

Angie shrugged. "Bobby shares your dislike of doctors. Even small-town cops end up with cuts and bruises sometimes."

Chris nodded, pleased when the room only tilted instead of beginning to fade. He was almost back. "Lambert as in Lambert Falls?" he asked, playing for time.

It was Angie's turn to nod. "He's my great-great-great-great-grandfather." She explained. "Some folks 'round here think it's a big deal still, but we don't much care anymore. Mostly, it just means Bobby's the grand marshal of the Founder's Day parade every year."

Chris chuckled lightly. It made his head hurt, but at least the room stayed straight. He realized Angie's response wasn't arrogant or timid. She and her family were simply who they were, without pride or embarrassment. Chris found himself envious she could just accept who she was so easily. "That sounds like a fun time. I have an image of him riding in the back of a baby blue convertible."

Angie grinned and agreed earnestly. "It is a good time. The whole town turns out. There are floats and music and games. And of course, the annual bake-offs."

"Of course."

"Don't take that too lightly, Mr. Montgomery," Angie scolded with mock sternness. "The jelly competition can get downright cutthroat. One year, Mavis Dunne was disqualified for trying to tamper with Margaret Jones's pear jelly."

"It seems I have stumbled into a den of scoundrels." Chris lifted an eyebrow.

Angie laughed outright at that. "It's never a good idea to screw with Margaret Jones."

Chris's laughter became a groan as pain shot through his head. "Okay, no laughing yet."

Standing, Angie crossed to the groceries still on the counter and began to put them away. "Why don't we call it a day and start fresh tomorrow. I don't think you're up to much housekeeping this evening."

Dammit, she was determined. He'd completed a mission with a dislocated shoulder and she thought he couldn't unload boxes because he'd hit his head. Did she dislike him that much? No. He knew better than that. She was really trying to take care of him. He had an idea.

"You're probably right." Chris nodded and pretended to try not to wince. "After all, I'm not paying you to nurse me." He stood and let the room sway just a bit. "And I'm sure I can manage dinner on my own." When Angie's eyes cut to his grip on the back of the chair, he managed to bite back a smile.

"Don't be silly." She changed her mind. "I'll make dinner."

"No, Angie. It's okay. You were right." Chris took a step and closed his eyes, as if to steady himself.

"You are the most stubborn man imaginable. Hand to God, can't a body even help out? Sit back down. I'm makin' dinner. And you're not payin' me for it. This is just bein' neighborly."

Chris sat back down again, smiling behind Angie's back. "In that case, what's for dinner?"

Angie swallowed hard and kept her back to him. She'd

almost had one more night to practice. But she couldn't just leave him to fend for himself with that lump on his head. Ah well. What would be would be. "Spaghetti with meat sauce."

"Excellent. I enjoy a Bolognese."

"Ummm . . ." Angie turned to face him. "A what?"

"I like spaghetti with meat sauce," Chris reassured her.

"Is that what Bolognese means?"

"Yeah. It's fancy for meat sauce."

"Then that's what you're having tonight. Spaghetti Bolognese." Angie went back to the ingredients and muttered under her breath. "I hope."

"What was that?" Chris asked.

"Nothing," Angie responded a bit too cheerfully. "Want me to put on some coffee while dinner's coming?" She had already moved to the coffee maker and was filling it efficiently.

Chris sat back and watched her as the aroma of coffee filled the room. Her curves were something to behold. The way her jeans cupped her bottom. Even the way, whenever she reached for something, her sweatshirt pulled up, exposing a tease of bare skin. With a pang, Chris realized that until his master plan worked, he was going to stay in a state of painful frustration if he wasn't careful.

"There." She put his mug on the table in front of him. "I've fixed it up the way you like it. Now go into another room until I call you. You're making me nervous back there watching me."

Chris blushed. So much for being subtle. Grinning, he picked up his coffee and stood. "Can't help but watch, Angie. The view's too good from back here."

With a laugh, Angie waved him out of the room.

It was . . . edible. And the sauce was indeed red. He'd give her that much. Chris picked at his plate again, grateful Angie wasn't there to see him. Somewhere along the line, they had gotten their signals crossed. He'd assumed she understood she was to stay for the dinners she would be cooking.

"Tomorrow night," he had said to her, hoping the disappointment didn't sound in his voice, "plan on staying." And he'd watched her leave. Twirling another forkful of mushy pasta, he almost wished he had gone with her. Still, she had tried to warn him. Lord, she was beautiful and kind and funny and soft—but the woman couldn't cook worth a damn. With a sigh, Chris swallowed another bite. It might be edible. It sure as hell wasn't Bolognese.

He had wanted her to stay. He had expected her to stay. In fact, she had planned on staying. But when he had pulled out two plates, just as natural as could be, she had panicked, plain and simple.

"O-oh," Angie had stammered. "Carter Anne is expecting me home for dinner." She had blushed deeply, but not because of a misunderstanding. No, she had known they would be having meals together. But she'd expected to do so after several hours of hard work, performed by her and her employer. Not after what had passed between them earlier. Not after the heat she had felt coming from him while she did something as ordinary, as comfortable—as right—as tending to him and making him dinner. No, that hadn't been part of the plan at all. So she had made her excuses.

Still, he *had* watched her. She had seen the look in his eyes. Angie wasn't as naive as all that not to know when a man was attracted to her. When he, well, wanted her.

Warmth spread through her tummy at the thought. Ducking her head against the wind, she couldn't help it; Angie smiled. Chris Montgomery had wanted her. The warmth took her all the way home.

"What are you doing back so early?" Bobby asked sharply

as she hung up her coat. He had two bowls of tomato soup in his hands, taking them to the table.

"There was a little accident, so we stopped early. Everything's fine." Angie looked at him, puzzled, and took the soup from him. Bobby followed her into the dining room, exhaling hard.

"Go tell Carter Anne you're here, then come in and tell us about it. I'm assuming that blood's not yours."

Angie looked down. That explained it. There were small streaks of blood on the cuff of her sweatshirt. She might have missed them, but Bobby never would have. She leaned over and kissed him on the cheek. "I promise, Bobby. And it's not as bad as it looks." She set the bowls down at Bobby and Carter Anne's places at the table.

"Didn't say it looked bad," Bobby muttered as Angie left the room. He didn't like seeing blood under any circumstance, but especially not on his girls, no matter how little there was.

Carter Anne was flipping a grilled cheese sandwich when Angie walked in the kitchen. "What are you doing back?"

Angie rolled her eyes. "If I promise to tell y'all, will you make me a couple sandwiches, too?" She put her head on her sister's shoulder. "Pleeease?"

Carter Anne laughed and reached for the bread. "Wash up. It'll be ready when you are."

Chapter 5

Technically, she wasn't snooping. Technically. The boxes had arrived yesterday and Chris *had* told her she could unpack them, after all. Okay, so maybe he'd meant for her to unpack them without looking through everything. And she had. Until she found the photo album. Still, he'd told her time and time again she could look through anything. So she wasn't snooping. Technically.

She just meant to look at the first few pictures. But Chris had been so young, so handsome, smiling out at her, that she had found herself turning page after page. Right before her eyes, Chris went from being a gawky teenager to, what appeared to her anyway, a cocky young man in military fatigues.

Several of the same faces showed up in the pictures. Sometimes they were fooling around. Other times, more serious. In a few of them, there were even women tucked under arms, smiling sweetly. Angie couldn't help it. She studied each of the girls who appeared next to Chris.

Each one was pretty, well dressed, and put together, even for obviously casual events. Perfect hair. Perfect makeup. Perfect bodies. Angie looked down at her dusty bib overalls and sighed. This was pointless. She should really get back to work.

She flipped the pages faster, curious but disheartened. Then she flipped back. Sure enough, the pretty redhead had made a second appearance. The first of the girls to do so.

Toward the middle of the album, this young woman became a regular. Not so many shots of Chris with the other guys. More of the two of them.

Chris and Red dancing. Red at a beach somewhere, splashing in a bikini, laughing at the photographer. Chris and Red embracing on an airfield, him in uniform, her in a light summer dress. Was he leaving? Or coming home? Angie traced the picture with a soft touch, wondering.

"That's Beth." Chris's voice was low in Angie's ear. She turned quickly, looking over her shoulder.

"I . . . I . . ." Angie stammered. "I didn't mean to pry. I'm sorry." She went to close the album, but Chris reached around and stopped her.

"It's okay, Angie," he reassured her. "That"—he tapped the picture—"that was just after the Maldives. We'd only been gone a couple months, but it felt like forever." Angie watched him as he turned the page. "And this one." Chris laughed, pointing to another picture. "That's my birthday. Don't ask me how she convinced the guys to do that." Angie looked down. Red—Beth, she mentally corrected herself—was dressed in a blonde wig and metal bra, apparently singing. Behind her, four men were dressed as backup dancers.

Angie laughed. "Madonna sings *Happy Birthday*?" She asked.

"Yeah." Chris nodded. "God I was embarrassed. But it was a good night."

Angie studied Chris's profile. He seemed very far away. "So what happened to her?"

Chris's shoulder twitched in a half shrug. "We were young.

Too young. That's only my twenty-first birthday there. We just . . . grew apart." He shrugged again.

"She's very beautiful."

"Yeah. She was. But there wasn't much more than that to her. And what's important at twenty and twenty-one isn't as important as you get older."

They sat in silence as Chris thumbed through the pages of the album. Sure enough, Chris's smiles started to look forced. Red—Beth—wasn't standing so close. By the end of the album, she was gone.

"We had some good times, though." Angie was surprised at how matter-of-fact he sounded as he closed the book. "How about you?" Chris turned to her.

"'How about me' what?" Angie asked.

"What happened to your guy? You must have had one."

Angie looked at her hands. Chris reached out and lifted her chin. He was in dangerous territory and he knew it. But hopefully, hearing about Beth . . . He made his voice as soothing as possible.

"You don't have to tell me, but I would like to know. Who hurt you, Angie?"

She squirmed under that intense gaze of his. "What makes you think I've been hurt?" She sounded tougher than she felt. At least, she hoped she did. Chris just raised an eyebrow.

"Come on." Angie stood up and dusted herself off. "Let's get some coffee. Dinner's probably almost ready anyway."

Chris sat where he was for a moment as Angie headed into the kitchen. Dammit! He had pushed too hard and she had closed down on him. With a shake of his head, he stood and followed her.

Angie was at the counter, already doctoring his coffee. She crossed to the table, both mugs with her, and sat down. God only knew why she was about to answer his question. And if

God didn't know then no one did, because she surely didn't. Chris joined her at the table.

"His name was Andy. I was a junior; he was a senior." Angie kept her voice steady, clinical. "He went away to UVa and never came back." She took a sip of her coffee.

"University of Virginia?" Chris asked. Angie nodded. Chris snorted. "That's not very far. What, two hours?"

"'Bout that," Angie agreed. Months of unreturned phone calls, long silences, and last-minute cancellations went through her head. At least it didn't hurt any longer. Time had taken care of that. And what time hadn't gotten rid of, she had.

"If he meant that much to you, did you consider going to school there?" Chris was trying to figure this all out. It was only two hours. Of course, they had been younger even than he and Beth.

Angie nodded again. "Sure. I applied and even got in. 'Course I didn't want to leave the Falls, but Andy always said we could come home after we'd lived a little, seen a little."

"So what happened?" Chris tried to keep his voice casual, but he thought he was beginning to understand. He'd been nineteen and stupid once, too.

Angie smiled. It was dry and bitter, nothing at all like her usual warm, open expression. "I couldn't sleep one night so I called him, round about one-thirty, two in the morning. He wasn't the one who answered."

"Ah." Chris grimaced. "One of those clean breakups, I see."

Angie laughed, as Chris had intended, the hard smile melting away. "You could say that. Anyway, we both ended up getting what we wanted. He never had to come back to the Falls, and I never had to leave it."

"You're really that happy here, aren't you, Angie?" Chris said.

She met his eyes directly. "I really am. I can't imagine living anywhere else, calling anywhere else home."

"That must be nice," Chris said. "Knowing where home is. Knowing where it's always going to be. I've always wanted a place like that, but we moved around too much."

"Yeah." Angie swallowed. He was looking at her *that* way again. "But I bet you've been happy, moving around, seeing so much."

"I suppose so," Chris agreed. "I didn't have to join up. But I'm looking for something different now. Someplace I belong, the way you belong here."

Angie cleared her throat, looking for something to say. The timer on the stove went off, making her jump. She pounced on the excuse. "See!" She stood quickly. "I told you dinner would be ready soon."

Behind her back, Chris smiled. His name had been Andy, huh? Well, Andy had met his match.

"So." Chris allowed the subject to be changed—for now. "What's for dinner tonight?"

"Pot roast and vegetables." Angie turned around, holding the heavy pan between pot holders. "But I think I might have overdone it."

Chris looked at the blackened piece of meat Angie was putting on the table and found a smile. "I'm sure it's delicious."

They settled in and filled their plates. Chris gnawed at his first bite. "See?" He smiled. "Delicious."

Angie nibbled at hers. God it was horrible. She looked over as Chris took another bite and forced it down. He was actually *eating* it. How could she not eat it if he was? Maybe Carter Anne would have leftovers at the house when she got home.

Chris rinsed his last bite down with a large swallow of coffee. "A meal like that deserves dessert. Can I buy you an ice cream? Or pie at the diner?"

"Oh, I don't . . ." Angie blushed.

"Come on, Angie. I could go for a hot fudge sundae."

"It's cold out there." Angie protested, but she could feel herself weakening. It was never too cold for a sundae.

At first, Chris just looked at her. Then the jerk batted his eyes, and Angie laughed. "Okay, okay," she relented. Why the hell not. "Let me just clear this away." She stood and started to reach to clear the table.

"Oh no you don't." Chris stopped her. "I'm not giving you a chance to change your mind." He grabbed her coat from the hook and held it out for her. "Miz Angie?"

She laughed and, with a last look at the cluttered table, slipped her arms into the sleeves.

The wind pricked at them outside, but Angie thought she could smell spring in it. At least it wasn't *as* cold, anyway. The lights of the ice-cream parlor shone warmly, and she stepped inside gratefully, breathing in the scent of fresh waffle cones.

Chris watched her as she worked the room. Not many people were out on a Wednesday night, but Angie seemed to have a smile and a friendly word for each of them. As empty as the place was, it still took them a good five minutes to get from the door to the counter.

"Hey, Angie." The girl behind the counter greeted them warmly.

"Hey, Amy." The young woman looked pointedly from Angie to Chris and back again. "Oh. Amy, have you met Chris Montgomery? Chris, this is Amy Tallis. Probably gonna be valedictorian this year and makes a *great* hot fudge sundae."

"Nice to meet you, Amy." Chris smiled at her, and Angie watched as the girl's heart melted just a bit.

"You too, Mr. Montgomery. Welcome to the Falls."

Angie noticed he hadn't told her to call him Chris. Apparently he had noticed the crush blossom as well. Smart man.

"So I take it you want a hot fudge?" Amy asked.

"With that kind of recommendation, how could I get anything else? And whatever Angie wants."

Amy turned her attention to Angie. "The usual?"

"Please." Angie cringed.

He wouldn't let her get uncomfortable now. He just wouldn't. "So what's 'the usual'?" Chris asked casually.

Amy answered before Angie could, busily building the sundaes while she talked. "Rocky road ice cream with marshmallow topping and extra nuts. But no cherry."

"No cherry?" Chris looked aghast. "What's a sundae with no cherry?"

Angie laughed, relaxing again. "Amy, be sure to give him extra cherries."

With a nod, Amy put three cherries on the hot fudge sundae and presented them with a flourish. "There you go. Seven bucks."

Chris handed her a ten. "Keep it. The valedictorian probably needs to save up for college, right?"

Blushing, Amy stuttered her thanks and watched, dreamy-eyed, as Chris took the desserts and led Angie to a table. Angie Kane was one lucky girl to be out on a date with a man like Mr. Montgomery. Wait until she told her sisters.

"You know you just made her night. Maybe her week," Angie said around her first bite of sundae.

"Well"—Chris shrugged—"if she's working evenings and is still making grades like that, she deserves a nice tip."

"She's also the captain of the cheerleading squad."

"Really?"

"Mm-hm." Angie nodded. "Her older sister got into a 'spot of trouble.'" She stressed the words in a perfect imitation of Margaret or Mary Jones. "So there was a bit of a family scandal there for a while. They got married, but she was out to there in the dress."

"And what about them?" Chris motioned to a young family who had just come in.

"Oh, those are the Greenes, Andrew and Jeannie. The little ones are Andy and Rob. Carter Anne babysits for them some in the summer. According to her, Rob's a good little guy, but she's expecting Bobby to start seeing Andy any day now down at the station."

Chris laughed. "He can't be more than ten!"

"Nine, actually." Angie smiled and took a bite of her sundae. As Chris watched, Andy Greene pinched his brother and knocked at his brother's ice cream when their parents weren't looking.

"See?" Angie asked.

Chris took a bite of his sundae to hide his laughter. Swallowing, he looked around. "And what about him? The guy with the hunting magazine you hugged on the way in?"

"That's Jimmy, Bobby's deputy."

"Really?" Chris looked harder. "For some reason, I expected him to be younger."

"He's only thirty." Angie giggled. "That's hardly old."

Chris nodded. "So what's his story? He happy being deputy?"

"Oh sure." Angie stated matter-of-factly. "Every now and then, Bobby offers him a transfer recommendation, but Jimmy always turns him down. The Falls is home and everybody kinda knows he'll be sheriff when Bobby retires."

There weren't even half a dozen other people in the shop, but Angie knew all of their stories. Chris loved to listen to her. Loved the way her eyes lit up when she talked about someone particularly special to her. The way her voice could change, bringing the town characters to life for him.

In no time, Amy was at their table. "We're closing in about five minutes. Just wanted y'all to know. It was good to finally meet you, Mr. Montgomery. You come back in for a hot fudge anytime." She flashed him her brightest smile before heading back around the counter.

Angie looked at her watch, shocked. Sure enough, it was nearly ten o'clock. She and Chris were the only ones left in the place. Standing, she called to Amy. "Have a good night, honey."

Amy waved back, watching them leave. Yep, Angie was one lucky girl. Maybe one day she would meet someone like that. But who would've expected him to show up in the Falls.

Angie buttoned her coat. The wind had brought a temperature drop. So much for thoughts of spring. She had expected Chris to say good-bye and head back to the old Montgomery place. Instead, he fell in beside her.

"Let me walk you home. It's late."

Angie started to protest then changed her mind. One look at Chris told her it would be pointless anyway.

"Thank you, Mr. Montgomery." She batted her eyes at him as Amy had done. Chris laughed.

"She's a sweet girl but very, very young." Casually, Chris draped an arm over Angie's shoulder. It was cold after all. He tried not to notice how perfectly she fit or how easily they fell into step together.

They walked in comfortable silence, enjoying the night, until Chris noticed Angie's steps had slowed. "What's wrong?" He followed her gaze toward the house she shared with her sister and uncle.

"That light." Angie pointed to the second floor. "It shouldn't be on."

Chris shrugged. "Maybe it's Bobby or Carter Anne."

"No. Bobby's workin' second shift and Carter Anne is at the movies with some girls from work. She won't be home 'til after midnight."

Chris could tell she was concerned. That accent of hers had gotten thick again. "Well, maybe one of them left it on by mistake."

"Maybe . . ." But Angie wasn't reassured. It was silly. Chris was right. Carter Anne had probably just been in a hurry, running late or something, and hadn't turned off the light is all. No reason to fuss over it.

Chris watched the emotions play over her face and made a decision. "Wait here." He gave her shoulders a squeeze and took the keys from her. Small town or no, he trusted the sheriff would insist his girls lock the door. He was right.

Angie stood, arms across her chest, listening for any sound of struggle. Finally, after what seemed like a very long time, Chris reappeared at the door.

"All's quiet. Looks like a light just got left on."

Angie crossed to him, up the stairs.

"The kitchen light is on, too," Chris said, asking the unspoken question.

"That's okay," Angie reassured him. "We leave that one on for each other."

"Then all's clear. Charlie Mike."

Angie stared at him, puzzled.

Chris laughed at himself. Old habits died hard. "It means 'continue mission.' In other words, you can go on in."

"Thanks." Angie smiled gently at him.

Chris reached out, gently stroking her cheek with one finger. "Lock up, okay?"

With a nod, Angie went on in the house. Chris stood on the porch until he heard the sound of the bolt being thrown. He could go on home. He should go on home.

Sighing, Chris walked down the steps and circled the house once. Bobby would be home in about an hour. And, if he was wrong, Carter Anne would be home in two or so. Besides, it wasn't that cold. Pulling his coat tighter around him, Chris sat down on the steps, keeping watch.

Bobby took his time in spite of the chill. His walk home when he worked second shift was his last chance of the day to check on his town. And it was his town. Not because he was related to anyone or any such nonsense, but because he loved it. As such, even after he'd clocked out, even when it was a cold night like tonight, he took his time.

He tugged on Jack Beddingham's gate to make sure it had caught. That crazy dog of Jack's would get out otherwise. The dog herself bounced over to the fence, wiggling happily at the unexpected company. Bobby slipped his hand through the fence and gave her a pat. She barked once, friendly, in response. Out of the corner of his eye, Bobby saw something move in the shadows of his porch. "Hush now, Daisy girl," he whispered, patting the dog once more and slipping his hand from between the slats. Instinctively, he unsnapped his holster. He'd rarely had to draw his weapon and hoped not to now, but someone was on *his* porch. Moving slowly, he crossed to the corner of the house, hand still on the butt of his gun. Finding a shadow, he squared his shoulders and called out.

"I'd appreciate knowing why you're on my porch."

"Bobby, it's Chris. I'd appreciate you not shooting me."

Shadow or not, Bobby could swear Chris's eyes met his directly. He relaxed and moved into the light of the street. "Chris? What are you doing here?" He snapped his holster closed again and walked up the steps.

"I walked Angie home tonight. There was a light on that made her a bit uncomfortable, so I thought I'd keep an eye out until you got home."

"Well, hand to God, why'd the girl make you wait outside? Come on in." Bobby slipped his key in the lock but felt the added resistance of the deadbolt. Chris was right; his girl had been spooked.

"Um . . ." Chris began as Bobby opened the door. "She doesn't exactly know I'm here."

Bobby looked over his shoulder at the younger man. "I see. Well, come on in now and have a beer for your troubles. I appreciate you looking after me and mine."

Chris followed Bobby in, closing the door quietly so as to not wake the woman asleep upstairs.

"Stay here." Bobby motioned for Chris to wait in the foyer. When he returned, it was with two beers, already open. He passed one to Chris. "Let's go in here."

Chris followed him into the den where Bobby relaxed into his chair with a sigh. Stalling for time, Chris sat on the sofa and took a sip of his own drink. Small talk was Champ's thing, not his. Bobby was obviously tired.

"Mighty nice of you to stick around." Bobby broke the silence.

Chris shrugged. "It seemed like the right thing to do."

"Well, I thank you for it. But I will say you gave me quite a start up there on my porch."

"You know, I almost couldn't see you." Chris spoke drily but Bobby heard the compliment.

"I'd've preferred it if you hadn't seen me at all," he said with a grin.

"It was close," Chris reassured him. He took a sip of his beer. "Of course I heard you coming a block away."

Bobby let out a bark of laughter. "You ever want a job, you let me know. Jimmy's all right, but he wouldn't've heard me 'til I was on top of him. Not even after I talked to the dog."

"I'll keep the offer in mind." Chris tipped his bottle toward the older man.

"What *are* you planning on doing now you're in the Falls?" Hopefully, the question sounded casual.

"I've been thinking about that." Chris leaned back into the couch. "I'm toying with the idea of starting up a private security firm. Maybe get some off-duty police or former military on the payroll."

"I should warn you. You might not find much call for that around here. Things are pretty quiet in the Falls." Bobby took a drink. "Might end up an investment that won't pay off quick, if at all."

A lightbulb went on in Chris's head. He kept his voice casual but looked pointedly at Bobby. "That's okay. The house isn't the only thing Pops left me."

The two men studied each other until Bobby nodded.

"Besides"—Chris relaxed again—"even if there's not much call for it here in the Falls, Danville, Charlotte, they're all close enough to give it a go."

"So long as you know it might be a long haul."

"Even after Pops died, I knew I couldn't just sit on my ass. It's not in me. And I'm not afraid of hard work or the long haul."

"Somehow, I didn't think you were."

Both men turned instinctively at the sound of the front door opening.

"Carter Anne?" Bobby called in a loud whisper.

"Hand to God, Bobby! You just scared the daylights out of me!" she exclaimed from the foyer. "What're you still doing . . . Oh. Hi, Chris." She stepped into the room and brushed her lips across her uncle's cheek. "You boys're up late."

"Yet oddly enough, *we're* not the ones who have to be at work in the morning." Bobby scolded her good-naturedly.

"I should be going home, though. Thanks for the beer, Bobby." Chris drained the bottle.

Carter Anne took it from him as he crossed the room. "I got that."

"Thanks, Carter Anne." He kissed her lightly on the cheek. "'Night, Bobby."

Carter Anne waited until the door closed behind him before asking. "What was that all about?"

Bobby looked at the closed door a moment then shrugged. "Nothing. Just met him on the street coming home and thought I'd invite him in for a beer." He turned to Carter Anne, ignoring her skeptical expression. "Turn the lights off when you go to bed." Whistling through his teeth, Bobby headed upstairs.

Chapter 6

Angie opened the door . . . and froze.

"Hi." Chris gave her a wave as he came out of the kitchen. "Sorry about this. Give me a second."

Feeling the blush run up her cheeks, she nodded as Chris passed her, dressed in jeans—and nothing else. This was when Carter Anne would say something witty and flirtatious, Angie knew, but all she could do was stare. Sure, she'd known he must have a great build by the way his shirts fit but, hand to God, she hadn't expected this. As he moved closer into the foyer, she couldn't help but rake her eyes across his chest.

"I like the way you look, too, Angie." He teased her with a twinkle in his eye. He had stopped just inches away from her.

Blushing harder, Angie dropped her eyes. They widened at what she saw. Just above the waistline of his jeans was the top of a ragged scar.

"Chris . . ." She gasped, reaching a hand out.

His hand closed on her wrist before she could touch him. "It's nothing, Angie."

Looking up, she realized the twinkle was gone. Chris's eyes were cold. "Sorry, I didn't mean to . . . I mean . . ." Angie stammered.

"It's okay." He loosened his grip, turning it into a light caress up her arm. "*I'm* sorry. I thought I could be dressed by the time you got here."

The ridiculousness of the situation struck her, and she laughed lightly. "Why aren't you?"

"Would you believe grand seduction?" Chris's eyes were softening again. Angie just lifted an eyebrow with a smirk. "Well, it was worth a try, anyway." He moved away from her and headed to the stairs as he spoke. "Sadly, it's no more interesting than oil on my shirt. It's probably ruined, but I wanted to get it in the wash immediately, just in case. I'll be back down in a minute." He paused on the first step, grinning. "Unless there's hope for the grand seduction?"

Laughing full out now, Angie shooed him up the stairs. "Go get decent. I'll put coffee on."

Chris winked and headed up. Angie stood long enough to enjoy the view from this angle before letting out a deep breath and heading into the kitchen.

Goddammit! Chris maintained his composure until reaching the privacy of his bedroom, then stormed over to his dresser. Goddammit! She would've seen it eventually anyway if he'd had his way, but not like that. Now the questions would start. They always did.

Women tended to have one of two reactions when they started asking the questions they only *thought* they wanted the answers to. Either they began to brag about dating Rambo—or they were horrified. Horrified by what he'd been through, what he'd seen . . . what he'd done. He wasn't sure which he hated more. Both reactions made him different in people's eyes and kept him from just being ordinary.

Sighing, Chris pulled on a clean T-shirt. Time to see which kind of woman Angie was.

When he got to the kitchen, she was staring into the refrigerator, a frown on her face, her eyes distant.

"Well?" He cleared his throat.

"Chris, I got a question for you." Angie shut the refrigerator and turned to him. Chris braced himself. "Would you mind orderin' a pizza tonight?"

Outwardly, he stayed calm. Inside, a small piece of him shriveled up. She didn't even want to stay. God, he'd wanted her to be different. . . .

"There's just nothin' in there I can do anything with. Carter Anne probably could, but I'm not as good makin' up recipes as she is."

"What?" Chris asked, unable to completely hide his shock.

"I thought we had the fixins for chicken soup," Angie explained, crossing to the coffeepot and pouring two cups. "But if they're in there, I'm not seein' 'em. And I don't have time to go to the store if we're gonna get any work done this afternoon. I know dinner's supposed to be part of my paycheck but . . ." With a shrug, she let the sentence dangle. Chris only stared at her. "I'm sorry," she finished. Damn, she should never have agreed to dinners. Still, he was looking at her like she'd just sprouted wings and told him she could fly. It was only dinner, hand to God. She opened her mouth to set him straight when he *grinned*. Her defense died in her throat.

"Pizza's a great idea, Angie." He wanted to wrap her up and spin her around. Instead, he reached for his coffee. "So long as you like it loaded. Otherwise, we'll have to get two."

Angie shook her head. Okay, she was confused and not at all sure what that had been about. She was, however, glad it was over. Grinning, she answered him. "Is there any other way to eat it?"

* * *

"You want a ride home, Angie, honey?" Bobby slowed the squad car and called out his window.

She was stuffed with pizza and her body hurt from scrubbing bathrooms after all day at the diner. "God, yes, Bobby. You're a lifesaver. Why're you out?" she asked, slipping in next to him.

Bobby shrugged. "The boys' wrestling team got a little rambunctious after tonight's win. Coach called, asked me to make it official that they quiet down and go on home, it being a school night and all." He laughed. "Figured since I was out, I might as well make rounds in the car. It's still a bit chilly on foot." Angie snorted in agreement. "Want me to take you on home," Bobby continued, "or feel like a ride 'round town?"

Angie decided. "I'll ride with you. But can I ask you about something while we ride?"

"'Course, honey." Bobby nodded.

"It's about Chris Montgomery."

Bobby squirmed slightly. "You sure you don't want to talk to Carter Anne 'bout this? She should be home from class by now."

"No. I think it's gotta be you." Angie looked out the window, not even seeing the lights of the town pass by. "He's got this bad scar across his stomach . . ."

Bobby nearly whimpered. "You *sure* you don't want to talk to Carter Anne about this?"

Angie glanced over and laughed, shocked at her uncle's obvious discomfort. "It's nothing like *that*, Bobby, hand to God! He just had to put his shirt in the wash."

"And?" Bobby still didn't like it, but it was a damn sight better than he'd feared.

"I don't think I handled it well. He wouldn't talk about it and, well, his eyes got all closed off and hard-like. You know how he does."

So Angie had noticed it as well. Probably a good thing she understood. "I do," Bobby replied. "Did you ask him about it?"

"No!" Angie was appalled. "Not when he was so obvious about not wantin' to talk."

Nodding, Bobby supported her. "Let it lie for now, Angie. When the man wants you to know, you will."

"Well . . . what do you think happened?"

Bobby just shrugged.

Maybe her uncle was right. Maybe she should be talking to Carter Anne about this. She'd at least be curious, too. "Come on, Bobby . . ." Angie needled him.

He sighed. "Angie, honey, the Green Berets are an elite unit. They go places and do things the rest of us never even know about. That's why they're called *Special* Forces. And, sadly, they've been a mite busy these last few years. Who knows what happened to the man. But again, he'll talk when he's ready."

Angie's eyes were wide. "You really think he was *shot*?"

Bobby cut his eyes over at her and grinned. "Or maybe he fell out of a tree and landed on a rock when he was young."

"Oh, Bobby!" She swatted at him playfully.

They were pulling up in front of the house. All was quiet in the Falls. How long had it been since she'd ridden rounds with him? Hand to God, she couldn't remember. But there'd been a time when she and Carter Anne both couldn't get enough of it. Sitting next to her uncle, looking so handsome and important in his uniform, had been a treat. So much so, he'd used it as leverage when they'd misbehaved. Angie looked over at his profile as he stopped the squad car alongside the curb. He was still handsome and important looking.

"You know I love you, right, Bobby?"

He cleared his throat harshly. "I know, Angie. And I love you, too."

She leaned over and kissed his cheek. "Be safe tonight."

"Always am, honey." Bobby assured her as she got out of the car. The front door was closed—and locked, he trusted—before he headed back to the station.

Chapter 7

Hands on her lower back, groaning slightly, Angie stretched. It had been a long week, hand to God. But tomorrow was Sunday and today had been payday at the diner. Maybe Carter Anne would want to go to Danville. Hit the Piedmont Mall. It had been a long time since she had done something girly. Too long. And Carter Anne was just the person to do it.

But that was tomorrow. There was still today to get through. Looking around at the dining room, she was pleased, though. One month and the downstairs wasn't just livable, it was presentable. When they'd started, she would've sworn this room itself was going to take a full month, let alone the entire first floor.

Now, every room down here but the ballroom was clean, the furniture dusted or aired out, and the place looked like a home. All it needed was decorating. Angie stared at the wall in front of her. Maybe a nice dusty rose. Or even a patterned wallpaper. It was old-fashioned but so was the house. And the rooms were certainly big enough to support bold colors. Yes, a patterned wallpaper.

Instinctively, she ran her hand over the old paint. The walls were smooth enough, too. A rose wallpaper with deeper red running through for the pattern. Maybe some gold flecks throughout, to pick up the candlelight for when they had dinner parties.

Angie froze. *They* wouldn't be having dinner parties in here. *They* wouldn't be doing anything in this room. And Chris would be making decorating decisions. Sure, she could make suggestions. Maybe he'd even listen. But that's all they would be. Suggestions. She stroked the wall lovingly. At least Chris would care for the place.

"Listening to the house?" His voice didn't startle her any longer. She had gotten used to how quiet he could be. "And what is it telling you?" Chris's question was teasing but not mocking.

"Rose wallpaper." She teased back, turning and taking the bottle of water he offered.

Chris looked around the room. "I wouldn't have thought of it, but you're right." His eyes twinkled. "Or the house is."

"The house is always right," she said, smiling as she tipped the bottle to her lips.

"I'm glad you think so, because the house is telling me we need to shut down early tonight. We've worked hard and deserve an early evening."

Angie groaned at the thought of an early night; a long, hot shower; her robe and slippers . . . Carter Anne's cooking. But it hardly seemed fair. Chris had worked as hard as she had. "Don't you want me to finish up dinner?"

With a wave of his hand, he dismissed her concerns. "You've got the sauce on already. I can boil spaghetti."

Nodding gratefully, Angie collected her things from the kitchen and headed to the door, Chris right behind her. "Oh." He stopped her as she opened the door. "Here." Chris handed her a slip of paper and took a long pull of his own water, watching her over the rim of the bottle.

"What's this?" Angie asked; then her eyes got wide. "This can't be right."

"But it is. I've kept track of your hours, and that's your paycheck. I've worked you hard this month."

Angie swallowed. The conversation about money seemed so long ago. And helping around the old house had been, well, fun, honestly. It didn't seem right to take money. Especially not this much money. "I really shouldn't."

Chris sighed, letting his exasperation show. "Angie, you really should. We've already talked about this, remember?

"Buy yourself something frivolous. Go away for a long weekend. Take Bobby out for a really nice dinner. But take it. You've earned it."

"You." Angie grinned at him.

"Me what?" Chris was puzzled.

"I'll take you to a nice dinner. Monday night. Feeding you is part of my job, so I'll feed you. Monday night."

Chris laughed, warm and full. "You're not supposed to use my money to take me to dinner."

"I'm not," Angie stuck her chin out at him, still grinning. "I'm using *my* money." She stepped out into the cool night air. It wasn't quite dark. It wasn't quite cold. Spring was definitely coming.

Chris leaned against the doorjamb, letting his eyes rake her top to toes and back again. "Well, well, Miss Angela Lambert Kane, I never thought you would ask me out on a date before I got around to asking you."

"Oh!" Angie stopped cold and stared at him. "No . . . that's not . . . I mean . . ." Her heart was somewhere up in her throat, blocking her words. And he was just standing there, smiling at her like a fox in the coop. "But . . ."

He looked her up and down again, enjoying the effect the

situation was having on her. Oh yes, this was working out nicely. "You're not taking it back are you?"

"God no!" Angie blurted. She should say something about friendship and gratitude and misunderstandings, but he wasn't giving her the chance.

"Then I accept. I'll see you Monday." With a wink, Chris closed the door.

She should knock. She should ring the bell and explain. Hell, she should just walk in there the way she did every afternoon and make *him* explain. She turned and headed down the hill for home.

Carter Anne and Bobby were sitting in the den, watching the evening news. He had his nose in a dog-eared book. She was flipping through the course catalogue from the community college. The house was warm and smelled of homemade soup and fresh biscuits. Angie hardly noticed any of it. She flopped down on the sofa next to her sister and stared blankly at the television.

"Hi, honey. You're home early." Carter Anne glanced up from her reading then looked closer. "Ang, what's wrong?"

Bobby automatically closed his book, thumb marking his place, and looked up.

"Chris Montgomery thinks I asked him out on a date."

"What?" Carter Anne giggled.

"I think I'll just go and check the biscuits." Bobby started to rise.

"But, Bobby, I didn't." Angie looked at him, eyes still blank.

With a resigned sigh, he lowered himself back into his chair. Carter Anne only bit her lip to keep from smiling. Some parts of raising girls never did get any easier.

"What happened?" Carter Anne didn't quite keep the giggle out of her voice.

Angie shot her a disgusted look and directed her answer to her uncle instead. "I got my check from him today and Chris suggested I do something fun with it. So I just said I'd take him to dinner. That's all. Now he thinks it's a date."

Bobby fought to control his own laughter. "Well, I admit it's been a while, but last time *I* invited someone to dinner and paid for it with my hard-earned money, it was a date. 'Course that's been a couple years now, so things might be different these days."

Angie narrowed her eyes at him.

"Yep." Bobby stood up. "Those biscuits are gonna burn all right if I don't go check."

"Coward." Carter Anne laughed at his back. "Ooh, Ang! This is so exciting. I didn't think you had it in you, hand to God. Where are you gonna take him? What are you going to wear?"

"Carter Anne? Haven't you been listening?" Angie looked hard at her. "I did not ask Chris Montgomery on a date."

Carter Anne looked right back at her sister. "I *have* been listening. And I've been *watching*, too. You like him. You've told me so yourself. And he's crazy about you. He's told me so himself. If you want to admit it or not, you asked him on a date. Now you can enjoy it or you can be bitchy. Your choice." She raised an eyebrow, waiting.

Angie looked at her hands. Dear God . . . she had. She actually *had*. A sound halfway between a laugh and a snort forced her lips into the smile she had been fighting back. "Carter Anne!" She squealed. "I got a date with Chris Montgomery!"

Carter Anne squealed right back. In the doorway, Bobby turned on his heel again, nibbling a perfectly baked biscuit, and headed back to the kitchen. He could always catch the eleven o'clock news later.

"Wake up. It's shopping day!" Carter Anne had always been the perky one in the mornings. Angie cracked an eye open at her sister. The younger woman was sitting on the edge of the bed, showered and dressed, grinning like a fool. Angie couldn't help it; she grinned back. Carter Anne held out a cup of coffee.

Sitting up, Angie pushed the hair out of her face, reached for the mug, and drank gratefully. Carter Anne waited until the first swallow had time to go down.

"So I'm thinking a little black dress."

"Carter Anne." Angie sighed, drinking deeply again. "You know the mall doesn't open until eleven, right?"

"I know. But it's already nine, and I'm not giving you a chance to back out of it."

Angie giggled in spite of herself. "A little black dress, huh? Won't that be too much?"

"A little black dress is never too much." Carter Anne grinned impishly. "That's why it's 'little.'"

Rolling her eyes but still laughing, Angie pushed the covers back. "Let me shower at least."

Carter Anne patted her leg. "Don't take too long."

Angie pulled her robe around but paused at the bedroom door. "A little black dress? You think?" she asked over her shoulder. Carter Anne wiggled her eyebrows.

Forty-five minutes later, Angie appeared in the kitchen wearing a skirt and an old pair of flats. Carter Anne eyed her once then nodded. "At least you thought to wear control top and flats instead of tights and your Doc Martens."

"Hey." Angie sat down and grabbed a biscuit left over from

last night. "I know how to be a girl." Her eyes twinkled merrily at her sister's teasing.

"Seems to me," Bobby spoke without ever looking up from his newspaper, "tights and Docs have worked just fine up 'til now anyway." At the silence that met his statement, he looked into the shocked faces of his girls. "The man said yes to the date, after all. And men talk, too, you know. Sometimes."

"Bobby! What do you mean?"

"Has Chris said something to you?"

The women erupted simultaneously.

"Look at the time." Bobby smiled. "I'm due at the station." Still smiling, he kissed both heads and walked out, whistling.

"But Bobby . . ." Angie called after him. "That man is insufferable."

"Hand to God," Carter Anne agreed. "Come on. Wish it was warm enough to put the top down."

They piled into Carter Anne's little red ragtop and took off. Even without the top down, the ride was beautiful.

"I saw you looking at the courses from Community last night." Angie spoke over the music coming from the radio.

"Oh." Carter Anne looked at her from the corner of one eye. "You saw *anything* last night? I'm impressed."

"Now hush." Angie hit at her sister.

"I'm thinking about going full-time in September. It'll be easier to transfer with more credits. And I've got enough saved to go part-time at work if they'll let me. It's not like I do all that much."

"Carter Anne, I think that's great. Seriously. Have you told Bobby?"

The merits of Duke versus UVa versus getting out of the area entirely kept their attention until Carter Anne pulled into a space just outside the main entrance to the mall.

"Now," she stated definitively, "it's all about you."

Looking at the mall directory, Carter Anne tapped her teeth. "What size are you?"

Angie looked around at the other people passing by and whispered in Carter Anne's ear.

"Then we have lots of options. Let's go here." Carter Anne touched the directory, pointing to a store known for its fashion as well as its range of sizes. Once there, she took over, holding up dress after dress.

"Carter Anne," Angie laughed. "I'm lookin' for one dress, not a new wardrobe."

"And what else are you gonna spend that money on, honey?"

Four dresses, three pairs of pants, and six tops later, Carter Anne herded Angie into the dressing room. Before she could close the door, Angie stopped her. "Carter Anne, is all this really necessary?"

"Angie, honey, tell me you're not enjoying it down deep. Truly and really not enjoying it and we will put all this away and go home."

Angie looked at the riot of colors and textures draped over her arm, and the corners of her mouth twitched. "That's what I thought," Carter Anne replied with a laugh. "Now get in there."

Once the door was closed, Carter Anne turned back to the store and looked around. The stuff Angie had in there was nice, real nice, but none of it was *right*. Chris knew she was beautiful. But hand to God, Angie didn't. And Angie should.

None of the dresses would have the effect Carter Anne was looking for. Damn.

"What do you think?" Angie struck a pose in the dressing room door.

"Girl, you look great!" The sales clerk responded before Carter Anne could.

"Oh!" Angie laughed, embarrassed to be caught by a stranger. "Thanks."

But the clerk was right. Carter Anne had thought the deep wine color would do nice things with Angie's complexion. She just hadn't thought it would do *such* nice things. Maybe they should rethink the little black dress and find a little burgundy one instead.

"Put that in the definitely-going-home-with-us pile."

"It's good, isn't it?" Angie agreed. With a shake of the hips that spun the skirt, she disappeared back into the dressing room.

Carter Anne immediately turned to the woman working the floor. "Did you see how good she looked?"

"Mm-hm. Red's her color."

"We need something that makes her look better. And if it's little and black, well . . ." She let the sentence hang.

"The girl's got a date, huh?" the woman asked.

"The girl's got *the* date, if I have anything to say about it."

"I've got just the thing. Came in yesterday with the new summer inventory. It's not even on the floor yet. Might be a bit cool though, if this date is soon."

"That's what wraps are for."

The woman smiled conspiratorially and went into the back room.

Angie reappeared in a pair of tailored black pants and an emerald green silk blouse.

"How come I've never seen you in jewel tones before, Ang? They're gorgeous on you." Carter Anne reached over and unbuttoned one of the top buttons on the blouse. "There you go. I'm cleaning out all your earth tones as soon as we get home."

"You don't think this is too much? I mean, where would I wear it?" Angie fiddled with the button but didn't refasten it.

"Once it's in your closet, you will find places to wear it,"

Carter Anne stated firmly. "Next!" She shooed Angie back into the room as the clerk came around the counter.

The dress was indeed little and black. The halter would show off Angie's shoulders while the low V neckline would show off her other assets. It was fitted at the waist before the skirt flared out to just under the knee.

This was it, Carter Anne smiled. This was the dress that would make Angie see herself the way Chris already did. After this dress, finding a place to wear black pants and a silk blouse would be easy.

"What kind of shoes does she have at home?" The clerk was happily getting into the project.

Carter Anne rolled her eyes. "Doc Martens."

"Oh no." The woman shook her head and strode to the shoe section. "What size does she wear?" she called over.

"What?!" Angie threw open the dressing room door. She was in another great dress, Carter Anne noticed, but that didn't seem to matter right at the moment.

"Shoe size, honey. Shoe size," Carter Anne reassured her.

"Oh." Angie looked relieved. "Eight or eight and a half. But I have shoes."

"Not for these clothes you don't."

Angie shrugged and ducked back into the small room. In for a penny, in for a pound.

"That dress was great, too!" Carter Anne called over the door. "Put it with the burgundy one."

The sales clerk and Carter Anne enjoyed watching Angie model the different outfits until they decided all but one top would work.

"After all," the clerk noted. "The child's got bosom. She might as well show it off."

"It's not as if I can hide it." Angie laughed through the door.

"It's not as if she hasn't tried," Carter Anne muttered to the other woman.

"I heard that!"

"Heard what, honey?" Carter Anne teased. "Here. Try this one." She passed the dress over the stall.

"Carter Anne, no more." Angie groaned but the dress was pulled over.

"With one of these." Carter Anne slipped a pair of three inch peep-toe pumps and a pair of kitten-heel slingbacks under the door. The two women waited. And waited. "Angie? You okay in there?"

"Sure" came the timid reply.

"Then open up." Carter Anne knocked on the locked door. Slowly it opened.

For a moment, Carter Anne could just stare. Sure, she'd always known Angie had a pretty face. Even a beautiful one. But when the rest of her wasn't covered by layers and loose-fitting clothing . . . "Oh, Angie," Carter Anne whispered.

"Girl . . ." The clerk whistled low. "You might as well throw everything else out and wear that every day for the rest of your life."

Chapter 8

All he could do was stare. He didn't care that he was being rude. He didn't care that he was standing in his doorway without yet asking her in. She was even lovelier than he had ever imagined—and, he admitted, he had imagined quite a lot.

Angie pulled her velvet wrap tighter around her shoulders more as a defense against the look in Chris's eyes than against the chill in the night air. She'd been appreciated before, even by him, but not like this. Never had a man looked at her as if he was starving, as if he wanted to feast on her until she was no more than a shell of herself and still want more. She shivered, feeling a heat inside of her that belied the weather.

The movement, as small as it was, broke into Chris's reverie. "You're beautiful, Angie." He backed up, clearing the doorway so she could step by him into the house.

Automatically, she moved toward the kitchen where they always sat, but with a firm hand on the small of her back, Chris guided her into the sitting room. He had found candles somewhere and scattered them throughout the room. A bottle of red wine sat on the low table between two glasses she had washed herself only days ago.

Feeling as if she had never set foot in the house before,

Angie struggled for something, anything, to break the tension building between them. "Told you we got the place ready for entertaining."

Chris slipped the wrap from her shoulders, trailing his fingertips lightly across her skin, encouraged by the low quiver that ran through her body. "And I can't think of anyone I'd rather have as my first guest in my new home." Taking her hand, he led Angie to the love seat, only releasing her once she had sat down beside him. Without asking, he poured the wine and passed her a glass. He lifted his and waited for her to join him.

"To possibilities," Chris said.

"Possibilities?" Angie wanted to be puzzled.

Chris's voice was low. "New town, new house." He indicated her with a shift of his head. "New friends. Possibilities."

"Oh." Angie swallowed then tapped her glass to his. The crystal sounded out, clear and pure. "Possibilities."

Taking a sip, Chris leaned back comfortably. Advance . . . and retreat. Two steps forward, one step back. He could do this, dammit. "So." He forced his voice to become casual again. "Where are we going for dinner? I'm starving."

Angie let out her breath. This was the Chris Montgomery she knew. Casual, comfortable, thinking with his stomach. Relaxing finally, she leaned back as well. "The Inn at Ashby. It's about twenty minutes from here. They have a nice restaurant. For breakfast and lunch, you have to be a guest, but they open it up for reservations at dinner."

"And you were able to get us reservations on such short notice?"

"It's Monday." Angie laughed.

Chris chuckled. "What time do we need to leave?"

Angie looked at her watch. "Now, actually." She took one

more sip of the wine, enjoying its warmth, then reached for Chris's glass. "I'll just put these in the kitchen . . ."

"Angie." Chris took her glass instead of relinquishing his own and put them on the table. "Leave them. You're not on the clock, and I promise you won't find them here tomorrow when you are." He corked the bottle and stood up, reaching his hand for hers. "Shall we?"

Much to Angie's relief, the conversation stayed comfortable on the drive. And if she occasionally glanced over at him, who could blame her when a man looked that good in a turtleneck and blazer? And if she caught him looking at her legs once or twice, well, there were certainly worse things than being admired by Chris Montgomery. Bottom line was, though, it *was* Chris. Just her friend, Chris.

As she pulled her Toyota into the winding drive of the inn, Chris couldn't help but be impressed. The main house and what had obviously once been the barn seemed to glow from the inside, promising warmth and hospitality against the dark night. A few buildings were scattered throughout the property, some with lights shining from the guest rooms inside, others waiting patiently for their current occupants to return. It was well done and would have a year-round allure as the seasons changed.

Following the drive, Angie pulled into a parking lot next to the barn and found a spot. "Right on time. The restaurant's in here."

Chris came around the car as Angie got out and put his hand on her lower back again, spreading a warmth along her spine and into her belly as if she had just drunk another glass of his wine. She couldn't do this. Angie stopped in her tracks and turned to him.

"Chris, I don't think . . ."

It only took him a second. He knew that look. Knew that

tone. Knew what was coming next. "Angie." Chris reached out and placed his hands gently on her shoulders. "Don't. Please. Just for tonight, relax and don't think. If tomorrow you still need to say what you're about to say, then all right. But give me tonight."

Chris's hands were strong and warm on her bare shoulders underneath her wrap. What he was asking for . . . Angie swallowed around the lump in her throat. "Tomorrow may be too late."

"That's what I'm hoping for." Chris smiled ruefully. "But just in case . . . ?"

How could she resist this? How could anyone? Angie smiled gently. "Then we will've at least had tonight."

Chris slid his hand down her arm and touched her hand. With a sigh, Angie entwined her fingers with his.

"Angie! Honey, is that you?!"

Angie had been pulling cash from her purse and hadn't seen the woman approach the table. When she looked up, Chris noticed the slight tightening around her lips and something—pain? disgust? something—pass through her eyes. It was only a flicker but it had been there. He looked at the woman. Her voice was just a bit too shrill; her hair just a bit too blonde; and her clothes just a bit too loud.

"It *is* you!" She exclaimed. "I told Clark it was, but he didn't believe me. You remember Clark, don't you, honey?" She pointed across the room to a man sitting in the corner. Just beginning to lose the muscle that had seen him through high school and college, Chris figured. He was still handsome, but in ten years . . . Chris watched as Angie forced a smile and a wave at the man. He tipped his glass, filled with brown liquor, at her in return.

"Well, don't you look all nice, dressed up tonight. Doesn't our Angie have a pretty face?" The woman included Chris in the conversation for the first time.

"She's a beautiful woman, yes," Chris responded coolly.

The woman looked at Angie pointedly. With a quiet sigh, Angie introduced them. "Langdon Hanes, this is Chris Montgomery."

She extended a limp, perfectly manicured hand to Chris. "Pleased to meet you. Only it's Langdon Howard now." She flashed her left hand at Angie, wiggling her fingers.

"Congratulations." Angie smiled. "And you didn't even have to change your monogram," she added drily. Chris hid his smile behind the last sip of his wine.

"So true!" Langdon gasped. She turned her attention back to Chris. "Chris Montgomery . . . Montgomery . . . Are you related to old Doc Montgomery?"

"He was my grandfather. I'm living in the house now."

"I had heard that someone had moved back in there. And here you are!"

"Here I am." Chris couldn't make eye contact with Angie. Couldn't even look in her direction.

The other woman leaned in, conspiratorially. "Clark didn't think I should come over here, even if it was you, Angie. Said you looked like you were on a date." Lifting one thinly plucked eyebrow, she glanced at the money still clasped in Angie's hand. "He'll be so disappointed to learn it was . . . something else."

"Actually." Chris reached across the table and enclosed Angie's free hand in his. "Clark won't be disappointed at all. She just wouldn't go out on a date with me until I agreed to let her pay. I figured a date with Angie was worth swallowing my pride. I can always pay for the rest of them."

"Oh." Langdon gasped, finally speechless.

"But it was nice to meet you," Chris continued. "Thanks for stopping by. Any friend of Angie's is a friend of mine."

"Well. Yes." She was thrown by the dismissal. "You, too. Angie, honey," Langdon soldiered on, "give me a call. I'd love to catch up."

"I'll do that. And congratulations again on the wedding. I'm sure you and Clark will have all the happiness you deserve." Angie spoke through her fakest smile.

She watched the other woman cross the room and start whispering to her husband as soon as she sat down. But when Angie turned back, Chris was watching her with a twinkle in his eye. "We'd better go."

Angie counted out the money and wasn't surprised in the least when Chris came around and helped her with her wrap. As they navigated the room, he looked back over his shoulder. Langdon Howard was still whispering a mile a minute, but unless Chris was very much mistaken, Clark Howard was watching Angie's backside over the rim of his drink.

Once in the parking lot, Angie threw back her head and laughed. "God! That was priceless! Oh, Chris, thank you." Her smile lit up her face, making her even more beautiful. "Although you probably think I'm horrible for laughing like this." Even with the disclaimer, Angie couldn't quite lose her smile or the twinkle in her eyes.

"Actually," Chris joined in, "I would say Mrs. Clark Howard got what she deserved." He opened the car door for her before getting in the passenger side. "Who is she, anyway?"

"Oh, she and Clark were the golden ones in high school. Homecoming king and queen. Football star and head cheerleader. But not like Amy at the ice-cream parlor. She's got a head on her shoulders. No, Langdon was just pretty and popular. You know the type."

Chris nodded. "The kind who will never leave town, never

accomplish much, and still be reliving the glory days twenty years from now."

He had said something wrong. Somewhere, during his response, he had said the wrong thing. But damned if he knew what it was. The shift in her had been subtle. If he hadn't been looking directly at her, he wouldn't have even noticed. But he had been.

"See, I told you you'd know the type." Angie's voice was hardly different at all. Nope. He wouldn't have noticed a thing. Quietly grateful he hadn't been able to take his eyes off of her, he decided he would just have to undo whatever mistake he had made. The unguarded Angie was too delightful to lose this evening.

They were getting close to town. He'd have to move quickly. Carefully, but quickly. "It's early yet. Want to join me for a bit of a stroll? I'll buy you a coffee or something."

"I'm so stuffed, I don't think there's room even for coffee." It was true, too, she realized. With other guys, she'd always felt required to pick at her food, claim to be full then raid the refrigerator when she got home. Although she'd never done that with Chris before, she had been just as comfortable with him on a real date. And wasn't that something . . . She opened her mouth to continue her refusal anyway, but Chris spoke first.

"Just a walk then. No coffee."

Angie pulled onto Main Street. "Mind if we stop by the house first?" Where had that come from? *So much for refusing*. She chuckled silently to herself.

Without waiting for an answer, she whipped the car into the driveway with ease. "Come on in. I won't be a minute."

"That you, Angie?" Bobby called from the den as they walked in.

"Just for a sec," Angie answered. "Chris is here, too, but we're going back out." She led Chris into the other room as

Bobby stood up. "I'll be right back." She smiled at both men then scurried upstairs.

"Seems the evening is going well," Bobby said with a knowing smile. He motioned for Chris to take a chair before sitting back down himself. Two books were open next to him; one upside down on the arm of his chair, the other on the small table under the lamp. Was he reading both of them at once? Chris wondered.

"Since it's Angie, I won't offer you a beer. She'll be right down. Now if we were waitin' on Carter Anne . . ." Bobby let the sentence dangle with a loving chuckle. "Where you off to now?" he asked, trying to keep his voice light. But it was nearly eleven. Ah well. They were young.

"Just thought we'd take a walk. Honestly, I'm not ready for the evening to end quite yet," Chris answered, almost shyly.

Bobby looked him over then nodded, as if coming to some decision. "Have her take you down by the statue in the center of town."

"Okay, but any particular reason why?" Chris asked.

Bobby shrugged. "It's a nice walk. Some interesting history there."

Angie appeared in the doorway before either man could speak again. Chris wasn't sure what he had expected, but it certainly wasn't for her to still be dressed the way she had been when they'd arrived. Then he looked at her shoes. She had changed from high heels into lower ones. Still, they weren't her usual clunky things and matched the dress as well as the others. Angie noticed his glance and blushed.

"They're easier for walking."

"I'm glad you didn't change."

From his seat, Bobby cleared his throat. Maybe he'd get a little television set for his bedroom if his den was going to be used for courting.

Angie jumped as if he'd goosed her then laughed. "I won't be late, Bobby."

"Lock the door when you come in," was his only reply as he picked up the books. Yep, Chris noted. He was reading them both. Angie leaned over and kissed the top of her uncle's head then reached her hand out to Chris. Bobby pretended to read until he heard the front door close. Smiling, he hoped Chris would take her to the statue—and would know what to do when he got there. He had faith in the man.

It was easy for Chris to steer them to town square, and they reached it quickly enough. He looked up at the large statue of Thomas Jefferson Lambert standing in the middle. It was him as a soldier, on his horse, riding into battle. One of the horse's legs was raised. Chris couldn't help but think of a hunting dog pointing to a downed bird. It was bordering on sacrilegious and he knew it; he just couldn't help it.

"So," he said, looking from the statue down to Angie, "tell me some more about this grand gentleman?"

"I've already told you about him."

"Nah, you've only told me he's your however-many-greats-grandfather." Chris waved her off, wanting to hear the warm honey of her voice when she talked about the town.

"Four greats. And I'm surprised someone hasn't filled you in already." Angie met his gaze briefly then looked away, up at the statue. "This is General Thomas Jefferson Lambert, originally from Virginia and named after her favorite son. He settled the land that would eventually grow up to be Lambert Falls."

"Of course." Chris was still watching her. She didn't notice it. She was already absorbed in the story of the town she loved so much.

"He came here before the war and raised a family. According to the story, he was in the military but thought mostly he would be a gentleman farmer. Then the South seceded. He was older than most other soldiers when the war broke out but still did his duty. Because he'd married late in life, he still had two teenage sons at home. They all three joined up to fight the Yankees. Only one of the sons returned, so the family name didn't die there, just almost. Still, everyone in town claims to be related somehow—through a mother's second cousin or something. I can't quite believe it. If all the claims were true, his ancestors multiplied faster than rabbits." Angie laughed. "But it's harmless, so I keep my mouth shut."

"Plus, you can trace your family back directly, so who cares, right?" Chris asked with a smile.

"Right," Angie agreed good-naturedly, still looking at her ancestor. "Your family and ours probably knew each other. I'm surprised you don't know the story yourself."

She looked at Chris and was thrown by the intensity of his stare. She had become accustomed to his intensity, his ability to focus so completely on a task or event. She was even getting used to being the target of that gaze—well, almost anyway. But it was different out here, under the moon. She found herself growing warm and slightly uncomfortable, though not in a completely unpleasant way. Oh, this was going to be such a mistake. "Do you also know," she continued hastily, "that you can tell how a soldier died by the way his horse is carved in the statue?"

"Really?" Chris responded, but she wasn't sure he was listening. He had moved closer to her and was rubbing his fingers along one of her arms. It tingled like nothing Angie had ever felt before. Her breath caught in her throat and she had to start twice before she could finally make her voice work again.

"Really. If the horse is rearing then the rider died in battle. If the horse has one leg up, then the rider died as a result of wounds sustained in battle. If the horse's front legs are down, then the rider survived the war and died of other causes. Probably old age. So, you can tell that the general here died of wounds sustained in battle."

"Actually, that's a myth. While it might have been true once, it hasn't been for a very long time. You can't tell how a soldier died just by the positioning of his horse." Chris's fingers pressed harder into her skin as he moved them on her arms. His eyes were penetrating and distracting. She wasn't sure what was happening or how to respond to this turn of events.

"Really?" Angie hardly recognized her voice. "Well, in this case it happens to be true. He did die of wounds sustained in battle."

"Anything else about this statue I should know?" he asked. His voice was husky and low.

"Actually—" Her voice cracked. Angie cleared her throat again but could only manage a whisper. "Town legend has it that if a boy gives a girl their first kiss under the statue and no clouds pass the moon or the sun, then the general has blessed her relationship and she's with her one true love."

"Maybe that myth is true, too." With that, Chris closed what little distance was left between them. He took her into his arms and lowered his lips to hers. He was gentle but demanding as he opened her lips with his tongue. When the kiss deepened, Angie thought she would faint. She felt her body lean into his, and she gave in to the kiss completely. Chris's arms were so strong, and his hands on her back so firm. She knew if she had fainted, he would have never let her fall. It was over all too soon.

He pulled back from her but didn't release her from his embrace. Advance . . . and retreat. "I should get you home."

"But . . ." Angie started to speak. Chris touched a finger to her lips.

"I don't *want* to take you home. But I should. The last thing I need is to get on the wrong side of a man with a gun who knows exactly where I live and who I'm with this evening."

Angie laughed, despite herself. Chris tightened his arms around her before turning them both in the direction of her house. God, she even fit right under his arm when they walked together. And she snuggled in there as if it was exactly where she wanted to be. The retreat part was going to be harder than he'd expected. He shook his head and sighed.

"You okay?" Angie asked, trying to keep the insecurity out of her voice.

"Yeah." Chris kissed her temple as they walked. "Just trying to talk myself into letting you go tonight."

"Oh," Angie whispered. "How nice." She snuggled in closer to him. The walk home seemed much shorter than the walk to the statue had been.

He walked her up the steps to the porch. "I want to see you again, Angie."

"You'll see me tomorrow, Chris." She tried to laugh.

"That's not what I mean." He lifted her chin. "I want to see you like this again. I want to take you out on another date."

Angie couldn't find the words she was looking for. Suddenly, it didn't matter that she was going to end up hurt. It didn't matter that she had tried to stop the evening before it had even started. But she couldn't find the words.

Chris studied her before speaking again. "I told you that if you still needed to have a conversation with me, we could have it tomorrow. So I'll see you tomorrow when you get to the house. But while you're thinking about everything tonight and what you may or may not say to me, think about this, too." He lowered his lips to hers and kissed her softly, teasingly, gently. As he felt her begin to deepen the kiss, he pulled back. "Good night, Angie."

She swayed on her feet for a moment before she could stop herself. The man could kiss. With a breath, she straightened up. "Good night, Chris."

Chapter 9

There was a thud above his head. Chris looked up at the ceiling. Was Angie here? How had he missed her? He'd been in the kitchen waiting for her to come make the pot of coffee she always put on for them. At the second thud, he decided to go investigate.

He found Angie in the first bedroom upstairs, struggling to move the bed itself.

"You're going to throw your back out," Chris said from the doorway.

"Oh!" Angie gasped. "Hi." She ran her hand over her hair and smoothed her shirt. Realizing what she was doing, she bunched the hem of it again, fidgeting it through her fingers.

"What are you doing, trying to move this thing yourself?" It wasn't the question Chris wanted to ask, but she looked so much like a trapped deer that he couldn't bring himself to push.

"I want to clean the floorboards today, so I needed to get behind the bed."

"At least let me help." Chris moved into the room, careful to brush her arm as he walked past her. Instead of just putting her hair up in a bandanna the way she usually did, it was in a thick braid down her back. And he wasn't sure, but he thought she might be wearing lip gloss. And mascara. The thought that she had made an effort with her appearance today reassured him after her sneaking in and upstairs.

Chris squatted at one corner of the bed. "On three, okay?" Angie took position at the other corner and nodded. "One, two, three."

They pulled and the bed jerked across the floor, spilling Angie onto her butt.

"Angie!" he shouted, kneeling next to her.

"I'm okay." Angie was laughing. "It's a lot lighter with two."

"And you're stronger than you look," Chris said. "I guess we both didn't have to give it our all."

"'Least I can get to the floorboards now," Angie said with a smile.

Several tendrils of hair had come free of her braid. Chris reached up and brushed them out of her face. She was very close; he could smell her conditioner and perfume. Perfume . . . and lip gloss. And yet she'd snuck in.

"You sure you're okay?" Chris asked.

"Oh yeah," Angie assured him. "My butt'll be sore, but that's 'bout it."

Chris stood and held out his hand to help her up. When he pulled, she felt as light as the bed had been with both of them moving it.

"How long have you been here?" Chris had to know.

"Not . . ." Angie looked away. "Not long."

"Come on." Chris took her hand. "I need coffee. Then we can start on the room."

Angie folded her hand into his and followed him downstairs. On the way over, she'd decided to talk about them being good friends, taking it slow, just enjoying each others' company. Something sensible like that. When she'd arrived, she'd chickened out. Now, with her hand firmly in his, she knew why. Nothing sensible made any sense when she was with him.

They walked into the kitchen hand in hand and Angie gasped. On the table were four white roses surrounding a single red one. Baby's breath and greenery rose up out of the vase, embracing the blooms.

"Oh, Chris," she breathed. "They're beautiful. Are they . . ." She hesitated. It seemed like a silly question, but she had to be sure. "Are they for me?"

Chris shook his head in disbelief. "Well, they aren't for Bobby." He turned her into him. "Yes, Angie, they're for you."

She looked back at the roses. "Nobody's ever given me flowers before. Well, 'cept Bobby on Easter Sunday."

"I think I should be offended," Chris teased.

"Why?" Angie was confused.

"The night we met. I brought you flowers then."

"That was different, though! You didn't mean to bring them to *me*, you just meant to . . ." She saw the mischief in his eyes. "Oh you! That was different and you know it. No one's ever brought me flowers like *this* before."

"Then they are long overdue. And I'm glad it was me." He leaned down and touched his lips to hers. Last night had been too special to scare her off. "I made the coffee, too." He grinned.

"Well, that was . . ." Angie searched for a word. "Romantic." She moved out of his arms, over to the coffeepot.

"Actually, probably not," Chris admitted. "It'll be my usual sludge so I probably should have just stuck to the flowers and let you make the coffee."

"I appreciate the gesture anyway." Angie brought two mugs to the table. She sat and took a sip of hers. He was right. But he ate her cooking, so . . . "It's fine." She smiled at him.

To hell with it, Chris decided. He was just going to say it.

"I really enjoyed last night, Angie, and I *would* like to take you out again."

Angie looked at her coffee and tried not to smile. "I'd like that, too, Chris. Just . . . slow, okay?"

Chris took his first deep breath since he'd left the night before. "Okay," he agreed. He could do slow. It was enough to know he had a chance.

It was a good evening. Her butt hurt from the fall; her thighs hurt from squatting at the floorboards; and yet the smell of her flowers made the rest insignificant. The meatloaf had even been less bad than some of the other dishes. Maybe if they started dating, Chris would let her off the hook with the whole cooking thing.

Angie opened the door to the lingering smell of Carter Anne's meatloaf. It was nothing like the way Chris's kitchen currently smelled. Not even close.

"Bobby? Carter Anne? Anybody home?" she called out.

"In here, Angie," Bobby called back from the den.

Angie placed her roses on the hall table and drifted in to find her uncle. He was reading, sipping Dr. Pepper. She kissed the top of his head before collapsing on the sofa.

"Have a good day?" Bobby put his book down.

"I did." Angie nodded. "Where's Carter Anne?"

"Out with some friends for drinks. Why?"

Damn! Angie was busting to tell someone, and Carter Anne would've been perfect. Bobby would have to do, if he liked it or not.

"I got flowers." She giggled.

Why, Bobby wondered, had Carter Anne and her friends gone out on a Tuesday night anyway? "The man shows good taste," Bobby said.

"And he wants to see me again." Angie's voice sounded almost surprised.

"As I said, he's got taste."

"Bobby?" Angie's eyes were still bright, but her voice was lower. "I think I'm scared."

Tuesday nights were definitely nights for young women to be at home. "Well," Bobby thought carefully. "Getting to know someone this way is scary. It can also be real nice."

"How come you never dated after Abby died?" Angie realized she'd never even thought about this aspect of her uncle's life.

Bobby shrugged. "First, I wasn't ready. Your aunt was a hard act to follow. Then I was raising two little girls. It didn't leave much time, and I couldn't bring just anybody into your lives."

"But once we were older—why not then?" Angie asked.

"I haven't lived like a monk, Angie," Bobby replied.

"You haven't?" Angie was shocked.

Bobby cleared his throat hard. "There were a couple of very nice ladies over the years. Just never got serious enough to introduce you."

"When though?" Angie couldn't get over this. "Seems you were always here or working."

Bobby was going to have to have a long talk with Carter Anne about her social schedule. "You girls would both be out doing your things—practices, sleepovers, stuff like that. There was time then. And I didn't exactly show you my work schedule. Then there were school days."

"In the afternoon?" She gasped. "You?"

Bobby cleared his throat again. Was Carter Anne too old to ground? "They were lunch dates."

Angie laughed loudly. "Sure they were. Why didn't you ever introduce us?"

Bobby sipped his drink. "Like I said, it never got serious enough. Introducing you and Carter Anne would've been a big step. There was one I was thinking about introducing to you, but her mother got sick down in South Carolina and that was the end of that."

"Miss Hendrickson? Miss Hendrickson from the high school?"

Bobby turned bright red. Surely Carter Anne would be home soon. "Didn't realize you knew why she left town."

Bobby and Miss Hendrickson . . . hand to God. "What about the others Bobby?"

"They were all very nice, Angie, but your aunt . . . Well, I just couldn't settle for less, especially not with you two to consider."

"What made Miss Hendrickson different, then?" Angie wasn't sure what she was hoping to learn, but she knew she'd recognize it when she heard it.

"Ah, Janet." Bobby smiled at the memory. "Janet was smart and funny and nearly as beautiful as Abby had been back before she got sick. We could talk, but we didn't have to. The silences were nice, too. And I trusted her. I trusted her to be honest with me. I trusted her to talk straight to me. And I would've trusted her with you."

"Sounds like you were in love." Angie was seeing him in a new light. As a real person, not just her uncle, possibly for the first time.

Bobby nodded. "I think we were very close to it. Plain old liking someone combined with trust can be a powerful combination, Angie."

"I can see that."

"What about Chris?" Finally, a way to change the subject. Maybe talking about his niece's love life wasn't the worst thing in the world.

"What about him?" Angie was caught off guard.

"I know you like him," Bobby explained. "Do you trust him?"

Angie thought about it. "I want to."

"Do you think he's trustworthy?"

She nodded. "I do."

"Then you're going to have to let yourself trust him, hard as that might seem. I didn't want to trust anyone ever again after Abby went and died on me, hand to God. But with Janet I finally had to. She just wore me down. It's easier if you don't make it so hard on them."

Angie sat forward. Somewhere along the line, she had gotten what she needed. She made a mental note to thank Carter Anne for going out.

"It's getting late, Bobby. I'm going on up." She stood up. "Did you ever give Miss Hendrickson flowers?"

Bobby's eyes twinkled. "Every time we had lunch."

"Dinner and a movie."

"What?" Angie wasn't used to Chris meeting her at the door. She certainly wasn't used to him making half-sentence declarations. She tried to move by him into the house, but he blocked her way, hands gentle on her shoulders.

"We should go to dinner and a movie. Isn't that a standard second date?" Chris's eyes were hopeful.

"Okay . . . fine." Angie realized she would never get to work unless she humored him. "When?"

"Tonight."

"You're crazy." She laughed and pushed by him, but Chris caught her by the arm and spun her into him.

"Tonight." His voice was lower, nearly a whisper.

And oh, his arms felt good around her. But they were tackling more of the second floor today. "Chris Montgomery." Angie tried to be serious. One of them had to be, hand to God. "We have work to do." He moved his hands slowly up and down her spine. "'Sides, look how I'm dressed."

"You're beautiful," Chris whispered.

"I'm dressed for cleanin', not for dinner." He wouldn't stop rubbing her back, though. She would be able to think so much more clearly if he would just keep his hands still.

"So, I'll take you home to change." Chris bent his head so he was speaking directly into her ear. "I want to take you out tonight, Angie."

She leaned into him, giving herself over for a moment to the touch of his hands, the sound of his voice. Just for a moment.

"Okay." She nodded, then her eyes sprang open. "No. I didn't mean to say that."

"But you did say it." Chris kissed her nose playfully. "And the upstairs has been dusty for years. One more night means nothing."

She couldn't help it; she giggled. "Okay, okay. Drive me home and I'll change." As Chris turned her around, Angie realized he hadn't even bothered to close the door.

When they got to the house, Carter Anne was in the kitchen making a salad.

"Is Bobby home?" Angie asked her.

"No. Why are you?" She looked from her sister to Chris. "Everything okay?"

"Oh yeah." Angie could feel the flush starting up her neck. "We're just . . . ummm . . ."

"We're taking a night off and going to the movies," Chris intervened.

"Well"—Carter Anne grinned—"good for you."

Somehow, Angie didn't think the comment was directed at her.

"I'm gonna change. You'll tell Bobby I might be late?"

"Sure thing, Ang." Carter Anne was still smiling.

Before she could think about it too much, Angie hurried up the stairs.

"That was good the other night, getting her to ask you out." Carter Anne leaned up against the counter.

Chris winked at her. "You're the one who told me to take it slow."

"So what are y'all doing tonight?" She returned to slicing vegetables.

"Dinner and a movie. But"—Chris reached around her to grab a cherry tomato—"before you ask, I have no idea what we're seeing." He laughed. "Hell, I don't even know what's playing. This was pretty spur-of-the-moment."

Carter Anne giggled and smacked his hand as he reached for another tomato. "'Least it's early enough for you to decide once you get there. Have dinner before or after, depending on movie times."

"You got it." Chris started to say something else, but Angie came in, seeming just as hurried as when she'd left.

"Is this all right? I figured we weren't going fancy 'cause you're in jeans."

Dear God, would the woman ever stop taking his breath away? Somehow, he didn't think so. Even in jeans, a cranberry V-necked sweater, and low heels, he was reacting as if she was dolled up for a big night out on the town—or a private night in.

"Perfect." Chris smiled at her. Angie felt her skin warm under his gaze.

Carter Anne watched the two of them. Oh yeah, he was getting to her all right. And good for him. She cleared her throat pointedly. "Y'all better get going if you want dinner *and* a movie. Or"—her eyes twinkled—"I could just close the door behind me and ignore any noises I hear comin' from in here."

"Carter Anne!" Angie gasped. But her sister's statement had been effective. Chris looked away from her, blushing a bit himself.

"Just offerin'," Carter Anne said nonchalantly.

"Why don't we go?" Chris said, laughter at the edges of his voice.

"You'll tell—" Angie started hesitantly, but Carter Anne interrupted her with a wave.

"I'll tell Bobby. Don't worry. Y'all just have a good time."

"Thanks, Carter Anne." Chris smiled, leaning past her quickly to steal another tomato before following Angie to the door.

"So, what are we seeing?" Angie asked as Chris pulled the car out of the driveway.

"No idea," he said simply. "I figure we'll decide once we're there. What kind of movies do you like?" Chris realized he truly had no idea.

"Honestly?"

"Well, I'd rather you not lie to me," he replied with a snort.

"I like action movies. The bigger the explosions, the better," Angie answered excitedly. "With lots of chase scenes, too."

"Really?" Chris was stunned.

"Since you didn't want me lying to you," Angie teased.

"John McLean or Martin Riggs?"

"Oh, that's easy: Martin Riggs. But I like the villain from *Die Hard* better."

"So you prefer Green Berets to New York cops, huh?"

"Oh." Angie realized what she had said. What the hell . . . "I'm coming to like Green Berets a lot, actually."

Chris glanced over at her, sitting turned in her seat so she could look at him. "Good. I'm glad to hear it."

"But not Rambo," Angie teased. "He's too mean."

"Oh, Angie!" Chris shook his head sadly. "And here I thought you were perfect." He cut his eyes to her suspiciously. "What about the Ranger training film?"

Angie looked puzzled.

"*Predator*," Chris explained.

She laughed. "Is that what you guys call it? Well, I love it."

Chris nodded. "Oh good. I was worried." He breathed a fake sigh of relief. "Back when everything was video tape, my boys and I probably wore out a dozen copies of that movie. Thank God for DVD. Although I am little surprised you know it."

"Please." Angie rolled her eyes. "Arnie's the king of the blow-'em-up. Least he was before he went and got all respectable."

It was Chris's turn to laugh. "Politics will do that to you. So, hopefully there's something with good explosions playing tonight."

They weren't disappointed because, as Angie pointed out, Will Smith was almost as good at blowing things up as Arnold. Almost. And she had wanted to see his latest, but Carter Anne wouldn't have anything to do with it and Bobby had been too busy. She nearly bounced as they gave their tickets over.

"I've heard really good things about this." Her enthusiasm bubbled over. "You know, 'rollicking good fun' and 'heart-stopping action.' I'm not sure how every movie is supposed to be heart-stopping, but I'm always hopeful when I hear that particular review."

"Critics do tend to pull out the clichés. We'll just hope they aren't lying this time." Chris stepped into the concession line. "You want popcorn or anything?"

"Aren't we having dinner later?" Angie was suddenly uncomfortable.

"Well, yeah." Chris just looked at her. "But that's later."

"I don't know." She hesitated.

"Do you like it with butter or without?" Chris asked, realizing her dilemma.

"With," Angie admitted with a shy smile.

"Perfect." He grinned, taking his place in front of the

counter. "One large popcorn, lots of butter, a Coke and a Diet Coke, please."

Next to him, Angie's heart tightened happily. Chris was such a nice change from other guys . . . *Careful*, the little voice inside her head whispered, but she silenced it determinedly. Hand to God, she was going to enjoy him and this. At least, while it lasted.

"Where do you like to sit?" she asked as they scanned the theatre. It was mostly empty with only a few groups scattered around.

"In the middle of a row, right up front," Chris replied without hesitation. "You?"

"I like the middle, but all the way in the back."

"Well"—Chris started moving up the steps—"sounds like the middle, right in the middle, then."

Smiling, Angie followed him to seats, just as the lights faded. Chris gave her a moment to settle in, watching her face in the light from the trailers. Her eyes were locked on the screen. His Angie was a quite a movie buff. His Angie. That sounded good. He would have to make it a reality.

Patiently, he waited through the previews and the reminders to be quiet. Once the movie started, he balanced the popcorn between his legs and entwined his fingers with hers. She didn't even look at him. Still, even in the dark, Chris saw the corners of her mouth twitch. As she curled her fingers around his, he sat back to watch the movie.

The moon was bright in the window, keeping Angie company as she lay awake. She had watched it cross the sky, remembering how it had shone down on them when Chris kissed her good night earlier. And, of course, how no clouds had crossed over it when he'd first kissed her next to the general last week.

That was a legend though, of course. Silly kids' stuff made up by romantic girls who wanted their prom dates to end up their husbands. Yet, Andy had never taken her to the statue, let alone kissed her there. But Chris had. Just as he'd kissed her under the moon tonight.

Rolling over, she buried her face in her pillow to help muffle her giggles. He had tasted like the coffee he'd had after dinner, and his arms had driven the chill from the air.

Carter Anne had been waiting up for her, pretending to read one of those magazines she loved so much. When Angie closed the door behind her, Carter Anne had taken one look at her and beamed.

"Get in here and tell me everything!" she'd demanded.

Angie felt like she floated into the kitchen. The first date had been wonderful, but it had also been almost a fluke. This one, though, this had been a real date. Not even she could deny it.

"It was just dinner and a movie." Angie tried to write it off.

Carter Anne exhaled sharply. "You don't come home all glowin' like that from 'just dinner and a movie.' And you don't spend nearly twenty minutes on the porch after 'just dinner and a movie' either."

"You timed us?" Angie was both pleased and horrified.

"I mighta glanced at the clock a couple times." She grinned. "'Least it was me and not Bobby."

"Hand to God." Angie shuddered at the thought. Unable to keep her own grin at bay any longer, she sat down across from her sister. "Was it really almost twenty minutes?"

"And not a lot of talking to overhear, I must say," Carter Anne teased. "Not that I tried or anything."

"Of course not." Angie rolled her eyes.

"So? Tell me!" Carter Anne insisted again.

"There's really not much to tell," Angie admitted. "We went to a movie. We went to dinner. He brought me home." Oh hell, she could feel the flush in her cheeks.

"And then you spent near on twenty minutes on the porch."

"Well . . ." The flush was deepening. "Yeah. But as you know about that, there's not much more to tell."

"What movie did y'all see?" Carter Anne prompted.

"Will Smith's new one." Angie grinned.

Carter Anne rolled her eyes. "Now there's romance. Where'd you go for dinner?"

"The Red Lobster at the mall."

"And?" Carter Anne couldn't believe this.

"And what?" Angie asked.

Carter Anne drummed her fingers and stared at her sister. "Don't ever try to write a gossip column."

And so they had decided to go to bed and Carter Anne to sleep, Angie was sure. She hadn't lied. There hadn't been any more to tell. How could she explain how nice just holding hands during the movie had been? And enjoying the wine Chris had expertly chosen to go with dinner? Or even the moment she had realized he was going to kiss her, right there on the front porch? Because those weren't the kinds of details Carter Anne was looking for.

Carter Anne had wanted romance, not good conversation, laughter, and comfortable silences. And if her heart had fluttered and her skin had tingled and her feet had hardly touched the ground all night, how did one explain that to a sister who was hoping for a grand, romantic story?

But all those things *had* happened, *had* been, well, romantic. So maybe there was some more to tell Carter Anne tomorrow. Just a little anyway. Still grinning into her pillow, Angie drifted off to sleep, the memory of Chris's touch still on her skin.

Chapter 10

"Chris Montgomery, you son of a whore, how the hell are you?"

Chris recognized the voice on the other end of the phone immediately and grinned. "Champ, that had better be you or else there's gonna be a killing for talking about my mother that way."

"Ah," Champ continued good-naturedly. "The colonel's wife is one of the best women I've ever met. Shame she never told you you were adopted."

Laughing out loud, Chris settled in for the conversation. While it was always good to hear from Champ, he never called just to chat.

"So, have you gotten bored living the life of a civilian yet, Sergeant?"

"Can't say I have, Major," Chris fired back.

"Ah, you're behind the times there. It's Lieutenant Colonel now," Champ answered.

"No shit, you made light bird?" Chris wasn't as surprised as he pretended. There had never been any doubt about Champ's promotion. "That why you're calling?"

"Yes and no, Chris." Champ's voice became serious. "I've got a proposition for you."

Fifteen minutes later, Chris hung up the phone. Well, this certainly put a crimp in his plans. But he couldn't deny the old excitement was back, even at the thought of only eight weeks. It wasn't the same feeling he once got before going overseas, but then Colorado Springs was hardly an overseas mission. Still, to prep a mission again. To help train up a team. And Champ was right; no one was better prepared to train up this mission than they were. It wasn't arrogance. It was the truth.

He grabbed a beer from the refrigerator and headed upstairs. Angie had worked him hard earlier and he needed a shower. Angie . . . What would she think of this? How could he tell her? They weren't moving along as fast as he would've liked, but they were definitely moving along. Champ's timing really couldn't have been worse.

Chris stripped down and stepped into the steaming shower. He wouldn't get this living in bachelors' quarters again, and he had gotten used to long, hot showers. The image of Angie and showers drifted through his thoughts, but he shook it off. Thoughts like that would *not* help him make this decision.

Because she would hate it. He knew that. He couldn't even fool himself for a minute about that one. She would hate him leaving and wouldn't even consider going with him. Not yet anyway. Not even for eight weeks. Maybe if they were further along.

His hands slowed then stilled around the bar of soap. She wouldn't come with him yet . . . They needed to be further along . . . Maybe he could make these eight weeks work for him. Grinning, Chris gave himself over to the heat of the shower and began to plan.

"Ladies." Bobby tipped his hat to the Jones sisters sitting in their usual booth.

"Sheriff," they answered simultaneously. Margaret opened her mouth to say something but closed it again as quickly, glancing at her sister. Mary nodded encouragingly but didn't speak either.

Bobby was used to a certain amount of . . . eccentricity . . . from two of his favorite townies, but something was definitely amiss. He'd never known either of them not to speak whatever was on their mind.

"Margaret? Mary?" He looked between them. "There something I can help you with?"

The women exchanged another look, decided something between them, and Margaret finally spoke.

"Bobby, do you have a minute?"

"Always for you." Mary slid over and let Bobby sit next to her.

"Now Bobby," Margaret continued, "we're two old biddies and we know it."

"Nonsense," Bobby said obligingly, but Mary waved him off.

"We are. And we enjoy a good chat as much as the next girl," she interjected.

"But when the chat is about someone we care for . . ."

"Someone we consider one of our *own* . . ."

Bobby was used to the tennis-match way the sisters spoke and settled in to wait until they got the point.

"We weren't even sure if we should say anything . . ."

"We agonized, actually . . ."

"Yes. Agonized." Margaret nodded, satisfied that her sister had found the appropriate word for their dilemma.

"But we finally agreed . . ."

"After all, Angie is a *dear*, *sweet* thing . . ."

Bobby's ears picked up. Without changing expression, he spoke calmly. "There's talk about my girl, is there?"

The women sighed in unison, relieved of the burden of having to spell it out for him.

"About her, yes." Mary spoke first this time.

"And that new Montgomery boy."

"And how much time she's spending at the house."

Bobby nodded thoughtfully. He probably should've seen it coming or heard the whispers himself, but he'd enjoyed seeing Angie so happy. He would always have a blind spot when it came to his girls. But that was just fine, he decided. Not everything needed to be about police procedure.

"We don't believe a word of it, Bobby," Margaret continued in her turn, her hand covering his.

"That's why we decided we had to say something."

The women's expressions showed identical looks of concern.

"Now Margaret." He patted her hand. "Mary." He looked to the other sister. "Don't you worry. Y'all did the right thing coming to me." He stood up and put his hat back on. "As you said yourselves, this is a small town, and in small towns, there's always some kind of talk."

The women smiled at him, pleased to have done their good deed for the day. With a smile of his own and another tip of his hat, Bobby walked out of the diner. It wasn't until he was outside that his brow furrowed. Looking up the street, he stared at the old Montgomery place. Yeah, small towns meant gossip. But when the gossip included one of his girls . . . He liked Chris. Liked him a lot. But it was time for a talk.

Chris couldn't help but feel like he had been summoned by the general. Or worse—and more accurately—sent to the principal's office. The weather wasn't helping the situation any, either. Somewhere between winter and spring, it was just cold and miserable. Hell, *he* was cold and miserable.

He'd been looking for a way to broach the subject with Bobby since the phone call from Champ. But how did one explain what he had in mind without it sounding like nothing more than an elaborate plan to get into Angie's pants? Of course, if things went well, that would be one of the more delicious results of the plan, he admitted, at least to himself. But there was more to it than just that. And it was the more that he had been trying to find a way to explain to Bobby.

Well, if he had found a way or not, the time had come for the explanation. Chris had no illusions that this was why Bobby had requested—if you could call it by such a gentle word—the two of them meet at the station. He took a deep breath before opening the door. Hell, it couldn't be worse than facing heavily armed insurgents with nothing but a cave at his back. At least, not *much* worse, anyway.

Bobby was at his desk on the phone when Chris walked in. He brought Chris over with a wave of his hand and indicated the chair opposite him. "Betsy, I understand, but I do think if you'll simply open a can of tuna this time, he'll come right down." Bobby rolled his eyes at Chris. The simplicity of the gesture relaxed Chris somewhat, if not completely. This was, after all, Bobby, a man he was coming to consider a friend.

"Tell you what," Bobby continued. "You give the tuna twenty minutes. If it doesn't work by then, me or Jimmy'll come on over and see what we can do.

"I know, Betsy. Yes. I hope so, too. You're welcome. Goodbye, now." Bobby hung up with a smile. "Betsy Abernathy's cat," he said in way of explanation to Chris as he stood and crossed to the coffee maker. Without a word, he poured two cups, tucked the creamer and sugar under his arm, and brought them back to the desk where Chris was waiting. "Every couple of weeks, that little bastard climbs up into something or other. Every couple of weeks, we gotta figure out a way to get him out or down or free or whatever." He added a large spoonful of creamer to his coffee. "Luckily today, he's just up a tree. A can of tuna and he'll come on down. Still, Betsy figures it's her civic duty to give me or Jimmy the chance to save him."

"Well," Chris spoke for the first time, "she wouldn't want to deprive you of the opportunity to be heroic."

Bobby chuckled. "That's about it, I suppose." He waited until Chris had finished doctoring his own coffee before deciding the pleasantries had been accomplished. "Son"—he kept his voice low—"I expect it's about time you and I had a talk." He had thought Chris's eyes would shut down, but they didn't. In fact, they'd been doing it less and less since he'd been seeing so much of Angie. Bobby wondered if the other man was even aware of that. If he was, maybe this didn't have to be too hard a conversation.

Chris nodded but refused to lower his eyes. "Yeah, Bobby, I expect it is." He waited. Bobby could take the lead on this one.

"I think you know I like you. And I respect you, which means even more in my book. I've always tried to let Angie and Carter Anne go their own way, especially since they've become grown women. It was easy to do with you *because* I like and respect you. And although I don't like to think about it, I do know that neither one of them lives in a convent. I do my best to be okay with that.

"But folks are starting to talk. Talk about one of my girls. You know what that means in small towns. And you also know that means I gotta have a talk with you.

"So, Chris, what do you have to say to me?"

Without flinching, without so much as blinking, Chris held the other man's gaze. It wouldn't work otherwise. Bobby would never believe him. "I think I'm falling in love with her."

Bobby's eyes widened then he blinked. "Well." He picked up his coffee and leaned back, crossing his ankles on the edge of his desk. "Does she know?"

Chris wasn't sure what he had expected—but he knew it

wasn't that. Sighing, he picked up his own mug. "I don't know. I don't think so. And if she suspects, I don't think she trusts it."

Bobby laughed. "That's Angie, all right. At least you got her pegged." He was beginning to relax. He *did* like Chris. Very much. And hadn't wanted to think about him simply using Angie. "How 'bout her? What are her feelings?"

Chris shook his head. "Damned if I know, Bobby. One minute, I think there's something there. The next . . . well, she's never rude. She's always friendly. She just gets . . . different." He shrugged. "I can't explain it better than that."

Bobby stared at his friend and made a decision. Angie's business was her business, but she could be as stubborn as a mule, hand to God. "She's been hurt."

"I know," Chris replied.

"You know 'cause you read a skittish horse well or you know because she's told you?"

Chris chuckled. "I know very little about horses. Angie's told me."

Bobby raised an eyebrow. "She's told you, huh? Then you're closer to where you want to be than you might have realized." He took another sip of his coffee, sitting in comfortable silence, thinking. "So," he finally continued, "what are you gonna do about it?"

Chris leaned forward, inviting confidence, and put his elbows on the desk. "That's what I've wanted to talk to *you* about. It's a bit convoluted." He took a deep breath, hoping Bobby would hear him out, hoping he was the ally Chris thought he was. Otherwise, he still might end up on the receiving end of one of Bobby's fists. "I've gotten a call from an old friend of mine. He was my captain for a long time. Then he was my major. We called him Champ. Now, he's Lieutenant Colonel Maynard. He's asked me to come to Colorado Springs."

Chris watched the other man carefully. Nothing moved.

Bobby was perfectly still . . . except for the hardening around the eyes. Good ol' boy, my ass, Chris thought. There were generals who weren't this cool. Still, Bobby hadn't said anything, which might mean he was still listening. Keeping his tone level, Chris decided to continue. "It's for eight weeks. Champ's got a team going into . . . going somewhere I know a lot about. He wants me to come in as a consultant, train them up. As a favor." He paused again, waiting.

"Go on," Bobby said. He still hadn't moved or looked away from Chris's face.

"I'm thinking about asking Angie to move into the house while I'm away. Tell her I don't want the place left empty again so soon. Ask her to keep working on getting it in shape.

"What I'm really hoping for is that she will get comfortable being there. Start to feel like it's home."

"And when those eight weeks are up?" Bobby asked coldly.

"When those eight weeks are up, I'll come back. Back home. Back to Angie." Chris's voice was just as cold and very determined.

Bobby exhaled hard. "Seems you've got a plan. Might be a good one, too. Why'd you want to talk to me about it?"

"Well . . ." Chris relaxed fully for the first time all afternoon. The corners of his mouth twitched and then grew into a full smile. "As you pointed out, small towns mean big gossip. There might be some speculation and talk, so I wanted your approval on the idea before I went to Angie with it."

"No 'might' to it. This *will* cause plenty of talk." Bobby smiled back. "Might be it's time for the town to have something interesting to talk about, though. I'll handle that end of business. You handle your end."

He stood up and Chris followed. The conversation was over. "Come by for dinner tonight. 'Bout six." Bobby winked at him. "Carter Anne is cooking."

Chris laughed. "I suppose I can choke it down. But it won't be the same."

Bobby threw back his head and laughed. "That was either the most diplomatic answer ever or you do have it bad." They were at the door before Bobby put a hand on Chris's shoulder. He cleared his throat hard before speaking. "You've got my blessing on this . . . and whatever comes after it."

Chris nodded. That was what he'd needed to hear and his friend knew it. He stepped back outside. God, it was a beautiful day.

Tonight, the hard part wasn't choking the meal down. The hard part was trying not to devour it as if he hadn't had a decent home-cooked meal in weeks. Which, Chris admitted to himself as he finished the last of his dinner, he hadn't. But damned if he'd say that in front of Angie. Still, he couldn't remember when a simple meal of ham, sweet potatoes, and green beans had tasted quite so good.

"That was mighty good, Carter Anne." Bobby leaned back in his chair.

"It was. Thanks," Chris agreed.

"There's more if y'all are still hungry," she replied, pleased.

Bobby shook his head and Chris lifted his hand. "I couldn't eat another bite right now."

"Make sure you send him with a doggie bag, though," Angie said. "He'll probably be grateful for it."

Chris looked at her but was relieved to see her eyes were twinkling in merriment. He shrugged. "I don't know what you're talking about. Food's food." The others laughed, and Chris was grateful Angie could not only take but join in the teasing. "Let me help clear." He stood and began stacking plates. Carter Anne followed him into the kitchen, her own arms full.

"Angie tells us the house is coming along real well." She scraped a plate into the trash and handed it to Chris with a nod to the dishwasher. He simply took it and started loading.

"It is. We're getting it done faster than I'd expected."

"Seems to me other things are going real well, too." Carter Anne grinned at him.

Chris smiled back. "I think they are."

"Good thing, too," Carter Anne noted, "since you're running out of reason to have her come over every afternoon."

He laughed outright at that. "Don't worry there. I have a plan."

"Somehow, I thought you might." Carter Anne poured coffee into mugs and put them on a tray. She waited, but Chris just kept loading the dishwasher, damn him. It was like pulling teeth sometimes with men, hand to God. "So?" she finally asked. "What's the plan?"

"That"—Chris winked—"is a secret. At least until I've had a chance to talk to Angie about it."

"Oh! You're no fun." Carter Anne pouted playfully. She reached for the cream and sugar. Fine. She'd just work on him later. "So what's next for the house?"

"You know . . ." Chris thought a moment. "I'm not sure."

"Bet it's nice inside."

"It is," Chris agreed. "Under all the dust. But it still needs work. You should come up with Angie sometime."

Carter Anne had an idea. If Chris wouldn't share his plan, she'd just have to work on one of her own. "'Needs work' how exactly?"

"Peeling paint and wallpaper. Rusty faucets. That sort of thing. The aesthetics. We're getting it clean, but . . ."

"You know"—Chris could hear the gears going in Carter Anne's head. She was up to something—"Angie is really good at decorating."

He looked up. She was holding the coffee tray, grinning at

him. Yeah, she was up to something, but it might be a good something. He leaned against the counter. "Is she now?"

"Remember what she did with those carnations you brought us that first night?"

Chris hadn't remembered, but he did now. They had gone from plain to beautiful under her hand. Still, flowers were very different from a whole house. Carter Anne seemed to read his thoughts.

"When we go back in, look around. She chose all the colors. It's not even her style, but it fits Bobby to a tee and she knew it."

Chris took the tray from her. "Might be something to think about."

Carter Anne winked. "Might be, at that."

As they headed back into the dining room, Chris realized he had never paid much attention to the decor. Mostly browns and tans, he understood what Carter Anne had meant: he'd never noticed the decor because he wasn't supposed to notice it. There was nothing flashy or eye-catching. The room was sturdy, solid, and unobtrusive—just like the man it had been designed for. And nothing at all like Angie. Yes, this could fit quite nicely into his plans. God, he was grateful Carter Anne was on his side. Smiling, he put the tray on the table.

"What're you grinning at, Chris Montgomery?" Angie asked.

"Just enjoying the evening, I guess."

Bobby and Carter Anne both looked away, trying to hide their own smiles.

Dinner was beef stew and biscuits. Chris had a serious hunch the stew was canned and the biscuits straight from the grocery store's refrigerated section, but he was too grateful to tease her. At least he wouldn't need the doggie bag Carter

Anne had indeed slipped him the night before. Anyway, he needed Angie in a good mood.

Their relationship had changed in subtle ways since he'd gotten her on that second date, but he still couldn't read her. And she'd been distant all afternoon. It didn't bode well. Still, because their relationship had changed, he didn't feel right keeping it from her any longer, either.

"Something's come up you need to know about." Chris plunged in.

Angie nodded as she took a bite of stew. She'd been waiting for this, expecting it. *Don't cry, don't cry*, she repeated to herself, hoping her face wasn't giving her away.

"I got a call from my old captain. He's asked me to go out to Colorado for two months. Help out with some things." Chris watched her carefully. Her face was unusually expressionless. "I'll be back once those two months are done, but I really feel like I should go. I owe him."

"So what are you sayin'?" Angie put her spoon down. Trying to swallow anything would be a bad idea right now.

"That I'm going away for two months. But that I'm coming back." He stressed the last sentence.

"You are?" It was hard to talk around the lump in her throat. Maybe . . . but she wouldn't let herself hope yet. She wouldn't.

"Yes." Chris took her hand. "I am. And it's important you know that."

Angie's fingers scrabbled for and found his. The lump in her throat started to ease up. "Why?"

Chris rolled his eyes. "Because *you're* important, Angie. You must realize that by now."

She looked away, unable to meet his eyes. Bobby'd been right. It was time to choose. "You're important, too, Chris."

Dammit, her voice broke. She had wanted to be able to play it cool.

He tugged gently on her hand until she finally looked at him. When she did, his eyes were soft. "I'm glad to hear that. I'd hate to think I was in this alone." Slowly, he leaned forward and brushed his lips against hers.

Angie giggled nervously and started eating again. Taking it as a good sign, Chris continued around mouthfuls of his own dinner. "I've got a favor to ask you, though. Would you stay here in the house while I'm away?"

"I guess." This was unexpected. "You just mean house-sitting, right?"

The truth jumped to the tip of his tongue, but Chris bit it back. "That's exactly what I mean. I just don't want it empty again so soon. You can have my bedroom, move right in."

"When do you go?"

Chris sensed the change in the conversation with the question. He couldn't quite keep the answer light, either. "Saturday."

"Oh." Angie looked away again. "I'm working or I'd take you to the airport."

"Thanks anyway." It was a relief. He wasn't sure he wanted her to take him. "I'll make a reservation with a shuttle service or something. There's bound to be one into Greensboro."

"I should be getting on." Angie stood. "You sure you don't want me to help with this?" She reached for the dirty dishes.

Chris smiled at their nightly routine. "Positive. You cook; I clean."

"All right then."

Chris followed her to the door. There was an unspoken agreement between them that their afternoons were professional. He had accepted it, even if he hadn't liked it. But he wasn't going to accept it any longer. Not after this conversation. He took her in his arms before she could open the door. Angie stiffened slightly. She didn't want this to complicate things.

"Angie," Chris said, soothingly. "I'm going to kiss you good night. And I'm going to be doing it every night."

"Is that really a good idea, Chris?" Angie searched for a reason to give him. "Shouldn't we keep this separate?"

"Good night kisses, Angie. Because you're important to me. And I'm important to you." He leaned down and found her mouth. His tongue teased her lips, asking rather than demanding. His fingers danced lightly along her back, offering to pull her in closer.

It was already complicated. Pretending otherwise didn't change that. With a sigh, Angie gave herself over to the kiss.

Immediately, Chris's arms tightened around her. She kissed him deeply, moving her hands into his hair. Tentatively, she stepped closer, barely touching her hips to his. It was enough. The groan came from deep inside him. Chris knew he had to slow down. He was leaving soon. The timing was all wrong, but oh . . . when he got back . . .

Careful not to reject her, he ended the kiss and stepped back. Angie's eyes were still closed, a small smile on her lips.

"I guess I can live with good night kisses." She opened her eyes and grinned at him. "So long as I'm off the clock before they start."

"I promise," Chris agreed. "Now go on home. I'll see you tomorrow afternoon." As she closed the door behind her, Chris rubbed his hands over his face. It was a good thing he was leaving. Too many good nights like that would kill him.

The counter was empty, but all the booths were taken. He wouldn't have much time with her. That was probably for the best, though, Chris knew. It would keep him from saying something stupid. He sat on a stool and waited for Angie to make her way over.

"Hi there." Her eyes lit up when she saw him. It was ridiculous for such a little thing to matter but it made him feel great inside.

"Hi," Chris said. "I'm heading out soon. Here are the keys to the place." He slid a spare key chain across to her, taking the opportunity to stroke her fingers as he did so. Although he'd finally gotten used to not locking his doors, he figured Bobby would have his ass if he expected Angie to do the same.

Angie returned the pressure before dropping the keys into her pocket. "I'm headin' over tonight after dinner at the house." She spoke as if nothing had just passed between them. "It won't be late, because Bobby's gotta get back to the station. Carter Anne might spend a couple nights with me, just 'til I'm used to it, if that's okay."

"It's fine," Chris said. "Really. Make yourself at home. Carter Anne is welcome any time."

"Thanks. It's just a big place, you know?"

Chris laughed. "I'm the one who's been sleeping there alone for how many months now? It's okay, I understand."

Angie laughed with him.

"There are blank checks on the table for bills and groceries," Chris continued. "Use them, okay?"

"I'll take care of everything, I promise," Angie assured him. "Yourself included."

"I'm gonna be here in the Falls. You're the one who has to be takin' care."

"It's only Colorado. I'll be fine."

The pick-up bell sounded behind her.

"I gotta . . ." Angie waved vaguely in the direction of the kitchen.

"Yeah." Chris sighed. "And the shuttle should be at the house any time now, so I should be there."

"Well." Angie had no idea what to say, especially with so many people around them. "Have a safe trip. I'll see you in a couple months."

"Yeah." Chris bit back his frustration. What had he expected coming to see her here? He headed to the door and had almost made it when she called his name. He turned, along with everyone else in the place.

"I'm gonna miss you. Call me."

"I'll miss you, too, Angie. We'll talk tonight."

Angie realized what she had done and blushed heavily. Without so much as a wave, she disappeared into the kitchen.

Chris looked at a table of construction workers staring at him. "My girl's beautiful, isn't she?"

When Angie came back out, he was gone. The day was busy enough to keep her distracted and tire her out. By the time a quick dinner with Carter Anne and Bobby was over, Angie was more than ready to simply collapse when she got to Chris's but Carter Anne was downright excited to see the place.

"I've always wanted to come in here," she spoke as Angie opened the door.

"You don't have to whisper, Carter Anne. It's just a house." Angie moved into the hallway, her bag over her shoulder and Carter Anne on her heels.

"Don't even try to tell me you weren't excited the first time you came in here," Carter Anne replied.

"You're right." Angie smiled, remembering it. "Come on. I'll show you around." She led her sister upstairs first so they could drop their bags. Angie stopped at the first bedroom on the right. It was the cleanest and most livable besides Chris's. Carter Anne put her overnight bag on the double bed.

"It'll be like when we used to share a room."

"Back when you were too scared to sleep alone?" Angie teased. Carter Anne stuck her tongue out.

"This isn't so bad. The hours y'all've been putting in, I expected the place to be condemned." She looked around. "I mean, it's old and ugly, but it's not gross." Looking over her shoulder at Angie, she wiggled her eyebrows. "Maybe y'all have been doing other things with all that time."

Angie rolled her eyes. "Follow me."

She led her straight to the smallest bedroom at the very end of the hall. "This is what they all looked like." The door creaked in protest when Angie pushed it open.

"Oh." There was nothing more to say. Carter Anne was amazed at the difference between this room and the one they had just left. If she'd thought that room needed work, she couldn't imagine even Angie rescuing this one. "Were they really all like this?" she asked, trying to hide her disgust.

"The whole house." Angie closed the door. "This one's still as bad." She tapped on the closed door next to the room they'd just left. "But this one . . ." She opened a third door with a flourish. It swung open noiselessly.

Carter Anne tried to hide her disappointment. It was definitely better than the other room, but in no better condition than the room they'd claimed as their own. If anything, it was uglier.

"It's green," she managed.

"I know!" Angie agreed with a strange enthusiasm. "Isn't it horrible?" She dragged Carter Anne into the room. "Look at this molding, though. Why anyone would paint it is beyond me, but it's original, all the way through the house.

"And the fireplace." She crossed the room, stroking the mantel with love. "This is real marble under all this soot. Check out the carving. It just needs a good scrub."

Carter Anne tried. She really did. But all she could see was a ratty room in ugly colors. It was, she conceded, clean.

"I'll trust you, honey, but . . . damn."

Angie laughed. "Oh, this will be the room all of Chris's friends want to stay in when they visit. At least once I'm done with it."

"So why aren't we sleeping in here?" Carter Anne tested the mattress. It seemed comfortable enough.

"Because," Angie said pointedly, "I'm *not* done with it, and right now it's still horrible. Come on, I'll show you the rest."

It only took a few more steps to show Carter Anne the bathroom at the end of the hall and Chris's space. As they headed downstairs, Angie felt herself getting excited about showing the place off. And Carter Anne was an appreciative audience. She oohed and ahhed at all the right times and actually gasped when Angie threw open the doors to the ballroom.

"I'm going to recommend he use a dusty rose color throughout the place, just as an accent to tie everything together." She walked them back through the house to Carter Anne's continued murmurs. "It's a very traditional color for the time. Of course, it'll be his decision in the long run. I don't know how modern he wants to go with . . ." Angie stopped. Her sister was staring at her. "What?"

"You really can see all this, can't you?" Carter Anne was impressed. This was more than just being able to decorate for Christmas or knowing where to place candles and knick-knacks in a room.

"Well . . . yeah." Angie thought about it. "Can't you?"

Carter Anne shook her head. "No. I can't. And I don't think many other people can, either. Not like you do."

"It's just decorating." Angie shrugged.

"It's more than that when you do it, though," Carter Anne tried to explain. "All I saw upstairs was an ugly green room I was grateful I didn't have to sleep in. But you see the bedroom people'll be fighting over. And believe me, most people would only see the ugly and the green."

Angie shook her head. She'd never thought of it like that. "You know what else I see?" she finally asked.

"What?"

"The two of us in front of a fire in the sitting room fireplace with a bag of marshmallows."

"And beer," Carter Anne added.

"Beer?" Beer and marshmallows? Was this really Carter Anne?

"Well we can hardly serve marshmallows with fine wine." Carter Anne laughed. "Surely Chris has beer." She went into the kitchen and began to rummage through the refrigerator.

"The marshmallows are in the cabinet to the left of the sink," Angie called to her. If Carter Anne was in charge of provisions, she would build the fire. It was blazing by the time Carter Anne reappeared with a tray of food and two six-packs of beer.

"No wonder he has you cook for him." She put the tray on the floor between them. "He eats like a teenager. And thank God for it."

Instead of just bringing the marshmallows, Carter Anne had a spread of junk food: a bag of peanut butter cups, two types of chips, several sticks of string cheese, and the intended marshmallows. Angie unwrapped a peanut butter cup and noticed there was also a small bowl of sliced apples. Somehow, she didn't think those were for her.

They had worked their way through most of the food and all of the beer when the phone rang, freezing them both mid giggle.

"It's gotta be after midnight," Angie said. "Who's calling this late?"

"Answer it and find out."

"Should I, do you think?"

"Of course! And quick," Carter Anne said as the phone rang a third time.

Angie scrambled up and jogged into the kitchen. "Hello? Chris Montgomery's residence." Please don't let her be slurring her words.

"That's awfully formal for my house." Chris laughed.

Angie relaxed. "Chris!" Carter Anne had followed her with the trash. Angie pointed at the phone. "It's Chris."

"Hi, Chris!" Carter Anne yelled from the sink.

Chris laughed again. "Hi, Carter Anne." His images of Angie moping around missing him had obviously been wrong. "I'm in Denver. We've still got to drive to the Springs, so I wanted to call before it got too much later there."

"Thanks." Angie yawned hugely. The beer and the long day were catching up with her.

"Sounds like I called just in time."

"We found beer." Angie rested her head against the wall. It was cool and surprisingly comfortable.

"Why don't you go to bed, then?" Chris tried to keep the amusement out of his voice but, oh, what he wouldn't give to be seeing her right now.

"I'm glad you called, though. I like your voice."

"I like your voice, too. Now go to bed." A chuckle slipped through, but he caught it. "I'll call as often as I can. Good night."

"'Night." Angie hung up and pushed herself away from the wall. Carter Anne had her head resting on her arms at the table.

"Bed." Angie patted her shoulder then pulled her up. They giggled their way to the bedroom and managed to change into their pajamas. Lying back to back with her sister, Angie sighed.

"Carter Anne?" she whispered into the night.

"Yeah, honey?" Carter Anne's response was barely more than a mumble.

"What am I doin' here?"

"Falling . . ." Carter Anne caught herself. "Asleep."

"Okay," Angie muttered. Yep. That's what she was doing all right.

Behind her, Carter Anne rolled her eyes at herself. No amount of beer should've made her answer that question honestly. Not yet anyway. But it was true. Angie was here because she was falling in love.

Chapter 11

Angie was grateful she didn't have plans that night. When was the last time she had done nothing all evening? Not worked on the house. Not stayed late at the diner. Not even helped Carter Anne or Bobby. Just done nothing. Honestly, she couldn't even remember. She was tired. The baseball team had come in right after school and kept her running for drinks and fries and more drinks. They were good kids, though. She smiled. Always polite, even the seniors who liked to flirt harmlessly. And, for teenagers, they tipped well. A full 15 percent from each of them. Although she figured Johnnie Thompson had probably helped John Hamilton out there. Everybody knew the Hamiltons were having rough times since his daddy had had the heart attack. Good kids who were raised right, nonetheless. But tiring, hand to God.

Slipping out of her shoes and into her slippers by the door, Angie bent down and picked up the mail where it had been dropped through the slot. Chris had asked her to go through it, pay the bills with the checks he had left her, and throw out the junk. It was just the mindless activity she needed for the evening.

She headed into the kitchen and pulled a Diet Pepsi from

the refrigerator just as the phone rang. It still felt odd to be answering Chris's phone, but she was getting used to it.

"Hello?" She stretched the cord all the way across the room to be able to grab a glass from the cabinet.

"Hi, honey, it's me." Bobby's voice was warm in her ear. "Carter Anne's making chops for dinner tonight, and we wanted to know if you wanted to come over."

"Aw, Bobby, thanks. Really." Angie poured her soda. "You know I love Carter Anne's chops. But tonight I really just want to crash out in front of the television and not move."

"Long day?"

"The baseball team was in," Angie said as way of explanation.

Bobby chuckled. "Suit yourself. Want her to put you up a plate? I can swing it by later. I'm on duty tonight."

"You're a sweetie, Bobby, but I don't even think I want to worry about that much. This way, if I fall asleep on the couch in front of the TV, I don't worry about it."

"Fine enough," Bobby said. Angie was grateful to know he meant it. "You get some rest then."

She hung up the phone and sat down at the table, pulling another chair over and resting her feet in it. The phone rang again before she could even start flipping through the stack of mail. "Hand to God . . ." she muttered, standing back up again. "Hello?"

"Angie?"

"Chris?" Angie tried to keep the excitement from her voice. "That you?"

"Yeah. We're on a break, so I thought I'd give you a call. Hoped you'd be home by now."

Angie settled herself back down at the table. "You just caught me. How are things out there?"

"They're good. Busy. We're spending the next couple nights in the field, so I'm really glad I got to talk to you."

"What are you doing out there?" Angie asked. She knew he couldn't talk much about what was happening, but maybe he could give her something.

"Mostly it's just classes. Presentations and things like that. But like I said, tonight we head to the field for a little while. I don't have too long to talk. How're things there?"

"Busy but good." Angie took a long sip of her drink. "Bobby and Jimmy are gonna come over this weekend and help me clear out some of the furniture from the third floor."

"Thank them for me, would you? And be sure to keep track of your hours. You still get paid for all this, you know."

Angie made a noncommittal noise. They'd discuss that later.

"And actually, I wanted to talk to you about that as well," Chris continued. "How would you feel about getting some of the decorating done for me while I'm gone? I was thinking it would be really nice to come back to a decorated house. You know I'm no good at that stuff." Chris held his breath.

"You really want somebody else to choose all that for you, Chris? That's awful personal stuff."

"No, Angie." Chris's voice was calm. "I don't want *somebody* to do it. I'd like *you* to. I trust you. You know me, know what I like. And you've got a great eye for things like colors and textures. Even if I was there, I'd be deferring to you most of the time anyway."

Angie laughed. "Bobby hates this kind of thing, too."

"It comes with the testosterone."

"It must." Angie laughed harder. "What exactly are we talking about? I don't want to overstep."

"Anything you think needs done, Angie. Floors, walls, furniture, hell, even the plumbing fixtures . . . whatever."

Angie sighed. It would be a challenge. And a fun one at that. How could she say no, really? "And how much do you want to spend?"

Chris gave her a number.

"I don't think I heard you right, Chris." Angie was shocked.

"You sure did. That's your budget."

"Chris, I'm not sure the house is worth that much."

"It would be if it was in Atlanta or Charlestown or Savannah." Chris was trying very hard not to laugh. "It'd be worth more."

"Chris Montgomery, this isn't Atlanta or Charlestown or Savannah. This is Lambert Falls, and the house ain't worth that much here."

"Then let's make it worth that much, Angie." She could hear his smile. "You up to it?"

She let out a long whistle. "What the hell. If you say so."

"I do. Listen, break's almost over and I have to look over the notes for the briefing I'm about to give." He paused. "It was really good to hear your voice, Angie."

Why was she suddenly on the verge of tears? It made no sense. But she was. "You too, Chris. Bye, now."

"Later." Then he hung up.

Angie sat with the phone in her hand, staring at it as if she had never seen such a contraption before in her life. With a shake of her head, she hit the disconnect button and then dialed home. Bobby answered after the first ring.

"Bobby, can I still come over for dinner?" she asked without preamble.

"Angie, this is your home. Of course you can be here for dinner. I'll pull another chop from the freezer. Everything okay?"

"Yeah. I just want to talk to Carter Anne about something."

"Then we'll see you in a couple hours."

The mail could wait. She really wanted a shower before dinner, though. And she had some serious thinking to do.

"How much?" Carter Anne gaped at her sister. The announcement had stopped dinner preparation cold. Carter Anne sat down at the table across from Angie.

"One. Million. Dollars," Angie repeated, taking a sip of her Diet Pepsi. She was still shocked herself.

"Is the house even worth that much? Truly and really?"

Angie shook her head, swallowing. "I don't think so, and I told him as much. Not here in the Falls, anyway."

"What did he say?"

"He just laughed and said 'Then let's make it worth that much.' As if it was nothing."

"The man's got it to spend." Bobby was leaning against the doorjamb, listening to his nieces. He should've told them he was there, but sometimes it was still nice to just watch his girls be themselves. "Let the man spend it. Or spend it for him." He crossed to the refrigerator and pulled out a Dr. Pepper.

"What?" Carter Anne exclaimed. "What do you mean?"

"I mean"—Bobby moved back to the doorway, taking his time—"he's got it to spend, so let him spend it. 'Sides, maybe he's got good reasons for wanting to fix the place up."

"Bobby, what do you know?" Angie asked. The man just looked back at her, sipping his drink.

"Aw, come on, Bobby." Carter Anne turned on the charm. "You're so smart. How do you know so much more?"

Bobby laughed. He'd been immune to her charm since back when it involved wrangling the car keys out of his pocket. "I'm older. I'm allowed to know more." He tipped his soda at them. "Let me know when dinner's ready." And he sauntered out, still chuckling.

"Ooo!" Carter Anne hit the table in frustration. "I hate it when he does that. He knows something." Turning back to Angie, she asked, "Do you think he's rich?"

"Chris?" Angie nearly snorted her drink.

Carter Anne rolled her eyes. "The president. Of course, Chris."

"I never thought about it, but he must be for a million dollars just to redecorate a house. And for Bobby to not even flinch over it."

"He's rich *and* he's crazy about you." Carter Anne's eyes twinkled as she got up to finish dinner. "I may be jealous."

Angie studied her soda quietly before speaking again. "What do you think Bobby meant when he said Chris might have reason for fixin' the place up nice?"

"I don't know." Carter Anne shrugged. "Maybe he wants to open it up, like a museum or something. It's mighty big for one person, after all. Maybe a bed-and-breakfast. That would be nice. Or maybe he just wants a nice place to live after so many years in tents or cots or whatever he's lived in." She stirred the cheese sauce thoughtfully.

Angie opened her mouth to ask Carter Anne about another option, the one she was most afraid of, when the other woman spoke first. "Pour this over the broccoli. The chops are ready."

"What?" Angie was pulled back into the moment.

"You already spending that money? Dinner's ready and I need your help. Bobby!" she called to the other room. "Come on! We're eating in here tonight."

Bobby came in and put the plates on the table as Carter Anne and Angie served them up.

"So you're going to do it, right?" Carter Anne asked once they were eating.

"Of course I'm going to do it!" Angie laughed. "How often do you get to spend a million dollars? 'Course, if I can do it for less, I will," she added.

"And can I help?" Carter Anne asked excitedly.

"I suppose. But"—Angie looked at her uncle—"it's your help I'd really like."

"You don't need my help, Angie," Bobby muttered into his dinner. Lord help him if he was gonna spend his days off looking at swatches and the such.

Angie giggled as Carter Anne rolled her eyes. Reading him was so easy. Reassuringly, Angie put a hand on Bobby's arm. "Just don't let me make the place too girly. If I've got a question, answer me honestly."

Bobby grunted. He supposed that wouldn't be too bad. "When have I ever answered you any other way, Angie?"

Angie smiled at him.

"Just stay away from pink and you'll be fine." Bobby took a bite of his pork chop.

"What about yellow?" Carter Anne teased.

"Or lavender?" Angie joined in.

"Ecru or eggshell?" Carter Anne continued in mock seriousness.

Bobby shook his head. No wonder the man had run off to Colorado while this was going on.

After dinner, Bobby helped load the dishwasher then excused himself. Knowing his girls, they had swatches hidden somewhere for just such an occasion and were waiting to spring them on him.

"Sit here," Carter Anne instructed Angie. "I'll be right back." Before Angie had time to pour two cups of coffee, Carter Anne reappeared, arms filled with magazines. "Here." She dumped them unceremoniously on the table.

"What in the world is this?" Angie asked.

"My contribution." Carter Anne smiled. She began to pass them over to Angie as she named them off. "*Southern Living. Southern Accents. Southern Lady.* Oh, and a couple of these."

Carter Anne's voice took on a distinctive sneer as she nudged at a few copies of *Yankee Magazine*. Angie raised her eyebrow at this addition, but Carter Anne just shrugged. "A year free with the bath stuff I wanted."

As Carter Anne handed them over, Angie put them in organized piles. Smugly, she noted there was indeed only one year of *Yankee Magazine*. Those she simply dropped to the floor next to the table.

"So what are you thinking?" Carter Anne asked.

Angie pulled several of each of the remaining magazines over to her and started thumbing through them. "The house needs to be traditional. I don't think he really cares about historical accuracy. At least he didn't mention that to me."

"You're right though," Carter Anne agreed. "It can be updated but not too modern."

Angie was pleased with her sister's grasp of the situation. "Updated but not too modern" was it exactly. "At the same time, it needs to reflect its owner, too, and not just be an anonymous showplace."

"Good thing its owner is kinda traditional, too, then, huh?" Carter Anne giggled. "What about this?" She pushed a magazine over to Angie.

Yes, it was lovely. And Angie could understand why someone would like it. It was also, well, it looked like the magazine spread it was, not a home. Still . . . the walls were nicely done. . . .

"Look at this. And this." Angie pushed two others across the table.

"Hm." Carter Anne eyed them. "What exactly are you going for? Because I don't like this one at all." Her pink polished nails clicked on one of the photographs.

"Honestly"—Angie stood and crossed the room, grabbing a pair of scissors from the drawer—"I don't either. But look at this." Sitting, she pulled the magazines back and started cutting.

Arranging the walls from the first, the curtains from another, and the furniture from yet a third, she pulled her hands into her lap. "Check *that* out," she said proudly.

Carter Anne came around the table and looked over Angie's shoulder rather than try to move the pieces. "How do you do that?" Her voice mirrored her amazement. "Those curtains were horrible before. Now they're perfect."

Angie shrugged. "I just . . . see it, I guess."

"Well." Carter Anne picked up another magazine. "Let's see what else you can see."

Walking in the door for the second time that day, she was even more tired than she'd been the first time. The excitement of Chris's phone call and his news had kept her going through dinner and a couple hours of planning with Carter Anne. Now it was time to stop.

As she entered the kitchen, the mail seemed to mock her from the table. She should let it sit until tomorrow. It would be fine. Only she had let yesterday's mail sit until today. . . . Sighing, she flipped through it, sorting quickly. Near the bottom was a letter with her name on it. Hand to God, someone had written her. Intrigued, she sat down and slit the top.

Dear Angie,

I know I can call you easier than write, but we're going to be pretty busy, so I don't know if the time difference will get in the way or not. The last thing I want is to finish up my day only to have your phone ring at one in the morning. Even without Bobby around to kick my ass for it. You need your sleep. When I can't call at a decent hour, I'll try to write some. I always wrote to my folks. I guess writing letters is part of the solder's life.

Speaking of that, it's great to catch up with old friends and see some familiar faces. The Falls is a long way from what I'm used to. I've only been here three days and Champ is already trying to lure me back into the fold.

It's really beautiful out here. All mountains and pine trees covered in snow, even now. You're probably thinking it sounds like North Carolina, but it's not. The mountains are so much bigger and the snow is real, not that dusting you get out there and call snow. You should see it some time.

Well, that's all for tonight. I start running PT with the guys tomorrow. We'll see how soft I've gotten over the last few months. Ha ha.

Take care,
Chris

Angie reread the short letter twice. She hadn't let herself miss Chris. Good grief, he'd only been gone a few days. And yet . . . he had touched this paper. He had taken the time to write these words. She had heard his voice today, and now this, too. Glowing happily, mail forgotten, she headed upstairs to the bedroom she had chosen.

It was a good night for a bath. To stretch out, surrounded by bubbles, and replay the letter. Maybe she would even think about what she'd write back.

She'd stayed in the guest room she and Carter Anne had chosen that first night, and the bath just down the hall. Chris had wanted her to sleep in the master bedroom with the bath right there, but Angie shook her head at herself. Nope. Chris's room needed to stay just that.

Wrapping herself in her robe, Angie wandered to the bathroom. This was perfectly functional. Just fine. So what if the tub was kinda shallow. And just a little too short. That big ol' claw-foot soaking tub was Chris's. "Aw hell," Angie muttered under her breath. Gathering her bubble bath and towel, she padded down the hall to the master suite.

Chris hadn't spent as much time on this room as he had the main living areas of the house. It was still mostly bare, without any of the small touches that were making downstairs feel homey.

The dresser tops were completely bare. The only thing hanging on the walls was a very basic mirror. Even the huge bed, a gorgeous dark wood piece, was made with spartan efficiency, covered by nothing more than a plain blue blanket pulled up over two pillows.

Angie traced her fingers over the cover as she walked by. Definitely an anonymous room. The only indication of Chris as a person in here was the picture of him and old Doc Montgomery leaning up against one wall.

How could anyone live like this? She sighed. To each their own, she supposed. Still, it was a great room and, with a little love and attention, could be a real haven to retreat to after a long day.

She sat on the edge of the bed, letting the room take shape in her mind. Peaceful colors. Blues and even some light gray for contrast. Masculine colors but feminine fabrics. Heavy curtains that would keep out the sun on a lazy Sunday morning but that could be drawn back once Chris was awake, showering the room with light through the huge windows. Maybe even some stained glass at the top of one or two of them, to send sparkles of color across the floor as the day wore on.

Yep. That's what she would do. Maybe she'd mention it to him in her letter. She loved the fact that Chris trusted and appreciated her style. Although it could be a little intimidating if she thought about it too long. This whole house was hers to decorate.

Happily, she stood, and her hand squished into the pillow next to her. Pure goose down, unless she missed her bet.

"Chris Montgomery, you old dog." Angie laughed out loud. Decorating might not be his forte, but the man knew comfortable.

"Hey boss?" Jimmy wiped his forehead with his bandanna. "What's that?"

"That," Bobby answered, balling up the dust cover he'd just removed, "is a chaise lounge."

Jimmy nodded. "In other words, another heavy piece of furniture Angie's gonna want downstairs."

"Yep." Bobby sighed. He couldn't remember ever wanting the radio on his hip to go off. Until today. There had to be five generations of furniture up here, and he and Jimmy had hauled down damn near every one of them, hand to God. At least this was the last room. "Angie," he called out to her.

She and Carter Anne fought their way from behind a stack of boxes. "Oh!" She gasped, seeing the piece. "Isn't it beautiful?"

"Ooh! Nice." Carter Anne stretched herself out on it. "Can't you just imagine it, laying on this, sipping a cool drink while someone fanned you by the window? That's the life."

Bobby cleared his throat. "'Course that someone fanning you would've been considered property instead of a person."

Carter Anne peeked out from under one closed eyelid. "You have to spoil it, don't you, Bobby?"

He laughed. "Well, I'm spoiling this anyway, because you've got to get up. It'll be heavy enough without you on top of it, too."

Carter Anne leaped up, waving an imaginary fan in front of her face. "Well, I never!" she exclaimed. "Hey." She turned to Angie with a grin. "That was pretty good."

"Sounded like Scarlett to me."

"Girls . . ." Bobby stopped them before they could get on a roll.

"Okay, okay." Angie studied the piece. Moving around, she spoke to Carter Anne. "Fireplace or window?"

"Window. Definitely."

Angie nodded and looked at her uncle. "The second bedroom. At an angle under the window farthest from the bed." Bobby and Jimmy groaned, but each picked up an end. "And thank you!" Angie called after them. Bobby's grunt made her laugh. "Poor guys." She turned to Carter Anne. "I think we should call it a day soon."

"You're probably right, but I just found a box full of pictures. You want to look at them first?"

"Hell yes!" Angie agreed. A thump followed by unintelligible voices drifted up the stairs. "Oh my." Angie looked toward the hallway.

"That sounded an awful lot like cussing." Carter Anne giggled.

"Be right back. You find that box," Angie said, crossing the room. Carter Anne followed behind her anyway. "Bobby! Jimmy!" Angie called down. "Y'all okay?"

"We're fine," Bobby called back. Angie bit back a laugh at his tone.

"My chase lounge all right?"

"It's a chaise lounge and the damn thing is heavy!"

"But is it all right?" Carter Anne called. The two women giggled harder at Bobby's silence.

"Think we better check out that box now?" Angie asked.

"I'm certainly not going down those stairs yet," Carter Anne replied.

"Bobby!" Angie hollered again. "You and Jimmy help yourself to beer. We'll be right down."

Carter Anne looked at Angie. "That sounded like more cussing."

"Definitely time to look through that box."

Angie followed Carter Anne through the maze of moving boxes and crates, both of them still laughing under their breath. "Here it is." Carter Anne knelt by one. It was labeled *family photos* in faded but neat, old-fashioned handwriting. Some of the pictures were loose, but most of them were in tarnished frames. There were several of a child who looked remarkably like Chris—but Angie knew it wasn't. His father, probably. As the child became a man, the resemblance both increased and became less definite.

"Think his father's still this handsome?" Carter Anne asked, handing her a picture of the man holding his newborn son.

"I would imagine," Angie agreed.

"Ooh! Look here." Carter Anne pulled out a large picture from the very bottom of the box. "Montgomery men get better with age. That's gotta be old Doc Montgomery there in the back."

Angie looked at the picture. Three generations of Montgomerys smiled at her, Chris's sister still young enough to be on her mother's lap. "Do you think he even knows this is here?" she asked.

Carter Anne thought about it then shook her head. "Probably not. I mean, do you know what's in *our* attic? Or stored over at the library?"

Angie groaned. "I don't know and I don't want to think about it."

"Exactly," Carter Anne agreed.

"I'm gonna get a new frame for this. Maybe mat it. Make it a surprise for him. The only picture he has out is the one of him and his grandfather. He should have this one, too," Angie decided.

"We can take it into Danville this weekend when we take the furniture to be recovered," Carter Anne suggested. "We can find a frame shop easy enough.

"You gonna redo that chaise lounge they just found?"

"Of course," Angie assured her. "I'm thinking a pale blue with maybe a dark blue velvet pattern. We'll see if the shop's got what I want."

"Have you told Bobby he's gotta move those pieces he just put *into* rooms out of those rooms and into a truck yet?"

"Well . . ." Angie hesitated. "I was gonna tell him tonight, but . . ."

Carter Anne nodded. "Probably better to wait. There's been enough cussing today."

Chapter 12

The bell jingled over his head as Chris walked into the diner. For a brief moment, he was struck with a sense of déjà vu. He'd only been gone eight weeks, so nothing much should've changed—and it hadn't. It could so easily have been that first day he'd walked in here back in January.

Sure, there were subtle differences. The sun was brighter. Winter coats and sweaters had been replaced by short sleeves. And he knew some of the names of the old guys, and some of the young ones, too, sitting at the counter now. Still, it was the same, down to the Jones sisters in the regular spots.

It was just as he'd left it. It was comfortable. It was home.

Adjusting his duffel higher on his shoulder, Chris moved toward the counter. The Jones sisters waved at him. "Welcome back, Chris," one of them—Margaret, no, Mary, he corrected himself—said with a smile.

"Thanks, Mary." He smiled back before sitting on a stool, dropping the heavy bag next to him.

Angie came out of the kitchen, butt first, four plates balanced precariously up her arms as if it was easy. She obviously hadn't seen him yet. Chris watched her. She was so beautiful. Her smile was warm and friendly, even now at the end of her shift. It had been a long eight weeks. Longer than he'd realized. And the picture he'd kept with him hadn't done her justice. As if a picture could capture everything Angie was.

With a laugh for the kids she had just served, Angie turned—and froze. Was Chris Montgomery really just sitting at her counter, big as sin and twice as handsome? She blinked, but when she opened her eyes, he was still there. Staring at her with that grin of his.

Oblivious to the crowded diner, Angie rushed to him. Chris stood and wrapped her up. God, she felt good. Soft and warm. He buried his nose in her hair and breathed in her coconut scent. Oh yeah. A very long eight weeks.

"You're home, you're home!" Angie wasn't sure if she was laughing or crying and didn't really care. He was home.

She remembered their surroundings before he did and reluctantly pulled away from him. Chris let her go but kept hold of her hand. Glancing around, Angie noticed most people look away quickly. Only the Jones sisters kept grinning at them.

"Couldn't wait to see you, dear. . . ." Mary spoke.

"Came straight from the airport. . . ." Margaret picked up the sentence.

"Or so it seems," Mary finished for them. They both looked pointedly at his duffel on the floor.

"Oh!" Angie blushed. "Did you need the key?"

"No," Chris reassured her. "I have mine. They were right. I just wanted to see you." Slowly, he released her hand and sat back on the stool. "If I can get a coffee, I'd love to walk you home when you get off work."

Angie bit her cheek and ducked her head, trying to hide her smile. "I'd like that."

"Angie," a voice whispered by her ear. It was Sarah, the young woman who ran the diner until closing. "I can handle the last thirty minutes of your shift. You go on." Sarah's eyes were soft and dreamy at the sight of such a romantic reunion. "I'll clock you out at four."

Angie didn't hesitate a moment. Looking at Chris, she said, "I'll be right back. Don't leave," and raced into the kitchen.

"You still want that coffee, Mr. Montgomery?" Sarah asked.

Chris shook his head. "I'm hoping I won't have time to drink it." He took his eyes from the kitchen door. "Thanks for this."

"Oh, no. No need for thanks," the young woman replied. "Y'all are like something out of a fairy tale or something. You shouldn't have to wait here."

Chris chuckled as she left to see to her customers. Ah, to be young. Angie came back out of the kitchen still smiling. He was back. At first, she felt strange, even shy, when Chris took her hand in front of everybody. She could've sworn everyone in the place was sneaking glances at them. The walk to the diner door seemed very, very long.

But why shouldn't they hold hands in public? So what if everyone knew they were keeping company? The whole town already knew she'd been living at the old place while he was gone. Now they would know why. Although Angie knew the town well enough to realize they had been speculating for quite a while already. Of course, she hadn't quite known what was going to happen when he got home today, either. Things between them had been so new when he left, and there was only so much a person could tell from phone calls and letters. So, she had hoped, but not known. Now it was looking like she had hoped correctly. Looked like she was indeed dating Chris Montgomery. A faint blush crept up her neck, warming her nicely.

As they reached the door, Chris opened it for her and Angie looked into his eyes. They were good eyes in a handsome face. Let people talk. She was dating Chris Montgomery and didn't care who knew it. When it was over, she would have some lovely memories and her town wouldn't think too badly of her. After all, who could blame her?

As they stepped into the street, Angie automatically turned right while Chris turned left. They laughed as their hands tugged in opposite directions. Chris took the opportunity to spin Angie into his arms and wrap her up, careful not to bump her with his bag. God, he wanted to kiss her. To feel her lips, to feel her body melt in his arms. Not here, though. Not on the street with everyone around. If they weren't looking now, they would be as soon as he lowered his mouth to hers on a public street in broad daylight. Soon though. Soon he would have her alone, and then he planned to kiss her thoroughly and well. Until then, though, he had to do something to clear his thoughts. "And where," Chris teased her, "did you think you were going, Miz Angie?"

Angie fluttered her eyelashes at him, enjoying the fun almost as much as the feel of his arms around her waist. "Why, Mr. Montgomery, I thought you were going to walk me home."

"I am." Chris nodded his head in the direction of the house on the hill.

"O-Oh," Angie stammered, the joke going out of the moment. "But I . . . I . . . well, I moved out last night. I'm back . . ." She waved a hand behind her, in the direction of the house she shared with Bobby and Carter Anne.

"Oh."

She watched Chris closely. Something closed down in his eyes, and she felt a pang of guilt. Well, he hadn't expected her to go on living there once he was home, had he? *Had* he?

Chris recovered quickly. "Then you can walk me home first. Give me a chance to drop this bag." Still, his eyes were different than they had been, Angie thought. But maybe she was just making that up.

"Okay." Angie smiled up at him, moving out of his arms. This time, though, Chris didn't take her hand as they started to walk.

She felt like a damn fool. Thinking those things, letting him hold her hand in front of everybody just moments before, and now . . . this. She struggled to find something to say that would break the silence that was so sudden and so awkward. "I hope you like what I've done with the place," Angie finally said.

"I'm sure it will be fine, Angie," Chris replied. Damn. That had come out far more abruptly than he had intended. Just because she wasn't following the scenario he'd had in his head all the way from Colorado wasn't her fault. She didn't deserve that. "You haven't mentioned much about it." He tried to undo the damage. Had he ever been this uncomfortable with her before? Seriously, he didn't think so.

"I haven't wanted to build it up only for you to be disappointed."

"Angie." Chris kept his eyes straight ahead. "I can't imagine being disappointed in anything you do."

Where was the warmth that usually spread through her when he said things like that? Maybe it was how flat his voice was that made her feel nothing but an unfamiliar emptiness in her stomach.

"Well." Angie forced herself to sound cheerful once they reached the door. "Here it is." She opened the door with a flourish, watching Chris closely.

This wasn't the house he had walked out of eight weeks ago. He could tell that just from the foyer. The old linoleum had been replaced with black and white marble squares; the dingy walls repainted a soft white. And the functional, if utilitarian, lights from his grandparents' time were now shimmering electric sconces. Looking down the hall, the kitchen held the same promise of change.

Chris turned slowly, his duffel sliding forgotten off his shoulder to the floor. Through the doors of the sitting room, the parlor and his office, he caught glimpses of warm welcoming colors and inviting furniture. Even the staircase leading up to the second floor had been returned to its former glory, the wood stripped, stained, and waxed to a shine.

Amazed, Chris turned to Angie. She was smiling, all doubts gone in the face of his reaction. "How much of it?" Chris asked.

"All of it. The whole thing. Well, 'cept the attic."

Chris could tell she was excited and proud. Hell, he was excited for himself and proud of her, too. He'd never expected this. Not in eight weeks.

"Angie!" He picked her up and swung her around. "You are the most amazing woman!"

Angie's surprised laughter was silenced as Chris's mouth found hers. He deepened the kiss as he lowered her feet to the floor, but Angie would have sworn she was still floating in his arms as if she was light as a feather.

There was nothing timid about it. Chris crushed her to him, holding on to her, exploring her with his hands, his mouth. A part of Angie was aware of the fact that she was reacting the same way, but it was a very small part. Mostly what she knew was her own hunger as she kissed Chris greedily, her own passion as her hands found his hair and pulled him closer to her. Her earlier concerns were forgotten as she lost herself in the kiss.

"Angie." Chris broke the kiss but wouldn't let her step away from him. He swallowed hard, trying to regain composure. Because, dear God, he *had* to regain his composure. She had never responded like that before. Not that there had been all that many opportunities for her to do so. Still, he either stopped this now or he was going to end up pushing her and, as much he wanted her, he didn't want that. Chris took a deep breath, steadying himself.

"I've missed you, Angie. It's good to be back."

"I've missed you, too."

Her lips were swollen from the force of the kiss, separated slightly because of her own desire. Her cheeks and those gorgeous cat eyes were glowing. Yeah, he had to stop this right now.

With an inward groan, Chris stepped away from her. "So." He nudged his duffel to the foot of the stairs for later and took her hand. "Show me the rest."

Angie was stunned. If the intensity of Chris's kiss had surprised her, it was nothing compared to her own reaction. Her heart was racing. How had he just been able to stop like that? Maybe it was a good thing one of them was in control. With a steadying breath, she led him deeper into the house.

It was nothing less than amazing. Angie was true to her word; every room was different and new. Chris recognized most of the furniture that his grandparents had used or stored on the third floor, but there were a few new pieces. Everything else had been rehabbed, down to the plumbing fixtures in the kitchen and powder rooms. Somehow, Chris realized, she had managed to combine elegance and comfort. He could invite generals and their wives over for cocktails, but he could also see himself kicking back with Bobby and a beer in every room.

From the dining room, he opened the doors to the ballroom. No, he wouldn't be kicking back with a beer in here. It was as if he had stepped back into the 1800s. The windows across the back wall were so clean they might not have existed. The lace curtains that hung around them were interwoven with thin gold thread that would sparkle in the light thrown by the candles placed throughout the room and along the walls. The hardwood floors reflected the few pieces of furniture in their wax shine. Even the iron spiral staircases had been refinished and polished. At each end of the room was a gathering of vintage chairs, tables, and sofas, perfect for sitting out a dance or catching up with friends around the fireplaces. Two magnificent chandeliers hung from the ceiling. Looking around, Chris found their switches hidden discretely behind wrought iron faceplates. Sure enough, they were both on dimmer switches so the room could be bright as noon or bathed in a soft glow, depending on the occasion. He simply shook his head, unable to believe what he was seeing.

"How did you do all this? And in such a short time?" he asked with disbelief.

Angie laughed warmly. "It's amazing what you can get people to do when you're waving a million dollars cash at them. Speaking of . . ."

Chris interrupted her before she could finish the question. "We'll talk about that later. Right now, I just want to see my house and everything you've done to it. Take me upstairs."

Angie shrugged indifferently but was pleased. She'd waited this long to know; she could wait a little longer. And he liked what she had done well enough to not want to be distracted from the tour. Trying to hide her smile, she led him back into the foyer to the main staircase.

Picking up his bag, Chris bowed to her. "After you, Miz Angie."

She tossed her hair over her shoulder with a regal look, which was only spoiled by the giggle that followed it. *Oh yeah*, Chris thought. *She could have been the mistress here. Maybe she still would be, one day*. Enjoying that thought and the view of her as she climbed the stairs in front of him, Chris followed her as she led him into the master suite.

Of all the bedrooms, she was the most proud of this one. As Chris's personal space, it had been the most challenging, but she thought she had gotten it right. Now she would find out.

The walls were a light gray color that softened the room without making it dingy. Navy and gray curtains hung from the windows, letting the dying light in. On his bed were gray Egyptian cotton sheets underneath a thick comforter that managed, he was grateful, to be stylish but not too girly. It even complemented the curtains without looking planned. He had no doubt, however, that particular trick had indeed been part of Angie's plan in spite of the accidental look of it. And bless her, she had even left him his old woolen blanket that had seen him through so much, folded across the end of the bed, looking as if it belonged there.

Next to the fireplace, she had found and placed a large navy leather armchair and a small table. The chair was situated so he could look out over the yard in the summer when the windows were open or gaze into the fire in the winter when it was cold. On the mantel was a framed collection of his father's insignia and a photo of his whole family, taken years ago. Where had she found that? He had no idea, but she had, and the thought that she had taken this kind of time made him feel, well, special. Finally, above the mantel, off center so as not to make it look like a shrine, was the picture he traveled with of himself and Pops. This was where this photograph had always belonged, Chris realized now. After years of being crammed into trunks, leaned up against walls, and slid under cots when there was no place else to put it, the picture had finally found its home. And Angie had known it.

She watched him closely. His face gave so little away. And yet . . . she was beginning to learn how to read him. The flick of his fingers on his blanket. The twitch of his mouth when he saw the leather chair she had been so pleased to find in an antique shop. She had done it. Chris liked the space, truly and really. When he turned to her, she didn't need to be able to read him well. Anyone could have read the smile on his lips and the pleasure in his eyes as genuine.

"I've never had anything like this before, Angie." Chris's voice was low. "I didn't think I'd have it here, honestly. God knows I wouldn't have taken this kind of time to decorate the place. Thank you." He reached for her, and she moved into his arms.

"You're welcome. I really wanted it to be special for you. A place you could come and get away from everything else."

Without another word, Chris kissed her again. This time, he was slow and sweet. Taking his time, teasing her lips open with gentle flicks of his tongue. Instead of grasping at her as he had earlier, his hands barely touched her back, her shoulders. Still, Angie felt as secure as if his arms had been iron. The slow exploration of her mouth gave her a chance to experience him as well. The taste of him. The smell of his hair as he moved his head while he placed soft kisses along her jawline. The feel of his muscles under her hands. Oh, this was what it was like to feel adored. To feel beautiful and wanted.

Chris kissed his way down Angie's neck. He felt rather than heard her low moan as his teeth nipped teasingly at her collarbone, and chuckled. His Angie had her own passions it seemed. Nonetheless, he expected her to resist, to stop him, when his tongue trailed into the V of her blouse. Instead, she leaned into him encouragingly. She tasted both sweet and salty, and the combination went straight to Chris's head.

He should stop now. Stop them both, in spite of his hunger and her willingness. Instead, his hands reached for the buttons on her blouse and slowly unfastened them until her flesh was exposed.

With another moan, Angie arched her back, lifting her breasts, offering them to him. God, did she even realize what she was doing to him? Somehow, he didn't think so, and that made it all better—and all the more difficult to do what he had to do. In a moment. Just one more moment.

Chris tugged at her bra, releasing her breasts. His teeth nibbled at her until his lips closed around one nipple. He felt it go taut under his tongue. With one hand on her back, he used the other to tease her second nipple, moving his fingers in motion with his teeth.

"Oh, Chris." Angie's whisper was hoarse.

He had to decide and he had to decide right now. Only there really wasn't any decision to make. Slowly, Chris raised his mouth from her, placed a soft kiss in the hollow of her throat, and gently closed her blouse, holding its edges in clenched fists.

Aching, Chris lowered his forehead to hers, eyes closed. If he looked into those emerald green depths now, he would lose what little resolve he had left.

"Angie," he whispered.

Angie reached up and touched his cheek. "Chris?" she asked, hoping to hide her confusion. She had been willing, ready, to give herself to him. But he had stopped—again—and she wasn't sure why. Could one person want so much and the other be indifferent? Or worse, maybe once he'd seen what was really under her clothes . . . Her chest tightened at the thought.

The uncertainty in her voice ripped at him. Surely she realized why he was stopping and what it was taking for him to do so. "Angie," Chris spoke again, finally opening his eyes to meet hers. He kissed her nose, forced himself to button her blouse, and took two definitive steps away from her. "If I hadn't stopped right then . . ." This was hard enough without her looking at him, trying so hard not to be hurt. He took a deep breath. "Angie, I want to make love to you. And if I hadn't stopped, we would have. If the time was right or not."

Unable to stop herself, Angie closed the distance between them. "Would that have been so bad?"

"Oh God, no." Chris laughed shakily. "No. But it wouldn't have been right, either." He sat on the edge of the bed and pulled her onto his lap. She settled in with her head on his shoulder. She felt so right there. Chris fought away such distracting thoughts and continued. "And I want it to be right for you, Angie. I want to do right by you. When the time comes."

Angie snuggled in closer to him. "You said 'when.'"

Chris smiled into her hair. "I said when."

"So . . ." She paused, gathering her strength. "So, it's not *me* that made you stop?"

He threw back his head and laughed, wrapping his arms around her tighter. "Oh God, no, Angie. It's you that made it so damn hard to stop."

She sighed contentedly and wiggled in his lap. Chris moaned. "But you have to stop that right now, woman, because you're killing me with that squirm of yours!"

Laughing, Angie stood up reluctantly. She had enjoyed the feel of him pressing up against her thigh and the thrill it gave her knowing Chris Montgomery wanted her in his bed that badly. "Would you like to . . ."

"I was hoping we might . . ."

They spoke together. Their shared laughter broke the last of the tension.

"Go ahead," Angie said.

"Ladies first," Chris insisted.

"Would you like to come to the house for dinner? Carter Anne's frying up some chicken."

Chris smiled. And here he'd been hoping to see her tomorrow. Tonight was even better. "I'd love to. Can I change clothes first? I've been traveling all day."

"Tell you what? Why don't you make your way down in about an hour. That'll give you time to get settled and me a chance to get a shower," Angie suggested.

Chris dropped his chin to his chest with a groan. "Just what I need, Angie. The image of you in the shower."

Angie's eyes twinkled at him. Oh yes, she was enjoying this. Who knew this could be so much fun? She knew having feelings for a man could make a woman feel vulnerable. She'd had no idea that having a man return those feelings could make a woman feel so powerful. "See you in an hour." She giggled and turned on her heel. Chris listened until he heard the front door close then flopped back onto the bed. He would be taking a shower before dinner as well. A very, very cold shower.

"Chris!" Carter Anne squealed as she opened the front door, throwing her arms around his neck. "Welcome home, honey. Come on in. Bobby and I were so excited when Angie told us you were coming to dinner. Tell us everything you did. Do you like the house? Angie worked so hard on it. Bet you're tired out from traveling all day."

Chris found himself happily overwhelmed by Carter Anne as she practically pulled him into the house. Bobby was standing back, waiting, with a patient smile on his face.

"Now, Carter Anne," he said slowly. "Let the man get a word in." Bobby stuck out his hand. "Welcome home, Chris."

Chris shook hands and accepted the clap on his shoulder. "Thanks, Bobby. It's good to be back."

"Come on." Carter Anne slipped her arm through his and started walking him to the kitchen. "I'll get you a beer and you can tell us all about it over supper."

Bobby trailed behind them, hardly hearing Carter Anne's excited babbling. He paused at the steps in order to call up to Angie when she appeared at the top of them. She was dressed in those pants that came to midcalf—caprees or something like that, he thought—and a silky looking tank top. Over the last several weeks, he'd noticed his girls going out more, coming back with shopping bags, and giggling a lot in Angie's room, but he hadn't seen any changes. Until now. Now, his girl was glowing. Bobby was glad he knew where Chris stood on the matter. Seeing Angie look like this, well, it wouldn't have been good if Bobby had even suspected the man was playing her.

"Did I hear Chris come in?" she asked as she skipped down the stairs. "Bobby? You okay?" He was staring at her with such a strange expression on his face.

"I'm fine." Bobby patted her shoulder gently. "Just thinking you look like your mama is all."

Angie gasped slightly. "Oh." She barely remembered the woman, but had always heard how beautiful and vivacious her mother had been. How much Bobby had loved his sister. "Thank you, Bobby."

Bobby cleared his throat roughly. "Anyway, Carter Anne's got him cornered in the kitchen, riddling him with questions she's not giving him time to answer."

Angie grinned, and Bobby couldn't help but be amazed again at the transformation.

"Let's go rescue him." Angie giggled, anxious to be with Chris again.

In the short time Carter Anne had Chris in the kitchen alone, she had already seated him at the table, gotten him a beer, and returned to finishing up dinner. Bobby noticed the other man's eyes light up as Angie entered the room.

"Can I help with anything, Carter Anne?" Chris asked, but his eyes followed Angie as she crossed the room to pull a Diet Pepsi from the refrigerator. Angie flushed under the heat of his stare. Yes, things were looking up, Bobby thought.

"Nope," Carter Anne replied. "Your only job tonight is to tell us about Colorado."

"Unfortunately"—Chris sighed—"there isn't much I can tell you. And what I can talk about is pretty boring. I gave a lot of briefings and answered a lot of questions."

"Surely there's something," Carter Anne protested.

Chris opened his mouth, but Bobby spoke first. "Carter Anne, leave it be." His voice was kind but firm.

Carter Anne pouted sweetly for a moment before continuing on, energy unabated. "Then tell us how you like the house! Didn't Ang do an amazing job on it?"

Angie leaned against the counter, blushing gently. Chris smiled at her, and she felt her whole body get warm.

"She did," Chris agreed. "I couldn't believe it was *my* house. It certainly didn't look like the place I left."

Carter Anne beamed at Angie. She had worked so hard, hand to God, and been so worried. No matter how often Carter Anne had told her it was beautiful, that Chris would love it. It was lovely being right. "Told you so," Carter Anne teased her sister.

"I'm just glad you're happy with it," Bobby said honestly. "Makes losing my kitchen table for two months worth it."

Everyone laughed and Carter Anne slapped easily at Bobby's arm. "It wasn't that bad and you know it."

"No, it wasn't." Bobby winked at her then turned to Chris. "Still glad you like it though. They worked hard."

"I could tell it was hard work," Chris agreed. "And I've been thinking about that. We should show it off."

Bobby leaned back in his chair, studying the other man. Carter Anne squealed in delight. But Angie went pale.

"What do you mean?" she asked.

"Founder's Day weekend is in what, two weeks?" Chris asked. He directed his comments to Carter Anne and Bobby. They already seemed on his side, and it would take all three of them, he knew. "How do we get on the schedule for an open house?"

"What a great idea!" Carter Anne exclaimed. "The parade is Sunday, so that might be kinda hard."

"So we try for Saturday. And make it an open house rather than a big event. That way people can just come and go in between other things. No one has to choose this over something else."

"Betsy Abernathy is the one you want to talk to, Chris," Bobby told him. "She's in charge of scheduling the weekend. It's been put off a little late, but she might make an exception. 'Specially if you were willing to make it a yearly event."

"Or make a donation," Carter Anne added.

Chris gave a snort. "I think both of those things can be arranged."

"Then you'll probably be on the schedule." Bobby nodded. "I think it's a fine idea."

"You do?" Angie croaked.

"Oh, honey!" Carter Anne answered for him. "It's a great idea. Give people a chance to see the old place looking all spiffed up. Everybody'll want to come."

Chris appreciated the fact that Carter Anne didn't mention people would also be seeing Angie's work. Somehow, he didn't think this was an oversight.

"I know Gran would want me to use the house for entertaining. She loved her parties." He had hit the right note. It was in her eyes.

"House like that should have people in it," Carter Anne agreed. "It's been empty way too long. Truth is," she spoke to Chris, "I was excited to see the inside when you moved to town."

"I'll get you Betsy's number." Bobby stood up, taking several dishes into the kitchen with him. Angie stacked the rest and followed him, still silent.

Carter Anne turned to Chris, speaking in a hurried whisper. "I'll work on her, too. This could be a great chance for her. We just can't let her know we know it."

Chris had leaned in to ensure they wouldn't be overheard. He grinned at her. "So we play dumb and act like it's about the house."

"Exactly." She sat up quickly as she heard the others returning. "That'll be the key." She spoke as if continuing a conversation. "Keep it simple, not try to go all out. Just some finger foods and something to drink." She turned to Angie. "Do you think mimosas will be too much?"

Angie sat back down and swallowed hard. It was, after all, Chris's house. "No, I think mimosas would set just the right tone. Very classic, like the house itself."

Bobby passed the phone number on a yellow sticky note over to Chris. "You understand, don't you, that this party of yours has just been taken completely out of your hands."

With a glance at Angie, he smiled. "I'm counting on it."

Chapter 13

Everything was ready. Angie knew that. She and Carter Anne had put in so many hours the past few days. Everything couldn't help but be ready. But was that a smear on the banister? Had Chris put the throw pillows back on the bed this morning the way she'd shown him or just thrown them on haphazardly? Maybe she should just go check.

"You stay right there," Carter Anne spoke, freezing Angie as she started to stand. "Whatever you're going to check is fine as it is."

Angie opened her mouth, but Carter Anne spoke first, answering the question before it could even be asked. "Truly and really fine, Angie. I promise."

With a sigh, Angie settled back into the love seat where she and Carter Anne were waiting. At Carter Anne's suggestion, Chris had retreated into his office until noon when the house would officially open.

"How did I let him talk me into this?" Angie moaned, leaning her head back and closing her eyes.

"Well, it *is* his house, Ang. You could hardly have forbidden it," Carter Anne reminded her.

"Not that. I knew once he'd decided to do this there was no

stopping him, but why am *I* here? How did I let him talk *me* into it?"

Carter Anne looked at Angie, her voice firm. "You *should* be here. What if someone has a question? Chris has no idea where all this came from. And, bless his heart, he doesn't know a Queen Anne chair from a lawn chair. But you do.

"And anyway," Carter Anne continued more gently, "you deserve to be here. This house is a showplace again because of you. You should get the praise."

"You're right." Angie sighed. "I'm just nervous."

"Chris?" Carter Anne called sweetly into the other room. He peeked out of his office. "Would you please bring Angie a mimosa?" As Chris headed to the kitchen, Carter Anne patted Angie's knee. "You won't have to be nervous for long. It's time to open the doors, and you know people will be showing up at the stroke of twelve." She crossed to the door and opened it wide. Sure enough, three women were at the foot of the walk. Carter Anne turned to tell Angie, but she was already at the door, drink in hand. By the time the trio was close enough to see her, Angie was smiling and ready to show them around.

The house was packed by one o'clock. Chris was amazed. Had he truly considered Lambert Falls to be a small town? If so, where were all these people coming from? It seemed as if everyone for 100 miles had come to get a glimpse of the old place. And yet every time Chris thought a person was a total stranger, one of his friends would slip in with an introduction.

"Joseph Kelley, Chris." Bobby introduced him to a man in a suit. "I went to the Academy with his dad."

"Chris? Have you met Bill and Diane Turner?" Carter Anne asked him with a smile. "Their kids go to my school."

"Christopher." Mary Jones tugged on his sleeve gently. "I'd like you to meet one of my oldest friends, Lalah Pierce. She and I have known each other since we were just girls. She lives over in Thomasville now, but has never missed a Founder's Day weekend."

And so many names and faces presented to him by Angie that he knew he would never keep them all straight. The politicking and schmoozing he and the captain had done overseas was nothing compared to the intricacies of a small, Southern town.

Every time he felt like retreating though, he noticed another person with one of Angie's cards or heard someone new asking her advice, setting up an appointment for Angie to *just come have a look* at a room or piece of furniture. Those cards had been a stroke of genius on Carter Anne's part. Especially how she'd just worked it into the planning. She and Angie had been sitting around the kitchen table, talking about what to serve. They had gotten as far as ham biscuits and mimosas when Carter Anne had simply said, "You know, I just had a thought. What if someone asks me a question I don't know the answer to? Or Chris? Or bless his heart, Bobby?"

Angie hadn't even looked up from her list. "Just send them to me."

"But that's three of us, all sending folks to you. Plus the ones who were smart enough to ask you in the first place. People'll be lining up to talk to you."

"Well"—Angie shrugged, absorbed in the menu planning—"give them the number to the house and have 'em call me."

"Business cards! What a great idea, Ang! I'll handle those. What about fruit and vegetable trays?" Carter Anne had simply looked back at their list.

"What?" Angie's head popped up.

"Fruit and veggie trays. Maybe with a poppy seed dressing."

"That's not what I'm talkin' about and you know it, Carter Anne."

"Think about it, Ang." Carter Anne's voice was no-nonsense.

"It just makes sense. You said it yourself, we should give them your number. How are we supposed to do that? Hand it out on scraps of paper?"

Angie had thought—thought hard—but in the end, hadn't had an alternative. Chris had watched her struggle before finally swallowing hard and agreeing. Carter Anne tipped him a wink before going back to the menu. And now everyone was here and, it seemed at least, everyone had a card.

Chris smiled at the glow on Angie's face. The madness of the open house was definitely worth it.

A hand touched his arm familiarly, and Chris turned into the fake smile of Langdon Howard.

"Chris!" she exclaimed. "I just *had* to tell you how much Clark and I *love* what you've done here." Clark was standing slightly behind his wife, clutching a mimosa but looking at it as if he wished it was something, anything, stronger.

"Thank you, Langdon," Chris replied, giving a nod to Clark as well. "However, I can't take the credit. Angie did it all."

"So I've heard!" Langdon gasped. "Who would've thought our little Angie had such a good eye?"

"Obviously, I did. And lucky for me."

"Well, of course." Langdon laughed. "You should have a real party here, soon. Open up the ballroom again. I was sorry to learn we wouldn't get a peek at it today."

"That's a good idea." Chris wasn't sure if he wanted to slap the woman or laugh in her face. "A party with just a few good friends. To inaugurate the ballroom."

"Well . . . that's nice." Langdon stood, expectantly.

"Now if you'll excuse me, I really should keep mingling. Thank you for stopping by. I'll be sure to tell Angie you were here." Chris nodded again in Clark's direction, who lifted his glass this time, with a wry smile in return.

Turning, Chris couldn't find Angie, but Carter Anne was over in a corner, so he made his way to her.

"Isn't this crazy and wonderful?" she said with a laugh.

"It is a bit overwhelming," Chris agreed. "Even when I decided to do it, I had no idea so many people would want to see Pops's place."

"Remember, Chris"—Carter Anne's eyes scanned the room for anyone looking bored or uncomfortable—"it's been closed for going on twenty years now. 'The Old Montgomery Place' is a bit of a legend in these parts. Looming up here on its hill, all dark and mysterious."

"I guess I never thought of it that way," Chris acknowledged. "To me, it's just my grandparents' old house. Still, the crowd should start thinning soon." He looked at the clock on the mantel. "Technically, this shindig ends in about twenty minutes."

Carter Anne nodded, her eyes still on the room. "We'll start herding them out at four and the talk will start about . . . oh my God." Carter Anne's eyes widened as she stared at the front door. Chris looked and saw nothing particularly noteworthy, just a woman in a peach linen suit and a tall man removing his sunglasses.

"Carter Anne?" Chris looked back at her, puzzled.

"Holy shit. It's Lydia Bain Carmichael. I've got to get Angie." And without another word, Carter Anne turned and was gone.

Chris knew it was something important from Carter Anne's reaction. It would be best, he decided, to simply watch. He had no idea who Lydia Bain Carmichael was but, he thought, he would wait and find out. The whispering spread through the crowd as the woman walked farther into the house, but Chris couldn't really make any of it out.

Angie appeared in the kitchen door as pale as he'd ever seen her, holding a champagne flute. Although he couldn't tell for certain from here, he thought she might be shaking. Carter Anne gave Angie a little push in the small of the back, and Chris watched as Angie made her way to the other woman. Intrigued, Chris moved close enough to hear the conversation.

"Mrs. Carmichael, welcome to the Montgomery House. May I offer you a drink?" Angie's voice was unusually high and, Chris could now see for certain, the hand holding out the mimosa was indeed trembling.

"No, thank you, dear. I don't drink in the afternoons." Mrs. Carmichael, whoever she was, declined politely.

"Oh." Angie flushed. "Of course not. I'm so sorry."

"Nonsense, you didn't know." Mrs. Carmichael was trying. Chris gave her credit for that. "Are you a Montgomery?" she asked Angie.

"No. Oh, no. I'm just Angie . . ."

Chris had seen enough. He closed the distance, extending his hand. "Did I hear someone ask about me? I'm Christopher Montgomery."

"Lydia Bain Carmichael." Her hand was as cool as she was. "Pleased to meet you, Mr. Montgomery."

"Please, call me Chris," he said with a smile. "And I see you've met Angie Kane." He put one arm around Angie and pulled her in close.

"I was just doing so, yes." Lydia Carmichael extended her hand to Angie. "It's a pleasure, Angie."

"Thank . . . thank you, Mrs. Carmichael."

"I'm in your home, dear. Call me Lydia."

"Oh, this isn't . . . I mean . . ." Angie stammered, but Chris interrupted her.

"Thank you, Lydia." Who *was* this woman who could fluster Angie this badly?

"When I heard the Montgomery house was going to be

open, I just had to come see. Michael wanted me to make arrangements. I hope it's all right that I didn't."

"What's the point of an open house if you have to RSVP?" Chris smiled. He turned to the man behind her. He was very tall, very stern, and radiated physical strength in spite of his wiry frame. "Are you Michael?" Chris asked.

"No, sir," the man replied, coolly professional.

"That's Scott," Lydia answered nonchalantly.

Angie stepped up quickly. "Mrs. Carm—Lydia, may I show you around?"

The two women wandered through the living room, leaving Chris behind. Somehow, Angie knew, she had to find a way to tell Chris what was going on. But letting Lydia Bain Carmichael, North Carolina's First Lady, wander around by herself was impossible. Thinking quickly, Angie moved the governor's wife into the parlor, hoping to find Carter Anne or Bobby there. Either of them could be dispatched to fill Chris in on the situation.

"You know"—Lydia studied the love seat, thoughtfully—"I think I saw a piece very much like this one in a magazine not too long ago. It was hideous, but here it's perfect. Who was the decorator?"

"Actually," Chris spoke from directly behind them. He and Mrs. Carmichael's security officer had followed them in from the other room. "You're getting the grand tour from her. Angie designed and decorated the whole place."

Lydia smiled warmly at Angie. "You have an excellent eye for color and space, dear. I've always envied people who could do this."

"Perhaps one day," Chris spoke again, "you and the governor might call on Angie for tips or suggestions."

The older woman looked at Chris, eyes twinkling with the

knowledge that he had put it all together. "Perhaps." She turned to Angie. "Do you offer professional consultations?"

"Let me get you my card," Angie answered smoothly. She left Chris with Mrs. Carmichael—she would never be able to think of her as Lydia, hand to God—and tried not to race to the table where Carter Anne had laid out several elegant business cards just a few hours earlier. The table was empty. Every single card had been taken. Starting to panic just a little, she turned toward the kitchen, straight into Bobby and Carter Anne.

"Here." Bobby had two of the cards in his hand for her.

"Angie, honey . . ." Carter Anne started excitedly.

"Not yet, Carter Anne," Angie answered, surprised at how calm she sounded. Squaring her shoulders, she looked at Bobby. He nodded and gave her a wink before pulling Carter Anne back into the crowd. Feeling composed, if somewhat numb, Angie returned to the parlor, only to find Scott standing in the doorway connecting the room to the kitchen.

"In here, ma'am." He indicated the kitchen and allowed Angie to go before him. Angie entered to find Chris leaning on the counter and Lydia sipping iced tea at the table.

"Thank you for the tour, Angie," Lydia said graciously. "I'm only sorry I didn't arrive in time to see more of the house." She stood.

"It was our pleasure, Lydia. And please, don't feel you have to leave. Chris or I can finish showing you around."

Lydia was moving though the house, back toward the front door. "Unfortunately, I have other engagements this evening. Still, I would like a card if you have one."

Angie handed over both of her spares, painfully aware that everyone within range was straining to hear the conversation.

"I'll be in touch," Lydia said with a last look around. "Thank you." And she swept out the door, Scott close behind her.

Angie spun to Chris, but he hushed her in spite of his own

grin. "Not now." He motioned to the still-full living room. However, Lydia Carmichael's departure, to Chris's relief, seemed to mark the end of the open house. He stood by the door, thanking people as they filed out. Angie, Carter Anne, and Bobby were clearing glasses and plates, but he could tell they were really just marking time until the door finally closed for the last time.

At last, he was able to call out to them in the kitchen. Angie and Carter Anne's squeals started immediately. Chris found himself smiling as he walked back to join them.

"Angie!" Carter Anne practically yelled. "That was Lydia Bain Carmichael!"

Angie collapsed into a chair. "I just about died when you first told me, Carter Anne. Hand to God."

"I thought y'all handled it real well," said Bobby, pulling two beers from the refrigerator and handing one to Chris.

"How'd you figure out who she was?" Angie asked Chris.

He sipped his beer and shrugged. "I asked Scott."

"Just like that?" Angie looked at him, stunned.

"Just like that." Chris smiled down at her.

Their eyes locked and held. Bobby took in the scene quickly and cleared his throat.

"Well." He set his nearly full beer on the counter. "Carter Anne, why don't you and I get out of here ourselves."

"I was going to stay and help . . . oh." Carter Anne could suddenly feel the heat between her sister and her friend. "Angie, give a call if you want help cleaning up."

"Okay." Angie forced herself to look away from Chris. "I mean . . ."

Carter Anne patted her shoulder. "Nothing that won't keep until tonight." She looked at Chris and winked. "Or tomorrow."

Bobby cleared his throat roughly again. Some things didn't bear considering too hard, and this was definitely one of them. "We'll see y'all tomorrow at the parade if not before," he said gruffly and headed out, trusting Carter Anne would follow him.

"Oh my God, Chris! Do you realize what we did today?" Angie finally let her excitement show.

Chris stood her up and pulled her into his arms. "Not me, Angie. You did all of it."

"No, Chris, I didn't." She leaned back so he could look into her eyes. "*We* did it. I was totally frozen when Mrs. Carmichael showed up."

"I wasn't that much help, not even knowing who the hell she was."

"That's my point, though," Angie continued. "We did it together."

"Oh, Angie . . ."

Chris was going to disagree with her, she could tell. Well, fine. If he didn't want to believe they were a good team, she'd have to prove it to him some other way. Before Chris could say another word, Angie rose up on her toes and kissed him deeply. He sank into the chair next to the table, taking her with him, onto his lap.

He pulled back from the kiss and looked into her eyes. "Angie . . ." he whispered.

"Shhh . . ." She traced one finger around his lips before replacing her nail with her mouth, nipping gently at him. Her hands moved from his shoulders to his chest, trailing her fingers along the skin exposed by the neckline of his shirt. And still, she was kissing him, playfully. Using her palms, she pushed open his shirt, revealing his chest. One nail flicked teasingly against a nipple, and Chris moaned. Pulling him to her, he deepened the kiss.

His hands found the hem of her skirt and pulled it up to her thigh. Two could play this game. Slowly, he let his hands move along the inside of her leg. When his thumb brushed the edge of her panties, Angie gasped.

Grinning at him mischievously, she took the break in their kiss to put her mouth to his shoulder, his collarbone. Her hair spilled over his chest, its silk arousing him further. One hand gripping her hip from passion as much as to keep her in his lap, Chris used the other to stroke between her legs. He could feel the heat through the thin cotton separating them. When he slipped a finger beneath the material, Angie nearly jumped out of the chair.

"Not here," Angie gasped.

"What?" Chris couldn't believe what he was hearing. "Angie . . ." he groaned.

"Just not *here*." Angie motioned to the kitchen.

It was cluttered with dirty glasses and used plates. With a sigh, Chris knew she was right. Dammit, he'd almost taken her on the kitchen table for God's sake. He closed his eyes, trying to control himself. Angie's arms went around his neck, and she resumed nibbling on his earlobe.

"Angie!" He tried to force her away, but she held on.

"Upstairs," she whispered into his ear.

Chris didn't stop to think, to give her time to reconsider. In one smooth motion, she was in his arms and they were moving to the stairs. Angie let out a squeal and closed her eyes against his shoulder, not opening them again until he placed her gently on the bed.

His face was hovering over her, his body pressed along hers. Chris had thought her curves would be soft, but he had no idea. Lifting her shirt, he felt the smooth skin of her tummy, her sides, her arms. Angie sat up and Chris supported her while he slipped the shirt from her head. He pulled back then. If she wanted to stop, it needed to be soon.

"Angie, are you sure?" Chris asked gently.

She never took her eyes from his, just reached around and unfastened her bra, allowing her breasts to spill free. Chris had no words. For all the months of wondering and fantasizing, he had never imagined she would be so beautiful. Her breasts were full and her nipples hard, her arousal as obvious as his own.

Angie reached for him. She wanted to see him and touch him. She needed to feel his flesh against hers. She needed him. His shirt was already mostly off, so she reached for his belt.

With a groan, Chris stopped her hands. "Just a second," he panted. He got to the closet in three long strides and began rummaging. Please God. Someone was listening. In a suitcase he rarely used any longer, he found three condoms. He was back on the bed in an instant.

Angie's hands were on him again, pulling at his pants. Once they were off, Chris leaned forward and grabbed her skirt. The elastic waist allowed him to free her of it and her panties in one tug. He looked at her then, eyes wide and inviting.

Chris was torn between a primal need to take her immediately and a longing to take his time. He took a deep breath and buried the need.

"You're so beautiful, Angie," he whispered, leaning forward to taste her skin. His lips moved from her abdomen lower. Angie's hips squirmed under his tongue, encouraging, inviting, demanding. Finally, Chris placed his mouth on her, using his tongue to discover her. He licked and nibbled until Angie cried out his name, her hands fisted in his hair, her hips bucking.

Then and only then did Chris raise himself over her. Pausing only to slip on a condom, he lowered himself between her legs. Angie's back arched, driving him deeper into her. She called out his name again. This was like nothing Chris had ever known. It was like he always thought coming home would be. They found their rhythm, moving together slowly at first and then faster as his need returned to the surface. When Angie opened her eyes and gazed at him, Chris realized he was lost. With a final thrust, he fell, taking her with him.

The sun was setting. Angie could see the sky turning pink through the windows. Next to her, Chris stirred.

"I dozed off," he muttered, nuzzling into her shoulder. Her skin was warm and smelled oh so nice. He kissed her softly. "I'm sorry about that."

Angie turned on her side to face him. "It was only a few minutes. Gave me some time to myself." She traced a finger along his chest, fascinated as the goose bumps rose under her touch.

Chris leaned in and breathed deeply. "You smell like coconuts. Coconuts and summer." Looking back at her, he whispered, "Are you okay, Angie?"

"Mmmm . . . I felt like Scarlett O'Hara."

"And that's good, right?"

"Every Southern girl wants to feel like Scarlett at least once in her life," Angie assured him.

"You know," Chris said in mock seriousness. "Technically, Rhett rapes her. It's very politically incorrect."

"You don't have a romantic bone in your body, do you Christopher Montgomery," Angie hit at him jokingly.

Chris trapped her wrist in one strong hand and rolled her on top of him. "I'll just have to prove you wrong on that one."

"Oh really?" Angie's heart was starting to beat fast again. "And how will you do that?" she asked breathily.

Chris's eyes darkened and he entwined his hands in her hair. "Like this," he said as he pulled her down to him.

Amazing. He felt absolutely amazing. Angie was amazing. This was amazing. Life was amazing. And he would tell her just as soon as he found the strength to open his eyes.

Next to him, Angie sighed. Chris peered out from under an eyelid and was grateful as Angie lifted her arms and arched her back in a contented stretch. The movement had him stirring again. Damn, but she was magnificent. Thank God the boys in Lambert Falls were too enraptured with stick thin supermodels to notice. He reached out and drew her to him.

"How are you?" Chris asked, kissing her hair. "Still feel like Scarlett?"

"No." Angie shook her head against his shoulder. "Now I feel like the cat that got the big ol' canary."

Chris laughed and hugged her tighter. "When you stretch like that, you remind me of a cat."

"A fat, old lap cat." Angie laughed at him.

"A magnificent lioness just back from the hunt and the feast," Chris corrected her. Angie ducked her head, embarrassed but pleased. "And speaking of feast," he continued. "Think there are leftovers from the party?"

"You hungry?" Angie asked.

"Aren't you?" Chris thought his ego was strong, but if after all that she wasn't even hungry . . .

"Starved." Angie grinned back.

"Let's go scrounge." Chris jumped up and was to the door before Angie could even reach her clothes. "What're you doing?" Chris asked.

Angie motioned to her clothes, scattered along the floor. "Getting dressed." She looked around. Her blouse was missing. "Or trying to, anyway."

"Why? There's no need."

Angie looked over at him. Chris was gonna go through the house naked as the day he was born, hand to God. "But . . ." Angie didn't even know what to say.

"But what?" Chris crossed back to her. His voice was gentle. "There's no one here but us. No one can see in. And you"—he put his hands on her waist—"are truly beautiful dressed just the way you are. Don't cover yourself up from me."

If she'd really protested, Chris would have let it go. Instead, to his pleasure, she giggled. It was enough. Chris took her hand and led her downstairs.

Although she was shocked at such behavior, Angie was also pleased. She felt daring, brave, and somehow sophisticated. Raiding the kitchen with Chris was decadent enough, but doing it naked, well, that was just a little naughty in a way that delighted her. As she opened the refrigerator, the cold hit her body, raising goose bumps, and Angie gasped. Talk about decadent.

"Anything good left in there?" Chris spoke from directly behind her, his chin resting on her shoulder.

"Not from the party, but look." Angie reached inside. "Pizza!" They had ordered it the night before, thank goodness.

"And one last bottle of champagne." Chris stretched around her, enjoying the feel of her skin as he brushed against her.

"With pizza?" Angie asked.

"Champagne goes with everything," Chris assured her. He found two clean flutes and popped the cork. "Besides, we should celebrate."

"Isn't that what we just did?" Angie giggled.

"So we'll celebrate the celebrating." Chris kissed her. "Come on."

"Where now?" Angie asked, following him.

"We can have champagne and pizza, but I refuse to do it at the kitchen table." He thought a moment. "At least while naked."

He settled Angie on the floor in the parlor with the food and champagne. Before he sat though, Chris lit the candles. "Now." He sat and snuggled her between his legs, leaning back against his chest. She handed him a champagne flute and clinked hers to it.

"Congratulations, Chris."

"Me?" he asked. "You're the one who should be congratulated."

"You're right." Angie smiled, taking a bite of pizza. "Congratulations to me." They sipped their drinks. "It was good, wasn't it?" Angie sounded shocked. "I can't get over how many people showed up."

"As Carter Anne explained to me, this old place has its own allure around here. People wanted to see."

"But so many of 'em."

Chris was content to watch and listen as she relieved the afternoon. She even, he thought anyway, seemed to forget she wasn't wearing a stitch of clothing. The more relaxed she became though, the more acutely aware of that fact he became. He'd been right earlier; she was amazing. Everything about her was passionate. She spoke passionately, ate passionately, and certainly loved passionately.

"Somehow," Angie said, "I don't think you're listening to me."

"Why would you say that?" Chris asked, embarrassed to have been caught.

"First, because the look in your eye is makin' me feel hunted. And second, well, because, well . . ." She lowered her eyes pointedly.

Ah yes, Chris realized. She wasn't the only one naked. Some things were more difficult to conceal. "Come back upstairs with me," he whispered.

"Didn't Carter Anne say something about us going over there for dinner?" Angie teased.

"Too much pizza." Chris leered at her.

"Let me just . . ."

"No," Chris said quietly. He stood and pulled her to her feet.

"But the . . ." Angie tried to continue, but Chris was kissing her neck and she couldn't quite remember what she was going to say. When his hand reached between her legs, she realized whatever it was couldn't have been important. He brushed her lightly until he heard a low moan and felt her body begin to relax into his touch.

"Come upstairs with me," he whispered.

"Yes," Angie whispered back.

Much later, snuggled in next to Chris, Angie realized she was tired but not sleepy. His breathing didn't sound like he was asleep either.

"I should've cleaned up," Angie spoke.

Chris wrapped his arms around her, enjoying the way she nestled in closer. "Tonight was not a night to do dishes, babe."

"But all that mess, just waiting for us."

"Hey, we blew out the candles." Chris stroked her arm.

"You did?" Angie hadn't even noticed, hand to God.

"I did. And that's the important part."

"Oh yeah." Angie chuckled. "At least if the place had burned down, there wouldn't be the mess in the morning."

"How's this?" Chris kissed her temple. "We'll get a maid. A live-in if you'd like. We've got servants' quarters, after all."

"That's not even funny." But she giggled.

"Okay. So maybe a live-in is a bit much. But we could bring someone in a couple times a week to help out."

"A couple times a week?" Angie sat up on one elbow and looked down at him. "That's crazy. How'd we pay for a couple times a week?"

"Angie," Chris said drily. "Haven't you figured it out yet?" Even in the dark, he could see her blush.

"I guess, well . . ." Angie buried her head in his shoulder. "I've tried not to think about it."

Chris laughed out loud. God, she was delightful. "Then you keep not thinking about it and I'll keep writing checks."

"That much?" Angie asked in a whisper.

"It's okay, babe." He stroked her back. The spot just at the base of her spine seemed to really be relaxing her. "But you're not involved with a slacker. I'd like to make my own money. Pops just made that easier is all."

"What do you want to do?"

His touch was working. Her voice was growing lazy and her body was softening into the bed next to him. Chris lowered his voice to help her. "I'd like a security firm. I did some research before moving here. Greensboro, Danville, even down to Charlotte. I think I could make it work."

"But you'd be based here," Angie mumbled.

"That's right," Chris assured her. "We'll be based here."

"Tell me more."

He had hardly understood the request but answered her anyway. Listening to Chris's dreams, feeling his fingers on her back, Angie drifted off.

Chapter 14

This was her favorite time of day. It always had been. The sky was pink with sunrise but the feel of the air was still quiet night. Now it was even better since she was snuggled down with Chris asleep next to her. Angie stretched, careful not to disturb Chris, and snuggled closer, her head on his shoulder. Tracing lazy circles on his bare chest was amazing. She was allowed to do this. Hell, she was practically supposed to do this. The smoothness of his skin still surprised her. She'd expected him to be rougher, somehow. At least until the line where the scar began. She felt along it, wondering at its story.

"Angie?" Chris muttered, not opening his eyes.

She tried not to jump. How long had he been awake? "Mmmm?" she answered.

"Tell me about your parents."

"What?" Angie propped herself up on an elbow and looked down at him.

Eyes still closed, Chris reached up and lowered her back to his chest, pulling her close. He stroked her hair and back. "I was just lying here thinking. You don't talk about them."

Angie shrugged. "I'm not sure what to tell you. I don't remember them too well. They died when we were so young."

"How young?"

"I was five. Carter Anne was only one. It was a car accident. Bobby and Abby were babysitting us for the night and ended up keeping us on."

"Where had they been?" Chris didn't want to push, but it was time. Her touch when she'd woken up had convinced him of that.

"They were both theatre fans. UVa had brought in a professional company doing *A Midsummer Night's Dream* by William Shakespeare. Daddy got them tickets. Momma's first real night out since Carter Anne was born."

"Sounds to me like you remember a lot."

"Oh." Angie shook her head. "That's not memory. I just know the story."

"What do you remember then?" Chris asked, keeping the pace of his hand on her back steady.

Angie smiled into his shoulder. "I remember Momma's laugh. It was rich and warm and full. Seems I started every day hearin' that laugh. And I remember how big Daddy was. 'Course, he seemed bigger 'cause I was so little but the pictures we have of him show he *was* big. And very safe. We used to dance in the kitchen while Momma cooked dinner and sang songs."

"Did you stand on his feet?" Chris asked, knowing the answer. His sister had stood on their father's feet, too.

"Of course. And sometimes he'd pick me up in his arms and we'd dance that way. Then he'd set me down and dance with Momma. When he did that, he'd sing to her instead of her singing."

"It sounds wonderful." Chris kissed her hair.

"It was." Angie was surprised by the emotion building in her. "You know"—she sighed—"I may not talk about 'em much, but I do think about 'em a lot. Wonderin' if they're watching over me and Carter Anne. And if they're proud of us."

"I'm sure they are, Angie." He tightened his grip on her. "On both counts."

"I guess that sounds kinda odd, thinking that way."

"Not at all." Chris took a deep breath. It was time. "I knew a guy once. Named Jim Edwards. He was on my team. We didn't always get along—the man would argue over the time of day—but we were still good friends." Chris smiled wryly. "He had a great laugh, too."

Not knowing what to say, Angie waited. Finally, Chris continued.

"I watched him die. He was only five feet away from me, but I couldn't reach him." Chris shook his head. "I still think about him a lot, too. Hope he's keeping an eye out for me."

"What happened?" Angie wasn't sure if she was supposed to ask, but she felt she had to.

Chris covered her hand with his and slowly moved it down to his scar. "This. We got hit. I think I was the first down, but it might have been Edwards. No one knows for sure. But I couldn't get to him. I was dying myself."

Angie did jump then. A ferocious, protective anger coursed through her. "But you *didn't*." She spoke through gritted teeth.

"No." Chris agreed. He pulled her up so they were face-to-face. "I didn't. My team saw to that, and I've always been grateful."

"I am, too." The anger was beginning to dissipate, but the need to protect wasn't. Hand to God, Chris Montgomery was hers now and nothing was going to threaten that.

The phone rang a second time, but Angie still hesitated to answer it. It just felt odd answering Chris's phone. She hadn't gotten used to it while he was gone, and it felt stranger now that he was home. They hadn't even really talked about her moving in. She had just sort of . . . stayed, slowing bringing more and more of her things from her room at home to the big house up on the hill as she needed them over the last few weeks. Planned or not, even Angie had to admit they were living together. But answering the phone felt stranger than having her own shampoo in his bathroom. Still, Chris was out back, planning what they would do with the gardens in just a few weeks. He'd never hear the phone.

On the fourth ring, she forced herself to answer it.

"Angie, honey, it's Langdon!"

Angie rolled her eyes. This was why voice mail had been invented. "Hello, Langdon."

"Imagine my surprise when I called *your* house and was told I could reach you *here* now." There was a pause while Langdon obviously hoped to get some dirt, and straight from the source at that.

"I'm glad you tracked me down," Angie replied, refusing to play along. "What can I do for you?"

Trying not to sound disappointed, Langdon continued. "I just wanted to tell you what a great job you did with the old Montgomery place. Clark and I were so impressed! And I *saw* Lydia Carmichael take one of your cards! You must be so proud!"

"Thank you, Langdon. I appreciate you saying so."

"Yes. Well."

Angie bit her lip to keep from laughing. She could practically hear Langdon pursing her lips in frustration.

"I actually have a proposition for you," the other woman said.

Angie perked up. "Oh yes?"

"See, I know once word gets around that the governor and his wife like your work, well you're just gonna be swamped, so I wanted to call you now, even if it is a leetle bit early." Langdon giggled. "You see . . . I'm pregnant!" She paused again.

Angie realized she needed to react to this news, although she couldn't quite see what it had to do with her.

"Congratulations, Langdon! I know you and Clark are so pleased." Angie hoped she had put enough enthusiasm into her voice that Langdon would get to the purpose of the call.

"Thank you, honey. I knew you'd be tickled for us. But that's why I called, actually. Clark and I have decided which room we want the nursery to be, and we want *you* to decorate it!"

Angie closed her eyes. The woman managed to make it sound as if she was bestowing the greatest gift, hand to God. Still, her first job offer. It *was* exciting, even if it was Langdon Howard.

"What did you have in mind, Langdon?"

"Can you keep a secret?" Langdon whispered.

"Of course." Angie assured her.

"It's a boy!"

"Oh. Well . . . good." Angie bit her lip again.

"So we want blues, obviously," Langdon continued on in a rush.

"Obviously," Angie agreed. This was getting silly. She had to stop it. "Before we go any further, let me tell you what I can offer."

"All right." Langdon pouted at being cut off.

"You and Clark will give me a budget for the room. Then you and I will discuss what you want and what's available within your price range. On top of that, I charge"—Angie thought quickly—"eighteen dollars an hour." Please God, let that be reasonable. She held her breath.

"Angie, that's practically a steal. With those kinds of rates, you are gonna be too busy to remember your old friends soon!" Langdon gushed. "When can we sign papers or shake hands or whatever we do next?"

Angie swallowed. What did they do next? She had no idea.

"Let's get together a week from today, next Monday. Say ten A.M.?" It was her day off from the diner and it would give her a chance to figure out what the hell she was doing. "I can have the paperwork drawn up by then." *I hope*, she added to herself.

"Ooh, Angie! I just can't wait to see you! Bye then." Langdon disconnected.

Angie stood, staring at the receiver. She had a decorating job. She had just accepted her first ever honest-to-God decorating job. Sure, it might be for Langdon's reputation, but it was also for Langdon's money.

"Chris!" she yelled as she headed outside. By the time she got to the back door, she was running.

Chris heard the kitchen door slam and turned to see Angie running across the yard. He took two long steps toward her before it registered that she was smiling and there was joy in the voice calling his name. Bracing himself, he was ready when, once she reached him, she launched herself into his arms, wrapping her legs around his waist and kissing him hard.

When she finally broke the kiss, Chris looked at her, puzzled. "I'm not complaining, mind you, but to what do I owe this?"

Angie threw back her head and laughed. "We did it!" She kissed him quickly then lowered her feet to the ground. "I got a decorating job!"

Laughing out loud, Chris grabbed her and kissed her again. "Tell me." Hand in hand, they headed back to the house as Angie filled him in on the call.

"All she wants is to be able to say Lydia Bain Carmichael used *her* decorator." Angie spun around the kitchen. "But I don't care!"

Chris watched and listened as Angie's enthusiasm came bubbling out of her. She was pacing the room, talking about shades and tones and textures already. Dressed in brown shorts, a thin red tank top, and loafers, she neither looked nor sounded like the woman he'd met just months ago. That woman had interested him. This one fascinated him. Plus, she still sounded like warm honey and had all those delicious curves.

"But Chris." Angie stopped, midpace. "I don't know what I'm doing."

"What do you mean you don't know what you're doing?" Chris laughed in disbelief. "Have you listened to yourself? I hardly know what half those words even mean."

"The decoratin', that's easy." Angie waved it off as she sank into a chair. "It's the business part. The contracts an' stuff. I don' know how to run a business, Chris." Dear God. What had she done?

"Whoa." Chris sat across from her and took her hands in his. "Slow down. Yes, you will need some business advice." Angie groaned, but Chris spoke quickly before she could get started again. "But not to decorate Langdon Howard's nursery. For that, a basic contract will do. I'll call my dad. See if he knows anyone who can help. If not, we'll figure it out ourselves."

"I need it by Monday." Angie sounded horrified.

Chris smiled at her. "Then I guess I'd better call my dad today."

Angie sighed. "I did get a little carried away there, huh?"

Chris couldn't bring himself to squash her enthusiasm. "It's good to be thinking ahead, though."

With a start, Angie jumped up. "What time is it? I want to tell Carter Anne."

"About four-thirty."

"She'll be home! Let me call her."

Chris stopped her as Angie reached for the phone. "Why don't you go over instead. Tell her in person. I'll give my dad a call, grab a shower, and meet you there. Tell her not to cook dinner. We're going to celebrate. Bobby, too, if he's not on call."

Angie threw herself into Chris's arms again. "That's perfect! Oh, Christopher Montgomery, I do love you."

They both froze. As Chris watched, Angie's eyes widened and the color drained from her face.

"I mean . . . that's not . . ." she stammered. She hadn't just said that. There was simply no way she had just said that. Angie closed her eyes and tried to pull away from him.

Chris tightened his arms around her. No way did she get to drop that and then pull away, emotionally or physically.

"Angie." She wouldn't look at him. "Angie," he repeated. Finally, she opened her eyes and met his. "I love you, too."

"You don't have to say that. You don't have to say it back."

"I love you." Chris spoke clearly, looking deeply into her eyes. "Not because I have to or because you said it first. Just because I do."

Tears sprang to Angie's eyes. She wasn't sure if she was laughing or crying. "Dammit, Chris Montgomery! You weren't supposed to say it back."

Chris laughed. Only Angie. He tucked her into his chest. "Well, Miz Angie, you weren't supposed to say it first, so I guess that makes us even."

Angie lifted her face to look at him. Slowly, Chris lowered his lips to hers. Before the kiss could deepen, could become more, Chris set her away from him. "Go see Carter Anne. Tell her . . ." He grinned. "Everything. I'll call my dad and be there by six."

All Angie could do was grin. She turned and headed to the front door. As she opened it, Chris called to her.

"Hey, Angie." She stopped in the doorway and looked back at him. "I love you," Chris said simply.

"I love you, too." Angie smiled wider. The walk to her sister's house was going to be very, very short.

Chapter 15

"I have to go away again." Chris's voice was low.

"What?" Angie looked up. She had been having a lovely daydream about decorating a nursery for her own child one day, instead of Langdon Howard's. Her child . . . and Chris's. Surely, she hadn't heard him correctly.

"Champ called again last night while you were getting paint cards. They need me back." Chris sat down next to her. The kitchen table had become her makeshift workspace. They were going to have to get her an office soon.

"For how long this time?" Angie wanted to cry. To scream. Something. Instead, she looked at her hands.

"Only a month, Angie. Half the time I was gone last time." Chris's voice was soothing, but it didn't help. He was going away again.

"Do you have to?" Angie looked at him, fighting back the tears.

Chris nodded slowly. "They need me, Angie. Men could die. I might be able to prevent that."

Angie choked. How could she possibly counter that argument? How could her half-formed daydreams be more important than lives? The tears filled her eyes in spite of her efforts to hold them back. "One month?"

"One month," Chris reassured her. He'd known this would be tough, just not how tough. Her tears ripped at him. But it was Champ . . . "You could come with me." The words were out of his mouth before he had known he was going to say them. And he regretted them immediately. It was too soon. He could tell from her reaction.

"No." Angie shook her head sadly, waving a hand over the baby blue clutter on the table. "I can't. 'Sides, Chris, I don't want to."

He reached for her hand and clasped it between both of his. "I know, Angie, but . . ."

She squeezed her fingers around his. "But I can be here when you get back."

"Angie." He pulled her into his lap, holding her tightly.

Angie let out one small sob. Lives. Sons, brothers, fathers . . . husbands. Lives. Against four weeks. She could do this. She drew a deep breath. It was shaky, but it helped calm her nonetheless. Sitting up, she looked at him.

"When do you leave?"

"Wednesday," Chris muttered.

"Wednesday!" Angie gasped. "But that's day after tomorrow!"

"I know, Angie. I'm sorry." Chris searched her face, looking for understanding. "I'm on a ten A.M. flight out of Greensboro."

Angie sighed. The Howard baby's nursery would have to wait thirty-six hours. It would be a good distraction, anyway. She stood up.

"Well"—she tried to smile at him—"let's go do something fun. And we should tell Bobby and Carter Anne this evening."

Chris's eyes twinkled. "I'll need a shower before going over there."

Angie buried her hurt. Lives. Chris was saving lives.

"Showers are fun." Her eyes twinkled back at him. She took his hand and led him upstairs.

Three hours later, Bobby opened the door. "Angie, honey, you do not have to ring the bell. You've still got clothes upstairs in your room." He accepted her kiss and shook hands with Chris.

"I know, Bobby." Angie laughed. "It just feels odd waltzing in here is all."

Bobby rolled his eyes at her. "Well, come on in. Carter Anne's just putting dinner on the table."

They crossed paths with Carter Anne, who was carrying a large, steaming casserole dish into the dining room.

"You're almost late," she said, kissing Chris on the cheek without missing a step. "Grab the drinks and come on in."

Bobby grinned at Angie. "Told you this was still home."

Laughing, Angie and Chris grabbed the glasses from the kitchen and followed Carter Anne into the dining room. Chris decided to wait until after they had eaten to say anything. Instead, they made small talk over Carter Anne's baked macaroni and cheese, green beans, and strawberry pie. Finally, when Carter Anne had cleared the dessert plates and refilled the coffee mugs, Chris spoke up.

"I've got news." He waited until Bobby was looking at him and directed his comments to the other man. "I've got to go back to the Springs again."

Bobby held Chris's eyes. "Got to? Or choosing to?"

Angie and Carter Anne exchanged glances, but Chris never took his eyes from Bobby's. "Choosing to," he admitted. "They've got some new intel. Champ thinks its right up my alley. I agree with him."

Sighing, Bobby looked away first.

"For how long?" Carter Anne asked before the silence could become uncomfortable.

"Only a month this time," Angie answered for Chris. She hated it, but she had to support him somehow. Directing her words to her uncle, she continued, "This could save lives."

The older man nodded, but his eyes seemed sad somehow. "You have to do what you feel you have to do, Chris." He looked to Angie. "You okay with this?"

"I am," Angie lied.

Bobby nodded again. "All right then. At least it's just Colorado, right?"

Chris couldn't relax yet. "And only a month. But . . ." He braced himself for Carter Anne's response this time. "I leave Wednesday morning."

She didn't disappoint him. "This Wednesday? As in day after tomorrow Wednesday?" At Chris's nod, she turned to Angie. "How long have you known about this?"

"Just this afternoon, Carter Anne. And," she continued quickly before her sister could turn on Chris, "he just found out last night."

Carter Anne's shoulders slumped. But Chris was watching Bobby. He had gotten up and crossed the room slowly. Surely this wasn't going to get ugly. Not with Bobby.

As Chris watched, Bobby opened the hutch against the wall and pulled out four glasses then a bottle of bourbon.

"Might as well send you off with the good stuff."

Finally, Chris relaxed. No, Bobby wasn't happy about it, but Chris hadn't expected him to be. At least he had accepted it. Chris could live with that.

The two men drank far more than either of the women. Angie would never understand male bonding. Still, it had worked. By the time they had left, Chris and Bobby were back on track. Watching Chris maneuver the stairs, though, she was grateful they had been running late so had driven down the hill. If he was having this kind of trouble with stairs, she wouldn't have enjoyed trying to help Chris walk home. In all her years, she had only seen Bobby drunk a handful of times, and it was a whole new side of Chris. They were happy drunks, at least, she'd give them that. Still, she wouldn't envy either of them tomorrow.

Tomorrow. Their last day together for a month. She couldn't think about it right now. She wouldn't think about it right now. Turning the light off in the house, she followed Chris up to bed.

Tuesday had, plain and simple, gone by too fast. As Angie stood waiting for the coffee to brew, she knew she was grateful for it, anyway. A quick call to Sarah and her shifts at the diner were covered for yesterday, today, and tomorrow. The rest of the day had been ordinary, sweet. A reminder to both of them, she supposed, why living through this separation was worth it.

She poured the coffee, still cringing at how much sugar he took in his, as his footsteps sounded on the stairs. Before Angie could turn around, Chris had slipped his arms around her waist. She leaned her head on his shoulder.

"I'm gonna try real hard not to cry. But I don't promise anythin'," Angie spoke.

Chris kissed her hair and rested his head on hers. She was trying, but her accent gave her away. "If you need to cry, you cry. It's not like you're sending me off to war."

"Oh!" Angie gave a half gasp, half chuckle. "I'm havin' a hard enough time with Colorado. I couldn't handle war." She squeezed him hard then moved out of his arms. "Here." She handed him his coffee. "Get some of this into you before Bobby gets here, else you'll grump at him all the way to Greensboro."

Chris sipped at the coffee gratefully. "I still think it's best you're not coming with us."

"I know. And I've realized you're right." Angie reached for his hand. "Best to say our good-byes here in private."

"And it's only Colorado," Chris reminded her. "I'll call so often, you'll think I'm still here."

Angie smiled sadly. "No. I won't."

Chris pulled her to him. Damn the coffee. He and Bobby could stop on the way down. "It's one month, Angie. Only one month."

Angie nodded into his shoulder until she could trust her voice. "I know."

The doorbell rang. Bobby had arrived. Chris kissed the top of her head. "Coconuts and summer," he whispered before letting her go and heading to the door. Angie wiped her eyes and followed him.

Bobby and Chris were standing in the doorway, with Carter Anne just behind them. Tears sprang into Angie's eyes at the sight of her sister.

"What are you doing here?" Angie sniffled, trying not to cry.

"I thought you might like company for a couple of days," Carter Anne replied simply.

"Thanks, Carter Anne." Chris hugged her.

Carter Anne hugged him hard before letting him move back to Angie.

He put his hands on her arms. "I'll call you tonight. I *promise*."

"You better." Angie tried to joke.

Chris wrapped her up, holding her hard but kissing her gently. "Tonight," he repeated. Angie could only nod.

Bobby picked up Chris's old duffel and the two men headed to the car. Angie stood in the doorway, her head on Carter Anne's shoulder, watching as Bobby's blue sedan made its way down the long driveway. As the car turned out of sight, Carter Anne closed the door and led Angie into the kitchen.

Angie burst into tears.

"Oh, honey . . ." Carter Anne went to put her arms around her, but Angie was reaching for the mug on the table.

"It's so *stupid*!" Angie cried. "But he didn't even get to drink the coffee I made him!" Standing there, one hand touching Chris's favorite mug, Angie let her sister hold her while she cried.

Carter Anne waited until Angie's tears had turned to sniffles before letting her go. Finally, she sat Angie down. Picking up the mug of coffee, Carter Anne paused. "You want to drink this, honey?"

"That would just be stupid," Angie said, wiping her nose on a tissue.

"But Angie." Carter Anne's voice was soft. "That's not what I asked."

Angie sniffed and tried to laugh at herself but couldn't. "Yeah. I do," she whispered.

Carter Anne put the mug back in front of Angie and poured herself a fresh cup, leaving hers black. Angie took a sip of Chris's coffee and cringed.

"How does he drink this? It's like drinking melted coffee ice cream, hand to God."

Carter Anne laughed gently but didn't move. Sure enough, Angie kept drinking it.

"How'd you get so smart?" Angie asked. Her voice was barely a whisper.

"I keep telling you." Carter Anne kept her voice light. "My magazines are good for more than just celebrity fashion."

Angie lifted her eyes and Carter Anne saw her lips twitch. It wasn't much, but it was a start.

"When do you have to leave for work?" Angie's voice was still low, but it was getting stronger.

Carter Anne shrugged. "I called out today and tomorrow."

"Oh, Carter Anne, you didn't have to do that." Angie felt the tears come again, but they didn't fall this time.

"Angie." Carter Anne was serious now. "I haven't called out once in two years. They can live without me a couple of days."

"You're gonna get me through this in spite of myself, aren't you?"

Smiling, Carter Anne sipped her coffee. "Sure am. So you can just stop fighting it."

Through the tears, Angie smiled. *Yep*, thought Carter Anne. *It was a start.*

Chapter 16

Hand to God, it was a slow day. Angie stifled a yawn behind her hand. Sometimes, she thought afternoons like this were more tiring than the days she never sat down. Sure, the days had been dragging ever since Chris left, but this was more than just missing him. This was just a long damn day. Her last lunch customer had left a little after one, and since then . . . nothing. She and Alvin had even run out of things to talk about, so he'd retreated back into the kitchen. Still, Sarah would be in soon. Maybe she would have something to talk about. And at least she would have enough silverware rolled for the dinner shift. Angie had rolled it all herself.

The bell over the door rang and she looked up. Maybe Sarah was in early. Nope, it was Bill and Diane Turner.

"Hey, y'all." Angie waved to them. "Have a seat and I'll be right there."

They both waved back to her as she turned to pour their iced teas—sweet for him, unsweetened for her. Why Diane Turner thought she needed to diet was beyond Angie, but everyone was different. She wandered over, teas in hand, menus under her arm.

"I don't think we need menus, Angie. Thanks, though." Diane smiled at her. "If I could get a fruit cup, please, that'll be fine."

"Of course." Angie managed to smile rather than sigh.

"And I'll take a slice of chocolate cake with vanilla ice cream," Bill added.

"I'll get that right out."

"And Angie . . ." Diane stopped her. "Do you think we could have a little chat when you come back?"

"I don't know, I'm pretty busy here." Angie laughed. "Maybe once the crowd clears out." Their chuckles followed her back to the kitchen. When she returned with their food, Diane slid over and Angie sat down next to her. "What can I do for y'all?" Angie asked.

"Well," Diane answered, "we were up at the old Montgomery place over Founder's Day."

Angie nodded. She'd seen them chatting with Chris—and taking one of her cards. Oh dear God . . .

"We want to redo the living room and were just wondering how much you would charge to help us."

"Really?" Angie looked from Diane to Bill and back again. Even with the cards and Langdon's phone call, she hadn't really thought anything would come of this. Hoped, maybe, but not truly and really *thought*.

"Honey, don't sound so surprised. What you did up there was nothing short of amazing. Of course 'really.'"

"Well." Angie took a deep breath and blew it out again. "Okay. First, let me tell you what I charge and what I do. Then you can tell me if you're still interested."

Bill nodded, businesslike, even with the cake in front of him, but Diane beamed with excitement.

"I'm chargin' eighteen dollars an hour right now, but I'll give you an account of the time I spend on it." One of these days, she'd have to figure all this out so she was ready for questions like this. For now, well, faking it had worked with

Langdon . . . "I'll have some questions about the room, and based on your answers, will present you with a proposal.

"Once you like it, you can either get your own contractors to do the work and just show 'em what I've given you, or I can get in touch with the folks who worked on the house and set you up with them."

"And what questions would you have for us?" Diane asked.

"First, are you just looking to paint? 'Cause if you are, you really don't need my help. Honestly, I'd feel bad takin' your money to pick out paint colors. So, assuming you're lookin' for more than that, what do you use the room for?" Angie grinned at Diane. "With three kids under twelve, it's gonna be mighty different if you want 'em playing in there or only on their best behavior.

"And then," Angie directed her attention to Bill. "There's budget. How much do you want to spend over and above my fee? 'Cause redecorating is expensive—but I can help you spend as little or as much," she added with a grin, "as you want. That would be part of my job; to find you the best deals for the look you want."

"Angie, I'm impressed." Bill wiped his mouth. "I had no idea you had such a head for business."

Angie laughed. "Honestly, neither did I until Chris asked me to do the house."

"Speaking of . . ." Diane touched Angie's arm.

"Diane." Bill sighed. "Don't be nosy."

"Oh hush, Bill. I'm not being nosy. Just sociable." She turned back to Angie. "Y'all do seem mighty cozy these days."

Blushing, Angie ducked her head. "We're very happy, yes."

"We're all expecting an announcement soon, what with you moving in with him and all."

Angie's head shot up, her eyes wide. A what? "Well . . . I . . . I mean, we . . ." *She* hardly knew what was going on between her and Chris and the *town* was waiting for an engagement? Hand to God . . .

Bill sighed, louder this time. "Angie, those are great questions. Can Diane and I talk about them and get back to you?"

Angie nodded, grateful for the change of subject. "Of course. Y'all take your time. Just let me know whenever."

"If you could come over some afternoon later this week, I'm sure we'll have the answers for you," Diane added.

"Oh." They wanted her. Angie bit the inside of her mouth to keep from squealing. "How's Friday?" I could be there by about four-thirty?"

"That's perfect." Diane smiled. "And thank you."

Bill reached for the check sitting on the table, but Angie got to it first. "This is on me." She stood up. "Y'all have a nice day and I'll see you Friday."

The Jones sisters were coming in as Bill and Diane were leaving. Luckily, Sarah was on the women's heels because Angie didn't think she could work right now. Laugh, squeal, jump up and down—those she could do. But not work.

"Sarah!" She grabbed the girl by the arm and pulled her aside with the news. Her squeals were as excited as Angie's.

"What are you doing to celebrate?" Sarah's voice was a whisper against the ears of the Jones sisters.

"I don't know," Angie admitted. "Chris is in Colorado. Carter Anne's in class . . ."

"Here." Sarah reached into her pocket and pulled out a ten-dollar bill. "Go get an ice cream. Fully loaded. On me." Angie opened her mouth to protest, but the other woman pressed the money into her friend's hand. "I mean it."

Grinning, Angie accepted. "So long as you let me buy you one once the paychecks start rolling in."

Sarah laughed and waved her off before heading over to serve the Joneses.

Once outside, Angie stood on the sidewalk and let the sun hit her face. Had she been tired just an hour ago? Two jobs. She had *two* decorating jobs. Sarah was right. Ice cream was in order. Shame Chris wasn't here to celebrate. Or even Bobby or Carter Anne. Well, next time. Because there would be a next time. And a time after that. And maybe even a time after that. With a giggle, Angie made her way to the ice-cream parlor.

"Angie!" Carter Anne slid into a stool at the counter, obviously trying to hold down her excitement about something. "Angie, come here!" She pounded the counter with the palm of her hand.

"One second, Carter Anne." Angie held up the coffeepot for her sister to see before making the rounds to refill. It was an odd time for Carter Anne to be in, but customers had to come first, especially since she wasn't crying.

Carter Anne drummed her nails impatiently until Angie returned. Angie couldn't help but laugh—Carter Anne was practically jumping out of her skin over something. "What is going on?" Angie asked.

"You got a phone call at the house," Carter Anne whispered, leaning in over the counter.

"So what?" Angie leaned in as well and lowered her voice teasingly.

Instead of answering, Carter Anne slid a piece of paper under Angie's fingers. Impatiently, Angie opened it.

"Carter Anne, I got a full diner here, so whatever it is . . ." Her words trailed off as she read the message in Carter Anne's neat handwriting. "Oh my God." She breathed. "Is this for real?" Angie looked up at Carter Anne, who was smiling proudly and nodding her head. "Truly and really?" Angie's voice was a legitimate whisper now, too.

"Truly and really," Carter Anne reassured her. "And you know what it's going to be about. You just know it. The phone was ringing as I was heading out after lunch. I almost didn't pick up."

Angie read over the note again then looked at the clock. "I'm not off until four, but I'll call her back the instant I get back to the house."

"But Angie!" Carter Anne started urgently.

The bell from the kitchen sounded. Angie shrugged to Carter Anne. "I don't like it either but . . . Just a second." She left Carter Anne at the counter while she delivered her order and handled two drink refills. "So, quickly, what did you say?"

"That you weren't available right then but that you'd call her back by end of business today. That's what I always tell people who call for the teachers."

"It's perfect, Carter Anne. I won't make a liar out of you. Thanks!" The two women clutched hands tightly, settling for grinning at each other instead of causing a scene.

"All right," Carter Anne spoke with a hard bob of the head. "I'm late back to the school. After you call her, call me. We gotta talk about printing up new cards so that people actually get you when they call you." She stood up then paused. "Maybe you need a cell phone."

The bell rang behind Angie so, with a wave, Carter Anne hurried out. Angie cut her eyes to the clock again. A couple more hours.

Watching the clock didn't make the afternoon go any faster but, luckily, the full diner didn't allow it to drag, either. Still, Angie was grateful when her shift was finally done. Trying not to race up the hill to the house, Angie smiled and called back to people who greeted her on the street, but she didn't stop to visit. Not today.

Once home, Angie crossed straight into the kitchen to the

phone without even changing into her slippers. Forcing herself to stop for a moment, she gathered her thoughts. Breathe. Be calm and remember to breathe. Slowly, she removed the number from her pocket and dialed the phone.

"Lydia Bain Carmichael's office. How may I help you?" The voice on the other end of the line was so cool. *Her* hands weren't sweating, Angie thought.

"This is Angie Kane, returning Mrs. Carmichael's call." She was proud of how controlled her own voice sounded.

"One moment, Miss Kane, and I'll see if she's available." Soft music played down the phone line. Angie leaned up against the wall, eyes closed, free hand over her heart. The music clicked off.

"Angie, thank you for getting back to me." Lydia Carmichael seemed genuinely pleased.

"My pleasure, Mrs. Carmichael," Angie replied. Her voice had suddenly risen. So much for controlled. *Just keep breathing*, she thought. "What can I do for you?"

"Well, first you can go back to calling me Lydia." Her voice was light and gently teasing.

Angie couldn't help but relax. "Of course, Lydia. And what else?"

"That's better. I was wondering if you might help out with our summer home on the Outer Banks. It's been in my husband's family for generations, and I think I've finally convinced him he's allowed to change the place."

"At least a little," Angie joked.

Lydia Carmichael laughed. "Exactly. So are you available?"

Angie swallowed before answering. She wanted to yell. Was she available for the governor's wife . . . hand to God. "When would you like to meet?" she managed to ask calmly.

"I don't know how long these things take. We like to keep

the house open for a little while after Labor Day, but the work could start sometime around there."

"Then I would recommend us meeting sooner rather than later." Had that really just come out of her mouth? Was she really standing here doing business with the First Lady of North Carolina? Angie reached over and pulled a chair to her, grateful Lydia couldn't see her.

"I like your attitude, Angie. I have a few hours free tomorrow, starting about ten-thirty if that works with your schedule."

"I can make that work." Angie lowered herself onto the chair before her knees could give out. "If you have picture of the house or ideas, you can show them to me then." She had to call Sarah for coverage tomorrow. . . . And get a fresh notebook; her current one had grocery lists in it along with her notes for her other projects. . . . And figure out what to wear. . . . Angie put her head between her knees.

"And *I* can make *that* work," Lydia said. "Come to the back entrance. That's where private guests are expected. Someone will show you in. Tomorrow at ten-thirty, then. Thank you, Angie."

"Thank you, Lydia," Angie replied, her ponytail brushing the floor. Before she could think, she disconnected the call, waited a moment, then, sitting up, she called Sarah at the diner. Sarah answered on the first ring. The evening must be as slow as the afternoon had been busy.

"Sarah, it's Angie. I know you've covered for me a lot recently, but could you take tomorrow? I wouldn't ask but . . ."

"Sure!" The younger woman interrupted enthusiastically. "I could use the extra money."

"Will the turnaround be too much?" Angie asked, only thinking of it then.

"Nope. I'll be here. It's not as if I am getting overworked tonight anyway." The bell over the door jingled down the phone line. "Well, what do you know." Sarah laughed. "I actually got a customer."

"I'll let you go, then." Angie was relieved. She had too much to do to chat. "And thanks again."

Just as she was about to call Carter Anne, the doorbell rang. Angie muttered and hung up the phone. Carter Anne was at the door.

"I got tired of waiting for your call. Bobby can cook his own dinner tonight. What'd she say?" Her words spilled out of her in an excited jumble as she followed Angie back into the kitchen.

Angie laughed. "I was just gonna call you and tell you to get your butt over here. I . . ." She placed a diet soda in front of her sister and paused for effect. "Have an appointment with Lydia Bain Carmichael tomorrow at ten-thirty to discuss redecorating their summer home on the Outer Banks." She grinned hugely.

"Angie!" Carter Anne squealed, hugging her. "Truly and really?"

"Truly and really," Angie insisted.

"I knew it! I just knew it!"

They spent the next two hours going through Angie's closet, finally deciding on a red linen sheath dress with a black jacket. Carter Anne made a quick run home and returned with a handsome leather briefcase and a leather folder with a fresh yellow pad.

The work paid off. When Angie looked in the mirror the next morning, she hardly recognized herself. Now, after an hour and a half drive, she was pulling up to the governor's mansion. If she only felt as professional as she looked.

"Ah, Miss Kane." The woman who opened the door smiled warmly. "We've been expecting you. Mrs. Carmichael is just in here."

Trying not to stare at the house surrounding her, Angie followed the woman through into a large room. Technically it was a parlor, but it had been made into an office as well. Angie was impressed with Lydia Carmichael's seamless combination of comfort and professional efficiency. What was she doing here?

"Angie." The woman herself rose from behind the desk and crossed the room, extending her hand warmly. "Come in. Would you prefer tea or coffee?"

"Coffee, please. If it's not too much trouble."

Lydia waved away the concern and turned to the other woman. "Coffee for Miss Kane, please, Nicole. And some peppermint tea for me if you would."

"Of course, Mrs. Carmichael," she agreed and left quietly.

"Now, come and sit." Lydia motioned to the love seat in the center of the room. The table in front of it was covered in photographs and a magazine or two.

Angie settled in and tried to appear professional. She would *not* be intimidated. This was just like the Turners' living room. And maybe, if she kept telling herself that, she would believe it.

"You said you wanted pictures?" Lydia asked, motioning to the table again.

"It helps to know what the space looks like," Angie replied. *No, really, Angie?* she thought to herself. God . . . She soldiered on. "Eventually I'll probably need to go down there myself to see it, unless the pictures are just really, really good. That's something I wanted to talk to you about, actually, Mrs. Carmi—" She caught herself. "Lydia."

The older woman smiled at the correction. "And what is that?"

"Well, as much as I would love to do this with you, wouldn't it make more sense to find someone local down there? Or at least here in Charlotte?"

Lydia waited while Nicole unobtrusively set out tea and

coffee service with shortbread cookies. Once the woman left again, Lydia answered the question.

"Of course it would make more sense." She poured Angie's coffee and presented it to her with two of the cookies. "Unfortunately, I can't find anyone whose eye I like and trust closer than Lambert Falls." Sitting back, she sipped at her tea. "Therefore, convenience be damned." She smiled and raised an eyebrow. "Does that answer your question?"

Angie sat back and smiled as well. "It certainly does."

"Then let's get to work." Lydia placed her china cup on the table and passed Angie one of the magazines. "That's the house. This ran about twenty years ago. It looks *exactly the same*." She stressed the end of the sentence with an eye roll. "Which is exactly the same way it looked for the twenty years before that. That is my one absolute requirement. You must promise it won't look exactly the same when we're done."

"This . . ." Angie gasped at the magazine spread in front of her. "This is your *summer* house?"

"A monstrosity, isn't it?"

"I just can't imagine where you live year-round." Horrified, Angie looked up from the magazine, but Lydia was laughing, thank God. "I am so sorry. That just kinda slipped out."

"Oh no, don't apologize," Lydia spoke through her laughter. "Before we lived here"—she gestured to the governor's mansion—"we had a lovely house just outside of town. Much smaller," she added, her eyes still twinkling.

"I just . . . well . . ." Angie couldn't seem to get back on track. Finally, she found her voice. "Lydia, I want to be honest with you." This was going to be tough, but she was determined. A magazine spread, after all . . . "I don't think I can do something this big."

Lydia sipped at her tea, slowly, watching.

"What you saw at the old Montgomery place," Angie spoke

to fill the silence. "That was just me and my uncle and his deputy busting our butts for Chris. We knew who to call and who to ask for what. But this . . . this will take people I don't know. Contractors and workmen and I just don't have that kind of experience. I really think you need a professional."

"Perhaps," Lydia agreed. "But what I want is a home. One day, Michael won't run again and we will retire. My biggest concerns will be keeping him out from under foot and spoiling my grandchildren. When that time finally comes, I want to be able to retire into my home, not just some anonymous house. Somewhere I'm comfortable and happy."

Angie could feel her resolve weakening in spite of herself in the face of this woman's force of will. Maybe politicians' wives ended up becoming politicians by proximity.

"If you truly believe you cannot help me with that goal," the First Lady continued, "I will respect your *professional* opinion. But my eyes tell me differently. The old Montgomery place is a beautiful showpiece, yes, but more, it's a home now." She finished speaking and sat back, holding her teacup, waiting for Angie.

Ignoring the magazine, Angie studied the personal pictures Lydia had provided. The kitchen was far too crowded. The living room too staid. The whole place was too dark. It was, despite its size and grandeur, a beach house. It should be bright and airy. And why was there carpet anywhere when it would just get sandy, especially with grandchildren running in and out. "Local men could do the work . . ." Angie muttered under her breath. Still looking down at the pictures, she missed Lydia's lips twitch into a small smile. Really, all she had to do was help with colors, make some design suggestions. So long as Lydia knew what she was asking the contractors for . . .

Angie looked up from the photographs. "So what colors do you just hate, because we'll need to avoid those."

Lydia smiled and reached for the coffeepot. "Have some more coffee and we'll discuss it."

"So we're meetin' again next week for me to show her what I've found so far," Angie finished telling Chris about the meeting. The story had come out in a rush, but she'd been jumping at the phone all evening, hoping it was him.

"Angie, that is unbelievable!" She could hear his genuine excitement and it warmed her to her toes. "I am *so proud* of you! What are you doing to celebrate?"

Angie giggled. "I took Bobby and Carter Anne out for extra-large sundaes. Even made Carter Anne eat every bite of hers."

Chris laughed. "Oh, babe, I wish I was there to celebrate with you." His voice had gotten lower, huskier.

"I do, too," Angie whispered back. That warmth was spreading, changing.

"When I get back, we'll have our own celebration, how's that? A bottle of champagne is in order."

"Followed by . . . ?" Angie was only a little shocked at herself. After all, she was a woman of the world now. She was the personal decorator to the First Family of North Carolina.

"Mmm . . . followed by extra-large ice-cream sundaes," Chris murmured. "But eaten in private. And naked."

"Oh really? Won't that be messy?" Angie teased.

"That's where the bubble bath and second bottle of champagne come in," Chris teased back.

At Angie's moan, Chris laughed deep in his throat. "Damn North Carolina feels a long way away tonight."

"I wish you could come home right now."

"Soon, Angie."

"I miss you, Chris." The warmth was changing again, turning to melancholy.

"I miss you, too." Chris could hear the change in her. Hell, he felt it himself. North Carolina *was* a long way away.

"All right." Angie nodded, even though she knew he couldn't see her. "Things going okay there?"

"They are." Chris was grateful for the change of subject. "I'm meeting Champ here in a minute to go over some new intel that's come in. Help him prepare for the briefing tomorrow."

"Tell me you're still coming home soon, though, right?" Where had that come from? Of course he was coming home soon. She was being silly.

"I am," Chris reassured her. "And I don't have to come back until the end of August. You did get that letter, didn't you?"

"No." Angie sighed. "You have to go back?"

"Just for a week. I didn't mean to tell you this way. I'm sorry."

"The letter'll probably be in the mail tomorrow, anyway. It's okay."

Chris paused. Now would be a logical time to discuss it. It had, after all, almost come up naturally in conversation. But he couldn't. Not after the exciting day she'd had today. It should probably wait until he got back there, anyway. In person. He waited a heartbeat longer to see if she would ask, then the moment passed. It could definitely wait. "Angie, I hate to do this, but I've got to go meet up with Champ."

"I understand. I'm glad you called though. I was bustin' to tell you about today." She tried to keep the disappointment from her voice.

"Me too, Angie. I love you."

"Love you, Chris. 'Night."

Angie sat holding the receiver. That hadn't been the conversation she had expected. How could she have had the day she had and now feel so numb?

Chapter 17

The little red convertible whipping around the corner was unmistakable. Angie stopped just outside the diner and waited for her sister to pull up. Anyone else and she would have just kept walking. It had been a long day, hand to God.

"What are you doing here?" Angie asked once Carter Anne had turned down the radio.

"Wanted to talk to you about something. Figured I'd give you a ride up the hill. Hop in."

Angie smiled, weary, and sat down. "It'll be rare day I say no to a ride up there, but especially not after a day like today. Thanks. So what's going on?"

Carter Anne pulled a quick U-turn and headed up to the old Montgomery place. "You remember my friend, Kerri Bartholomew?"

"The English teacher over at the high school?" Angie did remember. "Of course."

"That's her," Carter Anne confirmed. "She asked me today if it was true you were in the decorating business now."

"Really?" This should be exciting, but she was already tired and spread awfully thin. "What'd you say?"

Carter Anne laughed. "What do you think I said? I said you

were just starting out, but yes. She'll probably be calling you in the next couple of days. She wants a new kitchen."

They had reached the house. A kitchen would be fun. . . . Sleek and modern, maybe, with lots of stainless steel. Or warmer tones with earthen tiles and copper. She would have to meet with Kerri, get to know her better, of course. Angie slumped in the seat. Sure it would be fun but . . .

"What's wrong?" Carter Anne asked. "I thought you'd be excited. I told Kerri you would be."

"You what?" Angie gasped.

"I told Kerri what your rates are, what you do, all that, and when she asked if I thought you'd do it, I told her you'd be thrilled."

"Carter Anne." Angie tried to stay calm. "You can't just be committing me to jobs like that."

"First"—Carter Anne didn't much care for Angie's tone—"I didn't commit you. Second, you are in the decorating business, so you might as well get used to things like this. And third, Kerri Bartholomew is a hell of a lot nicer than Langdon Howard, and you're working for her."

"I can't take jobs based on if a person is nice or not, Carter Anne. And I'm *not* in the decoratin' business."

"Then why are all these people calling you, Angie?"

"It's just 'cause I'm new. Interest'll die down."

"No, it won't," Carter Anne insisted. "This is what? Four jobs in only a few weeks? Including the governor of North Carolina! I bet Lydia Bain Carmichael would be interested to hear you're not really in the decorating business.

"And you've only done one house. Imagine what'll happen when people *really* start talking. 'Cause you know Langdon Howard is already talking. This is your job, Angie."

"I have a job, Carter Anne." Why did this have to come up now, today, when she was already tired and irritable?

"So quit the diner and make this your job, Angie. You're the decorator to the governor, for God's sake!"

"I can't just up and quit the diner!" Angie burst out.

"Why not?" Carter Anne matched her tone.

Angie just stared at her sister and shook her head. "I'm not havin' this conversation." She got out of the car and slammed the door. Carter Anne waited until Angie was up the front steps of the old house before calling out.

"You're only mad 'cause you know I'm right." She headed the car back down the driveway, radio blaring, before Angie could respond.

Carter Anne was angry and confused. It had been such an overreaction, hand to God. And usually Angie was the calm one of the two of them. The only time Angie got this way was when she was tired and working too hard. Which meant she *should* quit the diner and focus on the decorating. Because, hand to God, she, Carter Anne Kane, was gonna kill her beloved sister if she didn't get some sleep soon.

Still angry, she pulled into the driveway and stormed into the house. Bobby was in his chair, right where she'd hoped he would be.

"Angie's such a . . ."

Bobby raised his hand. "You may be grown, but I still don't allow name calling in this house."

Carter Anne humphed and collapsed onto the sofa. "Well, she is one if you let me call her one or not."

With a sigh, Bobby closed his book. "What's going on with you two?"

"I suggested Angie quit the diner and focus on the decorating and she bit my head off."

"That doesn't sound like Angie." Bobby frowned.

"No. It doesn't," Carter Anne acknowledged. "I know the nursery job is making her crazy. Langdon Howard is a real . . ."

She stopped when Bobby raised an eyebrow. "Anyway," she continued, "the woman isn't making it easy. Plus, she's gotta be stressed over working with Lydia Bain Carmichael." Carter Anne sighed. She was beginning to feel guilty about how she'd handled the situation. Angie *was* under a lot of stress. "Add working full-time at the diner and Chris being away . . ." Her sentence trailed off. Definitely guilty. "I just wish she would do this decorating thing full-time. She's so good at it."

"Tell you what." Bobby picked his book back up. "I'll stop by tomorrow or the next day and see if she'll talk to me about it."

"Thanks, Bobby." She crossed the room to go make dinner. "You're the best."

Bobby accepted her kiss on the cheek then went back to his reading. He loved his girls, but hand to God . . .

Bobby eyed his oldest niece while she poured his coffee. She didn't look good. Truth be told, she looked like hell. Those dark circles under her eyes were new. And even though it was early, she'd managed to be cheerful first thing in the morning for years now. At least here at the diner.

"You feeling all right, Angie?" he asked before she could move along.

"Just tired, Bobby. Been staying up too late, I guess." She didn't quite hide the yawn.

"Won't do you any good to get sick, you know."

"Well find me more hours in the day and I'll sleep through 'em," Angie snapped. Before Bobby could even raise an eyebrow, she regretted it. "Bobby, I'm sorry. Really. I'm tired and grumpy and that's no excuse for takin' it out on you."

He reached out and patted her hand. Looking around, Angie saw the few customers she had this early were fine for the moment. She put down the coffeepot and rested her elbows on the counter, head in her hands.

"It's just not so easy with the decorating jobs and the diner. Especially now I've got Miz Carmichael. I was going okay before that. I just . . . well . . . so much rides on this one. But I can't ignore the others just for it. . . ." Her voice drifted off.

Bobby knew he had to tread carefully. "Maybe it's time to think about quitting the diner."

Angie rubbed her face. "You been talkin' to Carter Anne?" She even sounded snippy to herself. "'Cause she said the same thing a couple nights ago."

So much for carefully. "Maybe I have." Bobby sipped his coffee. "Doesn't mean I disagree with the idea." Angie opened her mouth to speak, but Bobby raised a hand. "First, I'll let you sass me because you're tired once but not twice. Carter Anne told me how you reacted to her when she brought it up, so I wouldn't speak too quick.

"Second, all we're doing is suggesting you think about it. Seems to me it's time to decide if you're serious about this. If you are, then the time's coming to do it. If you're not, then the time's coming to stop killing yourself over it.

"And third." He cleared his throat in that rough way Angie knew so well. "I've got some money put by if you need it. Might be enough to get you started at least. You're welcome to it."

Angie could only stare at her uncle. The desire to snap at him evaporated as quickly as it had come on. She took his hand. "I love you, Bobby."

He looked down into his coffee, not quite able to meet her eyes, but squeezed her hand in return. "I love you, too, Angie. I'm just looking out for you."

"I know."

"Now." With a final squeeze, he pulled his hand back. "Go pour somebody some coffee or something."

He left shortly after that, tipping his hat to the Jones sisters and dropping Angie a wink. Angie watched him go. How often did he ever give her unsolicited advice? And, on the rare occasions he did, she couldn't once remember him being wrong. She pushed the thought of the business out of her head as best she could, but it kept coming back throughout the day.

By the time her shift was over, all Angie wanted to do was talk to Chris. He sometimes called during their afternoon break and, hand to God, did she want him to call today.

The phone was ringing as she walked in the house. Angie jumped on it.

"Hi there." Chris's voice was warm. "I'm glad you're home already. I knew it would be close, but we broke early. How's your day?"

"Long and tiring," Angie answered honestly.

"Oh, Angie, I'm sorry." Chris was sympathetic. "Can you put your feet up and do nothing tonight?"

"I wish." Angie sighed. "It's just crazy right now." This was the time. "Actually, I wanted to talk to you about that. Do you have a minute?"

"Sure. What's up?"

"In the last three days, both Carter Anne and Bobby have suggested I quit the diner and try the decorating full time. When Carter Anne first said it, it seemed crazy. But now Bobby's said it too . . ."

"I think it's a great idea," Chris spoke without hesitation.

"You do?" She had expected a conversation about the pros and cons, not absolute agreement.

"I do. You love it. You're damn good at it. And you're already building a reputation. Pick one of the bedrooms upstairs. We'll turn it into an office until you can find space."

Angie laughed. It was happening so fast. "We just turned 'em into bedrooms."

"Then it's a good thing I know a decorator, huh?" Chris joked. "Look, Angie, to be serious a second, I really think this is a good idea. You've got talent, clients, space, financial support . . ."

"Wait," she interrupted him. "How do you know I've got financial support?"

"What?" Chris asked.

"Financial support. Did Bobby talk to you, too?"

Chris was getting confused. "What does Bobby have to do with this?"

"Aren't you talkin' 'bout him when you talk 'bout financial support?"

"No," Chris spoke slowly. "I was talking about me. I thought . . . Never mind. Why would I have talked to Bobby about this?"

Angie put her face in her hand. She really had to stop biting people's heads off, if for no other reason than it made her feel horrible. Sleep was becoming a necessity. "I'm sorry, Chris. Bobby offered to help me out. I thought the two of you, maybe even the three of you . . ." God, she felt stupid. "I'm sorry," she repeated.

"Hush, Angie. It's okay," Chris said soothingly. "You're tired, huh?"

"Yeah. I am," Angie conceded.

"Then know I think it's a great idea. I'd love to come home and find one of the bedrooms an office."

"And what are you up to tonight?" Angie wanted to change the subject before she flew off the handle again.

"We've got a couple more hours training, then Champ's taking me to dinner. He says he's got some friends he wants me to meet."

"That sounds fun." Angie was glad he was getting some personal time with his old friend.

"Angie, break's over. I'm sorry."

"No." She sighed. "I'm sorry for bein' so bitchy."

"It's okay," Chris reassured her again. "I'm going into the field, so don't worry if it's a few days before I call again. It's not because you were bitchy." He was rewarded by a laugh down the phone line. "I love you, Angie."

"Love you, too, Chris. 'Night." Angie hung up. Apparently, she was outnumbered. Maybe it was time to quit.

She went upstairs, wandering from bedroom to bedroom, finally stopping in the one at the far end of the hall. It was the smallest of all of them, perhaps had been used for a nursery once.

When designing the bedroom, she had used the muted rose that was consistent throughout the house but had added pale blue accents in here. It was a good room. The windows were oversized for the space, but that would give her plenty of natural light. Really, all they would need to change would be the furniture.

Replace the twin bed and dresser with a sturdy table. Add a couple of comfortable chairs around a small desk for consultations. There was even a desk still in the attic that might work. Angie turned slowly in the middle of the room. It would work.

Not forever but definitely for now. Until she could find a real space. Maybe down in the square. At some point, she realized, it had gone from a crazy idea to a done deal. She was going to have her own business. Standing in the middle of the room, she threw back her head and laughed.

"So you really did it?" Carter Anne stared at her sister in shock. She didn't even open their sodas but left them on her kitchen table, sitting between them.

"I really did it." Angie's expression matched Carter Anne's. "And he was very excited for me and understood completely.

Didn't even seem shocked. Langdon must be talking. Anyway, I've told him I'll stay until he finds someone, but he put the HELP WANTED sign up in the window before I even left."

"You're really doing this!" Carter Anne squealed.

"Tell me it's not a mistake."

Carter Anne took both her sister's hands in hers. "It's not a mistake. This is the smartest thing you've ever done."

"Truly and really, Carter Anne?" The reality was setting in.

"Truly and really, honey. I promise."

Angie took a deep, shaky breath. "Okay then."

"Okay then." Carter Anne popped open their sodas and lifted a can.

Angie picked hers up and clinked the aluminum together.

"To your new business." Carter Anne took a small sip. "Have you told Chris yet?"

"No." Angie shook her head. "I came straight here. Anyway, he's in the field, so I won't talk to him for a couple of days."

"He's gonna be so proud, Ang." Carter Anne could feel the tears coming. "I'm proud of you."

Angie looked up and saw her sister's eyes shining. "Oh, honey, don't. 'Cause then I'll get to crying, too."

Carter Anne wiped at her eyes, determined not to cry. "Do you have a name for it yet?"

"Oh God." Angie moaned and lowered her drink. "What about something classic and simple like Designs by Angie."

"Ugh." Carter Anne made a face. "We can come up with something better than that."

"Answers by Angie?"

"That's even worse. Makes you sound like a Miss Lonely Hearts or something."

They sipped at their drinks in silence until Carter Anne jumped up. "I've got it! A Touch of Home."

Angie thought about it. "I like it." That was it: A Touch of Home.

"So now we know what we'll drink to tonight when we're celebrating. Where are we going?"

"What do you mean celebrating? What are we doing right now if not celebrating?" Angie asked.

"This is not celebrating," Carter Anne explained. "This is drinking Diet Pepsi at the kitchen table. We do this way too often for it to count as celebrating. Besides, you know Bobby is going to want to do something special once he gets home and finds out. You might as well know where you want to go when he asks."

Angie thought briefly about the Inn at Ashby but couldn't picture Bobby enjoying himself there. Plus, to be honest, she hoped to celebrate there with Chris. Maybe even book a room for the night soon after he got home.

"Do you think he'd go down to Greensboro?" Angie finally asked.

"Tonight, Angie, I think he'd go all the way to Myrtle Beach if you asked him to."

"Lord no." Angie laughed. "Even I don't want to go that far. I was just thinking maybe that fondue place we went for the school's Christmas party last year."

Carter Anne remembered it well. The principal had taken all the administrative staff there for dinner. Dateless at the time, Carter Anne had brought Angie along and then proceeded to spend the whole evening fighting off the advances of the husband of the principal's senior secretary. She'd hated every minute of it.

"Sounds wonderful," Carter Anne agreed immediately. "And Bobby can get as much steak as he wants."

"Which may make leaving the Falls easier on him." Angie laughed. Carter Anne pointed a finger at her, but Angie defended herself. "Hey, at least I'm willing to go to Greensboro and Danville. And"—she put her nose in the air haughtily—"of course my personal appointments at the governor's summer home in Nags Head."

"Of course." Carter Anne matched her tone to Angie's. "You know," she dropped back into her normal voice, "steak'll get Bobby to Greensboro. I swear, I don't think even the governor could get him to Nags Head."

Chapter 18

The stacks of baby magazines, wallpaper patterns, and books on nineteenth-century furniture were taunting her. Angie stared at them through glazed eyes. She was tired, hand to God. Lots of people held down more than one job. She just had no idea how they did it.

In the time since she had taken on the governor's beach house, she'd gotten three more decorating jobs: the Turners wanted to wallpaper their formal living areas; Kerri Bartholomew was definitely interested; and Amy's mother had decided that she liked the old-fashioned look of the ice-cream parlor where Amy worked, so she wanted her living room done to look like it was 1890 or so. Angie had tried, albeit gently, to discourage this last one but had been unsuccessful. It would ease up once she was truly finished at the diner, but for now, she was, well, she was just damn tired. And the stacks were taunting her.

She should never have sat down in the first place. That had been her mistake. Sitting in the parlor instead of going straight upstairs and going to work. She was going to need an office soon. With a sigh, she reached for the mail she had brought in with her instead of getting up. At this point, it was easier than moving. Chris's handwriting made her smile, even though she was expecting the letter. Leaning back, she curled her legs under her and settled in to read his letter.

Dear Angie,

I hope this letter finds you well. How is the hot new decorator of Lambert Falls? By the time you read this, I'm sure you will have already told me about another job or two you've picked up.

The guys here are really getting in shape for what they'll need to do. I'm proud of them and how hard they're working. Of course, they wear the Green Beret, so I wouldn't expect anything less.

Have I told you about having dinner with Champ and the general, yet? They took me out for steaks. I had forgotten how great steaks are when they're fresh here in cattle country. They just aren't the same when they've been packed on ice and shipped cross-country. Maybe one day I can get you out here to taste them for yourself. Anyway, Champ had obviously been talking to the general about me and the general wanted to meet me. He has some interesting ideas I want to talk to you about. We did agree I will come back for one more week at the end of August, just to finish things up.

She paused in her reading. What? She reread the phrase "interesting ideas I want to talk to you about." They had spoken at least twice since he put this in the mail, and he hadn't mentioned it to her. That didn't seem like Chris. Shaking her head, she went back to the letter.

I know you probably don't like that idea. Still, it's only a week, Angie. Maybe you could come with me and

check out Colorado. I really think you'd like it out here.
Think about it anyway, okay?

Well, I need to close this down because it's getting
late. I think about you every night before I go to bed and
every morning when I wake.

Love,
Chris

Angie reread the entire letter slowly, trying to ignore the
knot growing in her stomach. She finished the letter a second
time and headed upstairs, the paper still in her fist.

All of Chris's letters were in her bedside table. The one other
from this trip was on top. Praying she was remembering incorrectly, she scanned it for the few sentences she wanted to double-
check. The knot in her stomach grew as she reread his words.

Champ says he's never seen a consultant connect so
well with the guys. That's high praise coming from him.
I think it's because I not only remember being in their
shoes but am really enjoying what I'm doing here.

I had forgotten the good parts of military life. The
friendships, the simplicity of it. Of course, in my current
role, I don't have to deal with any of the horrible crap
that made me get out in the first place. It's a nice change,
I must admit.

The letter had gone on, so she hadn't paid that close attention to these paragraphs. Until now. Surely he wasn't saying
what she thought he was saying. But . . . Her stomach hurt. She
sat down on the bed and put her head in her hands. Trust,
Bobby had told her. Well, she was trying. But it was hard. It
was really, really hard.

Squaring her shoulders, Angie sat back up. Very deliberately, she placed both letters in the drawer and closed it. She had work to do.

"Bobby wants you to come to dinner tonight." Carter Anne slipped onto a stool at the counter. "Thinks you're working too hard and is worried about you. 'Course, I'm not supposed to tell you that part, just bribe you with burgers and potato salad."

"Your homemade potato salad?" Angie asked.

"Like I'd serve anything else," Carter Anne huffed. "'Sides, it wouldn't be much of a bribe if you could just buy it at the grocery yourself."

Company tonight would be nice. Seemed all she did these days was go from work at the diner to work at the house and back again. And Carter Anne's potato salad was more than worth taking a night off from the decorating business.

"I'll make enough for you to take some home," Carter Anne added in a singsong way.

"Deal," Angie agreed. It was easier than arguing. "And tell Bobby I'm okay. Tired but okay." She couldn't tell Carter Anne about the letters. Not here.

"I'll tell him," Carter Anne said. "But he won't believe me. Come to dinner and let him see for himself. That'll put him at ease. That and you finally finishing up here."

"Yeah." Angie nodded. "That'll put me at ease, too. You want breakfast or coffee or something?"

"No, I'm heading into work now. Just wanted to stop in and get you to dinner." She stood up.

"I'll see you tonight," Angie assured her. "But there'd better be plenty of potato salad."

Carter Anne was as good as her word when Angie walked in the house later. There was a large Tupperware container of potato salad waiting on the top shelf of the refrigerator, all for Angie.

"Thanks, Carter Anne. I appreciate it," Angie said flatly. She pulled a Diet Pepsi from the lower shelf. Carter Anne watched her slump at the table.

"It's going to take a hell of a lot more than that to convince Bobby you're okay. In fact, I'm beginning to wonder if he's worrying enough."

Angie stood and crossed to the counter. "Tired, remember? What can I do to help?"

Carter Anne didn't like it, but she let it go. For now. "Slice the tomatoes and onions for the burgers while I make the salad."

The vegetables were on the counter, so Angie pulled a knife from the butcher block and started slicing. She yawned once, for show. Maybe she wasn't in the mood for company after all.

Bobby came in with the burgers on a plate, two of them covered in melted cheese. "Thought I heard your voice, Angie." He leaned in and let her kiss his cheek. "These are perfect, so let's eat."

Angie and Carter Anne followed him into the dining room with the rest of the meal. Someone, Carter Anne probably, had already set the table. Angie felt a pang of guilt for wondering if she should be there or not. She would just find some enthusiasm, for Bobby's sake.

"So the new girl starts at the diner next week. I got the word today." Angie wondered if her voice sounded as forced to them as it did to herself. "Saturday is my last shift, and then I'll be a full-time decorator."

"That's great, Ang!" Carter Anne exclaimed.

Bobby nodded. "Now maybe you can get some rest."

"I hardly remember what that word means." Angie tried to laugh.

"You know the decorating thing is going to work out, right?" Carter Anne asked reassuringly.

"It better since I don't have another job." Angie sighed.

"What's going on at the school, Carter Anne?" She had to change the subject. Please God, her sister would have stories.

Bobby looked warily at Angie, opened his mouth, and then closed it again. Angie would talk in her own time. The key was waiting her out and being there when she was ready.

The night was still warm but not uncomfortably hot, and the wind was rustling through the leaves. A perfect summer's night. Angie wished she was enjoying it more.

"I wondered where you'd gone to." Bobby lowered himself onto the steps next to her.

"Carter Anne got a call while you were upstairs, so I finished cleaning up dinner. Guess I just didn't feel like leaving yet." Instinctively, she rested her head on Bobby's shoulder and let him put an arm around her.

"Figured you hadn't just up and left without saying so."

"No, I'm just lookin' at the night."

Bobby sat in silence and waited.

"That house gets pretty big when he's not sharin' it with me." Angie sighed.

"So I would imagine."

"It wasn't so big last time."

"No," Bobby spoke gently. "It probably wasn't."

"I miss him, Bobby." Angie's voice was barely a whisper.

He kissed her head. "I know, honey." Bobby took a deep breath. "You can stay the night here if you'd like. Think there're even clean sheets on your bed."

Angie smiled a little into the darkness. Bobby had never mentioned her gradual moving out. It had to pain him to even mention it that vaguely. "I don't know where I want to be, that's the problem. When I'm here, I want to be there. But when I'm there, it's too big and I want to be here. What's wrong with me, Bobby?" She brushed at her cheeks roughly.

"You're in love, Angie. Simple as that. And he's not here. So

no matter where you are, it doesn't feel quite right." Bobby
stared out into the night himself. Please let him be saying the
right thing. "It'll settle down for you once life settles back down."

"What if it doesn't settle down?" she asked timidly.

"Why wouldn't it?"

"He's writin' stuff, Bobby. Stuff that makes me wonder if
it's gonna settle. If *he's* gonna settle."

"What's he saying?"

Angie managed to tell him what was in Chris's letters, but
her voice kept cracking. Bobby listened in silence then thought
for a moment. Damn fool man. Hadn't he paid attention to the
woman he was courting? He didn't speak until he was sure he
could be calm. When he did, his voice was under control.

"Well, that does sound like he might be thinking about
something other than full-time life in the Falls." Angie started
to speak, but Bobby continued before she could. "But until you
have a chance to talk it over, you don't know. And there's no
reason to be miserable 'tween now and then. Best to wait and
see what the man has to say for himself when he gets home."

"You're right." Angie sighed, then laughed weakly. "But
waitin' sucks."

Bobby joined her. "It sure the hell does." Her laughter,
weak though it was, was still better than her tears.

Angie stood up and Bobby followed her.

"I think I'm gonna go on home, now. Tell Carter Anne I'll
call her tomorrow."

"If she gets off the phone before I go to bed, I will." Bobby
nodded. He let her get a few steps down the walk before calling out to her. Angie stopped and turned back.

"Whatever happens, there'll always be clean sheets on
your bed."

Blinking back tears, Angie blew him a kiss. "'Night Bobby."

He watched her move into the light of the street lamp

before heading in himself. Carter Anne was coming down the stairs as Bobby came back in the house.

"Where's Ang?" she asked him with a glance over his shoulder.

"Went on home. Was feeling a little out of sorts," he replied.

"She did seem . . . funny tonight. Is she okay?"

"Come talk with me a minute, Carter Anne." He headed into the den and took his chair. Carter Anne sprawled out on the sofa.

"What's up?" she asked.

Bobby thought about it. Really, the girl only had suspicions. Still, if they were at all accurate, she'd need her family.

"Seems Chris has been writing things that have her a mite worried."

"Like what?" Carter Anne sat up, paying more attention.

"Nothing like that," Bobby said, reading his niece. "It doesn't sound like he's losing interest."

"He better not be!" Carter Anne was indignant. "I coached him on how to get her. I'll kick his ass if it was just playing."

"Now Carter Anne." Bobby knew he had to calm her down. Inside, though, he smiled. She could be a formidable opponent when she was riled up. "No one's going to be kicking anyone's ass. All she's got are a couple of letters she doesn't understand."

Not quite mollified, Carter Anne sat back again. *Oh yeah*, Bobby thought at the expression still on her face, *quite formidable*.

"So what *is* he saying?"

"He's got her thinking maybe he wants to spend some time out of the Falls." Bobby chose his words carefully. If Carter Anne turned against the man, he'd have a hell of a time winning her back, even if the suspicions were wrong. "Doesn't sound like too much to me, I'll be honest. All she's going on are a couple of phrases in some letters."

"Well . . ." It pained her to say it, but it was true. "Angie's been looking for him to break her heart since she first laid eyes on him. Might be she's seeing what she expects, not what's there."

Bobby nodded, proud of his youngest. "Might be. She needs you, Carter Anne. If her suspicions are wrong, she'll have talked herself into believing them anyway. And if they're right . . ." He let the sentence fade. He wouldn't believe it.

"Then can I kick his ass?" Carter Anne batted her eyes.

"Then you can kick his ass," Bobby allowed with a smile. *Once I'm through with him,* he added to himself.

"Thanks for telling me, Bobby. I'll keep an eye on her," Carter Anne said as she reached for the remote.

"I know you will, honey." He liked this show. Not many programs got police work right, but this one came close. Choosing one of the books from his side table, Bobby settled in to enjoy his evening.

"I'll go see her tomorrow," Carter Anne said as the commercials ended and the show began. "I got an idea."

"What're you thinking, Carter Anne?" She had the look in her eye that usually led to one or both of them being in trouble when they were younger.

"Hush, Bobby." She grinned. "Your show's on."

The next afternoon, Carter Anne arrived at the old Montgomery place, plan in mind. "Angie!" She opened the door and stuck her head in. "Angie!" she called again.

"Come on up. I'm in the bedroom," Angie called back.

Carter Anne took the steps slowly. Maybe if she lived here, she'd get used to their elegance and how regal they made her feel—but maybe not.

"What're you doing here?" Angie asked, pleased to see her sister.

"Came straight from work. I had an idea." She flopped onto the bed.

Angie pulled a T-shirt over her head. "Should I be worried?" she asked with a grin as her face popped out of the neck of the shirt.

"'Course not. Chris comes home in a few days, right?"

"Right," Angie said. She could almost give the time to the hour, but thought she'd keep that to herself.

"He needs a surprise." Carter Anne's smile was devilish.

"What kind of a surprise?" Angie was cautious. She had an idea already, but doubted it was what Carter Anne had in mind.

"A slinky surprise." Carter Anne popped up off the bed. "Let's go to the mall."

"Carter Anne, I'm tired. I've been on my feet all day after bein' up half the night working on the proposal for Langdon's nursery. The woman keeps changing her mind."

Carter Anne cut her off. "Then this is just what you need. Trust me." She put her hands on Angie's back and nudged her out of the room.

With an exasperated laugh, Angie let herself be herded downstairs. "What about Bobby's dinner?"

"He's working second shift. He and Jimmy can get sandwiches or Miz Abernathy will bring him a plate."

"You'd better hope it's sandwiches with Jimmy. He won't thank you for a night with Miz Abernathy."

"She doesn't give up easy, does she?" Carter Anne agreed. "Kinda pushy." She grabbed Angie's purse from the hall table and headed her out the door.

"A quality you know nothing about." Angie rolled her eyes.

Ignoring her, Carter Anne kept talking. "Do you think she puts that cat places so Bobby has to come rescue it?"

Angie laughed at the thought. "I wouldn't put it past her."

The top was down and the wind made conversation difficult as the pulled onto the highway.

"So you excited to have Chris home?" Carter Anne asked.

"Oh God, yeah. Carter Anne, it feels like he's been gone an age," Angie hollered back.

"Bet he's gonna be glad to be home, too," Carter Anne added. She watched Angie out of the corner of her eye. Her sister only shrugged. "Oh, come on, Ang," Carter Anne continued. "Coming back to you, to his fancy new house. 'Course he's excited."

"I don't . . ." Angie sighed. She didn't want to have this conversation yelling against the wind.

"Angie, Bobby told me what you're concerned about. Now don't be mad at him," she added quickly. "He just thought I should know."

While Angie wasn't thrilled Bobby had told her, she wasn't upset, either. It had been right. Besides, he hadn't broken any great confidence. This was family.

"What do you think?" she asked.

"I think you need to trust him. Wait and see," Carter Anne said simply.

"I have to, Carter Anne. 'Cause frankly, I've been miserable the last couple days, and I can't live like this."

Carter Anne patted her leg. "No, honey. You can't. And right now it's all in your head." She looked at Angie. "I don't mean that bad."

"No, I know." Angie squeezed Carter Anne's hand. "And you're right. I'm making all this up. I'm gonna put it out of my head, trust him, and live my life like all's well."

"And give him a welcome home he'll never forget." Carter Anne grinned.

"Actually." Angie turned in her seat so she was looking

directly at Carter Anne. "I've got something in mind I want to talk to you about." She smiled herself. It felt good.

It was good to be home. It would've been better if Angie had been able to pick him up from the airport, but he understood. At least she'd promised him he'd see her tonight. Because all he really wanted was a hot shower, a good meal, and Angie in his arms—and not necessarily in that order.

Holding on to that thought, Chris opened the door, hoping to find her already home. Dammit, the house was quiet and still. "Angie?" he called out, just in case. No answer. With a sigh, he stepped inside. The rich aroma of baking chocolate hit him. She *was* here. "Angie!" he called again.

Chris moved into the kitchen, following his nose. Angie wasn't in there, either, but there was a folded note card with his name on it on the table next to a glass of bourbon.

Chris, he read. *You are cordially invited to dinner in the ballroom at seven this evening. Welcome home. Angie.*

Chris tapped the card on the palm of his hand. He had been right; she was here. Somewhere. Still, he might as well enjoy whatever she had planned. It was six-thirty. Looked like he would get that hot shower first, after all. Picking up the drink, he headed upstairs.

From the pantry, Angie and Carter Anne peered out, trying to be silent, as they watched Chris read the card. Angie held her breath while he decided what to do. Only when she heard him on the steps did she risk turning to her sister.

"You sure this is gonna work?" she asked again.

"It's already working," Carter Anne whispered exasperatedly. "He'll love it."

"And this"—Angie held out the flowing black negligee she wore—"this isn't too much?"

"That, he'll love the most! You're going to make him crazy. It's perfect." With a quick peek to ensure the coast really was clear, Carter Anne led her back into the kitchen.

"It's not too revealing?" Angie asked with a tug on the bodice. She was practically spilling out of this thing.

"Angie." Carter Anne took a hold of her hands. "It's supposed to be revealing. You're beautiful in it. Relax."

Angie nodded.

"Okay," Carter Anne continued. The water ran through the pipes as the shower upstairs started. "I gotta scoot. Tell me again, one last time."

Angie rolled her eyes but did as requested. "In ten minutes, I fluff the rice and plate it. Ten minutes after that, I pull the chicken and steam the asparagus. Everything on the table by seven when he comes in. When the timer goes off, I take the cakes out of the oven. Serve them with the cream stuff in the 'fridge with the coffee and Baileys."

"Perfect!" Carter Anne grinned then lowered her voice with a glance at the ceiling. "And call me tomorrow." With a quick kiss on Angie's cheek, she slipped out as quietly as she could.

Angie checked the ballroom. *This* she knew. The small table in front of the open French doors was lovely. The night air blew in just enough to make the candle flames dance. She turned on the classical music Bobby had recommended and dimmed the lights. The candles on and around the table created an oasis of light in the room, just as she'd known they would.

The shower turned off upstairs and she scurried to the kitchen. Following Carter Anne's instructions explicitly, she had the plates on the table just before seven. She poured two glasses of wine and took a long, fortifying sip from one of them. Now, all she needed was Chris.

She was beautiful. *This*, Chris thought, *was what heaven must be like*. The smell of good food, light in the darkness, and, standing in the very center of it all, the woman he loved. The woman he loved dressed as he had never seen her before, at that.

Angie had her back to him, and the light from the candles outlined those fabulous curves through the sheer of the gown she wore. It was low cut, exposing her back almost down to the curve of her round bottom. She'd left her hair down, and it brushed low on her shoulders. Chris could just imagine moving her hair aside to replace it with his lips. He watched with this image in his head as she took a long sip of wine. Had *watching* a woman ever been this delicious or arousing before?

Chris took a step forward, hoping to slip his arms around her, but the old floorboards creaked beneath him. Angie turned at the sound and met his eyes.

"Chris," she murmured and then was in his arms. It felt as if it had been much longer than a month—and no time at all. He felt so right, so familiar.

All he could do was hold her. There would be time to talk, time to explore, later. Right now, Chris just wanted to hold her.

Reluctantly, he let go when she stepped away from him. "Come eat before it gets cold," she said, taking his hand. "And tell me everything. Or," Angie stopped him before he could correct her, "everything you *can* tell me."

Chris allowed her to lead him to the table. He sat but kept his fingers entwined in hers. "This is incredible, Angie. Thank you."

"I wanted your welcome home to be special," she replied with a smile.

"No one's ever done something like this for me before," Chris admitted, almost shyly.

"Then I guess no one's ever loved you like I do." Angie held his gaze.

Overwhelmed, Chris kissed her fingers.

"Now eat," Angie insisted with a laugh.

Chris took a hesitant bite of chicken cordon bleu. He loved her and she had obviously worked hard. He wasn't above lying. Automatically, he reached for his wine to help rinse it down, but stopped midreach.

"Angie." He couldn't keep the surprise out of his voice completely. "This is really good." He took a bite of wild rice. It was fluffy with a rich, nutty flavor. "Really good."

"Well, I . . ." Angie took a sip of her wine. "I've been practicin'."

"You can make this any time, babe." Chris sliced into his chicken enthusiastically. "How did you . . ."

"So tell me what you've been doin'," Angie said quickly. "Those guys gonna be ready?"

Chris swallowed. "They are." He filled her in as best he could but knew it wasn't much. Secrets were something else they would have to get used to. Finally shrugging, he finished. "I'm sorry I can't tell you more." God, he was a coward. What would Champ and the rest of the guys think of him now— nervous about bringing up a simple proposition. But how could he spoil this evening after she had worked so hard? And it would spoil it. She would hate the idea at first. It was going to be a long campaign to get her to change her mind.

"Chris?" Angie touched his hand. "You okay?"

"Sure." He found a smile for her. "Why?"

"You just went away."

"I'm sorry." He breathed deeply. Maybe he should . . .

A timer went off in the kitchen. Angie grinned at him. "Dessert!"

"There's more?" Chris groaned appreciatively.

"I'll be right back." Angie kissed him and padded into the kitchen, carrying away their empty plates. He watched her go. She was barefoot, he realized, pink-painted toenails peeking out with every step. Another woman would've added high heels or something with feathers to the ensemble, but not his Angie.

She had changed in the few months he'd known her, true. But she'd stayed the same at the core. Chris refilled their wine-glasses, trying not to stare at the door for her return but unable to stop thinking about her. How she had blossomed. Her new sense of confidence and style. Hell, she'd even learned to cook. Yet she still went barefoot for an elegant, romantic dinner.

His glass was halfway to his lips when he started to laugh. Oh Angie, not that much had changed.

When she returned, Chris was smiling into his wine. He stood and crossed to her, taking the tray of desserts from her. It was quite a spread: hot coffee, a bottle of Irish cream, and what appeared to be individual chocolate cakes on crème fraîche. Chris set the tray on the table and began to serve them.

"Let me do that," Angie protested, but Chris stopped her.

"I've got it. You've done everything else. I think I can pour coffee."

Why not, Angie decided. If Chris wanted to handle serving dessert, she'd let him. She settled back and accepted her coffee and Baileys gratefully.

Chris took a bite of his cake and moaned. "If I didn't al-ready love you, I would now. When'd you learn to make crème fraîche?"

"Crème . . . what?" Angie asked.

"The sauce." He twirled his fork in the liquid and licked it clean. "Crème fraîche."

"Oh. Is that what it's called?" Angie looked at her own plate.

"Didn't Carter Anne tell you?"

Angie's eyes snapped to Chris's. His mouth was twitching and there was a twinkle in his eye.

She laughed. "You caught us. But I really wanted it to be special."

"As I said." Chris took another bite of dessert. "If I didn't love you already, I would now."

"But you knew Carter Anne . . ." Angie looked puzzled.

"For going to the trouble of making it special, even if you didn't do the cooking." Chris winked at her.

Satisfied and only a little smug, Angie took a bite of her own cake. "So this is crème fraîche, huh?"

Chris reached out and took her fork, dipping it into the sauce. "It's not ice cream, but I bet it could be interesting." Angie smiled at him as he came around the table.

Chapter 19

"That's it!" Angie giggled, moving so the spray of the shower hit Chris directly in the face. "Some of us have to work for a livin'!"

Chris laughed with her and, reluctantly, stepped out of the shower. It seemed he was doing a lot of laughing these last few days. The one downfall was he hadn't found a good time to bring up Champ's offer. He didn't want to do it when they were having a good time—and they were always having a good time. But when she was working didn't seem fair, either. He finished drying off and went to his dresser, barely noticing what clothes he put on. There wasn't going to be a good time, Chris realized. And Champ needed an answer. It might as well be now. As if she had heard him, the water of the shower turned off. Chris sat on the edge of the bed and waited.

Angie came out of the bathroom, hair in a towel, wrapped in a robe. Chris noticed it was his and smiled to himself.

"Come here a second." He held out his hand to her. Angie took it and sat next to him. "There's something I want to talk to you about."

"This sounds serious." Angie grinned at him.

"It is, Angie."

Her grin disappeared immediately. He was holding her hand too tight, studying their interlocked fingers too hard. "What is it, Chris?"

"Angie, remember when I wrote you I'd had dinner with Champ and the general?"

"Yeah." Angie swallowed. "The general wasn't female, was she?"

"No," Chris assured her but didn't laugh at the small joke. "Nothing like that." He looked up at her, forcing himself to meet her eyes. "They've offered me a job out in the Springs. They want to bring me on as an official, permanent civilian consultant."

Angie shook her head. Her voice wasn't working. All her fears crashed back onto her. It was what she hadn't believed. What she hadn't *let* herself believe. "No." She finally managed. "No."

She threw his hand onto his lap and marched to her dresser. Flinging the robe from her body, she started pulling on clothes.

"Angie." Chris was behind her.

"Don't touch me!" She turned on him. "What did you tell them?"

"Angie." His voice was low, conciliatory, but Angie was having none of it.

"What did you tell them, Chris?"

"I said I had to talk to you about it," he answered honestly.

"But you didn't say no."

"That's right. I didn't say no."

"Well." Angie's chin rose. "I say no."

"Please, Angie, can't we talk about this?" Dammit, wouldn't she even listen to him?

She pulled the towel from her head and shook her hair out, not even bothering with a brush. "No." Her voice was ice. "I have to go to work, now." Without looking back, she headed to the room down the hall. Chris heard the heavy door slam, barricading her away from him.

Angie leaned her back against the door and closed her eyes. The tears had started before she'd even gotten all the way down the hall. How could he be doing this? They had made plans. Her business, *his* business, this house. They'd been building a life here, in Lambert Falls. She had trusted him. With a moan, she sank to the floor, buried her head in her hands, and wept.

Chris turned on the television there in the bedroom as loudly as he could bear. She wanted space? He'd give her space. And plenty of it. He hit the power button again before he could even register what was on. The hell he would. All he wanted was a real discussion about it, and dammit he deserved that. His feet carried him down the hall, but when his fist raised to pound against the door, he couldn't do it.

This was why he'd put it off. Because he'd known what her reaction would be. How could he be angry at her for reacting the way he knew she would? He rested his forehead on the door, breathing deeply. She needed space. Quietly, he turned and went downstairs.

The coffeepot was more than half empty. Chris had managed to drink it even though Angie had spoiled him with hers. When she came in the kitchen, he was at the table, just sitting.

Chris wanted to say something, reach out, close this gap between them. But he waited. Angie poured herself a mug of coffee and sat down across from him.

"I didn't react well. I'm sorry." Her voice was flat but sincere.

"I didn't handle it well, either," Chris acknowledged. "I want you to come with me. You know that, don't you?" Chris searched her eyes.

Angie nodded, sipping her coffee. "I do know that, actually."

She chose her words carefully. "And it's nice to know. But Chris, you know how I feel, too."

"I know you love me," Chris said.

"I do." The tears were back. "I really do. But I love the Falls, too. It's my home. Haven't you been listening this whole time?"

"I have been listening, Angie." He ran his fingers through his hair, fighting to stay calm. "I know you love it here, but I thought we could at least talk about it. That you'd at least think about it."

Angie nodded. That was fair. "Tell me about it."

"Technically, I'd work for one of the contractors the military uses, but Champ and I would be training missions. You and I, we wouldn't even have to live on post. It would be like me having any other civilian job. Occasionally, I'd spend some time in the field, but not often. And lots of jobs require people to do some traveling."

"But you gotta do this out in Colorado? You can't do this from Fayetteville?" Angie asked. The pain in her voice stabbed at him.

"It's something Champ's put together. Pulled some strings. It's Colorado."

"Colorado's so . . ." Her voice broke. She swallowed twice before she could continue. "So far away."

"But it's beautiful, Angie." Chris reached for her hands. She let him take them. "The Rockies make the Blue Ridge look like ant hills. And up at altitude, the air is so clean. The people are as friendly as they are down here. Come with me next week. Just come and see for yourself."

"Chris, if I go, it'll have nothin' to do with the place. How beautiful it is and how nice the people are, that won't matter." Angie squeezed his hands, willing him to understand. "It won't be home." He didn't understand. Not really. She could see it in his eyes. Chris Montgomery had needed to be at home wherever he ended up. The ties she felt to Lambert Falls were roots he'd never really had. "I wish you could understand how important the Falls is to me."

Chris sighed. "I do, Angie. But this is important to me, too."

"Why, Chris?" She struggled against the tears. "If you got outta the military in the first place, why is goin' back so all-fire important now?"

"Because it's Champ asking me." Chris's jaw was tight. He pushed his head into his hands, elbows on his knees.

"You've said you owe him. What do you owe him? Hand to God, Chris, I know what you've been through. What more could you possibly owe him?"

"Everything!" Chris snapped. He closed his eyes. They had finally stopped arguing. It wouldn't help to start again. Angie seemed to come to the same conclusion, because she reached for his hands and held them. Taking a deep breath, Chris looked at her. "I owe him everything, Angie. During the ambush, I should have died."

"I know . . ." Angie started, but Chris held up a hand to silence her. His hands were back around hers before he started speaking again.

"It was Champ who gave me cover fire, but he did more than that. The guys told me. Later. He knelt over my body and used himself as a shield, Angie. Even once they'd shot his legs out from under him, he lay on top of me, firing back.

"When the rest of the team cleared the unfriendlies, it was Champ who hauled me over his shoulders and carried me out. With two bullets in his own body."

Angie didn't want to hear any more, didn't want to think about how horrific it must have been, but she couldn't look away.

"A wound like mine," Chris continued, "Angie, he would have been well within his rights to leave me for dead or even put a bullet in me himself. It's sheer luck that an artery wasn't hit and I didn't bleed out. But luck had nothing to do with my survival beyond that. Beyond that, it was all Champ."

The silence at the end of the story battered Angie's ears. How could she ever compete with that? How could she say no? But hand to God, how could she say yes? It was too much to take in all at once. She needed some time. She needed to think.

She pulled her hands away, wrapping them protectively around her mug. "What happens if I say no?"

Chris stared over her shoulder. "Angie, it's Champ. Don't say no. Please."

Tears fell onto her cheeks. "I see." And she did. The answer to the question how could she compete with that was that she couldn't. He would go. The only question was would she be going with him. "Then I guess I've got some thinkin' to do."

"He's what?!" Carter Anne exploded. She could not be hearing this.

"Please, Carter Anne." Angie's head was in her hands, her elbows on the table. Bobby had stayed calm, but Carter Anne was now pacing the dining room.

"Angie, how could he do this?" No wonder Chris hadn't been to dinner. Bastard couldn't show his face. No wonder Angie had only picked at her food.

"He hasn't done anything yet." Maybe telling Carter Anne had been a mistake. At least until she'd gotten her own feelings in order.

"But Angie . . ."

"Carter Anne." Bobby's tone was the quiet one he'd used when they'd been girls. "Sit down. You're not helping your sister or the situation."

She turned on him, but Bobby just raised an eyebrow. Carter Anne sat down and crossed her arms over her chest.

"Well, I don't like it."

"I don't like it either, Carter Anne." Angie looked at her sister, eyes glistening.

Carter Anne softened, unfolding her arms and reaching her hand out. "No. 'Course you don't, honey."

"Do you know what happens next, Angie?" Bobby's voice was gentle again.

"He leaves Sunday to be gone all week." The knot that had settled in her stomach tightened. Chris had chosen to leave on Sunday instead of Monday so she could take him to the airport. She kept talking, forcing each word to follow the next. "I've asked him not to call while he's gone. I gotta think clearly about this one."

Carter Anne's voice was steely. "You want me to talk to him? Help *him* think clearly?"

Angie gave a watery laugh. "No, honey." She gasped. Everything hurt. "He's made his decision. It's up to me now."

"I know." Carter Anne sighed. The fight was going out of her.

"You coming back here while he's away?" Bobby asked.

She had thought about it. Hand to God, she'd thought about it hard. It would be easy to come home, hide in her room, and lick her wounds. But she couldn't. "That makes it feel too final, Bobby. I gotta see this one through 'til it's done."

Bobby nodded. She'd've been welcome—but this was the right decision. Thank God she could see it.

"If I go . . ." The tears in Carter Anne's eyes made it impossible for Angie to look at her, so she spoke to her uncle. "I can still come home, right?" Her voice was tight.

Bobby blinked once. "This is your home. This town. This house. And we're your family. Nothing can change that, 'specially not something like where you live."

Angie looked away. The words could not even be forced out any longer. Instead of making it easier to think, to breathe, telling Bobby and Carter Anne had only made it harder.

"I have to go now," Angie managed.

"Oh, honey, are you sure?" Carter Anne didn't want her to go. Angie nodded.

"Let me drive you." Bobby stood.

"No, no it's okay . . ." Angie protested.

"Angie." Bobby's tone was back. "Let me drive you."

Silently, Angie followed Bobby to the car. He didn't speak during the short ride up the hill, and Angie was grateful. If he had, she would've started to cry. Once she started crying, she didn't think she'd ever stop.

The next few days passed in tense silence. Angie spent as much time as she could at work in her office. Chris gardened and prepped the last trainings he would be giving the guys before they headed out. At night, though, they clung to each other, joining together, sometimes angrily, sometimes slowly and gently. Angie even thought Chris had cried once. She knew she had. But the sun would rise and bring back the distance between them.

Angie found herself relieved when Sunday finally came around. She had gotten up first and was waiting for the coffee to brew when Chris appeared.

"I'll pour this into travel mugs and we can get going."

"Oh." Chris was surprised. "I've . . . well, I made reservations with the airport shuttle. I didn't think you'd want to."

Angie met his eyes for the first time in days. Her words were hard but her tone was soft. "Oh Chris. You were wrong. You were so wrong."

Dropping his duffel, Chris reached for her. He couldn't leave like this. He couldn't live like this. Angie didn't even hesitate but folded herself into him.

"God, Chris." She sobbed into his chest. "Don't go. Just don't go."

"Angie," he whispered. "I have to. You know that."

Angie only sobbed harder.

"Come with me. Please. Angie, we can book a later flight and go together." It was a last-ditch effort, but he had to try.

"I've got work to do here, too, Chris."

"Picking out paint colors for other people? It can wait a week, Angie. It's not important."

Angie pulled back and looked at him, pain etched in her face. "You didn't mean that," she whispered.

God, what a low blow. He'd been reduced to fighting dirty. Disgusted with himself, he shook his head. "No. I didn't. I'm so, so sorry, Angie."

There was a horn blast from the driveway. "Dammit. Angie . . ." Chris didn't know how to make this right.

"Go on." Angie brushed the tears from her cheeks and kissed him lightly.

"Remember I love you," Chris said.

"You remember it, too."

As Chris left, Angie filled a coffee mug for herself and poured the rest down the sink.

Chapter 20

She had a week, so she would use it. By the time he got back, she would have made her decision. But, Angie sighed, that would require sleep. Rolling over, she looked at the clock. 4:47 A.M. Less than four hours. At midnight, she'd finally allowed herself to take a very light sleeping pill and even that had taken an hour to kick in, to counter the pain that had settled into her body after Chris left. Chris . . .

Even thinking his name caused her chest to tighten. Blinking at her tears, Angie sat up and wrapped her arms around herself. Everything hurt. How could everything hurt? Unaware she was doing so, she started to rock and let the tears come. If this was what losing someone you loved felt like, then she didn't want to ever love anyone ever again, truly and really. Nothing could compare to this. Nothing could be worse than this.

Not even leaving Lambert Falls? a small voice inside her head asked. *If nothing could be worse, then go with him.*

But this is my home another voice answered. *I don't want to go. Everything I am, everything I know, everything I love is here.*

Except Chris, the first voice insisted.

With a deep cry, Angie threw back the covers. This same conversation was what had kept her up until one. The conversation . . . and the pain. Getting up, she decided. If she couldn't sleep, she wouldn't just lie there. There were things to do, so she would do them, even if it meant forcing herself to put one foot in front of the other. A shower, then coffee, then work. Thinking and feeling would have to wait. A shower, then coffee, then work. Okay.

Angie wiped her eyes, went into the bathroom . . . and sobbed. He was everywhere. Why did he have to have a travel bag? Why couldn't he pack his toiletries, same as other people? Then his toothbrush, his cologne, his damn robe, wouldn't be staring her in the face. She buried her nose in the heavy blue-and-red-patterned cotton and breathed deeply. The smell of him bombarded her. God, she couldn't lose him. She couldn't.

Then go with him, the first little voice was back. *You haven't lost him and he isn't dead. Go. With. Him.*

No! the second voice insisted.

With a gut-wrenching groan, Angie forced herself to straighten up and let go of the robe. One foot in front of the other. Turning, she grabbed her essentials from the counter and headed down the hall to the second bathroom.

The shower hadn't helped. Neither had the coffee or the work but, hand to God, she was getting through the morning. Not even the continuous argument going on in her head or the even more constant ache in her body could make time stop. The clock on her desk actually read ten-thirty. She'd done it. Angie nodded. She made it until time for her appointment with Amy's mom.

Looking down at herself, Angie thought briefly about changing clothes. Sweatpants and a T-shirt weren't exactly her style any longer, but she couldn't find the energy to care. Mrs. Tallis would just have to understand. Or not, Angie laughed bitterly. Honestly, she didn't care one way or the other.

The notes and clippings were scattered all over the desk.

She was going to try one more time to change Mrs. Tallis's mind about the decor, offer some alternatives. The place would still be gaudy, in her opinion, but it would be better than what Mrs. Tallis had originally requested. If she liked them, great. If not, well, right now, Angie didn't care about that, either. She wasn't going to have to live there herself. But she did have to do the job. Methodically, Angie gathered the information into the folders and headed out.

"Angie, honey!" Mrs. Tallis threw open the door. "I'm so excited to see what you've brought me. Come on in."

Angie found the strength to return the woman's smile and followed her into the room in question. It inarguably needed work—the gold shag carpet was awful—just not late nineteenth-century ice-cream parlor, either.

"Mrs. Tallis," Angie spoke as she placed the file on the table. "Before I show you these, I want to explain what I've brought." The other woman sat back expectantly. Now was the tough part. Angie would have to be very diplomatic. Like Chris. Chris . . . She had to clear her throat twice before the words would come again. "I think I understand the look you want. I also think you can achieve it a bit less, well, drastically. What I've got here"—she patted the folder—"are bits and pieces that will suggest the look you're going for without overwhelming the room."

"Really? You can do that?"

Angie nodded. "Let me show you." She opened the file and spread out the pictures. "First, instead of red carpeting, make use of those hardwood floors we found under the shag. Use these runners and area rugs instead.

"A single, large gilt mirror across this wall"—Angie indicated the wall behind her—"instead of gold faceplates and outlets will keep it simpler, less fussy.

"And finally, instead of the red and gold wallpaper they have at Amy's work, hang these velvet curtains there on your big window." As she had spoken, Angie had laid out the pictures she'd found, creating the room she was describing. Mrs. Tallis looked at it, eyes wide.

"That's really nice, Angie. And you're right. A lot less fussy. Oh, honey, I knew I could trust you to do right by me. It's always best to work with people who care about you instead of strangers who just want your money. Why I heard from . . ." Mrs. Tallis stopped talking. Angie had tears in her eyes. "Angie, honey, what's wrong?"

"I'm sorry, Mrs. Tallis." Angie sniffed, blinking hard. "It's nothing."

"Of course it's *some*thing," Mrs. Tallis insisted. "If you don't want to talk about it, that's just fine, but you're crying. It's *some*thing."

"Thank you." Angie smiled weakly. "I just really needed to hear those nice things you just said about me."

"Well, you come by any time you need to hear nice things said about you. Tell you what." Mrs. Tallis stood up. "Let's finish this another time. Next week maybe? Would it be better then?"

Oh yes, Angie thought. *One way or another, it will be better then*. "Thank you, Mrs. Tallis. I'll call you once I'm in front of my calendar, and we'll set up a time."

"No rush." They walked to the door. "And I really do like your suggestions."

Angie smiled and went to her car. Noon. At least she'd made it through the morning.

Carter Anne's car was in the driveway. Angie breathed a sigh of relief. With the elementary school out for summer, there was no telling when her sister might take off for the mall or even just a drive. Get out of the Falls for a bit. What a joke that would have been if Carter Anne had needed time away just while Angie was struggling over staying.

"Anybody home?" she called out as she opened the door.

"Hey!" Carter Anne called back from upstairs. "I'm up here!"

Angie climbed the stairs and found Carter Anne in her room.

"Hi, Ang." Carter Anne was standing in front of her closet, holding two blouses. "What're you doing here?"

Angie shrugged, sat down on her sister's bed, and started to cry. Carter Anne pitched the shirts into the closet and moved across the room, wrapping Angie in her arms. "Oh, honey, shhh. It's okay. It's okay."

"But it's *not*, Carter Anne," Angie cried. "It's *not* okay. I don't know how to make it okay. If I go, I'll be so alone and unhappy, but if I stay, I'll be just as alone and unhappy. How am I supposed to choose, Carter Anne? How?" Her words dissolved into sobs.

Damn Chris Montgomery anyway, Carter Anne thought as she tightened her hold on Angie. And *she* had told him how to get Angie in the first place. Everything had been fine until he'd shown up. Maybe he'd made Angie happi*er* but she hadn't been *un*happy. She surely hadn't been miserable like this. Carter Anne did the only thing she could do: hold her sister and let her cry. Only when the tears had turned to sniffles did Carter Anne stand up and get the box of tissues. "Here, honey. I guess I know why you're here now."

"It's just so quiet at the house," Angie explained. "And there's all this noise in my head. I can't concentrate on work. All I can think about is Chris." She shook her head. "And I'd managed to stop crying but, when I saw you . . ." She shrugged again. The tears were threatening but she wouldn't—wouldn't—give into them again so soon.

"Have you made your pros and cons list like Bobby always

told us?" Carter Anne asked. If Angie was fighting the tears then she'd fight them, too.

"I have." Angie let out a tired sigh. "It's all I *have* done is run the pros and cons—only it doesn't matter." She rubbed her eyes. "I can't get past losing Chris or losing me."

"Losing you?" Carter Anne sat back down next to her.

"That's what leaving the Falls feels like. Losing a big part of myself. But losing Chris feels the same way. So it goes 'round and 'round, not making any sense and not getting any easier.

"You know, I was actually relieved when he left? Hand to God." She laughed bitterly. "It was so tense around the house, I thought I'd actually be able to think clearly with him gone. Now I just want him home again and not *have* to think." Her voice cracked and she buried her head in her hands. She was so tired of crying.

"Well, I can't bring him home any sooner, but maybe I can help you not think for a little while." Carter Anne patted Angie's knee. "Come on. I know just the thing."

"Carter Anne." Angie lifted her head. "I don't want to go shopping."

"For your information"—Carter Anne stood with her hands on her hips—"I wasn't going to suggest it. Shopping is *my* cure-all, not yours. And who knows you better than I do?"

"No one," Angie conceded.

"That's right. So come on." Carter Anne reached for her hand and pulled her off the bed.

Even after Carter Anne's statement, Angie was surprised when they pulled up in front of the ice-cream parlor. "You go in and get two of the biggest, gooiest sundaes Amy can make and something to take home to Bobby for later. I'll run to the video store and meet you back here." Carter Anne put money in Angie's hand.

"Carter Anne . . ." Angie started.

"Stop." Carter Anne's voice was no-nonsense. "You just stop it, Angie. This is what family means."

Angie nodded. It was too much work to argue right now. And besides, Carter Anne was right. "Meet you back here."

The parlor was bright, crowded, and noisy—the perfect summer afternoon hangout. She stepped in the door and looked around. John Hamilton was sharing an ice cream with his girlfriend while Johnnie Thompson watched Amy behind the counter. The Turners gave her a wave. She knew just about every name and did know every face. This was home. The now-familiar pain in her heart hit again. Before the internal debate could start back up again, she walked up to the counter.

"Hey, Angie." Amy's voice was gentle. "You okay?"

"Sure," Angie lied. "Why?" Word couldn't have gotten around. Not even here in the Falls. No one knew but Bobby and Carter Anne and they would never tell. How could people possibly know?

"You just look sad today is all. It's not like you," Amy replied.

"It's nothing, Amy. Really." Angie tried to find a smile but knew it was a weak one. "Could I have my usual and a caramel sundae, as well, to go, please? And I'll need a half gallon of butter pecan, too."

"Taking some home to Sheriff Granger?" Amy asked as she started making the sundaes. Angie nodded. This time, as small as it was, the smile was genuine. "You know," Amy continued, "maybe you should go to a movie or into Danville or something. That helps me when I'm feeling sad."

"Thanks, Amy. Maybe I will."

"'Cause I know you must miss Mr. Montgomery. How long is he gone for this time?"

Angie sighed. Maybe looking for company hadn't been a good idea after all. Still, if they thought she was just missing him, that was better than everybody knowing the truth. "He's back Saturday."

"That long again?" Amy gasped.

The girl obviously wanted to keep talking about it, but Angie . . . couldn't. She just couldn't. "When are you going to say yes and go out with Johnnie anyway? He's over there pining for you now."

Amy shrugged. "I figure before the summer's out. But I'm not letting him kiss me by the colonel." She put lids on the ice cream, bagged them, and passed them over. "Not at first, anyway."

"You're a smart girl, Amy." Her heart hurt. Her stomach hurt. Everything hurt. God, she just wanted to go home. "How much?" she asked, taking the bag.

Momma was right. There was something wrong with Angie. Seriously wrong. "Angie . . ." Amy started but stopped. What did she know anyway? "Tell you what, these are on me."

"Oh, Amy, I can't let you do that," Angie protested. "Carter Anne's paying anyway."

"One of these is for her?" Amy asked, surprised. When Angie nodded, Amy just shrugged. "Well then she can pay for hers and the Sheriff's butter pecan. But, really, yours is on me. And I really hope you get to feeling better."

"Thanks, Amy." Angie handed over the money and slipped an extra dollar in the girl's tip jar. "I'm sure I'll feel better soon."

Amy watched her leave. She sure hoped Angie was right and she got to feeling better soon. Angie not smiling was just wrong somehow.

When Angie got to the car, Carter Anne was already in the driver's seat, on the phone. "So next week then? Great. I gotta go now. Bye."

Angie slipped in next to her. "Everything okay?"

"Sure is." Carter Anne pulled into the street. "You get me caramel?"

"Of course." Angie lifted the bag. "And butter pecan for Bobby."

"He'll love it. And speaking of loving it, check this out." She handed Angie the video bag. "This is how we're spending the rest of the day."

Angie opened the bag and pulled out four DVDs: two Stallones, a Willis, and her favorite—Schwarzenegger. "Thanks, Carter Anne, but I was hopin' we might do somethin' together. That is if you don't have other plans."

"Well"—Carter Anne slipped easily into the driveway— "I've just cancelled my other plans and we are doing something together. We're watching those movies and eating those sundaes."

Angie could only stare. Her sister. Watching action movies and eating ice cream.

"Now come on." Carter Anne smiled. "It's time to not think."

It wasn't an easy decision. It was, however, the only decision she could've made. Even the events of the week had pointed her to it: Amy and the sundae; Mrs. Tallis; even Carter Anne and the movies. It had taken twenty-five years to build that here. How long would it take to build out in Colorado Springs?

This meeting with Lydia had simply been the final step, Angie realized as she drove back to Lambert Falls.

"Angie, it's Lydia." The woman's voice was warm, as it always was when she called. Didn't she ever have a bad day, Angie wondered? Even with the numbness that had begun to replace the pain, she couldn't pull that off. "I have a proposition for you. Michael and I are going to the summer house Friday. Why don't you and Mr. Montgomery join us for a long weekend? You can get a look at the place and have a bit of a vacation as well."

"Lydia." Angie sighed. "Thank you for the offer, but Chris is out of town. He's coming back Saturday, so I really couldn't."

"What a shame." Lydia sounded truly disappointed.

Angie made a decision. "I could drive down Friday and come back that night if that's okay with you."

"Five hours each way is an awfully long drive just for an afternoon, isn't it?"

It was also, though Lydia didn't know it, ten hours away from the ghost of Chris Montgomery and the pull of the town. Somehow, Angie knew she would make the final decision better if she could get away from both, even just for a few hours. "I don't mind at all," Angie assured her.

"Why, thank you, dear. Michael and I will be there by noon, so any time after that."

"I'll try to get there between two and three." Angie figured out the timing in her head.

"Perfect. I'll have Nicole e-mail you directions and tell Scott and his people to expect you. See you Friday."

So Angie had made the drive to the coast, arriving at two-thirty. Lydia had greeted her more as a friend than a business associate, with lemonade and an offer to freshen up, but Angie had wanted to get to work. The house held such promise, could be so beautiful.

The two women wandered, Lydia telling her which rooms were used most often and for what, while Angie took copious notes. Carter Anne had suggested bringing a camera and Angie was grateful for it. There was simply too much to remember. Finally, Lydia insisted they sit on the deck to discuss Angie's thoughts.

"The biggest problem," Angie started right in, "is the house isn't bright enough. We can do some with color but, well . . ."

She hesitated. "Depending on how much you want to do, you could take a few walls out. That would help more."

"Which walls?" Lydia was intrigued.

"The one between the kitchen and breakfast area, to start. It didn't look load-bearing to me and would open up the whole area. Not just when people are around but for the person cooking to see out to the water. That'll be nice even when it's just you and the governor."

"Is someone talking about me?" Michael Carmichael came out onto the deck.

"Michael." Lydia smiled. "Come meet Angie Kane, the woman who's helping me with the house."

The man moved to Angie and shook her hand with a firm grip. If he was impressive on television, he was more so in person.

"Mr. Carmi— Sir . . . Governor . . ." Angie stammered.

"Please, Miss Kane. I insist anyone who drinks lemonade on my deck call me Michael."

"Thank you, sir. It's a pleasure to meet you."

"You as well, Miss Kane." He turned to his wife. "I'm taking the boat out. Just wanted you to know."

"Thank you, dear." The look they exchanged was loving and private. Angie looked out at the beach, fighting back tears.

The governor kissed his wife's cheek and turned back to Angie. "Just please don't let her turn my office into a sewing room, Miss Kane."

"That's a promise, sir." Angie laughed, pleased to have regained her composure.

Lydia turned back to Angie before he had even gotten back into the house. "You said we could work with color as well?"

"Of course." Angie reached into her briefcase and pulled out several large, colored squares. "You said no greens and no reds or pinks. That's actually helpful because the house doesn't call for them. Here's what I've been looking at. If you really want carpeting, I would suggest you only use it upstairs. Let down here be linoleum or tile so you can stop worrying about sand."

Lydia laughed. "Oh, the housekeepers will be so grateful."

"I'm sure." Angie laughed gently as well. There was something peaceful about Lydia. This trip had been good for lots of reasons, not just the long drive. "Down here," she continued, "I would suggest natural materials to help complement the nature you're surrounded by. Earthen tiles that will clean up well and not be too slippery when they get wet and yet bring out the beauty of the place.

"In the formal areas, marble or hardwoods. The grandkids won't be running in from the beach to a cocktail party or sit-down dinner."

They spent the next hour exchanging ideas, Angie explaining why—or why not—certain things would work.

"Miss Kane," Nicole spoke discreetly. "Will you be staying for dinner?"

"What time is it?" Angie hadn't even been aware she'd been so wrapped up in the work.

"Almost six-thirty," Nicole informed them.

"Dinner will be in about an hour if you'd like to stay," Lydia said.

"No, thank you, though," Angie spoke to both women. "I've got that drive ahead of me."

"Very well." Nicole nodded and left the room as Angie began gathering her notes and paint samples.

"I do love your ideas, Angie. I would never have thought to take down walls. And I like that it's nothing like the Montgomery house. You've really listened to me. Thank you."

"They're two different houses," Angie explained. "They shouldn't be decorated the same. That's part of the problem you've got now. Whoever decorated last, decorated for a plantation home, not a beach house."

"Well, I'm going to tell people about you, Angela Kane." Lydia's eyes twinkled. "Get ready to be busy."

Angie took a deep breath. "I appreciate that, Lydia, but I might not be here long. I'm thinking about moving to Colorado."

"Are you now?" Lydia's eyes widened.

"It's only just come up, but"—Angie made a production of putting her things into her briefcase—"but it's something I'm thinking about."

Lydia sized the young woman up. Something was amiss, but she wasn't sure what it was.

"I mean, I'll absolutely finish this job," Angie reassured her. "And there'll be work for me out there."

"The governor of Colorado is a lovely man, but far too busy to worry about his house. I'll give him your name, if you'd like, so you can worry for him."

"See? There's work for me, even in Colorado. And really, I can do this anywhere."

Lydia wondered who the young woman was trying to convince. "Do you think so?"

Angie stopped packing her bag and looked up. "What do you mean?"

"You might not know this, but Michael was a senator for Tennessee many years ago. The party needed him, so we moved there, got his residency established, and he won the election. Served two terms. I'll tell you a secret, though." Lydia dropped her voice. "He wasn't a very good senator for Tennessee. He did his best and served them well, but his heart wasn't in it. They weren't his people. So we came home. Back to North Carolina. And he's an amazing governor. Because he really loves this state and these people." Lydia shrugged.

"Maybe this is different. Perhaps you really can do this anywhere. I would simply suggest you be sure."

"Thank you Lydia." Angie shook her hand. There were tears in her eyes, but she didn't think that mattered to either of them right now.

"Drive safely, dear. I'll give you a call next week about the house." Lydia's businesslike manner was back—almost.

The whole five hours back to Lambert Falls, Angie replayed their conversation in her head. And remembered the rest of the week. And thought about the rest of her life.

She would lose him. Chris was too much of a soldier to stay in one place for very long, in spite of what he claimed to want. She had known this from the beginning. When her heart broke, she'd have no one to blame but herself. But at least she'd be here. She'd have the Falls. And the voice in her head that had always been so plaintive before sounded with some shy strength. *Maybe a man who made her choose wasn't right for her anyway.* The thought startled her. This was *Chris* she was talking about. Of course he was right for her.

Except, the voice answered, *she had fallen in love believing he wanted to stay. Hadn't he believed her when she told him she wouldn't leave? If not, did he really love* her*, Angela Lambert Kane? Could he really love her if he didn't understand such an important part of who she was?*

It was time to stop thinking again. Angie turned up the volume on the radio, hoping to drown out her own thoughts.

Pulling into the driveway, she realized how late it was. Hardly a light shone below in the town. Angie opened the door, dropped her briefcase, and headed to the phone to check messages.

"Angie, it's me." Chris's voice was the last one she'd expected to hear. "God, I wish you were there. I know I'm going to see you Saturday, but . . . Well, I guess I just wanted to talk to you now. Hopefully you're okay. I . . . damn . . . okay, I'll try to call again tomorrow, and I'll definitely see you Saturday. Love you."

Angie replayed the message twice more before finally saving it and hanging up. It was too late to call Carter Anne, and she had no idea what that phone call meant. She did know that she wished she'd been here for the call as much as she was grateful she hadn't been. She pulled a Diet Pepsi from the refrigerator.

Although it was late, there was still time to get her notes in order for Lydia. She should get them done while they were still fresh in her mind. Especially because she didn't think she was going to be getting much work done next week.

Sighing deeply, she headed up to her office, the small room that had become *her* space in this big house. It would be good to throw herself into work. It would be.

She stood at the door, looking into the room. Chris swore it was chaos, but she knew what was in each pile, which stack belonged to which customer. And soon, she'd have to move all of it. Start over somewhere new.

The tears came again. She'd spent the last couple weeks crying, it seemed. If this was the right decision, and she thought it was, why did it hurt so bad? And what if she thought wrong? What if it wasn't the right decision? But what if being with a man who would ask her to leave was the wrong decision? The internal debate started again in spite of everything. Had she actually thought she knew what she was going to do? Work wouldn't help tonight.

It was too late to call Carter Anne, yes, but Bobby had the graveyard shift. If it was slow, he might be up for some company. Instead of going all the way back downstairs, she called him from the extension in the bedroom.

"Lambert Falls, Sheriff." He answered on the first ring. That was a good sign.

"Hey Bobby, it's me."

Bobby looked at the clock. "What's wrong, honey?"

"I'm just thinking. Wanted some company. You slow tonight?"

"Come on down," he answered without hesitation. "I'll even make fresh coffee."

"'Kay." Angie hung up and forced herself to move at a decent pace. If she let her feet drag the way they wanted to, Bobby would worry. The man knew exactly how long it took to walk everywhere in this town.

She walked into the station just as he was pouring two cups of coffee. "Let's sit over here." Bobby took the cups to the old, plastic-covered couch against the wall. It was uncomfortable but better than putting his desk between them tonight. Once Angie sat down, he handed her a coffee and sat next to her.

"So, what're you thinking about?" he asked.

Angie stared into her coffee then put it down without taking a sip. "Day after tomorrow."

Bobby nodded, waiting.

"I love him Bobby but . . . I can't. I just can't go all the way out there."

"I figured that's what this was about." He sipped his coffee.

"And"—Angie's voice dropped to a whisper—"I'm starting to think I shouldn't have to."

Bobby raised an eyebrow but stayed silent.

"Still, I need to know my own mind on it," Angie whimpered.

"I'd say you already do, Angie."

"I think I do but . . . what if I'm wrong, Bobby? What if I stay here and it's a mistake?" She looked up at him, eyes full of pain.

"What if you go and that's the mistake?" Bobby asked

plainly. Angie just stared at the floor. He rested his elbows on his knees and rolled his cup between his palms. "'Bout a year after your aunt died, friend of mine from the Academy called me. He's up in Alexandria. Said he could get me a place on the force there.

"Everybody said it was a good idea. Told me a fresh start—that's what every single person called it, 'a fresh start'—would be good for me, good for you girls. And I thought about it, Angie, hand to God I really did. You and your sister had gone through so much, losing your folks and then Abby.

"But I couldn't do it. I love the Falls. It's my home. Abby and I had a good life here. That was part of it. But I also knew this was a good place to raise you. If I was going to have any chance at all of raising you right, on my own, it had to be here. The town I know and trust and can trust who I am when I'm here. 'Cause I do know who I am when I'm here. Some places, they just get into you like that."

"So you think I should stay?" Angie asked.

"I'm not saying that," Bobby said, his voice more severe than he'd intended. He took a deep breath before continuing. When he did, he was calm again. "I'm not saying that at all. My decision might not be yours." He gave a sharp laugh. "It sure won't be Carter Anne's. She'll leave soon as she's able.

"I *am* saying you might be one of those people tied to a place. And that's not bad. Knowing who you are and where you are, those things are important. Some people go their whole lives without ever learning them. And no one, man or woman, is worth giving up the strongest parts of yourself."

"Thanks for staying." Angie leaned her cheek against his arm.

"All those years ago?" Bobby clarified. Angie nodded. "It was the right decision for me. Now it's your turn to decide what the right decision is for you."

"I wish I was Carter Anne." Angie sighed.

"And what would happen to Carter Anne if she fell in love with a man who never wanted to leave here?"

"Oh." Angie thought about it. "She'd be as torn as I am."

"Life's never as easy when you're living it as it is when you're looking in on it." Sitting up, he gave her shoulders a squeeze. "Any chance you'll be able to sleep any time soon?"

"I think so. Listening to you always did relax me." Her smile was sad, though.

"'Fraid we're past the point of Pooh helping much." Bobby sighed.

"Good ol' fashioned talkin' helped tonight. Thanks." Angie leaned in and kissed his cheek. She left the station, walking slowly, head down, more confused than ever.

"Damn you, Chris Montgomery," Bobby muttered. "Damn you to hell."

To say she'd slept would have been an overstatement. Dozed in and out would probably be more like it and, Angie realized, it was catching up with her. She stretched, not wanting to get out of bed. Anyway, it was nearly ten. When was the last time she had stayed in bed until ten? Hand to God, she couldn't remember. And Langdon would be arriving at eleven-thirty. Still, even with Langdon's appointment looming over her, the thought of getting up made her want to cry. The promise of a hot shower and fresh coffee finally got her up and moving. It wasn't much, but it was something, and right now, she'd take whatever she could get.

The hot water beat down on her shoulders. Giving the faucet a twist, she made it hotter. Anything to distract her from the debate raging in her head. Dammit, she'd thought she'd made her decision, but the debate continued on. Yes, it had begun to change subtly, but it wasn't any less painful or confusing. Still, she had work to do today: appointments with Langdon and then Kerri Bartholomew. And tomorrow . . . well, Chris would be home tomorrow. She'd just have to hope she had a *solid* decision by then. For now, Angie turned off the water and stepped out of the shower. There was still one foot to be put in front of the other.

Fortified with coffee, Angie figured she was ready, or as ready as she was going to be, for Langdon's arrival. Although she still hadn't found the energy for makeup, she had managed a pair of capris and a pretty T-shirt with lace around the collar. It was better than sweatpants anyway, hand to God. Right at eleven-thirty, the doorbell rang. With a sigh, Angie went to answer it and knew immediately she should have found the energy for makeup.

"Angie! Honey, what's wrong? You look awful. Everything okay?" Langdon Howard spoke in her usual prying rapid-fire.

"I'm fine, Langdon, but thank you for asking. Come on in." Angie stepped back from the door.

"Missing Chris, I bet, huh? I think I would just die if Clark went away so often."

Not even being this sad and this confused could tempt Angie into confiding to Langdon. The predatory, greedy look in her eye was too obvious. "Actually, I was just up too late with my sister watching movies. It's nothing. Now why don't I show you the final design for the nursery."

Langdon wrapped her hands around her disturbingly flat tummy and grinned. "Yes, the nursery."

Somehow, Angie managed not to grimace. Had she always been cynical, or was everything about Langdon really so calculated? Truth be told, she thought it was probably a little of both. Ah well. Her part of the nursery would be over today, and then Langdon was the contractors' headache.

Langdon settled in on the love seat in the parlor while Angie pulled out samples and the large paint cards she preferred. "I really think you'll be pleased with this."

"Before you start"—Langdon put a hand over Angie's—"I'm thinking about yellow again."

Inwardly, Angie rolled her eyes, but outwardly simply patted Langdon's hand. "I'm sure you are. Still, as we discussed when you went back to blue, it depends on how soon you want to redesign the room. What I've got here will grow with him until he's almost a teenager. I just can't see a son of Clark's having a yellow room, can you?" Angie smiled her sugariest smile and got one in return. The woman thought it was a compliment, hand to God.

"You're right, as always, Angie." Langdon sighed. "Thank God I've got you to do this for me. You don't know how the mind goes when you're pregnant, of course. It's hard to make a decision and you get all flighty. I'm surprised Clark puts up with it." She giggled.

"I'm sure he's already learned to make concessions for you, Langdon." Angie patted her hand again. "As we all have."

"And I'm just so grateful to everyone," Langdon simpered. "So let me see the blue room."

Relieved, Angie pulled out several pictures. "See how the shades blend from lighter at the bottom to darker at the top? The ceiling is the darkest blue, and kids love the glow-in-the-dark stars."

"Like the night sky!" Langdon clapped her hands happily.

"Just like that." Angie spoke through a gritted-teeth smile. "You can hang these planet mobiles that help babies learn and these bright suns and moons while he's still an infant. But again, it can very easily become a boy's room instead of a baby's."

By the end of the hour of discussing furniture, curtains and flooring, Angie was tired, hungry, and very low on patience. Yes, the situation and lack of sleep were definitely taking their toll. It was bad enough snapping at Carter Anne and Bobby as she tended to do when she was tired. She could never afford to snap at a client, not even Langdon Howard. Giving thanks for Kerri Bartholomew, Angie pounced the very next time Langdon paused to take a breath.

"As lovely as this is, Langdon, I'm afraid I have another appointment this afternoon." Really, there was no reason to tell Langdon it wasn't for another four hours yet. She did have another appointment, so she wasn't lying. Not really.

"Do you? Oh, Angie, how wonderful! Didn't I tell you this would take off for you? Honey, you are gonna be the toast of Lambert Falls."

"Thank you, Langdon. I hope you're right. But I'll be happy with just a small clientele." Angie stood and began to move them toward the front door. "Now, about the contractors . . ."

"Oh, don't you worry about that," Langdon interrupted her. She leaned in conspiratorially. "Clark knows people."

"That's just fine. Then I'll give you this now." Angie handed her the final file. "And put a bill in the mail." Langdon took the folder with a manicured wave and headed out.

Leaning against the closed door, Angie rubbed her forehead. On top of everything else, she was getting a headache. It was so tempting to crawl back into bed and stay there until she had to meet with Kerri. Instead, she went to the medicine cabinet. The one good thing about Chris going away was he always came back with 800mg ibuprofen. 'Ranger candy' he called them. Angie sighed. If it meant keeping Chris, she could manage with good ol' fashioned aspirin.

Tears came to her eyes again but she held them off. If she started crying, she'd end up back with the bedcovers pulled up over her head. She headed upstairs and forced herself to walk past the bedroom, down the hall to her office. There was always work to be done.

The sound of the doorbell actually startled her. About one-thirty, she'd stopped working on the Turners' living room and made herself a sandwich, but since then had been totally absorbed with the governor's office. It was plain fun working with another history buff. Before Kerri could ring the bell again, Angie picked up her folder and headed down. She thought she'd found exactly what they were looking for in flooring, and within their budget, too. So maybe, Angie smiled for the first time in weeks, doing the job was just delightful.

"Hi, Kerri." She opened the door, still smiling. It was easier with her because Carter Anne had been right; Kerri Bartholomew *was* nicer than Langdon Howard. "Come on in. I'm excited to show you what I've found."

They headed into the parlor. Yes, she would need a storefront soon. She couldn't use Bobby's den this way once she moved home.

The suddenness, the certainty, of the thought stopped Angie cold. Where had *that* come from?

"Angie?" Kerri looked at her, concerned. "You okay? You just went pale."

"I'm fine." Angie shook her head.

"Maybe you should sit down a minute." Taking her arm, Kerri helped her to a chair.

"Really," Angie insisted, "I'm fine. It's just been a busy day is all." But the tears were coming back, in spite of her best efforts.

"I bet there's a kitchen right through there." Kerri motioned down the hall. "I'm going to go get you some water." Practically before Angie could protest, the other woman was already back with a glass of water.

"It's okay, really," Angie tried, wiping her eyes.

"Whatever it is, Angie." Kerri sat on the love seat next to her and passed her the glass. "It's not okay."

Angie was horrified. This was the third client this week she'd cried in front of. It wouldn't do to keep behaving this way. "I'm so very sorry, Kerri. I just haven't been feeling well. I should probably have rescheduled."

"Then that's what we'll do." Kerri patted her hand. "Would Tuesday next week work? Same time?"

Angie nodded. "Thank you."

Kerri leaned in. "Do you want me to call Carter Anne? Or I can take you over there? It's on my way home."

"No." Angie sighed. "I think I just need to rest some. But thanks so much."

When Kerri stood, Angie started to get up with her, but Kerri stopped her with a gentle hand on her shoulder. "I can see myself out."

Angie tried not to cry. "Thank you again. And I'm sorry."

"Don't even think about it, Angie," Kerri reassured her. "We take care of each other 'round here, right?"

Angie waited until she heard the door close before heading upstairs. Embarrassed but grateful, she crawled into bed. Were people like this out in Colorado? Somehow, she doubted it. She didn't want to leave.

"Carter Anne!" Angie shook her sister's leg with a loud whisper. "Carter Anne, wake up!"

"What! Shit!" Carter Anne sat up and backed away from the person in her room.

"Carter Anne, it's me. It's okay," Angie assured her.

"Hand to God, you just scared . . . Are you okay?" Why was Angie in her room in the middle of the night? She turned on her bedside lamp. It didn't *feel* like a dream.

"I'm fine. Bobby's fine. Take a minute to wake up." Angie sat back so as to not crowd her sister.

"Okay. Wow." Carter Anne breathed. "What time is it?"

"A little after three."

"Oh, honey, couldn't you sleep?" Carter Anne hated what Angie was going through. If she couldn't make it better—and damn him anyway—at least she could keep her company at three in the morning. "You could've called. I would've come to you."

Angie waved her off with a shake of the head. "You didn't hear your phone. Anyway, it's not what you think."

"What is it, then?" Carter Anne asked.

"Damn Chris Montgomery to hell and back," Angie spat.

"What?" Carter Anne was shocked. Maybe this was a dream.

"Damn him. Who the hell does he think he is anyway? Wasn't he paying any attention to the person he was dating?"

Carter Anne sat up straighter. Apparently, it was time to pay attention. "Okay." She rubbed her face and brushed the hair out of her eyes. "Start from the beginning."

"I've been thinkin' the past couple days. I *don't* want to leave the Falls. I've *never* wanted to leave the Falls. And I told Chris that from the very beginning. It's who I am, and maybe . . ." Angie faltered. She didn't know about this part—or didn't want to admit it. "Maybe if he would ask me to leave, then he doesn't really love *me*."

"But, Angie, he *does* really love you," Carter Anne insisted. "You can see it in him."

Angie looked away, staring out the bedroom window. "You're right. He does. And I really love him." She looked back at her sister. "But this connection he's got to the Green Berets and his loyalty to Champ—I wouldn't ask him to give those up or expect him to change just because he loved me."

Carter Anne nodded, wondering where Angie was going with all this.

"Don't you see? It's the same thing. He can't or won't give up the important parts of himself for me, but I would never ask him to. Well"—Angie took a deep breath. It was right . . . but it was hard—"I can't and won't give up the important parts of me just 'cause I love him, either. Because then I wouldn't be *me*."

"And it's hard knowing he asked you to. Or that he doesn't know you well enough to realize what he was asking. Or something like that, right?"

Angie could only nod.

"You know I've never understood your connection to little old Lambert Falls, right?" Carter Anne kept her voice low so Angie wouldn't think she was being teased, or worse, criticized.

"I know," Angie admitted.

"But if I understand it or not, I do understand it's there and it's real."

"I just wish Chris had," Angie whispered.

"Not that I think it'll help much right now, but I'm proud of you and how strong you're being. If it's this important, you should be standing up for it." Carter Anne stroked Angie's hair. "You want to spend the night here?"

"I do," Angie admitted. "Thanks." She pulled off her sandals and shorts and slid in next to her sister. Carter Anne reached over and turned off the light.

"He did love me, though, right?" Tears filled Angie's eyes. Carter Anne wrapped her up.

"Oh, honey, yes. He did. And you loved him. Y'all just . . . need different things." Tears were pricking her own eyes now. "But yes. He loved you. Truly and really."

Chapter 21

The driver took his tip with thanks and a nod toward the parking area just off the house. "Nice little car you got there. How fast can she go?"

"I don't know," Chris said. He had seen Carter Anne's car as they'd pulled up. If she was here—and the car was proof she was, as much as he wanted to believe otherwise—it didn't bode well for the conversation he was about to have. "It belongs to a friend of mine."

The driver dropped a lascivious wink. "Can't understand why you look so hangdog then, with a friend like that inside waiting for you. Bet she's a spitfire, drives a car like that."

The man had no idea. "Thanks for the ride." Chris dismissed him.

Shouldering his duffel, he paused at the door. Would Angie even be here? Or was Carter Anne his only welcome home this time? Chris took a deep breath, squared his shoulders, and opened the door.

He saw them both, out of the corner of his eye, sitting on the love seat in the parlor. This wasn't how he'd wanted it to be. He dropped his duffel by the stairs and joined them.

Neither woman stood up as he walked in the room. Chris

went over to Angie and brushed a quick kiss on her cheek. She made a low noise in her throat but didn't pull away.

"Angie?" he asked, hoping for some warmth.

"Chris, you better sit down." Angie's voice quivered. He saw her tighten the hands she had clasped around one of Carter Anne's until they were white knuckled. He took the chair directly across from them and pulled it in close before sitting down.

"Carter Anne." He looked directly at her for the first time. The anger he'd expected wasn't there. Just a deep, penetrating sadness. "Could I speak with Angie alone, please?"

Carter Anne looked at her sister. He was hurting as much as she was. Maybe, if they could just talk . . . She was surprised at the sympathy she felt flood over her for him. For Angie. For both of them.

"I need her here, Chris," Angie answered his question.

"You've obviously made a decision," he said. But maybe it wasn't too late. Was she cold because she was protecting herself? Or because she had truly pushed him out of her heart forever? Damn, he wished he knew if it was even worth trying.

"I have." Angie took a wavering breath. It wouldn't get easier. "Chris, I've thought and thought. I really tried to make it okay. But it's not. I can't go to Colorado with you. I just can't." Tears filled her eyes but she blinked them back. There would be more than enough time for tears soon.

"Angie." Chris reached for her and this time she did pull away.

"Don't, Chris. Please don't."

It was time to find out why. He rested his arms on his knees and leaned into her. She looked away.

"Do you love me, Angie?" His whisper was intense. Next

to her, Carter Anne closed her eyes. A tear leaked from beneath her lids.

"Why are you doing this?" Angie asked, her voice breaking.

"Because I need to know, Angie." He waited.

The anger that had been building in her the last few days erupted through the pain. "Why, Chris? Why do you need to know if I love you or not? You've made your choice and you asked me to make mine. Well, I have, Chris Montgomery, and *my* choice is the one I've *always* wanted. What I always *told* you I wanted. And, if you think about it, it's the same choice you made: to put us aside for something else. So, I don't know why my feelings suddenly matter when they so obviously haven't before." She was running out of steam. The tears and the pain were coming back. "I'm thinkin' maybe we should go now, Chris." Angie stood and Carter Anne followed, but slowly.

"Angie, wait." Chris reached out but didn't touch her. "Just *tell* me. Please."

"Carter Anne . . ." Angie looked to her sister plaintively.

"Damn you, Chris," Carter Anne spoke though tight lips. "Can't you just leave well enough alone?"

"No!" Chris insisted. "I can't." His frustration took him out of the chair and across the room. "Because I love you, Angie. I want you with me. I want to be with you." Goddammit, how could he make her understand, because he *had* to make her understand. It was what Carter Anne had warned him about that first night—if he didn't do this right, Angie would never trust him again. Perhaps she wouldn't anyway.

He turned back to her, trying to find the words. Carter Anne tugged gently on Angie's hand until they were both seated again.

"Thursday," Chris continued, "I'm standing on a tarmac at an airfield, watching the guys get ready to roll. All these women, holding on to them, saying good-bye. Nobody looked happy, but there were no tears either. And I was standing there, so proud of the guys, and proud of the wives and girl-friends, too, dry-eyed, every one of them.

"Then the plane took off. Angie, I've never been left on the ground when the plane took off. These brave, strong women . . . they just melted. Oh, the captain's and the ser-geant major's wives stayed strong because they had to. But the rest . . ." Chris shook his head, part of him back on the tarmac. "They were clinging to each other. All the strength was gone, the entire facade they'd put up for their men was gone. I realized for the first time, it *was* a facade. Made to make the men feel better about going into combat and noth-ing more." He looked over at Angie. She and Carter Anne both had tears streaming down their cheeks.

Angie shook her head. She couldn't trust what she thought Chris was saying. It was touching, but something was miss-ing. "What about Champ?"

"Champ . . ." Chris smiled gently. "He was with me, there on the tarmac, watching the women behind his sunglasses. I'd told him, of course, about us, about you." God, she was so beautiful—and so sad. "He didn't even look at me, just kept watching the women. He said, 'Maybe we should all be forced to see this side of it before we join up. It's different down here.' Said he'd never thought about what his family went through every time he deployed until he stopped going." Chris laughed bitterly. "Of course, by that time, he was divorced three times and didn't have anyone to wave him off anyway."

Chris was torn. Champ had said things in confidence, but this was Angie. This was his life. There was only one choice. "He and I are close. I think I probably know him better than anyone else. And, as he explained, that was part of the problem.

"I've seen Champ bury men. Tell their wives and mothers a mission went bad. Take fire himself. And I've never seen him

even close to breaking until standing there on that tarmac."
How could he explain? He wasn't even sure it could be put
into words. From the look in Angie's eyes, though, he knew he
had to keep trying. Champ was the one who was good with
words—so, fine, he'd use Champ's words. Closing his eyes,
Chris tried to remember.

"Before his third wife left him, they fought a lot. They fought
because Champ didn't understand how much more he loved and
trusted his team than he loved and trusted her." The bitterness
in Champ's voice sounded in Chris's ears. "He denied it. Denied
it for a long time, but he finally realized she was right the first
time he stood on the tarmac with the people being left behind.

"See, Angie." Chris opened his eyes and looked at her from
across the room. This was going to be the turning point. If she
got angry now, he'd lose her forever. But if she listened . . .
"Champ's ex was right. We don't love or trust anyone the
way we love and trust each other. Not our parents, not our
siblings . . . not our wives."

He watched Angie's eyes go hard. Goddammit, he had to
talk fast. "And that's why Champ thinks we should see what
happens on the tarmac before we agree to leave it. Because
how can you *not* love and trust someone who is willing to do
that for you, go through that for you? Love and trust them
completely. After all," Chris heard Champ's voice as he spoke
his friend's words, "these women are willing to live for us.
How can we not give them as much as we give the men willing to die for us?"

Chris sighed. He was almost done. Tired, and scared even
if he'd never admit it, he crossed back to his chair and sat down.
"Then, for the first time since he'd started talking, Angie, he
looked at me. And I realized he knew why I was there."

Angie leaned forward. She wanted to believe. Dear God,
please, she prayed.

"Because," Chris's voice was strong, "he said 'I didn't save your life for you to spend it alone and giving it to the wrong people.'

"The only thing I owe him anymore, Angie, is to live a good, happy life." In spite of himself, Chris's voice finally broke. "I can't do that without you. Please tell me I don't have to try."

"I won't leave the Falls," Angie said simply.

"I know," Chris replied. "I should never have asked you to."

Angie slipped off the love seat and knelt in front of Chris's chair. Her cheeks were still wet with tears. She took his face in her hands and stared deeply into his eyes. After days of struggle, *this* decision was easy. "You listen to me, Chris Montgomery, and you listen good. You don't have to win me back 'cause I never stopped loving you and I never will. I love you, truly and really."

She tried to embrace him then, but Chris held her wrists and guided her back onto the love seat. He reached into his pocket. It had been close, he understood that. The knowledge shook him to the core. Damned if he was going to risk losing her again. Dropping to one knee, he pulled out his grandmother's ring.

"Angela Lambert Kane, will you be my wife? Will you build a life with me here, make Lambert Falls my home, and help me raise more Montgomerys to fill this house?"

"Oh, Chris. Yes. Oh yes." The tears spilling from her eyes were finally happy ones.

Chris slipped the ring onto her finger and pulled her into his arms. She smelled of coconut and summer.

Quietly as she could, Carter Anne dried her eyes and slipped out. It wouldn't be easy to keep her mouth shut, but she would. Angie would want to tell Bobby herself. In a little while.